THE
HEADHUNTER

Paul Kilduff

CORONET BOOKS

Hodder & Stoughton

Copyright © 2003 by Paul Kilduff

First published in Great Britain in 2003 by Hodder and Stoughton
A division of Hodder Headline

The right of Paul Kilduff to be identified as the Author
of the Work has been asserted by him in accordance with the
Copyright, Designs and Patents Act 1988.

A Coronet paperback

A CIP catalogue record for this title is available from the British Library

ISBN 0340 81931 6

Typeset in Centaur by Palimpsest Book Production Limited,
Polmont, Stirlingshire
Printed and bound in Great Britain by
Mackays of Chatham Ltd, Chatham, Kent

Hodder and Stoughton
A division of Hodder Headline
338 Euston Road
London NW1 3BH

ACKNOWLEDGMENTS

Thanks are due to Patrick Walsh, Wayne Brookes, Lynn Curtis and Nick Austin in London for their editorial input. Location advice was provided by former colleagues Achim Holz in Dusseldorf and Mark Doherty in Luxembourg, and by Michelle Ong in Singapore.

'**headhunter**: a person who identifies and recruits personnel to fill business positions, esp. at senior levels and from other firms – a member of a people that collects the decapitated heads of defeated enemies.'

Oxford English Dictionary

PROLOGUE

PARQUE RETIRO, MADRID: 6.45 P.M.

He follows the target along the wide avenue. A few lost souls stroll in the opposite direction towards the bustling streets outside. The public park closes in fifteen minutes. His timing is perfect.

Notes from a post-mortem examination of a thirty-nine-year-old white male. The body was recovered from the lake approximately twelve hours after death. There are multiple stab wounds to the upper torso.

The four-hundred-acre Retiro is at its best in springtime as Madrilenos come to enjoy the free concerts, carriage rides, rose gardens, blooming tulips, horse chestnuts, puppet shows, fortune tellers, red squirrels, open-air cafés, and other impromptu entertainments. White stone figures of the kings and queens of Spain peep out from among the park's lofty trees and thick bushes. This former royal preserve, with its palaces and elegant formal gardens, is an oasis for the three million inhabitants of this cosmopolitan metropolis.

On the right side of the chest, immediately inferior to the nipple, is a deep laceration. This wound is oval in shape and measures 30 × 12 mm, and both ends are pointed. There is a small notch at the mid-point of both edges of the wound. Immediately below this and 5 mm distant from it is a blue/grey bruise with green margins, which measures 30 × 20 mm.

Today the park is chill and barren, its branches stripped bare, almost devoid of human life. Its hidden secret paths are shaded and deserted. Darkness pervades. The target draws nearer to El Estanque, a broad lagoon where locals hire paddle boats and canoes in season. Nearby, a giant statue of Alfonso XII on horseback stands proudly. No king ever did less to deserve such a grandiose memorial.

Another stab wound entered the right chest cavity — completely penetrating the bone of the sixth rib — perforated the lung and the main pulmonary artery, and terminated in soft tissue to the right of that artery. The wound was accompanied by about 350 millilitres of blood in the chest cavity and about 100 millilitres of blood in the pericardial sac cavity.

The target stands at the edge of the lake, takes out a paper bag and starts throwing lumps of crusty bread into the stagnant water. There are no ducks. It seems odd. Suddenly masses of fish surge in the putrid water and devour the sodden morsels. They are primarily carp, huge orange aggressors, but also black bass, goldfish and sweet-water turtles. There are fifty or more thrashing about in the water, churning it white with surf. The carp are ravenous and bloated to the gills, their teeth sharp and white.

Another stab wound track is 10 cm deep and passes in the interspace between the fourth and fifth ribs to penetrate the right ventricle of the heart. There is a 10 × 2 mm wound to the anterior wall of the left ventricle near its apex and a corresponding 8 × 2 mm wound to the posterior wall. The left chest cavity contains 1,500 millilitres of fresh blood and clot.

The two men are alone. He steps towards the target with one specific purpose.

The penetrating wounds of the chest caused comminuted fractures of ribs, with bone fragments driven into the lung substance. The trauma to the visceral and parietal pleura disrupted normal negative intrapleural pressure resulting in pneumothorax. The penetrating wounds caused both direct and indirect injury to structures encountered by the weapon.

The target crumples to the ground without protest, instantly expiring in visible gasps of breath.

The wounds were produced by a weapon with a double-edged blade at least 30 mm wide at a point 10 cm from the tip. The resultant wounds to the heart are inevitably fatal as a consequence of haemorrhage and are expected to produce immediate incapacitation.

He pushes the body firmly with his right foot. The target rolls into the murky water and sinks.

The injuries from these stab wounds are such that death was likely to have been relatively rapid; that is, within several minutes of the infliction of the injuries. The infliction of such wounds required significant force since the weapon was thrust into the chest to a depth of 10 cm and because it involved the penetration of bone.

The fish are confused. They surge about in the water, biting in vain at loose splaying limbs and layers of wet clothing. Their gills sift and strain the red liquid that spurts and spreads into the water.

The mode of death is likely to have involved a combination of breathing impairment from the collapse of the right lung and the inhalation of blood into the right lung, blood loss from both the internal and external haemorrhage and interference with the pumping action of the heart.

He strides to the exit gate on Plaza de la Independencia. An aged park warden padlocks the heavy iron gates to the city behind him. The rain begins.

In my opinion, death was the result of a haemorrhage due to multiple homicidal stab wounds to the chest.

OCTOBER

CHAPTER ONE

LONDON WALL, LONDON EC2: 9.50 A.M.

'Are you long or short?'

Adam Lewis looks over at his more experienced yet invisible colleague on the far side of the floor.

'Neither. I'm square.'

'What's the bloody point of that?' comes the retort from behind a Union Jack pennant.

Adam sits up and peers over the bank of Reuters trading screens to make better eye contact.

'It's what Wolfie told us to do today.'

'Forget about Wolfie. You've got ten minutes to decide before the ECB does it for you.'

Adam slowly stands up, stretches his lean frame, scratches his cropped dark hair, then his remaining stubble from a rushed seven a.m. shave. He feels the first tingle of adrenalin since the early-morning research meeting as he looks at the international wall clocks. There are ten minutes before the monthly announcement by the European Central Bank in Frankfurt. It's the last Thursday of the month.

'We need to talk, Beamer.'

He walks around, passing the more experienced foreign-exchange traders. These are the guys trading dollars, sterling, yen, the volatile exotics and the lesser-known emerging-market currencies. He wonders what the desk head really thinks of Adam's market knowledge and innate ability.

'Wolfie told us not to take a view on the ECB,' he observes in a carefully neutral voice.

The head of the FX desk keeps his gaze fixed on the screens, his forty-something face expressionless, the bags under his eyes heavier with each trading day, the wear and tear of the City increasingly evident. Beamer rarely smiles. Instead he gets a new bank 3-series every January at bonus time. The current love of his life, apart from Julia and two children, is a metallic silver 320i coupé with alloys and all the extra kit.

'What's your gut feeling today, Adam?'

For the first time since his arrival on the trading floor at 7.30 am, Adam is under pressure.

'EURIBOR interest rates might come down.'

'By much?' asks Beamer.

Adam's suddenly conscious that the others are gleefully observing his dilemma, listening in to their conversation.

'Twenty-five basis points maximum.' One quarter of one percent.

'Are you sure?'

He hates this attention, wishes he'd stayed in his seat, wishes he'd never replied to Beamer's question.

'No one can know exactly what the ECB will do . . .'

Beamer sees Adam's deliberations.

'I need a straight yes or no. An up or down. Show us you've got the balls to be a top trader. Show us that you can take on the foreign-exchange market and win. Otherwise, maybe you're in the wrong job.'

Adam's doubts crowd in. The pressure from the others is intense. Unseen, intangible, yet omnipresent.

'Rates to come down,' he decides. 'The euro will weaken. We should sell euros and buy dollars.'

Beamer doesn't divert his attention from the screens.

'So do it. Trade now. Get out right after the announcement. Your short euro position will only be on your trading book for a few minutes. It's all part of the education process.'

Adam resents the jibe after a full year's service. He's about to go back to his own seat but hesitates.

'And what about Wolfie?'

'Wolfie won't hear about this from me. He never knows if our trades are client trades or bank trades.'

'It's a hell of a risk, Beamer. What if I'm wrong?'

'If we knew that in advance, we could all retire and day-trade FX from home on the web as a hobby. Bite the bullet, Adam. Go and make me some money. It's what you're here for.'

Adam walks back and sits down. Wolfgang, the former FX trading supremo from head office and soon-to-be-retiree, has his door closed. With his bloodhound's nose, he'll sniff out any trading loss in the weekly P&L. Reuters shows the euro is moving lower. The wall clocks now confirm Adam has five minutes. He sees the others looking over, wondering if he is going to make the trade that matters. He hesitates.

Then an idea. The FX desk in head office is always closer to the action. He dials Germany on the dealerboard. A girl with a wonderfully husky voice answers on the first ring, efficiency personified in the Kapital Landesbank AG head office. He thinks he might know her.

'Who's that?' he asks.

'Natalia,' she rasps back. He's met her the few times she's come over to London. Adam is momentarily distracted from the euro and the prices on the screens. She still sounds great. Way out of his league, though.

'Adam here. You got a moment?'

'Are you kidding? At the time of an ECB rates meeting?'

The clocks show three minutes to the hour. He can't wait any longer. He must decide.

'Natalia, do you see a rate cut today?'

'Hard to say. The Bank of France governor made some loose comments on Monday to the press. The Bundesbank chief economist is bearish. Euro-zone economic growth is slowing in most countries. Concerns over inflation are subsiding. Industrial confidence fell last month. Our research guys say a cut is possible. Others on the desk here think rates will be unchanged. Maybe a fifty-fifty chance.'

Jesus! Natalia is light years ahead of him in the global intellectual capital game. He'll take her advice.

'Worth a punt?'

'Always, Adam.'

'Thanks, Natalia. Bye.'

He must trade now. There's still no sign of Wolfie on the floor. Two minutes left. Adam daren't ask Beamer again, in case his boss thinks he's scared to deal, too indecisive to act, too lacking in confidence or worse. He has to seize the moment and build his reputation. He sits at the Reuters 3000 spot-FX trading terminal, one of seven and a half thousand traders trading thirty-three currency pairs in forty countries worldwide on a twenty-four/seven basis. The best rates on screen flash upwards and downwards with amazing rapidity. He selects Chase and keys his indicative interest into the trading screen.

ADAM > EUR 10

Adam's looking for a price on ten million euro versus dollar.

STU > 10 20

A guy in Chase who he's never met, maybe he's called Stewart, is showing him the bid/offer on euro/dollar. The .99 is implicit. The actual rates are .9910 to buy and .9920 to sell. Adam is a seller today.

ADAM > 20

STU > RISK

Done deal.

ADAM > THKS TO CONFIRM AT. 9920

I SELL 10 MIO EUR VAL 27 OCT

MY USD TO KAPITAL BANK AG NY A/C NO
45637387
STU > CHEERS

'Sold ten euro,' he shouts to the desk as is their practice. The 'million' is implicit.

Adam sits perfectly still, watching the screens, waiting for Judgement Day, as the minute hand ticks towards ten.

Henry Simpson is a fan of the new Jubilee Line extension eastwards. He loves the clean stations unsullied by human life, the chrome walls and marble floors, the air-conditioning and all-pervading sense of order. He enjoys the audible announcements at Waterloo about the connections to European destinations, as if he can hop on any Tube to Paris or Brussels. Most of all he likes the glass partitions and automatic doors that separate the platforms from the electrified tracks. If one feels the sudden and compelling urge to push someone off the edge, then it's impossible all the way to Canary Wharf.

He exits the Tube station feeling calm, almost exalted, riding the final escalator into the natural daylight, staring upwards at the vaulted ceilings. He walks through the Canada Square shopping mall. It's all here for the smart yet casual bulge-bracket bankers. Vodafone and Orange to stay in touch. The Gap and Thomas Pink for Him, Dorothy Perkins and Monsoon for Her. Starbucks and Costa Lot! for caffeine shots. Moshi Moshi sushi and Pret-à-Manger for easy eats. Vision Express and Links to look good. Tesco Metro for those who don't live in restaurants. ATMs on every wall for fast cash. Barclays Premier Banking and Chase Private if you ever need advice. Essex Boys in waistcoats and on their knees, doing shoeshines for a fiver. McDonald's and Burger King banned by the freeholders. An oasis of work and play for the chosen few.

Mid-morning is quiet. Henry's aware that the expansive concourses are meant for the growing army of workers steadily colonising this easterly extension of the City. He kills a few minutes out of necessity, standing on the cold pavements in the shadows of the Citigroup and HSBC twin towers, collar upturned, sheltering from the thin rain, waiting for the appropriate time to enter the revolving doors to Cabot Square.

'Henry Simpson, here to see Lloyd Weinbaum.'

The bored security guard with the peaked cap doesn't remember him from last time. Henry takes an anonymous visitor's badge and rises in the bank of lifts to the scary heights of floor twenty-one. Inside he checks his appearance in the smoked glass and is wholly satisfied. Six foot, broad shoulders, good shave, tight ex-army haircut, neat side parting, no sideburns, no glasses due to 20/20 vision, a crisp blue shirt and gold-patterned tie, dark single-breasted suit and navy coat. He looks the part. He alights to join a polished PA, checks his coat at a veneer wall cabinet and follows her sheer stockings and high heels along the main trading floor. The heels ahead stop momentarily by the largest office. The PA is puzzled.

'Lloyd's not here.' She discreetly checks the few papers strewn across the desk and assumes it's safe to leave the visitor alone briefly. 'Take a seat. He's around. I'll get him.'

Henry sits in the corner for the optimal view of the trading floor and watches the traders and sales staff scurry about in their smart business-casual attire. The eager guys outside look too young to hold down such important jobs. Henry feels overdressed. He loosens his own Windsor-knotted tie and unbuttons his suit jacket. He looks in vain for some familiar faces. Some of them must surely remember him.

Weinbaum appears from the far end of the floor and strides into his personal domain. He looks tired, even addled. They shake hands. There's no need to hand over a business card. The First Vice-President of Global Foreign Exchange already has Henry's in his Rolodex. In contrast to his casually dressed staff, Weinbaum wears a white button-down shirt and Barney's tie, the shop's logo visible on the twisted silk. In the City, the organ grinder still dresses differently from the monkeys.

'Henry, we can't seem to live without you.' The FVP slides into his seat of power with some difficulty. His waistline expands with every year of corporate excess. He loosens his tie, then his humorous cufflinks, stroking his silver hair. He looks in dismay at the relentless wave of incoming corporate e-mails on his screen, most still in bold text and unread, and refocuses on his invited visitor.

'What's up?' Henry enquires.

'I need a body.'

Henry is surprised. 'Another one?'

'Sure thing.'

He glances outside. 'So soon after Samantha?'

The FVP looks out also until his gaze rests on a twenty-something girl sitting alone at the end of the desk. They both study her for too long; watch her swivel in her chair and ignore colleagues who pass, ever aware of her presence and looks, and of the fact that she doesn't look too happy today. She leans back in her chair and removes a pair of narrow-framed black Gucci glasses. She stands up, walks nearer and bends low over the water cooler, paper cup in hand. Some body. The FVP refocuses.

'We're doing more business. Making more money. We need more capacity. So I need another body.'

Henry nods in anticipation. He mentally rehearses his usual sales spiel. This pitch matters. Lloyd is a big shot. This is Mitchell Leonberg & Co. Inc., his bluest of blue-chip clients, as blue as the summer skies over London, which are a distant memory. He can see a lucrative five-figure placement fee coming his way, and smiles.

'That's what I'm here for, Lloyd.'

'You got any decent bodies?' asks the FVP.

Henry tries to forget Samantha's. 'What sort, exactly?'

'A spot-FX trader with, say, a year or two's euro experience at a lesser bank who wants to work with a top-tier name like Mitchell's.' Then, after a slight pause: 'Maybe someone impressionable.'

'What do you mean, "impressionable"?'

'Someone I can easily direct and tell what to do. Someone less feisty than Samantha on a bad day.'

'Profile?' asks Henry.

'A graduate. Keen. Insomniac. Early twenties. Male this time. The women call in sick for a few days every month.' The FVP doesn't seem to worry much about political correctness, ageism or sexism at work.

'Personality?' asks Henry.

'Yeah, we need one of those.'

'Salary and bonus?' asks Henry.

'Yeah, there will be one too,' Henry smiles and waits. His host gets up, closes the door with a firm thud. A few heads outside look over at them. 'Sixty K plus fifty per cent bonus in year one if they perform.'

'I'll send you over some excellent CVs later today.'

The FVP rises. 'If they're so excellent, why are they looking for jobs?'

'They're waiting to work in a place like this and for someone like you, Lloyd.'

'Smooth talker.' They shake hands. 'Remind me of your usual terms, Henry?'

'Thirty per cent of basic once they pass your three months probation. Mitchell's always get the best deal.'

'Goddamned extortion, Henry!'

'Cheap enough for the right body, Lloyd.'

CHAPTER TWO

LONDON WALL, LONDON EC2: 10.01 A.M.

The scrolling words on the Reuters screen hit Adam like a kick in the groin.

'The ECB, which sets monetary policy for the twelve-country euro zone, left the minimum bid rate for its regular refinancing operations unchanged. It also held steady its other two key rates – the deposit rate and the marginal lending rate. Some economists were expecting a downwards move this week, as recent weak euro-zone data had led some investors to think the bank would spring a surprise rate cut on the markets.'

Rates are unchanged . . . Unchanged. Adam reads the words again slowly, vainly hoping that second time around it will be different. The word is the same. *Unchanged.* Meaning there is no change. No twenty-five-basis-points cut. Rates are exactly as they were ten minutes ago. One of the other guys has this annoying habit of reading out the bleeding obvious on the screens for all on the desk.

'ECB leaves rates unchanged.'

Adam is in shock. Beamer let him do this. *Made* him do this. Forced him into a corner. No way is Adam holding on to this position. The prices flash back at him. The euro is on the up and up and he is caught short. He needs to buy immediately.

He keys in the buy trade. Again he trades with Chase. He has his face ground into the dirt by Stewart, the trader who has just made what he lost in this global zero-sum game.

'Bought ten euro,' he admits aloud.

The exchange rate is crap. He hits the desk calculator and checks the trades in his front-office trading system. He has churned and burned seventy K in ten minutes. Beamer looks over.

'How much?'

'Seventy K.' He can hardly get the words out. It's more than his entire remuneration blown away in ten minutes.

'Profit or loss?' someone else asks.

'Ha-bloody-ha.'

Suddenly the door to the nearest glass office opens. Wolfgang appears in his trade-mark open grey cardigan and heavy spectacles, puts his hands in his deep pockets and looms over Adam, facing Beamer.

'Rates are unchanged?' Beamer nods. Wolfie looks at him directly. 'Were we flat, like I said?'

Adam sits numbly, wondering why he traded, why his natural instinct is so wide of the mark, wondering if he's really meant to be a spot FX trader or if there is some other, better vocation in life. He's about to say something premature, to look for the optimal presentation and the minimal downside.

'Yeah. We were flat. Like you said, Wolfie,' advises Beamer.

'Anything else I should know?'

'Nope.'

Adam is unsure what's happening here. The boss walks off and closes the door to his office. Bewildered, Adam peers over the flags.

'You told him we were flat, Beamer. We weren't. I was short ten euro. Naked.'

'I know you were.'

'So you lied?'

'I was long ten euro. I heard you trade with Chase, did an

equal and opposite trade with Paribas. Overall the desk was flat. I just sold out and made eighty K. You lost seventy. We made ten K net.'

Adam is still bewildered.

'Like you said minutes ago, what's the bloody point of that? What if I'd been right and rates had fallen?'

'Then you'd make some money, I'd say nothing, and that would be it.'

'I still can't see the point.'

Beamer gets up and walks around. He places a hand on Adam's shoulder.

'How did you feel when Wolfie came out and stood behind you?'

'I almost wet my pants. I've heard of traders who've been fired from here for less. Jesus, some of the guys who were let go in that head office downsizing this year were even making money for the bank.'

Beamer offers the benefit of his fifteen years' experience in the global foreign exchange markets. 'Remember this feeling. You only lost seventy K. Imagine if it was seven mil. If that had happened, you'd have deposited a large pile of fresh excrement on the seat of your executive swivel chair before being sent on your way out the revolving door with a pink slip and a kick up the backside from Wolfie. And from me. You'd never work in the City again. All part of learning to trade the markets.'

'Thanks!'

Beamer sits down again, chuckling at Adam's grey pallor. 'Relax. At the end of the day it's only someone else's money that we play with at this desk. Fortunately, there is more to life than FX trading profits. Like having a wife and kids. And happiness. And, of course, the ultimate driving machine from deepest Bavaria.'

Henry triumphs over the best efforts of London Underground and arrives back at the office by late morning. Not just any old office. The polished brass nameplate on the ground floor announces Henry Simpson & Associates, Executive Search Consultants. It's his Covent Garden base, his personal empire.

Upstairs, Trish, his efficient Irish temp of three years' almost permanent standing, is on a telephone call. She toys with some long strands of auburn hair, lips curling into an easy welcoming smile. Trish was a great find, courtesy of another recruitment firm, and the temporary contract arrangement suits them both. Someday she will return to Dublin. She's dressed eclectically in garments garnered from retro shops, Camden Market and second-hand stalls. He opens his briefcase and places a box of fine Lindt chocolates on top of her desk.

'You look wonderful today,' he whispers. 'Hope you like these.'

She mimes reciprocal gratitude, then transfers the call to the outer office. Trish gives the junior associates there some serious competition with her proven feminine intuition and natural people skills. She's wasted as a PA. She runs her perfect nails along the wrapping and opens the box, eyeing the tempting selection.

'I can't touch these. Think of my figure.'

He looks at her. 'I try not to. Amanda would complain. Ration yourself to one of these a day and you'll be fine.' He stops by his door. 'Any decent post today?'

Trish has a sixth sense. 'So did you got a role from Mitchell's?' Henry nods. 'Samantha couldn't stick it there?' she asks.

'No, she's still there. It's another junior FX trading role. We need to move fast for Lloyd. Again.'

'We got a few more CVs. Some came in by e-mail.' Trish knows Henry hates e-mails. He's more a face-to-face people person. 'I printed them off. They're on your desk. They're pretty average CVs.' Trish is never short of ideas. 'And I'll ask the guys outside.'

Henry doesn't hold out much hope of anything useful from the associates. It's a misnomer for the young guys at the desks.

They are cheap. They wear M&S suits and polyester shirts so he'll never allow them to meet the top clients. They'll never be Associates. Henry owns the firm, save for one token share held by his wife Amanda. The associates focus on the dull finance and operations roles. They're working the telephones and PCs exactly liked he showed them, screening incoming calls and e-mails from potential candidates, replying to the best ones and trashing the aspirational fiction they often encounter.

'Ask them. I could do with a good laugh today,' admits Henry.

The associates revel in bringing Henry the worst lines in the CVs. 'I failed my final exam with relatively high grades. I finished eighth in a class of ten . . . Marital status: often. Children: various. Personal interests: donating blood, six gallons so far . . . My goal is to become a meteorologist but since I possess no training in meteorology, I will continue in banking . . . I worked for my parents until they decided to move away . . . The company made me a scapegoat, just like my previous employer.' Henry likes typos most of all. 'I received a plague for best equity saleswoman of the year . . . As indicted, I have years of trading derivatives . . . I was instrumental in ruining the entire trading operation.'

'And I'll check our database for anyone who needs a move,' offers Trish.

They both know from experience that this is a bad time of year. No one good ever moves in the City in autumn. It's too near bonus time to jump ship like a rat. Henry will soon have to place another of those job adverts in the *FT* on a Wednesday or Thursday, with his glossy logo and contact details smeared everywhere. One of those impressive quarter-pages, announcing some phantom jobs in sales and trading, in advisory and mergers and acquisitions, in research and quants. He'll use some cliché-ridden description for the anonymous top-tier global-player transatlantic investment bank. If some eager candidates follow up their CVs with a telephone call, he'll tell them they didn't make it to the shortlist. But he'll have their CVs and the competition will see the advert and know he is still big in the City.

'Good idea. Otherwise it's an advert again,' he observes, taking one proffered white mint chocolate.

Henry sits in his office, wondering how he'll find another suitable body for Mitchell's. Samantha was a great find but to source another quality candidate for Lloyd so soon afterwards is pushing it. His reputation for delivering is on the line again. He checks the CVs in his in-tray in vain. This recruitment lark was easier in the boom years of the nineties before he went out on his own. In those heady days he had twenty CVs for every job and he could be selective.

He remembers fondly the classic CVs, the ones from the old days, that they had framed. The banker who was endeavouring to master the fine art of vegetable gardening. The fixed-income girl who said music was an aesthetic pleasure that helped her transcend her normal emotions. The analyst who admired Hitler because he got things done. The options trader who said he was single but had been with the same girlfriend for the past six years. The M&A guy who was a vegetarian on moral grounds, as if the grounds mattered. The syndicate guy who said he had a high metabolic rate, whatever that meant. His favourite was the covering letter from the equity trader who wrote that he worked in a shit bank for a bunch of wankers on crap money with fuck-all chance of advancement and so he wanted to move.

Trish arrives with a printout from their database and another easy smile. 'I got you some bodies.'

His hopes rise. A few of the bodies are overqualified for the junior role. The last body on the file is circled in red. Trish is rarely wrong. He looks ideal on paper. The body works on an FX desk. Henry hasn't had any business from Kapital for months due to some downsizing programme. He can afford to poach their staff for a better client and not suffer any adverse consequences. He runs his finger though his Rolodex at speed and finds the Kapital direct number. The first call is his because it's all-important.

He's about to hit the first digits on the console when Trish walks closer to his desk, holds a dark orange truffle in her hand, places it between her lips, allows it to melt, swallows slowly, then speaks.

'I forgot to ask. How was your trip?'

CHAPTER THREE

LONDON WALL, LONDON EC2: 11.45 A.M.

Adam's mind is still fixed on his screw-up on the euro when his direct line flashes. He's glad to see on the trader board that the telephone call is external. Maybe it's got nothing to do with FX trading.

'Adam Lewis.'

'Hi, Adam. It's Henry here.' Adam is lost. The line remains silent, as if the caller is waiting for some sort of recognition. None comes from Adam. More information is required. 'We met a year ago.'

Adam racks his memory. A year ago he joined Kapital . . .

'That Henry?'

'That's me.'

The incoming call is necessarily ambiguous. They both know that telephone lines at investment banks are taped for recourse purposes in the event of a trader error, a client dispute or some other argument. But both know too that others on the trading desk are only feet away and that colleagues have sharp ears for news.

'Adam, can we meet?'

'Why?'

There's an uneasy pause on the line.

'You know what I do.'

Adam appreciates what is being implied. 'If it's about me, then I'm okay. I don't want to be called.'

'Adam, trust me, like last time. This is in your interest. Have you got some time?'

Adam reckons reluctantly that Henry isn't taking no for an answer. Beamer is looking over, curious.

'When?'

'Lunchtime. Today.'

Adam looks at the five wall clocks, ignoring New York, Frankfurt, Hong Kong and Sydney.

'Possibly'.

'I'm still in Covent Garden. Trish will look after you when you get here.'

Henry knows how to hit the right spots. Adam remembers Trish well and the memories are good. He knows he can be there and back in an hour by black cab but he still isn't keen.

'It's a waste of your time.'

'Let me be the judge of that. See you in an hour.'

Adam hangs up and ponders the call, wondering why the prospect of a meeting with a headhunter doesn't make him so anxious. He realises the wonderful difference. This time he is a wanted man, he holds the advantage and all the cards. Unlike the last time, Henry needs Adam more than Adam needs Henry.

He tells Beamer he's taking a long lunch to meet a friend from back home, walks out onto the wet streets of the City, eventually hails a black cab near Bishopsgate, curses the traffic of the West End and alights at the Strand. He finds the office more by luck than from the distant memories of a year ago.

Trish has matured since last time. She wears a tight lilac top over her full figure, with a few too many top buttons undone. Her long hair is gathered neatly in the small of her back. There is still no important ring of commitment upon her left hand. She smiles as they shake hands. He loves her soft accent.

'Good to see you again, Adam. You're looking very well.'

He wonders if she really means it or whether it's the party line she sells to every candidate. Trish has a bundle of today's post in her hand. There's also a BA envelope.

'Come on in and meet Henry. I'll give him these. It's mostly CVs but there is some good news. A free flight to Dublin! Henry uses his Air Miles for me to have a weekend at home.'

'Adam, welcome.' Henry interrupts Adam's lustful dreams, placing a firm hand on his shoulder. They sit together in his office. 'I have a very special opportunity and the first person I thought of was you.'

Adam's thinking of the ramifications of moving jobs again. All that hassle and sense of the unknown.

'I know how you guys operate. As soon as you get the placement fee for one job, you want me to move.'

Henry shakes his head. 'We're not that mercenary. I'm putting no one else forward for this.' He leans forward, using the tried-and-tested sales patter. 'This is a once-in-a-lifetime opportunity for a junior spot FX trader.' Henry's pushing all the right buttons, whetting Adam's appetite, piquing his taste buds. 'It's a better package than you have at Kapital, with a guaranteed fifty per cent bonus. It's a big name.'

Adam grows worried. Big names mean big pressure, big profits, big losses. But Henry is working that same magic as last time. It's exactly like when he told Adam that Kapital was the best place to work.

'Who is it?' he asks casually.

Henry sits back in his chair. 'So you *are* interested?' He grins broadly. 'I knew that you would be.'

'I'm interested in the one piece of information that is relevant.'

Adam sees Henry's eyes light up like some cash register on overtime.

'It's the biggest name in the City. They're the best FX desk. It's Mitchell's.'

Adam's thinking that Henry is making some serious inroads.

'Why would they want me?'

'Don't be so pessimistic. Be optimistic.'

'I'm being realistic.'

'They want your experience.'

'I've only got a year's trading experience.'

'There aren't that many good candidates out there at present.'

'Thanks.'

Henry worries that he's losing his touch. 'You're the man. You get first refusal.'

'Henry, you're forgetting one thing. Mitchell's haven't made me an offer. There's nothing to refuse.'

''Course they'll make you an offer. Once they meet with you and see how good you are.'

'I'm not prepared to do an interview.'

'Who mentioned an interview? This is just a friendly chat with Lloyd Weinbaum, the FVP of FX there.'

'Henry, thanks, but I'm not interested. I'm happy where I am.' Adam stands up. 'I'm off back to Kapital.'

He sees Henry's demeanour change. His face tightens up, his expression becomes grim and intense. Adam senses he's about to be on the receiving end of a torrent of abuse but then the glossy veneer returns.

'I told Lloyd you'd drop by this time tomorrow. If that goes okay then you'll meet the desk head next week. He's away on business in Europe this week. What's the harm? Trish has all the details.'

Adam leaves ten minutes later, wondering whether Trish really means it when she says she hopes to see him again and asking himself now he's been cornered into an imminent job interview that he simply doesn't need. He sits in the cab and wonders if someone like Trish is ever single, available and interested. He definitely is.

*　　*　　*

Henry sits at his desk, catching up on another day's worth of bad CVs, when Trish barges in.

'Lionel Roberts is here.'

Henry recognises the corporate name of one of the biggest recruitment firms in London, the firm he acrimoniously left five years ago with a legally binding one-year non-compete clause; the firm that now shares the same building. In the sense that Henry has a few offices there and they have five and half floors.

'I think you'll find that's the name of the firm, Trish. What's the guy's actual name?'

She's adamant and stands her ground by the door.

'His name is Lionel Roberts.' She muses for a few seconds. 'So I guess he owns the firm.'

Roberts immediately enters, shakes hands and sits down without an invitation. He is often in the recruitment press and can be glimpsed from afar at black-tie industry functions. Roberts exudes wealth close up, with the fashionable cut of his dark hand-tailored suit, glistening gold watch and rings, a well-buffed set of Colgate teeth, manicured ageless hair and a permatan from the yacht he keeps near Marbella.

'Do you have an appointment today, Lionel?'

'Sure do,' replies Roberts. 'And if this isn't quick, then I'll be late for it.'

'Very droll.'

Roberts is still the major shareholder in the firm he founded years ago, since floated off as a listed plc on the LSE in the buoyant nineties. Henry still watches the share price, more out of envy than any commercial interest. Roberts is worth tens of millions on paper and the evidence is now before Henry.

'How's business, Henry?'

'That'd be telling.'

'Do you ever worry about being a minnow?'

'If I was, then I'm sure you wouldn't be dropping by.'

'Do you ever regret leaving us all those years ago?'

'Nope —' Henry's having a brief flashback '— Mr Roberts.'

'Call me Lionel. Everyone who works for me does. My firm is an informal, open-door type of company.'

Henry's thinking that he doesn't work for Roberts so he'll call him whatever he likes. He wonders what brings Roberts down from the sanctuary of the top floor to visit a tiny competitor like Henry Simpson.

'Is this a business or a social call, Mr Roberts?'

Roberts frowns at the second mention of his surname.

'I want to discuss a proposition. I hope you'll hear me out.' Roberts waves an open hand and gestures towards Henry's associates who sit outside in the open plan. 'I want to make you an offer for all this.'

Henry had guessed as much. He has one thousand square feet of scarce floor space in a prime West End location and now the bigger tenant wants the entire building for his sole use. It's an offer to buy out his long lease. Henry will have to move elsewhere with all the associated hassle and grief. No dice.

'Forget it. No can do.'

'Surely we can discuss this? Usually I find it all comes down to money and timing.'

Usually? Henry doesn't think there are any other tenants in the building. He is lost.

'Money and timing?'

Roberts leans forward and places his open palms upon Henry's desk.

'How long do you intend to carry on running this business on your own? Don't you plan to retire before the age of sixty-five? I do. I intend to quit work when I can. So don't dismiss my offer out of hand.'

His offer. Henry's slowly catching his drift. Roberts hasn't mentioned floor space at all.

'You're offering to buy my firm?'

'That's what I said.'

Henry's amazed.

'Why would you want to buy my firm?'

'I know your client base in the City and that you work for the best blue-chip names. I know the roles you filled in the recent past. I know it all. I know your retainers. I know you have a magic database of some of the best guys and gals in the City. Shit, I even know you got an unknown called Samantha Perry an FX job in Mitchell's and you have one more FX trading role to fill there right now. My CVs are on the way too.'

'How the hell do you know all that?'

'Market intelligence. That's what got me where I am today.'

Henry dares to push his luck, to see how much.

'What do you think my firm's worth?'

'Maybe you have a figure in mind.'

'Maybe you could have come down here better prepared.'

Henry lets Roberts stew, knowing he has to make the running. He finally acquiesces.

'I've been through your last set of annual accounts filed two years ago at the Companies Office. Tut-tut. You need to get your accountant to file in a more timely manner.' Roberts is doing some mental arithmetic at speed. 'The numbers show you made a net profit of just under two hundred K. I expect you made more last year but you're not going to tell me exactly how much.'

'Correct.' Last year was good. Henry is not going to volunteer that this year is tough and profits might be down.

'We value recruitment firms by applying a price/earnings multiple. My firm trades in the stock market on a p/e of fifteen because it has a good record of stable earnings growth. I don't expect a firm like yours to warrant a p/e of more than ten. So ten times your annual profits is about two million quid. You are the majority shareholder, with one share held by your wife. So that's my offer. Two million quid.'

The two men sit in silence. Henry already knows that he's well off. But now he can be liquid too.

'You're not expecting an answer here and now?'

'Take some time to think about it.'

Henry rises from his seat.

'I don't need time to think. I know the answer now.'

Roberts rises too, suddenly looking excited and almost relieved at the ease of negotiations.

'Excellent.'

'The answer is no.'

Roberts frowns but retains composure – on the exterior, at least.

'You know where I am. The offer stands. You'll come round in time. I know you too well.'

Roberts leaves. Henry sits alone, basking in the sudden attention, aware that he now has a lucrative exit route. As Roberts says, money and timing are everything. For Henry, though, money is a non-issue. Two million is a bad opening gambit from his former boss based on pre-historic data. He'll get Roberts up to three or four million quid once he shows him last year's accounts. Timing is the only issue that matters.

CHAPTER FOUR

TRINKHAUS STRASSE, DUSSELDORF:
5.35 P.M.

The cream E240 Mercedes taxi glides off to his left, only to stop abruptly at a set of red lights at a T-junction. An exhaust-wheezing estate pulls up next at the deserted rank. A bent elderly woman stumbles closer, hoping that it's her ticket home in the steady drizzle. He waits. They make eye contact. He smiles, opens the rear door and helps her inside, shopping bags and all. The OAP nods in gratitude, puzzled by a stranger's kindness, mumbling something like *danke*, her faltering speech leaving a visible trail in the chill evening air. In fact, life is too short for him to be seen dead in a battered VW Passat.

The lights at the junction are now green, the blurred reflection glinting off pools of rainwater. The next taxi stops alongside. It's the ultimate mode of transport, crafted in Stuttgart and here just in time. Another Merc. He jumps onto the rear leather seat and points ahead past the incessant motion of the single-sweep windscreen wiper. Despite his adequate command of German, he fakes a bad accent.

'Follow them, buddy. Don't lose 'em.'

The stubbled driver grunts in acknowledgement, surges forwards, but hits the pedals at the now amber set of lights. No way.

They must stay on the move or this opportunity dies an early death. He leans forward, ignores the unpronounceable surname on the dashboard and prods the reluctant Turk in the back.

'Break the lights. Keep going.'

'*Nein.*'

'There's twenty euro in it. Do it!'

They're past. He moves to sit directly behind the driver. The legroom is less on the left-hand side but he avoids being in the line of vision of the rear-view mirror. The side windows are badly misted up on the inside. He runs his coat sleeve over the wet glass and stares out at the depressing eternal darkness, punctuated only by overhead sodium lights reflecting onto the barren tarmac streets.

The frustrations of today return. The early-morning departure by cab, the delayed BA flight, the time-waster who invited him over, the laborious loquacious liquid lunch, the anticlimactic meeting. This day trip was a waste of time and money. The Turk behind the wheel is too enthusiastic.

'Not so near,' he instructs. He establishes his sole authority. 'Keep your distance.'

If the Turk loses the other taxi, if the journey drags on for more than, say, thirty minutes, if they stop in a built-up well-lit densely populated street, then he'll give directions to go directly to the airport. Otherwise he will continue. There is no downside. There never is. There is only unlimited upside, the chance to relieve his frustrations before the civilised comforts and fine cuisine of Club Europe.

The brief kerbside encounter is fresh in his mind. The target is in his late thirties, professional, affluent, probably socio-economic grouping ABCI. Occasionally the rear window of the taxi ahead is well lit by street lights. The target sits with good posture in the rear seat, has a full head of well-combed fair hair, is lean and of only average height. He thinks he recalls the glint of a gold wedding ring on the left hand and wonders if the target has any children. Pity. He takes an unnecessary pair of spectacles from the inside of his suit and places them on the bridge of his nose. The glass in them is clear and unmagnified.

He mentally rehearses the Ten Commandments. First Commandment. Be overseas. Second Commandment. Not in the USA. Third Commandment. Select a different country. He's never before worked in Germany. Fourth Commandment. Not spring or summer. It's autumn. Fifth Commandment. Avoid those who may resist. The target poses no overt physical threat.

He takes his left hand in his right and holds his wrist. He estimates his pulse to be about seventy-five beats per minute. Ten over normal. It's not fast enough to suggest any change of plan. He is in full control. He rubs his hands together. His palms are cold. No sweat. He feels the adrenalin rising. He exhales and contemplates the latent energy he has within, the frustrations that he is about to exorcise, the control that he is about to exercise. He takes his pulse again. He estimates ninety beats per minute.

Sixth Commandment. Choose the optimal location. The span of a bridge looms ahead. A road sign points west along the Rheinkniebrucke. There are road signs for Oberkassell and Niederkassel. They're heading across the Rhine. Suddenly there are fewer buildings and offices, more private homes and shuttered shops, then some hedgerows and open green spaces. The taxi ahead brakes, red tail lights bouncing erratically off the slippery road, and hangs a right onto a narrow street. There are imposing houses set back from view with high trees and wrought-iron gates. Ideal.

Seventh Commandment. Avoid complication. He sits back into the seat, sure that the Turk has his jaded eyes on the road, exhales slowly and silently, drops his shoulders, and slides his slim briefcase up onto his knees. The case opens to his touch. He shields the contents from the Turk, removes the pair of black leather gloves without taking his eyes off the slowing taxi ahead. From memory, he feels along the metal spine of his briefcase near the pair of solid brass hinges, extracts his weapon of choice with his right hand and carefully slides it under his coat and inside the left sleeve of the jacket of his suit.

Eighth Commandment. Get home safely afterwards. He opens his worn copy of the *Official Airline Guide* inside the briefcase. He looks at his Tissot again. He may miss the BA flight but there is a Lufthansa flight in ninety minutes. He has a fully flexible Club Europe ticket. No worries. He opens the complimentary city map from the airport tourist office. Checks where the main railway station is in the city. He folds away the *OAG* and the map, places the briefcase alongside him on the seat and sees the taxi ahead take another right to stop abruptly by a smart residential entrance.

The Turk by now senses what to do and kills the engine on a corner a hundred yards away. The target is in full view as he crouches into his taxi in the drizzle and pays the fare, his collar upturned against the increasingly hostile elements. The target's trench coat hangs open as he takes the cash from his pocket. There's a glimpse of a white shirt. The watcher leans forward as he opens the rear door with a gloved hand.

'Wait here, buddy,' he drawls deliberately.

The target strides past a low stone wall, stops at two stone pillars and opens and closes some creaking gates. The watcher hears footsteps upon a loose gravel path. Through the railings, he sees that the house ahead is in complete darkness. He quickens his pace and opens the gate in turn. The footsteps ahead stop suddenly. The target stands at a mailbox. He's ten feet ahead, removing a bundle of envelopes and magazines.

Ninth Commandment. Crave anonymity. The target turns at the sound of footsteps on the gravel. He holds the post in one hand and his house keys in the other. They stand just three or four feet apart, two men with absolutely nothing in common. Or so he hopes. The curious local speaks first.

'*Ja?*'

He watches the cold air exhaled into the night as the single word is uttered. He opts first for German.

'*Sprechen Sie englisch?*'

The target is wearing neat oval spectacles. Individual drops of rain settle upon the glass, partly obscuring his vision. The raindrops look like clusters of tears about to run down his puzzled face.

'*Ein bisschen.* I know English.'

They're close enough. No lights inside the home. All is quiet. The time is right. The time is now.

'Fucking excellent.'

The target looks back, almost bemused, expecting a smile in return. None is offered. The house keys go back into his suit pocket with his right hand, pulling back his coat and jacket again to reveal a pristine white shirt. The thin layer of cotton is all that lies between a deadly weapon and the inner chambers of his heart. The target takes one step back, as if moving nearer to his home gives him some additional protection.

'I'm sorry?' The target exhales.

It might be an apology or a rhetorical question, it doesn't matter which to the recipient. He brings his gloved hands together, produces the weapon, steps forward with confidence and practised ease, smiles reassuringly and thrusts it cleanly between the third and fourth rib on the right-hand side of the target's chest. It makes a near-perfect entry wound and goes straight into one of the two main chambers of the heart. He retracts it smoothly and steps back as the blood begins to pump rhythmically onto the loose gravel below.

The target's surprised facial expression doesn't change much. It never does, seemingly frozen by the elements. He makes successive futile gasps for incremental air, which are inaudible yet visible. He staggers on the gravel, his white shirt now Burgundy red as he collapses onto the unforgiving stones with a heavy crunch.

'I'd say you're fucking sorry now.'

He crouches over the target, sufficiently close to complete the job yet far enough away not to be splattered with the bloody evidence. There is no need to add to the already burgeoning wound.

'You took my fucking cab.'

Tenth Commandment. Eliminate the motive. He doesn't bother to run through the target's pockets, to purloin a stuffed wallet of euros and Amex plastic, to make it look like some robbery or a mugging. He's going to steal nothing from the body and nothing from the silent home. Some still say you need a motive to kill. What do they know?

He wipes the weapon repeatedly on the wet grass by the path, then removes a few blades of grass with the tip of his gloved index finger. He looks around. All is still quiet. He walks down the driveway and back to his taxi, its engine dead yet meter still running, heartbeat pounding ever faster. He carries the weapon in his right hand out of view of the Turk and sits back into the warm womb of a rear seat.

'Let's go to the railroad station now,' in another bad attempt at an accent.

They retrace their immediate route, back over the span of the bridge following the signs towards the Hauptbahnhof. He opens his briefcase and places the weapon, then gloves, into an anonymous self-sealing clear plastic freezer bag, one of the type that is never missed from the kitchen. He estimates from the flickering meter that the fare will be forty euros. He counts out the cash well in advance, ensuring no remnants of blood taint the notes. They stop at the rank at the main terminus in Konrad Adenauer Platz.

'Can I catch a train to Bonn from here?' he asks.

The Turk nods, swears as he looks at the long queue of taxis, and defaults to the usual trite answer.

'Information desk. Inside.'

The explicit question and suggestion of intent matter more

than the quality of the reply. He avoids eye contact as he hands over the cash, but takes a covert look at the driver as he suspiciously checks the money, as is if he still isn't used to the euro banknotes. The Turk has potholed eyes and three days' growth of grey stubble. Clearly hasn't slept in as many days. He gets out of the Merc and walks away slowly.

'*Halte.*' He stops, turns, wondering if he has somehow erred. The Turk holds out some paper. 'Receipt.'

He takes the scrap, deciding that refusal is an unnecessary evil. The Turk crawls off to join the long line of waiting taxis. His last fare watches him do an illegal U-turn, skid across the cobblestones, get out of his car and light a cigarette in the shelter of a wall. A green and white Vectra roars close by at speed, the word *Polizei* emblazoned on the side doors. He smiles. They can't be looking for him just yet.

A glance inside reveals that the station concourse is teeming, the departures board humming, everyone apparently running for a departing train. The locals know that here at least trains run on time. It's an ideal place to dump the evidence in a left luggage locker for just a couple of euros. But he's not going inside. He can see the glass globes hanging ominously from the roof. CCTV rules inside. Perish the thought.

The Vectra pulls up alongside. Four police officers jump out with a definite purpose in mind. Three big guys and an even larger woman. He freezes. They wear peaked caps, khaki trousers and green jackets with holsters. They're serious competition. They run past and burst through the swing doors. He looks inside. They lift an anaemic guy off the floor and drag him outside into the back of their car. White powder in cellophane bundles falls from his hands, evidently selling something to passers-by, and it wasn't picture postcards of the Rhine. False alarm. He walks away from the station. The whole point of being here is not to go inside.

He walks along Karl Strasse for five minutes, ignoring the

neon lure of the sex kinos and video *Welten* that cluster in German main-line stations. Every pavement step, every dithering pedestrian, every dodged oncomer becomes a private celebration of his primary purpose. He seeks the inside track and takes cover from the incessant drizzle under awnings and roofs on this now glorious evening.

The bright lights of the Konigsallee draw him off to the right. He passes the glossy Joop, Gucci and Guess shop windows, with single mannequins in plum-red trouser suits illuminated by single spots against sheer white backdrops. He circumnavigates the local couples, tall Teutonic women in sable furs and long leather coats window-shopping hand in hand with their equally well-pickled sugar daddies.

There's a sign for the Steigenberger Park Hotel, five gold stars, a row of international flags and an excess of taxis outside. He bounces up the steps, past the clipped topiary and welcoming staff, into the brassy lobby and through to the toilets. Inside there's a chrome bin with the visible edges of a black plastic refuse sack. A typed schedule on the wall confirms the staff visit hourly to discard the contents of the bin.

A genuine hotel guest hovers by the washbasins so he goes to the farthest cubicle and opens his briefcase on the toilet seat. He takes out the plastic bag and carefully removes the gloves and the blade, handle first. He rolls down a sufficient wad of toilet paper and wraps the blade inside the paper, then places the contents back into the bag. The guy outside whistles a few solo bars of some unrecognisable tune.

More paper. He wipes his gloves repeatedly with a wad of it until the black leather gleams, throws the paper down the bowl and flushes away the evidence. Running water now gushes from the taps outside. He leaves his gloves on as he removes his glasses. Next he throws off his trench coat, folds it into a tight bundle and crams it inside his briefcase. He presses the case closed with some difficulty until the lock clicks shut.

The banal whistling fades, the door to the lobby opens and

all is quiet. He opens his cubicle, goes past the basins and thrusts the plastic bag and its contents deep down inside the bin. He examines his face in the mirror, then his clothes. The hot tap is turned on with a gloved right hand. He removes his gloves and places them inside his suit pocket, washes his hands meticulously and turns off the tap with the edge of his right elbow, enough to stem the flow but not to stop an occasional drip. Outside he takes another taxi.

'*Zum Flughafen, bitte.*'

The journey takes twenty minutes at some speed. He approaches the BA ticket desk in the functional Terminal C and eyes up the middle-aged customer-service girl from a safe distance. She toys with the keyboard of an unseen monitor below the desk. Smart uniform, good height even allowing for the raised platform of the desk, well-groomed fair hair with give-away darker roots, sufficient make-up, a skirt that comes just above the knee, good legs in black stockings, moderate heels. Her name badge proclaims 'Emma Fischer' with a small German flag to indicate her second-language proficiency. She has a wedding ring on her left hand. He's about to speak when a sweaty guy pushes past.

'Excuse me, mate, you don't mind, do you? I'm in a real hurry.'

'Not at all,' he fakes, suppressing the look of death. The Ten Commandments must be followed.

Emma speaks to the other passenger in perfect English. He can make out a hint of a distant northern accent. He deduces that if she's now stationed permanently in Dusseldorf, then she married a German. The guy Fischer is a lucky bastard. The queue-jumper leaves. His own turn comes. He places his Club Europe ticket on the counter, safe in the knowledge that he knows more about Emma than Emma will ever know about him. He gives her his best corporate smile.

'I missed the 18.50 to Heathrow. I need to change this ticket to Lufthansa.'

'That won't be necessary, sir.'

He'll have to pull rank here, whip out the BA gold card and cause a scene.

'What do you mean?'

'You haven't missed the flight, sir,' she advises. He doesn't understand, unsure if greater forces are at work here. 'The incoming flight was late. BA 943 leaves in twenty minutes.' She points behind. 'See?'

He looks up at the display boards in the departure hall. BA is flashing a revised departure time. There was no need to engage in unnecessary conversation, to even approach the ticket desk, to stand out from the mass of anonymous suits wandering about the hall with their latest-model hands-free mobile kits and carry-on metal suitcases on wheels. He should have gone straight to check-in.

'Excellent.'

'You only have that briefcase.'

He wonders what she means. He nods. Emma looks at the clock on the wall.

'I can check you in. Aisle or window, sir?'

'Aisle.' Better views.

'You're in 6C, sir.'

'Thanks.'

'I hope you haven't been inconvenienced too much today, sir.'

He takes his boarding card.

'Not at all.'

CHAPTER FIVE

CANARY WHARF, LONDON E14: 12.45 P.M.

Adam is collected second time around from Mitchell's reception by the same pleasant yet utterly bored middle-aged PA. She doesn't help matters as they stand in the rising elevator, each watching in utter silence as the numbers light up towards twenty-one. He wishes he didn't have to make this covert lunchtime trip out east but the first meeting with Weinbaum went rather too well. Now he has to impress Bruce somebody.

'Wait here,' the PA advises.

He sits in a plush glass office, big enough to house two corner sofas. After ten minutes spent examining the revolting corporate art on the walls, bought by the metre, he wonders if the delay is part of a plan by this Bruce guy to soften him up before they meet. His mind rambles over what he will be asked and the answers he has rehearsed. He even thinks about leaving. The PA returns after another fruitless ten minutes.

'I'm sure he knew about this. He can't have gone far. Want a coffee?'

'I'm okay,' he mutters.

The PA walks away. He looks out at the trading floor and the few others sitting nearby who occasionally stare over at him. They're all in their smart casuals. Mitchell's are supposed to be casual about everything except for FX trading. He wonders why he wore his best suit. They look back like they know who he is. An unknown looking for a job. Many are called but few are ever chosen at Mitchell Leonberg & Co. Inc.

A tall guy with a bag from a deli slouches back into a seat at the far end. The PA approaches him immediately, they speak, he looks over at Adam, feigns lack of interest as she hands over a few A4 pages, probably his CV, and walks away. The guy sits down, picks up a telephone handset and begins an earnest conversation. It's already a quarter-past. Beamer will miss him. This is a disaster. Adam blames Henry.

'Bruce will be with you in a minute.' The PA opens and closes the door in almost the same instant.

The guy outside finally gets up, throws the bag in a bin and approaches the office. He's impressive from afar, swarthy, imposing. Adam wonders if he should look away or stare back, wonders which is better, which is expected. He is ever aware that an interview is always won or lost in the very first minute.

'Hello.' They shake hands. Adam thinks it went well. Firm and decisive yet not too prolonged to be embarrassing. 'No one get you a coffee, Adam?'

He's clearly made the wrong decision.

'I said I was okay . . .' He tries to recover the moment. People like to hear their first name. 'Bruce.'

The guy sits down opposite, stretches long muscled arms under rolled-up shirtsleeves but says nothing. He must be six-two or -three. His hands are huge. His shoes might be size twelve. He's radiating sheer naked power, oppressive body language, bottled confidence, eyes darting with energy, skin shaved close to the bone. Adam thinks he can detect the smell of drink – beer. He wonders if these traders play hard. Bruce runs his hands along his jawline and past the open top button of a blue Oxford shirt. There's silence. Adam's wondering if he should open the conversation and seize the moment. He's already picked up some clipped accent.

'Are you Australian?'

'Guess again.'

There's definitely an accent from down under. Adam regrets he made the wrong choice.

'So you're a Kiwi?'

'I think you'll find that's a small green fruit.' Adam's in deep. 'You'll never guess. I'm South African.'

'Been in the UK long?'

Bruce is looking back at him like the question is an invasion of his privacy. Adam still doesn't know his surname.

'Long enough to run an FX desk.'

'Are you going to go back sometime?'

'No way. Country's being run into the ground. Don't believe all that Mandela, Biko, Robin Island shit.'

There's another pause. Adam waits.

'So you survived the first interview with Lloyd?' asks Bruce.

Adam fakes it. 'Looks like it. Decent guy, I thought.'

There's no agreement. Bruce reluctantly picks up the CV like it's sort of contaminated.

'Twenty-three. From Faversham. Never heard of it. A good primary business degree at college. Some vaguely relevant summer-intern work experience at UBS. A year's spot trading at a well-run, boring place like Kapital.' Bruce feels obliged to open with a stock question. 'So why do you want to leave Kapital and come to Mitchell's, which as it happens is the best FX desk in the City of London?'

'Kapital's a small player. Mitchell's is a bigger player.' His rehearsed answer sounds trite.

'Don't you mean payer, not player?' Bruce is now grinning back at him. Adam's beginning to see the light. This isn't an interview. The guy's having a laugh with him, maybe at him.

'Yeah, I only came here today for a bigger package.'

Bruce is showing off his shining teeth. It's all one big joke. He's just going through the motions of interviewing someone whose second-hand CV he has first read five minutes ago over a prawn and avocado sambo with Thousand Island dressing on wholewheat to go. The pressure is off. Adam's wasting his time. He can say whatever he likes. It doesn't matter.

'Sell me a paper clip.'

'What?' Adam exclaims.

'You heard me. You're a trader and you're making a market in paper clips. Make me buy one.'

He's lost. 'I don't know what you mean.'

'Most people can talk about an expected fall in the supply of paper clips or huge demand from offices or even unprecedented paper-clip inflation. Doesn't really matter if it's paper clips or euros, it's all about supply and demand. Most people who work here can think on the spur of the moment.'

'I'll sell you this paper clip for a tenner,' offers Adam. 'Others are buying them for twenty.'

'Better. But too late.' Bruce leans back. 'Try this. You're driving along in your car on a wild stormy night and you pass a bus stop. There are three people waiting ages for the bus. There's an old lady who looks as if she's about to die, there's your best friend who once saved your life and there's the perfect woman whom you've been dreaming about. Your car can only take one passenger. Which person do you offer a lift to?'

Adam can't think any more. 'I dunno. Maybe you don't stop at all?'

'Wrong. You stop and give your car keys to your best friend and let him take the old lady to the hospital. You stay behind and wait for the bus, alone with the woman of your dreams. She'll be dead impressed. You can't fail to score. Easy. It's called lateral thinking. That helps here too.'

This is a waste of time for both of them. Adam's attention is drifting. He sees the wall clocks outside and coloured flags. That has to be the FX desk. He looks at the faces sitting in rows, increasingly uncertain if they will be his future colleagues, if he will work with them, what they will think of him. Bruce suddenly gets personal.

'So, what do you do after work?'

Adam is suddenly distracted. He sees her standing up from an end seat. Every FX desk in the City has one. A slim well-dressed twenty-something girl with perfect make-up and shortish dirty-blonde hair that can be worn a million different ways but still look great. Even her glasses are a turn-on. She has spextacles.

'Go out. Meet people. See friends.'

Bruce is moving on, his back to the world outside.

'You single?'

It's an unexpected question. The blonde's side profile reveals high cheekbones, full lips and strands of dangling hair. She's all in black and has sparkling eyes when she turns around. She'll be waiting to garner Daddy's self-made wealth, working as a mere hobby to enhance her already extensive social life. Adam is sure that Bruce Whoever can't ask questions like this but he acquiesces.

'Yeah. I'm single.'

'You got a girlfriend?'

She'll have some posh accent from the Home Counties. She'll be able to give as good as she gets from the beery blokes nearby. Adam already has an answer for Bruce. Every trader has to be a player.

'I'm in between girlfriends,' he lies.

She'll be an Ice Maiden, so cold to the touch, even colder on the inside. They make eye contact briefly. The ordeal of the interview is over. It's a waste of half an hour except for Adam's imaginings about the blonde. He stops by the office door as he leaves. They never mentioned FX, spot and forwards, inter-banks and corporates, bids and offers, volatility and curves, ECB and the Fed and all that technical FX jazz.

'Did I miss something here? We didn't discuss the job.'

'I know from your CV that you can trade FX,' advises Bruce. 'Anyone who joins Mitchell's is on three months' probation so if they're useless, or even vaguely mediocre, then we drop them from a great height.'

Samantha Perry worries about the poor bastard sitting with Bruce in the hermetically sealed glass office. The guy is insulated from outside reality. She recalls the buzzwords that Bruce used with her. Bulge-bracket blue-chip investment banking. Leading global presence. Best FX desk in the City. Three months' probation only a formality. It's all corporate bullshit. She fell for the diatribe only months ago and now knows the truth about life on Mitchell's FX desk. She's almost tempted to run over and cut in to warn the candidate to get out while he still can. There's always more to life than a big name and a bigger salary.

'Sam, I need your professional opinion.' Muppet suggestively dangles his handset in his left hand, letting it swing back and forth at waist height. On her first day Bruce told her that the fat bloke traded euro with French banks, which were all frogs to the paranoid Europhiles at the desk, and that while Kermit is a stupid name for a FX trader, Muppet is so much better. She still doesn't understand. It's somewhat ironic too, she deduces. Muppet is a blue-blooded Tory Eurosceptic who hates all things Continental. He told her weeks ago that the only good thing ever to come out of France is the Channel Tunnel. She's half tempted to ignore him, but it's too near year-end bonus-deliberations time. This must be a wind-up.

'What do you want?'

Muppet uses the mute switch on the telephone connected to the dealerboard by metres of coiled cable.

'I got this saleswoman on the line. Says I shafted one of her best clients on a spot euro trade on the day of the ECB rates meeting last week. I haven't even met the client. How could I have shafted her? She says that the rate I quoted her over the phone is different from the one that I wrote on the ticket, and the trade has gone tits-up on the client. The client has a hard-on and wants the rate changed. What do I do?'

Samantha speaks clearly for the benefit of the intellectually challenged in the immediate vicinity.

'If you've got it wrong, split the difference and give her half. Then wash your mouth out with soap.'

Muppet nods back, scratches his crotch, shakes his head and shouts into the handset, 'I'm busy. I'll call you back.' The others laugh. 'Fucking sales force! Who needs 'em? Who's on the bun run today?' he asks.

Samantha keeps her head down but senses the pairs of solely male eyes boring into her. It's a grim day. The guys had one of their infamous all-night bars last night. Work all yesterday, off to the pub in the late afternoon, rack up a few hundred behind the bar, stay at a club till five a.m., get a cab home, have a shower, shit and shave, change, back into the same cab to the office for a seven a.m. start. Brewing up coffee beans and buying pastries was not on the syllabus of her three-year Maths degree at Bristol.

'Not me?' she hazards.

'Sure thing, Sam,' confirms Muppet.

'My name is Samantha. I've told you before.'

'You're Sam to us. One of the blokes,' confirms Muppet. 'Bun-run time.'

Samantha stands up reluctantly. 'Why me again?'

'Because you're the position keeper and we're the traders who make the money to pay for the coffee.'

True enough. She *is* the position keeper, helping the others to monitor their long and short currency positions. But the offer letter said her job title is junior FX trader. Only they won't let her trade yet. Bruce says it's just a matter of time. 'And, more importantly, tradition has it that the most junior person at the desk gets in the coffees,' Muppet patronises her as he points. 'Might not be long now.'

Samantha looks over at the office with the closed door with mixed feelings.

'So if that guy in there joins us then I'm free from these daily duties?'

'Except at home, obviously, and for your eventual hubby,' advises Muppet. The others snigger out of sight. 'And that guy isn't joining us. He's wasting his time. Lloyd wants to hire someone new but Bruce will veto everyone. Unless it's your twin sister, Sam.' He pauses. 'You haven't got a twin, have you?'

She's that close either to giving up work or else complaining up the line about the constant sexist jibes.

'Same order?' she sighs.

'Yep. Coffee. Black. No sugar. Neat. On the rocks. Straight up. To go,' advises Muppet.

'Coffee, two sugars, very milky,' advises Spoon who trades Far East, has titled ancestors, a plum stuck deep within his vocal cords and a family estate in Middle England almost as large as his ego.

'Tea for me. The stronger the better,' advises Cable Guy, who trades sterling versus dollars, the so-called cable, but spends his nights and weekends watching Sky Sports and dodgy movies on Red Hot & Dutch. Decades ago there even was a cable laid on the floor of the Atlantic to connect London and New York traders. Hence the term.

'Decaff coffee,' advises Bookie, who trades the exotics like Turkish lira and Mexican pesos, but usually spends his lunch hour putting a pony on a nag at Sandown at the nearest Ladbroke's.

Samantha looks over at the glass office. The candidate is still with Bruce, then he turns to look directly at her. It's as close to a smile as you can do in an interview. Samantha looks back at him, past the PA with immaculate dress sense who partly obscures her view. She likes what she sees, even from this distance.

'Do I get Bruce something?'

Muppet leans back to examine the interviewer and inter-viewee. His chair creaks with the disposition of his weight. The candidate is sitting comfortably, at his ease, is making good eye contact. Bruce is nodding, but it's clear his interest is waning. It's all in vain.

'Bruce won't be long. I know him well enough. I can tell he's unimpressed.'

'I'll get him a coffee.' Samantha turns to Muppet. 'If he's not finished when I get back I can always pour it in your lap.'

'Promises, promises.' Muppet's on the phone again. The saleswoman has rung him back. He fumes.

Samantha walks off down the row of desks, looking inside the office as she draws nearer. The candidate has a sharp suit, a good side profile, strong features, clear skin up close and close dark hair in excellent condition. Bruce should make him a job offer. Then he'll get her a regular latte on the next bun run.

Henry's having a bad day at the office. One of his candidates is at Goldman Sachs for his ninety-third interview because Goldman's want potential employees to meet everyone, including the tea lady and her mother. An equity sales candidate has late doubts because he thinks there might be office politics at his new bank, it being the sort of place where you go for a leak only to return and find half your client list has been nicked. Some senior Italian M&A guy pulls out of a long-agreed move from a Milanese bank to a US bank in London because his wife is suddenly now expecting their second kid in six months' time. A fixed-income salesgirl turns down an offer to move to London with a Swiss bank because she doesn't want to leave Frankfurt, of all places. Jolly exciting Frankfurt, where nightlife consists of watching the traffic lights, entertainment consists of jaywalking and even the public-park trees are boringly straight.

He wonders why overseas staff don't want to work in wonderful London. You can get a decent meal out for a few grand a head, service, VAT, cover charge, wine, water, bread rolls, gratuity and food excluded. You can get mugged in St John's Wood for a fake Rolex, or killed for a real one. You can buy a broom cupboard in the Barbican or a bijou garage in Chelsea for a few million quid up front. You can walk the streets paved with gold, phlegm and dog turds. What does somewhere like Paris or Madrid have to offer apart from sun, culture, history, good food, friendly people, a working transport system and gorgeous women?

He walks outside to Trish. 'Any news from Mitchell's on Adam Lewis?'

'None yet,' she replies. 'You want me to call them?'

'Let's leave it a while longer. Don't want to seem too desperate.'

This job market is damn' difficult. There are too many headcount freezes, cost containments, downsizing exercises and other corporate PC slang. There are too many mergers and takeovers among the banks so his client base diminishes by the day. Henry's heard a rumour that the next big merger is between ABN, Rabobank, Salomon, Erste, HSBC, Oesterreich, Landesbank Berlin, Ergo Bank and SBC. He hears senior management is still considering a suitable acronym for the newly merged entity.

He's toying with some names in his Rolodex when Trish bustles into his office mid-morning. 'It's that time of the year again.' He looks up blankly. 'The best time of the year. It's Christmas time!'

Henry looks at his desk calendar. 'I think you'll find that's months away.'

'Selfridges don't agree. They've sent their corporate gift catalogue today. We need to choose.'

'I'm too busy with difficult clients. You know, if we didn't have any this job would be so much easier. Do me a favour – can you organise everything? You did such a good job last year.'

Trish sits down. 'I'm already one step ahead of you. I circled a few items for your approval.'

'Let's get what we got last year.'

'We need to be original.' Trish thumbs through the glossy pages. 'I thought maybe this time the cufflinks for the gentlemen.' Henry looks and nods. 'And maybe the compact for the ladies?'

'A BMW 3-series compact? At thirty grand a pop, I fear not, Trish.'

'Make-up compacts. Sterling silver. Sixty-five pounds a pop, as you say. I'll order twenty of each and we can mail them out to our best clients in early December.' Trish gets up. 'Easy.' She makes to leave.

'Is that enough gifts?' he wonders. 'We must have more clients now.'

She points to the cupboard in his office. 'We still have some items left over from last year.'

'I thought you said we have to be original?'

'We can. We use last year's surplus items for our newer clients. They'll never know. Remember we got those silver desk sets last year. Look.' Trish leans over, opens the cupboard and rummages about inside.

Henry closes the cupboard with his foot.

'I gave some away during the year. Special occasions, I think. Better order a few more.'

She leaves, then calls from the outer office.

'Lloyd Weinbaum is on the line.'

CHAPTER SIX

VICTORIA STATION, LONDON SW1:
10.05 A.M.

An anaemic stubbled youth gets into Adam's standard-class carriage before the train is due to depart.

'I've got some copies of the *Big Issue* to sell. I know it's complete crap but I need the money.'

The embarrassment in the carriage is overpowering. Heads are suddenly buried in newspapers. Others stare away. An elderly woman buys a copy. Adam offers up a quid but doesn't bother with the magazine. They are soon left alone to their solo thoughts. The train leaves twenty minutes late due to engineering works. Not bad for Connex, apparently. Adam watches platform five slowly disappear through a grubby window, grateful to have what all rail passengers ultimately desire, a double seat all to himself.

The ugly part of South London — terraced homes and disused railway sidings — gives way to No Man's Land. Gillingham station has a handwritten sign announcing that the ladies' toilets are out of order due to vandalism. Sittingbourne car park has a car-boot sale with rubbish on discount. Rainham has a giant Aldi store for bargain groceries. A lost-looking Connex employee who seems almost too embarrassed to collect tickets breaks the monotony. Adam's rolling back towards his early years. There's barren farmland, crumbling outhouses, aluminium fences, skeletal trees and sparse copses. It's another world. It's home.

Seventy minutes later he alights at Faversham station. He telephoned last night as usual but there's no one waiting to meet him on the platform. It's their unspoken agreement. He's now independent so will make his own way in life. He takes a minicab outside the station for the ten-minute trip. With every twist and turn along the claustrophobic roads and encroaching hedgerows, he relives his early life in this rural retreat. He passes the parochial all-boys Modern School where he studied for his stellar A-level results and nurtured a burgeoning secret ambition to get the hell out of here.

The garden of the family home is unkempt, its biological imperative for seasonal growth long ago overtaking his parents' ability to curtail it. The trusty Ford is in the driveway. His father greets him at the door like the delay is his fault, not Connex's. 'You're late.' He wears a loose cardigan. He's more bent and stooped than last time. His Sunday-best trousers show stains by the fly. Up close Adam can see that he misses more than he catches when he shaves with his old Wilkinson.

'Sorry. Train trouble. Smells good.'

'Should do.' His father limps on inside ahead of him. 'Your mother went to a lot of trouble.' Adam has given up asking how his father is keeping. His father has given up talking about the accident at the factory.

The house is small, with low ceilings, busy wallpaper, oppressive curtains and dark carpets. There seems to be more narrow corridor and long hallway than actual living room. Adam avoids the low beams of the ceilings. He knows where to sit at the dining-room table. There are always only three place settings. Such is the hazard of being an only child. There was no one to play with, no one to amass toys with. Sometimes, when his parents dispensed immediate and rough justice, he wished there were someone else to distract them.

His mother welcomes him but they don't kiss. She is wrapped up against the winter elements and prefers layers of woollen clothing to turning the central heating up to high. 'You're looking well,' she comments.

'Must be the high life in London,' observes his father from the hallway.

She carries in the burnt sacrificial offering. In a former life it was a side of lamb. Adam wonders how much of the weekly state invalid pension went on the meat. His father carves parsimoniously, as if the rest of the joint has to last them all for the following week. Adam makes do with three crisped wafer slices. He fulfils his usual familial duty and opens the bottle of modest red he bought in Oddbins at Victoria.

'What's London like these days?' asks his mother after a token grace.

Adam is tempted to say that it's a big city with lots of buildings and people. 'Great. I still love it.'

'Never fancied it much myself. Looks awful from the train,' she observes.

'Most big cities do,' he replies, then eats.

There's a lull in the conversation. His father pours a huge globule of HP sauce onto his lamb. His mother prefers a polite modicum of mint sauce. Adam is dying to talk to someone about his fantastic news from Henry. He can wait no longer. No one else knows.

'I've got some news.'

His father puts down his cutlery. 'You moving back?' Adam shakes his head. 'Got a new girlfriend?'

'Something else. I think I'm going to move jobs.'

'Again? After being only a year at that ... German place?'

'It's called Kapital.'

'What's wrong with it?'

All Adam wants is some encouragement. 'Nothing's wrong with it.'

'Then why leave?' his father perseveres.

'I got a job offer this week from Mitchell Leonberg.'

There's a blank look from his father who has returned to chewing gristle. 'Never heard of them.'

'They're huge.'

'Is that a good thing?'

All Adam wants is some enthusiasm. 'Mitchell's are the best in the City.'

'Says who?'

'Only everyone I know.'

The parental interrogation continues. 'Do you know anyone who works there?'

'No one yet. It'll be okay, I'm sure.'

'I don't know why you want to work in London. What's wrong with a nice bank job here, in Barclays?'

Here is nowhere. Lifeless. Dead End. Cul-de-Sac. Road to Nowhere. 'The best careers are in the City,' he says patiently.

His father looks through him. 'Only if you're a toff who went to public school. It's a closed shop. You should stick to what you know. I don't know of anyone from Faversham who ever made it in the City.'

'Gimme time.'

'You make it sound so easy.'

His mother intervenes. 'What do Brian and Cheryl think of the move? They're such nice people.'

'I haven't told them yet.'

Next up is a warm trifle that sags against a chipped glass bowl when his mother inserts a spoon. Conversation is still limited but seems irrelevant to Adam. He's made the effort to visit them. Nothing has changed. The room feels smaller with the walls closing in by the hour. He's tried his best, tried to involve them in his new life, but once again they are unresponsive. Adam knows the Connex timetable verbatim.

'I gotta go soon. Thanks for lunch.'

His father stands expectantly by the door. He's not volunteering a lift to the station in the Ford. With his game leg, he drives only in emergencies, when he's going to Asda or the local pub at the crossroads. Adam senses the time is right. He takes the folded cheque from his pocket. His mother can't see them.

'That's something for you both. It might help, coming up towards Christmas.' His father never thanks him. 'I'll let you know what I decide to do with the new job,' offers Adam.

'Sounds to me like you've already decided what you're going to do.'

Bruce Villiers slouches with his feet up on the edge of the FX desk. He's come a long way from growing up in Fishhoek with its ludicrous alcohol ban: a modest economics degree at Stellenbosch University, lazy BBQ summers on the beaches outside Cape Town, fraternal rugby on the dusty playing fields, a job with Standard & Merchant Bank in downtown Johannesburg and finally taking the Chicken Run on SAA to the UK when the going got tough and the smart got going in the early 1990s.

He surveys his personal kingdom. Muppet is on the telephone to his ex-wife. Bookie is on the telephone to his bookmaker. Spoon is on the telephone to his private banker at Coutts & Co. Cable Guy is on the telephone to ntl about his monthly bill. Samantha is doing some sort of research on euro/dollar FX rates on Bloomberg. He hired her principally for her looks but she seems to be the first girl he knows able to resist his tall frame, swarthy looks, lilting accent and ebullient personality.

Bruce stretches his hands behind his head. This year has been a good one. The desk has made millions. He manages Lloyd rather than the other way around. This week should be no different from the others. He remains in full control of the destiny of this particular FX desk. He waits until the others hang up. It's time for management in action.

He likes to address the important issues of the day on his feet.

'Gimme all your business cards,' he says, standing up. The others oblige but they're puzzled. Bruce explains. 'We got a new name at the desk, a new role, a new function. We used to be foreign exchange, but not any more. Now we're gonna be *global* foreign exchange. We're nothing if we're not global. So I'm the new head trader of global foreign exchange.' He hands out boxes of new business cards. 'Use these, global guys.'

'Congratulations on your elevation, Bruce,' Muppet crawls to him.

Samantha looks at her card and then back at him. 'This even says I'm a trader?'

'All in good time.'

Muppet reads aloud from the *Sun* as usual. 'There's a scary look at the future of medicine, further proof that the long-term implications of drugs must be considered. Says here over the past few years more money was spent on breast implants and Viagra than on Alzheimer's. Shit! In a few years we'll have a lot of people running around with huge breasts and erections who can't remember what to do with them.'

The others are impervious to Muppet's edited highlights. Instead they watch the lack of a reaction from Samantha. Tranquillity returns. They graze the screens but the market is dead today. Becalmed. Bruce takes a telephone call on an internal line. He recognises the number but can't place it immediately.

'Bruce, you got a minute?'

He looks up and sees Lloyd replacing his handset. He's twenty feet away but Lloyd can't be bothered to get up and drag his lardy ass over to the FX desk. Bruce deliberately waits a few minutes as if he has better things to do, then wanders reluctantly over to Lloyd's office.

'What's up?'

Lloyd holds up a travel and expense form.

'I have to sign this for Finance. It's yours. What were you doing in Zurich last month for two days?'

'It was the Euromoney Annual FX conference. You approved my trip months ago.'

'I don't remember doing that. These are hard times. And where were you on Wednesday?' asks his boss.

'I was here.'

'I mean, in the afternoon.'

'I took the afternoon off. A half-day's vacation. We're allowed vacation, you know.'

'You're supposed to okay time off with me in advance.'

'I'll do it next time.' Bruce wonders if that's it. He's going to leave.

'So where were you this time? Another junket?'

Bruce knows his privacy is being invaded. 'I don't need to tell you what I do outside of work.'

'Someone on the floor thought that you were in Germany? Odd sort of a place to go for a vacation.'

Bruce can't believe that Lloyd knows his exact movements. 'Who told you that?'

'Doesn't matter who told me. So you *were* in Germany?'

'What if I was? It's not a crime.'

'So you flew all the way there just for a few hours and then back here again?'

Bruce looks himself up and down. 'Evidently so.'

'Frankfurt, was it?'

It must be a wild guess. Lloyd couldn't know any more. 'You don't need to know where I went.'

Lloyd leans closer. 'Are you being headhunted?'

It's a perfect alibi. 'Who knows? Maybe. Maybe not.' Bruce makes to leave. 'Is that it?'

Lloyd holds up one hand. 'We need to touch base on Adam Lewis.'

'Who?'

'Last week's interviewee. Adam Lewis.'

'There's nothing to talk about.'

'Glad we agree on something. I've made him an offer to join us.'

'He'll never make a top FX trader. He's not aggressive enough. He's reactive, not proactive.'

'I think he's intelligent. Malleable. Will grow into the job. I think he's worth a speculative punt.'

Bruce stands by the door. 'You can hire him for whatever you want, but not for my FX desk.' He walks out to the desk, waits a few long minutes until Samantha goes off alone in the direction of the ladies' and lowers his voice. 'Who the hell told Lloyd where I went?'

There's silence until Muppet speaks. 'I might have said too much to a PA by the vending machine.'

'Well, don't fuck up again. No one needs to know where I go on my time off from Mitchell's.'

Henry alights from the Northern Line at Angel, walks along Upper Street, turns left along Theberton Street and through Gibson Square to his six-hundred-grand three-storeyed Georgian terraced home. It's peaceful. There's no one about and no traffic. It's the way he likes it. Some of the homes are dilapidated. Some are renovated. Dead marigolds hang down from wrought-iron balconies. He knows Amanda is at home tonight because her car is still in a residents' bay out front. Inside she's standing by the hall table, her favourite black Karen Millen coat in one hand, the keys to her sporty Z4 in her other.

'Hi,' he says.

'Hi,' replies his wife of eight years' standing. She seems preoccupied. 'Good day?'

'Not bad. I placed another candidate at Mitchell Leonberg.'

They kiss. Henry's uncertain, wondering if she's arrived home or is about to go out. It's difficult to tell until he sees her check her face in the wall mirror, ruffle her bobbed fair hair, pat her light make-up and finally touch up her lip gloss. Under her coat he can see flared culottes and smart heels.

'You going out again tonight?' he asks. 'Another launch?' She nods enthusiastically. 'Some space shuttle at Cape Canaveral?' he hazards with a mock grin, pushing his briefcase under the hall table as usual.

'More like another new girlie-magazine launch at a hotel off Leicester Square.'

Henry's a widower. A PR widower. Amanda explained the mysteries of the marketing industry to him once like this: you see a gorgeous girl at a party and go up to her and say, 'I'm fantastic in bed.' That's Direct Marketing. You're at a party with a bunch of friends and see a gorgeous girl. One of your friends goes up to her and, pointing at you, says, 'He's fantastic in bed.' That's Advertising. You're at a party and you see a gorgeous girl. You get up and straighten your tie; you walk up to her and pour her a drink. You open the door for her, pick up her bag after she drops it, offer her a lift home, and then say, 'By the way, I'm fantastic in bed.' That's Public Relations. You're at a party and see a gorgeous girl. She walks up to you and says, 'I hear you're fantastic in bed.' That's Brand Recognition.

'So is business still good?' he asks.

'Only because we work so hard. We got a new radio-station account and some sports events this week.'

Amanda was never one of those bubble-head bimbos who get into the PR business thinking that it's all champagne and canapés. She knows that there's far more of stuffing envelopes and getting paper cuts. She's managed to lose the rubbish clients who think that just because they're paying her a fee, it entitles them to a guaranteed front-page picture of their useless product in a national daily – 'That's called advertising, mister.' She knows that the majority of her eloquent press releases go straight into the 'round filing tray'. Once a *Guardian* journalist said to her on the telephone, 'Yes, I'm looking at your press release now', so she asked him straight up –

'Yeah, really? Well, read the first line of it to me, then.' He hung up.

Henry takes the *Standard* and a glass of Volvic into the living room. He doesn't know tap water is safer. There's hardly space on the low table for paper and glass. The beech top is piled high with glossy coffee-table interiors books. He derives a modicum of satisfaction from putting his shoes up on her pile of Conran interiors hardbacks.

This is no longer his room. It's Amanda's sample room. She changes the interior weekly. Her obscure prints adorn the walls, which in turn morph from pear-white to apple-white emulsion. She's taken his last personal effects from the room, one by one, down to his basement haunt. Henry misses his pair of framed red Rothko prints. He ordered them after a visit to the Tate Modern on Bankside. The Rothko room is his favourite. All those dark heavy solid colours. So much easier to assimilate.

Amanda still hasn't left. It's approaching eight o'clock. 'Will you be okay?' she asks.

'Sure. I'll potter about.'

'More TV and DIY?'

'Could be worse.'

'I'll be home by eleven. You can wait up, if you like.'

'I've got some work to do. And I have a busy day tomorrow.'

'I've left something for you. Zap it. And feet down, please.' She blows him another kiss before she closes the hall door behind her. He hears the sonic boom of the car alarm, hears the driver's side-door slam, then the two-litre engine rev to her expert touch and she's gone from the London Borough of Islington.

He walks through the ample rooms of the three-bedroomed turn-of-the-century house. There's a picture frame of their wedding standing further along the hallway. He knows the cleaner dusted it recently because the frame stands at the wrong angle to the light from the transom above the door. He moves the frame to the left so it stands exactly the way he left it last time.

He descends the half-stairs to the basement floor. They blew ten K on a remodelled Shaker-style kitchen, with bright colours, recessed spots, granite worktops and chrome fittings. Amanda saw it in an interiors magazine at the much-frequented hair salon. Bowls of assorted citrus fruits, fresh cut flowers, deserted gleaming surfaces, unused steel utensils abound. It's all an illusion to be admired, never to be used.

Amanda insisted on a double-door GE fridge with icemaker, for some phantom two point three children family unit that will never enjoy this kitchen. Inside there's a huge slab of congealed lasagne and a yellow post-it note with cooking instructions. He recognises the food from two days ago, recognises the corner portion, even recognises the garnish that remains. Henry opens the pedal bin with his left foot and drops the food into the black plastic bag from an unnecessary height, pleased with his accuracy. There's a frozen Tesco carbonara something in the freezer. He zaps it for five minutes in the Sanyo and eats half of it at the kitchen table. Then he walks down the next flight of stairs to his DIY room.

Three hours later he lies awake in bed until he hears the hall door open below. He listens to Amanda tiptoe unnecessarily up the stairs, an occasional step creaking, then hears her spend longer than usual in the en-suite, running taps and the like. He watches her undress in the semi-dark and slip in beside him. Their bed's huge, big enough so that he and Amanda needn't touch each other unless he wants them to. All he can see is the back of her head, her bare shoulders and her bobbed hair that he hasn't run his hands through for months. She always lies towards the door, facing away from him.

He rolls closer to her and inhales. He can't smell any alcohol. Only the lingering remains of cigarette smoke from too many hours mingling in some function room with freeloading leeches and luminaries.

'Not tonight, Henry,' she mumbles.

'C'mon. That's why I stayed awake.'

She rolls over and stares up at the ceiling. 'I was on unsweetened cranberry juice all evening.'

'So? You were driving.'

'You don't get it. I feel like I drank gallons of the stuff. I drank a few litres of water today. I haven't touched any coffee. All I had for breakfast was a few tubs of live yoghurt. Lunch was chicken, green vegetables and kiwi fruit. I had an hour-long hot bath before I went out. I tried everything. Even a bloody hot water bottle.' He stares. 'You still don't get it, do you?'

'Get what?'

'I'm in pain. It's excruciating, sickening. My bladder and kidneys are sore. I'm bleeding. You don't know real pain until you have this cystitis. Do you even know what that is?'

'Don't take it out on me.'

'It's your fault. It's too much sex.'

'What's wrong with that?

'Last weekend was too rough. Way too vigorous.'

'I thought you liked it that way. Why don't you take some drugs for it?'

'I'd prefer to heal naturally. And I am not the age I was. Leave it out for this evening.'

Henry pulls her closer. 'But I need it tonight.'

Amanda resists. He insists.

CHAPTER SEVEN

LONDON WALL, LONDON EC2:
11.10 A.M.

'Did you guys hear about one of our staff in Dusseldorf?' The desk staff shake their heads. 'Killed.'

Someone nearby pipes up from behind the screens, 'What are you on about, Beamer?'

'I'm telling you, it's on the wires. Reuters say that one of our syndicate bankers in head office left work, took a taxi home and was later found by his wife, stabbed in his own front garden. Guy called Ulrich somebody.'

Adam looks up. 'I know an Ulrich somebody from my head office induction course. He gave us a talk about international lending and all that.' Beamer passes over the Reuters printout. Adam reads it quickly, then turns cold as realisation slowly dawns. His own career suddenly seems less important. 'Jesus, it *is* him. Ulrich Karst. 42. Married with two kids. Time of death believed to be in the early evening. No witnesses. No immediate leads. No known motive. Stabbed several times in the chest. Jesus, what a way to go! I remember him now. He was a good guy.'

'My condolences,' offers Beamer. 'We'll send something to his wife. A card. A wreath. Whatever.'

'I'll organise it. I'll ring Natalia over there. She knows most of the people in head office.'

'Any excuse to talk to Natalia,' observes Beamer with a smile.

Adam dials the dealerboard on the inter-office leased line. Natalia can't be located. She's gone to the funeral. Head office is in mourning. One of the other guys tells Adam that Natalia knew Ulrich's wife very well. Adam gets the impression that FX trading doesn't matter as much to head office today.

He sits at the FX desk, his thoughts a million miles away from trading euros. Lloyd called Henry again. Henry called Adam twice. Once to tell him the good news, then again to encourage him. One of the telephone calls was made to his home. Henry talks a good game. It's hard to say no.

The morning drags. The atmosphere is subdued. Adam can't put it off any longer. Henry says that he did well. They like him. No, love him. Lloyd wants to move fast. Mitchell's are making a firm offer. It's twenty K more than his basic at Kapital plus there's in-the-money stock options on the NYSE-listed parent. Only a lunatic declines free money. Mitchell's need a yes immediately. They don't take no for an answer. Now comes the difficult part. It's time to tell his boss. Adam looks over at Beamer.

'Can we talk for a few minutes?' Beamer rolls over his chair. Adam gets to his feet. 'Wolfie is over in Dusseldorf today. Let's use his office.'

The two walk off, others nearby aware that something is up. Beamer instinctively shuts the door.

'Have you got a problem with a trade? Something you shouldn't have done? Maybe screwed up?'

Adam knows there's no easy way to break the news. Once he utters the words, there's no going back. He can make this move, become a player at a name, begin a new life all in one fell swoop.

'I got an offer to work somewhere else.'

Beamer's running his hands through his greying hair, like he's trying to rip out the follicles one by one.

'From who?'

Adam knows Beamer's going to be jealous. He savours the moment for an impolite second. Already he feels like he's working on the Canary Wharf floor, trading away, beating the market every time.

'Mitchell's.'

'For fuck's sake!'

'I didn't know you'd take the news like this.'

'Look.' Beamer's hanging on to his patience – just. 'Banking is a job for life, like the church, nuclear waste disposal and burglary. We all gotta move on sometime, somewhere. Otherwise we're part of the bloody fixed assets. But to Mitchell's, of all places . . . They're a bunch of complete assholes.'

Already Adam feels like defending his future employer. He will soon be a company man, true to the image.

'They seem okay to me.'

'Who'd you meet there?'

'I met Lloyd Weinbaum. He's cool.'

'He is but he's a one-off.' Beamer nods. 'I met some guy, the FX desk head, at the Euromoney Conference in Madrid last year. He was so damn' arrogant and in my face. Full of it. A South African, I think.'

Adam makes the required admission. 'He's my new boss.'

'I rest my case. Jeez, this gets worse! You gotta tell Mitchell's you're staying here.'

But Adam's committed. He's told Henry. He's signed the couriered offer letter. It's a done deal.

'I can't.'

'Adam, you'll sink without trace in Mitchell's.'

They've not had a conversation like this in a year or more. Adam's getting edgy.

'What do you mean?'

Beamer moves closer. It looks like he genuinely cares about his staff.

'A bank like Kapital is where you belong. I've seen you work here. I know you. You started off slow, needed a chance to learn the job and settle in, but we gave you enough time to develop. We nurtured you.'

'So?'

'So here you're a small fish in a small pond. In Mitchell's, you'll be a fucking minnow in a bottomless ocean full of circling sharks with razor teeth. You will drown in the first high tide.'

'That's rubbish. I'm a good trader. That's why Mitchell's want me. I interviewed well and got the job offer. You don't want me to leave. It's just sour grapes. Nothing more. Nothing less.'

'We can forget about this conversation, you know, walk out of here like it never happened. You go back on the desk with the benefit of my experience.'

It's vaguely tempting but Mitchell's want him. Henry insists. 'I'm definitely going,' Adam explains.

Beamer sighs. 'So you've made up your mind?' Adam nods. 'It's your funeral.' Adam reluctantly accepts the facts. It's his last day in Kapital. 'We can't have you trading for the bank now. I'll tell Wolfie later. I'll call HR now. Wait here and do nothing.'

Thirty minutes later, Adam signs the pro forma resignation letter and shakes hands with the other guys. It feels like going to a funeral of a friend without being able to express any genuine words of condolence. He catches an empty Central Line Tube in the late morning, sits in the carriage, wonders how his life can change so much in a few weeks.

Samantha listens to Muppet standing at the photocopier. He's in obvious trouble. 'This damn' machine must be female. Once it's turned off, it takes ages to warm up. And I gotta push all the right buttons.' He walks over to her. 'Do you enjoy Sex in the City?'

'The TV programme is called Sex *and* the City,' she retorts.

'Who said anything about a TV programme, dear?'

Bruce arrives over to the desk from the elevators, playing pocket billiards with his left hand, holding a single piece of paper in his right. He seems satisfied about something as he shows the page to the others.

'It's finally arrived.' Most of the others immediately hang up their phones. 'You know what to do, Sam?'

She nods, remembering the most important month-end task in her menial role at the FX desk.

'Let me see it,' she asks.

'Not yet. You do your bit first.'

'Gimme five minutes.'

Muppet enjoys eavesdropping and is the first to stand up.

'We can't wait five. Let's have it in two.' He walks over. 'How does it look, Bruce? Ballpark.'

The desk head waits for complete silence on the desk. The squawk box is turned down to mute.

'Ballpark, Finance say we made three million dollars plus in September.' Bruce looks at his attentive and expectant team. 'Divided by five, that's more than half a mil each.' Samantha's conscious that Bruce and four traders make the five bodies. He doesn't yet include her in his trader headcount. She's the recent hire, perhaps just passing through their lives for a few short months. Slave labour of sorts. 'You guys want to cash it in now or wait till the end of year?'

'We wish,' advises Muppet, moving even closer. She inhales his noxious BO. 'Hurry up, Sam.'

She toys with the Excel file for the month of September. It amazes her that the world's greatest investment bank's technology infrastructure is essentially a series of vital spreadsheets connected by unseen macros. The systems suck. Every day each trader advises Bruce of his estimated trading profit by five p.m. Bruce nets all their estimates together, adds in his own profit and gives Samantha the final number for her to record. The alleged greatest FX trading mind in the City won't lower his ego to use an Excel file if he can find someone cheap with long elegant fingers and neatly painted nails to key in the data.

'So what do we show?' asks Bruce.

The desk usually makes a few hundred K or so per day. They drop the same on a bad day when they get burnt by the market, stung by other smarter counterparties and investment banks, shafted by pushy senior salesmen or ripped off by eager clients. She checks that each weekday cell is completed and that the original currency-to-dollar conversions are correct. The file looks okay. She reads the down tot aloud.

'Our own estimates say that we made three million, one hundred and thirty K.'

She wonders why she uses 'we' in the announcement, whether she is slowly being absorbed into the team.

'Perfect.' Bruce grins. 'Finance have three million two twenty K on this page.'

They cheer but then shut up as other cut-throat traders in the vicinity look over. Finance has screwed up again. If the desk shows more profit than Finance then they prove Finance wrong and get the Finance number revised upwards. If the desk shows less profit than Finance then some accounting error occurred and some other desk's FX profit is included in their FX figures. Tough. They say nothing and accept the acclaim.

'It's looking good for year-end. How much to date, dear?' asks Muppet.

Samantha tabs back to the summary sheet, enters the September number and reads the down tot.

'Eighteen million dollars of trading profit since January.'

'That's all net profit,' exclaims Muppet. Bruce stares over. Muppet reconsiders. 'Except for essential related expenses, of course.' A few knowing looks are exchanged. A smile or two. Samantha's lost. It's in some unknown code. 'The five of us make more than entire metal-bashing companies in the Midlands.'

'Lunch in Corney and Barrow in thirty minutes' time,' announces Muppet. 'Samantha, you gotta come.'

She ignores the smiles of the others at the simple yet ineffective double entendre. They leave her in peace. The same Excel file is glowing back at her. She wonders if she will spend her career staring at Excel, Word, Access and PowerPoint, never allowed to use a Reuters screen to trade the global markets. She's alone with her thoughts, always looking for an opportunity to expand her market knowledge.

The trading profit in September is consistent from day to day. She eyes the numbers, always in awe of the way five complete tossers can make so much money, and wondering whether a group of highly trained chimps would make more or less than Bruce's motley crew. One day's number jumps out at her. On the last Thursday of the month the desk made one and a half million dollars. Some day. Half the month's revenue crystallised on a single day.

She doesn't remember that day. She checks her Outlook diary and nothing of note appears. She wonders if the figure is right, wonders how she'll break the news to Bruce if not, then remembers the number came from him. She'll never learn the business if she doesn't ask questions. Bruce has walked away. She speaks to Muppet against her better instinct.

'What happened on the last Thursday in September?'

'I might have scored. Can't recall exactly.'

'We made one and a half million dollars' profit that day. That's ten times the daily average.'

He shifts in his seat, preferring to stare at cross-currency rates on screen than look her in the eye.

'Forget about it, dear.'

She's never noticed it before. She tabs over to August, always a quiet month in the City with the players jetting off to borrowed pads in the Indian Ocean or to rented yachts in the Caribbean. One day's dollar number jumps out again. The most profitable day is the last Thursday in August. She goes back through July, then June. The best day of the month generally seems to be the last Thursday.

'No. I won't forget about it. What happens every last Thursday? Why do we make so much?'

'Leave it,' snarls Muppet. 'I said, forget it.'

'You must know.'

'I fucking don't!' She hears his tone change. He's mean under pressure.

'Who knows, then?'

'Ask Bruce, if you dare.'

It is a dare. Muppet leers over at her. She has to accept the challenge. Bruce is coming over.

'I want to know what happens on the last Thursday of every month. We make millions almost every time.'

Bruce shifts on his feet for a moment, looks around and seems to lower his voice instinctively.

'You're such a clever girl.' He pauses, looking for the optimal words, the minimal damage. 'That's the day that the ECB meets to fix interest rates for the euro. We take a big position and try to make a profit.'

Samantha is unconvinced.

'But we always seem to make money. It seems too good to be true. How is that?'

She sees his attention span wane. Bruce is already mentally celebrating in the wine bar.

'Don't worry your little head about it. Just leave the trading to us. You do the position keeping so well. Get your hat and coat and go with Muppet for an early beer. That'll be nice. Just the two of you.'

Muppet is on his feet. Samantha shakes her head. 'I need a sandwich first.'

'Yeah, that's right, darling,' Muppet sneers. 'You need to get something inside you.'

Henry sits in his favourite seat on the Northern Line on his way home. It's the seat next to the glass partition and the sliding doors, the seat where no one can sit to his right to dig their elbows into him, the seat with the orange window sticker asking him to give it up for some phantom elderly or infirm passenger. If they want a seat they can stare away at whoever else is sitting directly opposite. Henry's moving for no one today. His arms are folded in defiance. His leather briefcase lies across his knees.

The Tube driver is a failed comedian. 'Hello, this is Lee speaking. I'm the captain of your train. We'll be departing shortly. We'll be cruising at an altitude of zero feet. Our scheduled arrival time in Edgware is 7.25 p.m. The temperature in Edgware is approximately five degrees Celsius. Edgware is in the same time zone as Moorgate, so there's no need to adjust your watches.' Others smile. Henry isn't that amused.

He despises the Tube. There's an e-mail going about that a year ago a bunch of forensic scientists removed a row of passenger seats from a Central Line carriage. They found hair upon the seats: human, dog, mouse and rat. They found seven types of insect, mostly fleas, mostly alive. They found human vomit, human urine, human excrement, rodent excrement and human semen. Trish says that the e-mail is a hoax. Others in the office worry that it might be true. Henry's arms stay folded and off the arm rests.

Cosmopolitan London is alive and well. He eyeballs the others sitting nearby. Directly opposite him is a brittle Filipino girl, maybe twenty years old. She's eating an egg-and-something sandwich from a plastic box. She's eating directly from the box, as if she doesn't want her fingers to touch the food. He stares over at her but she refuses to acknowledge him, preferring to keep her tired sad black eyes fixed on the windows with a view of the tunnel. She wears some sort of uniform. He reckons she's a maid or servant in some big house. She knows her true place in the world, daren't look back at him.

There's a sad Indian gent in his fifties who seems either utterly bewildered or unconvinced by the Tube. He's turning to look at every station platform earnestly, reading off the station names one by one – Goodge Street, Warren Street, Euston and the rest – then looking for reassurance above Henry at the Tube line map, as if someone might have reordered the Northern Line's stations since this morning.

There's a solo vacant teenage girl in a denim jacket, sitting with a ridiculously conspicuous Gucci shopping bag up on her knees. Henry doesn't think she looks the type, with her bad skin and split ends. He wonders if there's anything inside the bag, or whether she carries it with her just for effect. She looks the sort who knows the price of everything in New Bond Street, but the value of nothing.

His eyes drift upward to the elongated advertisements above the window, mostly covered in stickers and graffiti. There's an aerial shot of the Sydney Harbour Bridge and the white domes of the Opera House. It's a blurb for Singapore Airlines long-haul flights down under with a three-day stopover in Singers en route. Henry dreams. If ever he needs to get away from it all, then this is where he will go.

Off to his left there are two Asian youths sitting across from each other. They're wearing baggy denim trousers where the crotchline hangs somewhere near their knees. They're talking in some sort of street slang, short punches of conversation, monosyllables and one-liners. It sounds like Swahili to Henry.

The woman who sits beside him is reflected in the window. She's white with short neatly combed grey hair, bland clothes, socks and comfortable shoes, and is reading the media section of the *Guardian*. He reckons she likes those flat shoes, might be what bankers call a Libyan, likes to take a holiday on sun-drenched Lesbos.

Henry is suddenly distracted. He sees the flash of fluorescent yellow first, then they board his train, his carriage, and stand on either side of his set of doors. On the back of their jackets he can read 'British Transport Police'. There are two of them. The male stands facing Henry, removing his crested helmet and bowing his head below the overhead lights, like he's too tall for the carriage. But it's all an illusion because in fact he's a short fat git who's carrying too much heavy paraphernalia around his large waist for his own good.

The female might be eighteen and is horizontally, rather than vertically, challenged. She leans against the glass partition, the shiny seat of her dark trousers belying her apparent inexperience. Her rear is huge as her flesh pushes against the clear pane to the right of Henry's face. He's wondering if it might give way. They are too close to his personal space. He can hear them talking.

'And then . . . I said we needed a statement . . . in writing . . . but they didn't get one.'

The male sounds stupid. He's too loud, even above the sound of metal wheels upon metal rail. Henry wonders if the policeman wants the carriage to overhear his great legal mind at work, to be so easily impressed. Henry knows that all they need for the job is to be able to stand on their feet for an entire eight-hour shift.

'I see . . . see what ya' mean,' the woman replies in awe.

The male is staring back at Henry. Henry holds his gaze, trying to look vacant, but it's not easy. He doesn't want to draw attention to himself. He looks away, expressionless. He wonders why the male stares.

Suddenly Henry sees the old lady. She's in his face, wants a seat. His seat. The male is looking around the carriage. Henry doesn't want to get up yet although the next station is his stop. He's nearly there and he's not going to be defeated at the very end. The male is looking at him. The Filipino stops eating, gets up and offers her seat to the elderly lady who accepts with a smile. Case closed. The train stops.

Henry stands between the coppers as the doors open onto platform mayhem. They both alight behind him and also make for the main-line station. Henry stands on the right-hand side of the escalator as is his custom and watches the policewoman pass him by, but she reconsiders, stops and moves in to stand two steps in front as they rise upwards. The male moves to stand directly behind Henry. He's trapped, his eyes still facing her huge rear end and swinging truncheon. He can't ride the escalator like this.

'Like I said . . . we had to get the statement . . . otherwise the CPS wouldn't wear it.'

'I see . . . see what ya mean,' she replies again monotonously.

Henry moves left into the human traffic without indicating and runs up to the top, feeling his heart rate quicken, through the tiled tunnels, then the ticket barriers. He's left them in his wake. It's a sort of freedom.

CHAPTER EIGHT

WEST HAMPSTEAD, LONDON NW6:
3.15 P.M.

Adam crams the last of his life's possessions into the boot of the modest Vauxhall Astra, its rear seats folded down flat for maximum storage capacity. The biggest single task of his week off between day jobs is almost finished. His loyal flatmates bring out a couple of dying house plants, some broken CD cases and a box of tattered paperbacks. He packs the items reluctantly and closes the boot with some regret.

'Thanks for all the help.'

Cheryl steps off the edge of the pavement. 'Adam, please reconsider.'

'I'd love to. I really would. I'm sorely tempted.'

Cheryl is shivering, suddenly feeling the cold of being outside without a coat, but she hasn't given up.

'You must be mad to leave us, Adam.'

'I agree. I love it here. But much as I'd like to, I can't stay for ever.'

She walks over to the car, holds him close and kisses him lightly. On the cheek, not the lips. Her vocation as a natural carer shines, even on her day off from paediatric nursing at St Mary's, Paddington.

'Won't you miss me?'

He holds her, then moves away, conscious they are not alone. 'Of course I will. Look on the bright side, though. You two lovebirds get to share the flat without me cluttering up the place.'

'But it's so bloody far away,' she insists.

Adam jangles the car keys in his hand, trying to minimise the feelings of real loss.

'It's not, like ... New Guinea. It's only East London.'

'Might as well be New Guinea.'

'You can visit me any time you like.'

'We gotta find our passports first. Why choose there?'

'It's nearer work. Mitchell's are in Docklands and the FX team start at seven a.m. I need my sleep.'

'It's soulless down there. All offices and towers, no homes. There's no other people.'

Cheryl steps back onto the pavement, signalling a conclusion of sorts. Her boyfriend Brian, a reliable part-qualified CIMA accountant, has other ideas. His turn comes. He takes Adam's hand and shakes it.

'It's the end of an era. Six years at school. Three years rooming together at Uni. A year here. Are you sure you can survive out there in the big bad world without me, mate?'

Adam is genuinely moved. 'I'll give it my best shot. I'll miss you both.'

'Like hell! You're going to miss here like a hole in the head. The creaky floorboards, the draughty windows, the old boiler, the tepid shower, the leaking taps, the queue for the bathroom ...'

Cheryl shopped, cooked and cleaned. Brian slept, surfed and vegetated. Adam looks for the positives.

'I'm going to miss Cheryl's stir-frys and your Sky Sports subscription.'

Brian steps back onto the pavement and closer to Cheryl.

'How much are you paying again?'

Last week Adam put down a month's rent in advance in cash to the eager agent but he hasn't the nerve to tell the others it's three hundred a week. It's the going rate for modernity. It's obscene.

'Don't ask.'

'You flash City boys are all the same.'

'Don't believe the stereotypes. I'm not that flash at all. Look at my Astra.' Adam opens the car door. 'Thanks for the help. I'll call later. We can go for a drink in the local again. This time I'm buying.'

'You'd better,' they respond in unison. 'And we want an invite round for dinner soon.'

His last view of the happy couple is in the rear-view mirror as he drives past the Victorian terraces of Fourdytch Road, then he loses sight of them as he turns right towards the Euston Road. The traffic is manageable, better now than the other recent trips, late evening being the optimal time to move house. Twenty minutes later he arrives at his destination, his third and final such journey of the week.

He found the apartment when he surfed the web for rental properties near Canary Wharf. From the road the complex looks like a giant ocean liner of a prior era, beached on the riverside at right angles to the Thames, with starboard portholes of light and visible interior stairwells like gangways. His remote control opens the security gates. He drives past the uniformed guard and the overhead CCTV camera. The remote opens the underground car park and he parks the Astra with difficulty in space 1205, due to the rather garish canary yellow VW Beetle badly parked in space 1305. He shifts some of the boxes into the lift but grows impatient. He'll leave the others till tomorrow. He is home.

Welcome to Barrier Park, E16, land of eastern promise. 1205 is a two-bedroom, two-bathroom eight-hundred-square-foot apartment. The clean smells of fresh cream paint and newly laid wooden floors are still evident, an added attraction of the first letting. The property cost the best part of three hundred K, major league and still out of his price range. But if all goes well at Mitchell's, if he makes a good start, if he becomes an FX player, then he will soon be an owner rather than a tenant, living the dream courtesy of the Halifax. 1205 is an apartment fit for a potential star FX trader at a bulge-bracket global US bank.

He walks the fitted carpets and ceramic floor tiles, then admires the barren designer kitchen with pelmet lighting and integrated stainless steel units. He swings the door of the en-suite walk-in power shower open and closed several times, hoping it will revive him at six a.m. on his first day of a new dawn. He looks out of the double-glazed windows, insulated against the elements, almost insulated against life itself.

In one drawer there's a Barratt Homes glossy brochure: 'Aspire to the Heights of Exclusivity'. Adam eyes the photographs of the role-model couple at home. She is slim with tresses of hair falling onto a beige sofa. He is muscled and dark. She wears glasses to enhance her sex appeal and her intelligence factor. His sallow skin glistens as if he might have just returned from the ground-floor residents' gym. They both wear T-shirts and baggies in neutral colours – charcoals, khaki, greys, whites, tans. Light streams in from behind them as if the sun always shines in this land. She is barefoot with toes curled. His teeth gleam. There is a tall vase of white lilies. She holds a glass of white wine. He plays with an open laptop. Dream on.

French doors lead onto the small balcony. The vantage point from the rotunda tower is impressive, its architecture and presence as bold and confident as Adam himself hopes to be next week. He examines the flickering lights and the depths of the Thames, the metal façade of the flood barrier reflecting off the dark water and raw landscape. A twenty-three-acre park surrounds the development, an arid wasteland or an oasis of tranquillity, a buffer zone between poverty and wealth, a chasm between old and new. He listens for traffic, trains, anything, but nothing is really audible from twelve storeys above ground level, only the engines of a distant BAE whisper jet hovering on its final approach to the nearby City airport.

He inhales the cold yet invigorating air, part of him wishing that Cheryl and Brian were here too to share in the excitement of newness. He imagines siting out on the balcony in the summer with them, drinks in hand, *Sunday Times* half-read. Some day his parents might even visit. This is a new beginning. New home. New job. New salary. New colleagues. New opportunities. New lifestyle. Game on.

Diane Rubin takes the telephone call in the late afternoon and leaves the trading desk immediately for the executive floor. She rarely gets the opportunity to visit the gods upstairs. Instead the head of global capital markets usually comes down to visit his leading female Managing Director after a long lunch, to walk the walk and talk the talk with the troops in the front-line trenches. She enters and sits down, puzzled and sensing his apparent unease, yet always distracted by the awesome vista of uptown Manhattan from his ample suite on the thirtieth floor of Mitchell Leonberg's global headquarters.

'Sorry to drag you away from the desk.'

Diane winces at his weakness. She never apologises to anyone, no matter what. 'What's up?'

'Have I got a job for you!' exclaims L. Jeremiah Horowitz II. At his sky-high level in the organisation it's important to have a juxtapositioned initial, a weird surname, and not to be the first to succeed in your family.

'I already have a job. I run the FX options desk,' Diane counters. She crosses her legs and arms in a defiant display of defensive yet aggressive body language. She's all in black, as is her custom. Less decisions to take at six a.m. Her long jet-black hair is gathered back. Easier too than all this hair-salon hassle. Her severe visage, heavy eyeliner and Fifth Avenue jewellery do the rest. Glamour, much like greed, is good.

Horowitz stalls as he plays with his silk tie and checks the top knot. He's conclusive proof in Diane's opinion that American multinational corporations are still run by the tallest oldest males with the best real hair.

'You *used* to run the FX options desk.'

'As far as I'm concerned, I still do.'

Diane watches Horowitz toy with her uncertainties and emotions for far too long. She thinks he's debating how to begin a sales pitch of some sort so braces herself for some serious corporate bullshit.

'Do you know Lloyd Weinbaum?' he asks deliberately in his Southern drawl.

'As in FX. As in London.' She nods.

'Only Lloyd isn't in London any more. Nor is he in FX. He came home last night on the last flight outta Heathrow. Lloyd won't be going back there for a long time on our tab. If ever.'

She knows Horowitz enjoys dumping on others from a great height. From the thirtieth floor, to be precise.

'What happened to Lloyd?'

'I got Human Resources to call him and tell him we had a new organisation chart for London. Only he wasn't on it.'

They both know the culture and the politics of the thirtieth floor. One day you're a megastar running a trading desk with carte blanche. The next day you're on the window ledge, ready to jump or be pushed.

'So what's Lloyd doing back here now?'

'He's pursuing other management opportunities,' he sneers. 'Meaning he'll never run a desk again.'

'That's a surprise,' she observes, preferring not to place other more personal opinions on public record. Diane has long ago learnt that it's as important to be popular as it is to be effective.

'That's the way the firm operates.'

'Only if someone screws up or knows too much.' Diane recalls Lloyd's wild lifestyle from the old days when they both worked in dollar swaps trading. 'Did someone finally check Lloyd's travel and expense claims?' she hazards.

'You don't need to know. Lloyd will be okay. He has millions in stock and options. He can retire aged forty-nine and lie to his wife and kids as to why he left us. But it leaves us with an opportunity.'

He plays with her HR file. She knows what's inside. He's surely not going to dredge up her glorious past, her NYU degree and Harvard MBA, her career-diplomat father and equally successful legal mother, her brilliant performance on the Mitchell's induction course a decade ago when she blew away the males.

'So you need to find someone desperate enough to work in London?' she says.

'Sure do. Might suit someone like you.'

Last year the firm branded her an Alpha Woman, the term originally used for aggressive American politicians. Diane almost ran her high-school class with a few other like-minded girls. They were as competitive, predatory and assertive as any male bully, yet subtle and cruel with it. They were brighter and sharper than any of their peers, undermined the weak, excluded others, developed back-stabbing techniques, demolished rivals, yet never exposed themselves to physical risk. Diane is indeed a dominant member of any pack. She can see the game plan already. He's in the end zone. She's not even at first down.

'I'm not interested.' She stands up.

'Sit down. Hear me out.' He shrugs. 'What's so bad about London?'

Diane sits down. 'It's the world's biggest lunatic asylum and all the patients are running loose.'

'Jeez, it's not like you're gonna die there. I know how much you hate long-term commitments and want your independence. Relax. It's only an overseas posting for two years.'

She's beginning to relax, aware that he's not making any significant inroads.

'People get less for a hit-and-run these days. I've been there often enough on work. I'd go stir crazy after a week. I'd need to see the arrivals hall of JFK every Friday evening. I'd have to commute. Forget it.'

She enjoys watching his reaction, enjoys the power she knows she wields. He shifts in his seat, knowing he has an ace card still to deal. She's hoping he'll produce it soon.

'It's an ex-pat package. The gravy train we all hope to ride at the shareholders' expense. This is an all-expenses-paid assignment. You will have a luxury condo, generous allowances, health clubs, flights home . . .'

She shakes her head vigorously, arms folded even tighter. Although Horowitz is in his best suit, sometimes he feels that it's Diane who wears the trousers in Mitchell's.

'Bullshit! I know why you want me to go, and not some guy on another trading desk. He'll have a trophy Barbie wife, three point two kids, and want a family home not a single apartment, flights home for all on every trip back and school fees on top. You're asking me because I'm cheaper, thirty-eight, and unmarried.'

She watches Horowitz finger her personnel file, both of them knowing that everything is relative, especially when it comes to his enormous annual package, stock options and cash bonus. She knows that only Microsoft offer more stock options than Mitchell's. In Microsoft the staff just hit F7 for more options.

Sometimes Horowitz wonders how Diane manages to look better with each passing year, apparently ageless, always alluring, often feline, and sometimes dangerously feral. He avoids displaying some overt Pavlovian reaction, such as drooling.

'You are married, Diane.' She looks at him incredulously. 'Married to this firm. Been here for more than a decade. You're locked in with restricted stock and options that don't vest for years. We have you. If you were a guy, I'd say we have you by the balls. But I couldn't be so non-PC, could I?'

An uneasy truce hangs in the room. Diane moves in her seat, about to leave. She thinks that it's an opening gambit, only a matter for discussion. He knows it's a done deal. Time to seek closure.

'Diane.' It worries her when he uses her name. 'You gotta work overseas if you want to get on here.'

'I'm doing okay so far.'

He opens the HR file and goes for the killer blow.

'You're a Managing Director.'

'So?'

'There's a promotion in this.' He sees her pupils immediately react and dilate. He waits. She's hooked. He senses the lust for power, her jealousy of others higher up the corporate food chain.

'Tell me more.'

'We'll make you an FVP. Like Lloyd.'

It's what she desperately wants. It's been promised by the male hierarchy for years, but never delivered.

'You will?'

'Sure thing.'

'When?'

'Once you take off from JFK, you're an FVP.'

'I get this in writing?'

'I can give you the promotion letter later today. Once HR type it up and I sign it.'

Diane weighs up two years overseas in a firm career spanning a lifetime. It's no choice at all.

'When do I go?'

'Next weekend. I need you on site immediately.'

'That's too soon. I got personal things to do first.'

'You don't. The firm comes first.' They lapse into silence, each deciding if they have the mutually agreeable outcome they desire. There are no further protestations. He takes her silence as acceptance. 'I'll advise HR.' He takes her hand in his palm. 'Congratulations, I'm sure you'll do a great job for us.'

He slams the door as she leaves and returns to his e-mails and some hard-core XXX internet site. He's got mixed emotions. The upside is that he shifts a difficult demanding subordinate to a desk four thousand miles away and simultaneously meets his covert HR targets to have four token female FVPs in the capital markets division by the year-end. The downside is that he will no longer get to fantasise about Diane and she might at some stage cause trouble in London. Like Lloyd did before her.

Trish ambles into Henry's office with some late-morning paper-work and a problem.

'I called Mitchell's HR department about Adam's contract.'

'There's not a problem, is there?' he asks.

'Not really. It's all signed and delivered. Only HR told me that Lloyd went to New York.'

Henry is puzzled. 'So? That's their head office.'

'I mean, he's relocated. I think. He may not be there when Adam joins on day one.'

'Impossible. Lloyd signed the offer letter. That's good enough for me. Adam can sort it out with Bruce. Anything else?'

'There's an enquiry from a bank in Dublin. They want to lure two fund managers back home.'

'Leave it with me. I'll see if it's worth a phone call.'

Later, near one o'clock, Henry tells Trish he's going out for a sandwich and a *Standard*. He strides briskly along Long Acre, past Stanford's map shop and into the dingy Indian newsagent with the best international press selection. He takes a *Standard* latest edition, ignores the *FT* and the skin mags and looks at the shelves of European newspapers, searching for the right dailies. He waits until the shop is relatively devoid of other customers before selecting and paying for extortionate copies of *Die Welt*, *Die Rheinische Post* and *Die WestDeutsche Zeitung*.

He finds a favourite café on a side street, eyeballs the interior through the plate glass, sees there's no one whom he recognises inside, confirms sufficient table space amidst some lazing tourists, and orders.

'A BLT on brown and an Evian. To stay.'

He takes a discreet table at the rear and wolfs down his sandwich. Then a gulp of water as he opens *Die Welt* first. He knows sufficient German from his two-year Army posting to decipher the headlines on the home news pages. There's nothing of interest in the paper. He's deep in thought when moving chairs and then footsteps disturb him.

'*Entschuldigen Sie bitte, haben Sie einen Moment Zeit?*'

Henry looks up slowly. A party of five is bearing down on him, a husband and wife in matching lurid Patagonian fleece jackets with three freckled juvenile offspring. They have street maps, pastel scarves, baseball caps, cheap cameras, and bulging backpacks.

'What?'

The father's the self-elected spokesman for the party.

'*Sprechen sie deutsch?*'

Henry answers instinctively.

'*Ein bisschen.*'

The father's looking down at his open newspaper on the table. They assume he's German?

'*Koennen Sie mir bitte sagen, in welche Richtung Trafalgar Square ist?*'

The father's right in his face. Henry stares back. Hard.

'Never heard of it, mate. Sorry.'

They move off slowly in disbelief. Henry opens the *Rheinische Post*. He finds what he's looking for on page eight. He ignores the other newspaper. He has what he wants, a name and enough personal details. He downs the last of the water, tears out the relevant article, taking care not to lose any of the column inches, neatly folds the unwanted newspapers and throws them into a nearby bin. He needs time to think, time to be on his own, time to prepare to return to the office, to Trish and the Associates.

St Paul's Churchyard is his favourite haunt, hidden away down Inigo Place and solely used for relaxation purposes by locals in the know. Henry sits alone on his usual wooden bench, one of many provided gratis by benevolent corporate donors over the years, and takes in the view. A row of small trees forms an arch up to an imposing façade atop tiered steps, with a paved walkway up the centre and grassy areas and flower beds upon either side. He comes here for Mass on rare occasions.

He loves this rampant unkempt garden. The wild standard roses, so wonderful in the long dry summer, are now dead to the world. Pigeons scavenge for the remnants of recent lunches. There are no tourists, no dogs, no radios, and no bloody investment-banking types. The noise of traffic, of people, of pressure, of London itself, recedes. A prominent clock face ticks remorselessly towards three o'clock.

The entrance signs remind everyone of the consecrated nature of the ground and ask visitors to show respect. The deceased are buried below the pitted paving and include many who perished in the Great Plague of London in 1665. Henry looks down on the uneven flagstones and moves his feet to the left out of a sense of guilt. The nearest cracked and sunken flagstone is now visible, with a chiselled dedication to a young woman who died in the early 1800s. All around, he can see the newer tilting gravestones of others.

Henry stands up and glances back at the weather-beaten wording inscribed on his favourite bench. 'Whosoever comes here, may you find rest and peace of heart.'

CHAPTER NINE

BARRIER POINT, LONDON E16: 9.35 A.M.

Adam wakes late on Friday morning. It's his last weekday between jobs. The apartment is quiet, with his neighbours all departed for work. He misses the newspaper in the hallway, the smell of a greasy fry-up and the sound of laughter and anecdotes. Most of all he misses Cheryl and Brian. He wastes ten minutes admiring the views of the calm Thames, empties a box or two of possessions, checks the designer yet barren kitchen and out of necessity decides to explore the suburban wilds of East London for the first time on foot. He's seen the optimal and nearest street from the Astra.

The row of shops is familiar, like any other. Awnings sponsored by cigarette companies, hanging National Lottery and Pepsi signs, dodgy personal ads on cards in the windows, stringy mongrels tied to posts outside, enough litter strewn about on cracked paving. Inside Raj's Newsagent's, he scans the newspapers but selects a boring *Financial Times*. He doesn't know why he buys it. He really wants to buy something racy like the *Sun* or *Mirror* or the even the ludicrous *Sport*, but a guy in the City about to start a new job with a global player like Mitchell's needs to be well read.

Adam's going to enjoy shopping here on a regular basis

because Raj has a sense of humour. There is a gleaming deli stall in one corner. Over it hangs a sign announcing 'New Deli'. Adam smiles. Bloody brilliant. He inhales the smell of fresh croissants. They seem to be self-service, but there's no tongs in sight, nor paper bags. Then the jangling bell on the door behind him rings, others arrive, so he picks up the first three croissants with his hands but he needs milk too so he goes to the other end of the shop, takes a litre of low-fat and tries to pay quickly to get out of this sudden heaving invasion of the masses, but the staff serve an elderly gent first as Adam tries to hold three croissants with the milk and the *FT*, and others select their croissants with the tongs that he never saw and they use the paper bags he missed.

The female shop assistant has a welcoming smile but he doesn't see it as she advises him he has a plain, an almond and a chocolate croissant, and all three are at different prices, so she does some really slow mental arithmetic as the crowds in the shop queue impatiently behind him and he only has a twenty note in his pocket to pay up with so getting all the small change takes years, and he rushes out of the shop.

Adam stands outside by the tethered dogs and the rubbish on the pavement and looks back inside the plate glass window, immediately realising that there are in fact only two other customers inside. One is the elderly gent who is slow to leave the shop. The other customer is a fit-looking girl wearing a loose grey athletic sweatshirt and jogging pants, her long hair tied back neatly for convenience. She has a Lucozade Sport in her hand and looks like she might have jogged to the shop. He likes what he sees but she turns away. He never even saw her face inside and dreads to think what she made of his mad exit.

He knows what it is. It's all the change. Moving house. Leaving Brian and Cheryl. The wasted trip back to his parents' home in the vain hope of a closer relationship. Hanging around killing time at home. The insecurity of being between jobs. Leaving good friends at Kapital. The uncertainty of Mitchell's.

Wondering if Henry has got him the best FX job in the City with Lloyd and Bruce, or whether it's going to be the hell on earth promised by Beamer. Adam slowly walks back to his apartment wondering how buying ten million euro is often so much easier than buying an *FT*, a litre of milk and three bloody croissants.

Samantha knows she is on to something. She is a veritable Bloomberg virgin yet knows the basics from watching the others. She runs a print of the euro versus dollar exchange rate for the year to date. She drills down into the biggest movements and sees that the biggest daily FX rate changes mostly happened on the last Thursdays of the month. She checks some of the related news stories and gleans the reason. When the ECB changes interest rates, the market reacts and Mitchell's make a profit. When there's no change on a Thursday, rates don't move much and Mitchell's break even. There is definitely a pattern.

She tries to focus but it's not easy. Muppet is stuck on another confrontational telephone call with another unhappy Mitchell's salesman. He breaks into her stream of consciousness as he yells over to Bruce, his left hand on the mute button on the handset.

'I'm getting some grief from a salesman. He says I told him a different euro/dollar rate on the telephone from the one that his oh-so-important client got when we booked the trade. What do I do?'

'Like I told you before, hang up and call him back on your mobile,' advises Bruce. 'Avoid the taping.'

'Not this time. No point.'

'So you think you're right?' asks Bruce.

'I sure do.'

Samantha is distracted. She's listening to the guys, trying to learn more about the job.

'Is he asking about a recent deal?' asks Bruce.

'One from last Thursday.'

Samantha grows more interested. Last Thursday was the day of an ECB rates announcement. And this trade is euro/dollar. She looks up but doesn't interfere in the evolving conversation.

'You should listen to the tapes,' advises Bruce. 'That'll shut him up.'

'Will do.' Muppet hangs up, scribbles some trade details on a page and throws it over. 'You gotta sign the authorisation.' Bruce signs the page with an illegible scribble. Muppet stands. 'I'll be back in ten.'

Samantha looks up, suddenly more curious about what happened at the trading desk that Thursday. There is an opportunity here with some upside. The downside is a voluntary conversation with Muppet.

'What are these tapes?' she asks.

'They record what we say on the phones twenty-four-seven.'

'I've never listened to the tapes before,' she advises.

'It ain't that exciting, dear,' advises Muppet.

She smiles. 'Can I see how it works?'

Muppet looks over at Bruce who issues his decree immediately.

'No unaccompanied staff in the tapes room.'

'I'm not unaccompanied,' she protests. 'I'm with Muppet. And I'm trying to learn more about the job.'

Muppet warms to the idea.

'Okay by me, Bruce. She can come along for the ride.' A few male faces grin.

'Jeez. Okay, go.'

They take an elevator that unfortunately is too small for Muppet's BO to dissipate. They get out on sixteen and make for ITS. Muppet knows where to go and eyes a warren of cubicles until he finds the main man.

'Krish, I need to pull some tapes.'

Krish is twenty-something, with long gelled hair, two days' stubble and extended pointed sideburns. He wears a tight pair of black Valentino jeans which breach the firm's smart-dress code and a navy Hackett polo shirt with a huge white number one emblazoned on the back, which Samantha deduces is more aspirational than any sign of some sporting prowess. She reckons that Krish fancies himself, which is just as well as no one else would. He seems distracted, perhaps now wondering why he had chosen to work in the pits of information Technology Support and not at a glossy trading desk with the top talent upstairs.

'Who's this?' he asks.

'Sam.'

'Never seen her before.'

It's like Samantha is some invisible interplanetary being. She explains. 'I joined a few months back.'

Krish offers his clammy hand.

'Any time you need anything, you call me.' She wouldn't. Always the same old story with ITS. If a bloke calls them for help with his PC, they tell him to pull the plug out of the wall and reboot it. If a fast girl calls they appear in person within nanoseconds. Krish stares for a while. 'You got the form?'

'Here. Bruce signed it,' advises Muppet.

'Is she okay to come along too?' Krish is now looking at Samantha yet talking to Muppet.

'Sure she is.'

They walk down some corridors to a door with a CCTV camera atop and a few signs. Authorised Personnel Only. ITS Access Only. No Food and Drink Allowed Inside. All in big red bold letters like it matters more. Access is by a keypad and a swipe card. Only Krish can oblige. He holds open the door. Samantha walks in first as the door is held for her. She's knows they're both watching her rear. She turns.

'Why all this security?'

'This is the central core of our systems infrastructure — all our servers, modems, hard drives, tapes, cabling and back-ups.' Krish seems proud of his modest empire. 'If anything happens to the systems here, then you won't be trading FX upstairs. Period. You need us more than you realise. The tapes are kept here because it's the safest room in the building. No one gets in here unless a desk head signs off and I am here.'

They stop by a tall stack of Racal tape machines, each voice-recording thirty-two channels.

'What day you want?' he asks.

'Thursday the twenty-sixth.'

Krish looks at the orderly row of tapes on a nearby shelf and selects the correct day. Samantha watches him work a control panel, all glowing red numbers and lights everywhere but it looks usable. There is a blank screen. It even has play, pause, rewind and forward buttons like her hi-fi at home in the flat.

'So it's just like a CD player?' she asks.

'Yeah. A CD player. You got it in one.' Krish turns to Muppet. 'Your extension?'

Muppet nods. '8203.'

Samantha watches Krish key in the extension number.

'What time?'

'Say three to four o'clock.'

She watches Krish key in 15.00 hours. Then 16.00 hours. The screen shows twelve calls made and received in one hour. He offers Muppet a set of headphones and hits play. They stand together, both watching Muppet fast-forward, stop, then fast-forward. He shouts over the headphones. 'This is it.' They watch his face grimace and contort as the conversation flows though his vacant head. He takes off the headphones, frowns, swears and hits the stop button. Krish reclaims the headphones.

'You want a cassette copy of that bit?'

Muppet is already stepping back towards the door.

'No fucking point! The salesman's right, I screwed up.' He walks off in a rage and slams the door. Alone at last. Krish is getting off on just the two of them being in this humid pulsing hothouse.

'You impressed by all this?' he asks.

'Like you say, it's just a CD.'

'This is not some Discman where you can play Britney! These are serious pieces of hardware. This is three hundred Ks worth. They record five hundred lines twenty-four hours a day, three-sixty-five days a year.'

Samantha has an idea. She can use Krish. He's like a pet waiting to please her in any way he can.

'Can I try it, then?'

'Why?'

She's thinking on her feet. 'I want to hear how I sound on the phone.'

'Take it from me, you'll sound great.' It's his first stupidly obvious play for her. He's getting all excited for nothing. She'll use him and that's all. 'Any particular day you'd like?'

'That same Thursday is fine.'

'Your extension?'

'Sure.'

'What is it?'

He can't know all the extensions in the firm. It's worth the risk. She takes the gamble.

'8207.'

It's not her extension. She knows it. Krish doesn't.

'What time?'

She knows the best time to ask. Eleven a.m. CET. ECB Frankfurt time. Ten a.m. GMT.

'Say between half-nine and ten o'clock.'

Krish keys in the start and end time and hands over the headphones. The screen shows eight calls. One of the calls is at ten minutes before the hour. He stands closer to her, preening his oily hair in the reflection of the smoked-glass cabinets that house the hardware. She uses fast forward and instantly recognises Bruce's voice as he makes successive aggressive phone calls to others in the market. As the time ticks towards ten o'clock he mentions the ECB once to someone and the imminent interest-rates decision. She wonders again what happens and how the desk makes so much money so easily. At ten minutes to ten Bruce takes an incoming call from an outside line. His voice is clear enough on the tape.

'Mitchell's.'

A man's voice speaks very quietly. Faltering speech. Old? Continental accent, she thinks. Dutch? German?

'It's me.'

'I told you not to call me on the landline. Use the mobile number.'

'I tried. It's not working.'

'Hang on.' A long pause. 'Shit, the battery's gone. Fuck.' A pause. Bruce suddenly speaks softly. 'Well?'

'No change.'

'Bye, Karl.'

Henry pulls the hall door shut behind him, walks across Gibson Square towards Upper Street and the Tube and sees the roadkill. A cat lies dead in the gutter. It's a short-haired male tortoiseshell. Some of the cat's innards lie in a trail of blood and guts that stretches from the painted median lines in the centre of the street. The rain drifts down and the water runs red in rivulets. Henry stops, fascinated to be first at this rare scene.

The cat's two front paws are crossed, like it's praying in vain for a saviour. The torn body is neatly arranged on the two yellow lines in the gutter. Someone, must be the killer driver, dragged it there after whamming it full on with a bumper or a grille, as if the act of removal lessened their guilt. The cat has a smart leather collar with an engraved brass name and number. Rover. The owner has a sense of humour. There's probably some happy family out there, the kids having Cheerios and Sunny D juice, oblivious to their loss. Someone's not yet missing Rover. Henry is distracted, his mind drifting off to times past.

He's maybe ten or eleven years old. It's the height of summertime. He's staying again at his grandfather's bleak dairy farm in Devon. His father is away on another government posting in Africa. He hasn't seen him since the end of term at his boarding school. Before that short day it was six months since the last visit. Some of the masters at the school know Henry better than his father does. They like the fact that he's in the top quartile of his year and sails through their exams with ease. His report card says that he should mix more with the other boys but that's down to his parental situation. It's four years since his mother left them to live in the States with a man with money whom he's never met. His father calls the American a cunt. Henry is breakfasting, raiding the cold pantry for what he can garner, when his grandfather grabs him.

'Come on. We gotta job to do. We'll make a man of you yet.'

His grandfather is a bull of a man in his early sixties with an unkempt beard and huge muscled arms from hard days of manual labour. He admires his grandfather, likes his energy and his drive. Except yesterday he beat him because he caught Henry lighting small successive bonfires of dry hay in the farthest field.

He is pulled by the scruff of his neck to the farmyard. Every day he spends alone on the farm becomes tougher to endure. Henry sees too much of life and death here. Stillborn calves, and lowing animals trucked off to abattoirs. Yesterday a local boy showed him how to turn ants and beatles into smoke with a steady magnifying glass. Later Henry crushed the older boy in a brief struggle for ownership of the lens.

The two stop in one of the corrugated barns. It's almost empty inside, pending the imminent summer replenishment. His grandfather pushes him onto a stack of bales and pulls back some loose hay.

'Now what do we have here then?'

Henry can see a cat, another tortoiseshell. It's a female. There are four kittens suckling their mother's teats alongside. They're newly born, their eyes hardly creaking open, their skin still raw pink. The mother wants to run and hide, perhaps aware of what will happen and the inevitability of it all. Henry is bewildered.

'Kittens.'

'What a big litter,' observes his grandfather. 'But four is too many for a farm like this. We don't need four and neither does old Mum here. They'll suck her tits dry. So we'll do the right thing by them.' He reaches in and selects the two smallest kittens. They squeal as he holds them up by the hair on the back of their necks. 'Mother Nature has to be helped. These two are the weakest. This one is the runt. Come on.'

Henry wants to run away but dares not. Last time he ran was a few weeks ago when a hired hand was cutting the throats of some old hens that were past their best-by date. His grandfather beat him with a belt and made him watch the rest of the job up close. He suffered so much that he wet his bed in the early hours of the morning and had to conceal the evidence from the local girl who kept house for them.

Henry is dragged by his grandfather over to a limewashed outhouse. Outside there's a rusty oil drum with its top sheared clean off. It exists primarily to collect rain from the weed-ridden gutters. His grandfather lifts him up so he can see over the edge. It's three-quarters full. Full enough, apparently.

'I'll do the first. You watch closely.' He takes the smallest kitten in his right hand and plunges it into the stagnant water. Henry counts the seconds. It takes less than half a minute. The hand is removed. The kitten is discarded on the ground, a motionless sodden mass of fur and fear. 'One done. Your turn.'

Henry has the other kitten in his hand. It's tiny. Its eyes open for the first time and look back at him. He can't do it. It's only days old but that's a lifetime for some. It's weak and pathetic but wants to live. Henry hesitates.

'Don't get all sentimental on me. Put the fucking animal in the drum. Do it! Now.'

Henry plunges the kitten into the water. He feels it struggle at first, moving around below the surface. He looks away.

'Watch it, boy.'

It's an eternity. The kitten stops struggling. It's over. Henry removes the little body and places it alongside the other one on the ground, wondering what he has done. But the tiny kitten moves. It's trying to get up. It's clinging to life.

'Jesus Christ! Do it again. Do it right.' As his grandfather cuffs him around the head.

Henry wishes he could run. He picks up the kitten, its life ebbing away. Thirty more seconds in the drum is enough. The litter is culled. His grandfather hands him a spade and clips him around the ears.

'Bury them in the orchard near the apple trees. Bury them a foot deep or the rats will get them.'

NOVEMBER

CHAPTER TEN

BARRIER POINT, LONDON E16: 5.55 A.M.

Adam sets the alarm for 6.15 a.m. but the noise wakes him first. He can't deduce the source, then recognition dawns as he comes to his senses. He hears running water, someone having a quick shower, wardrobe doors opening and closing. Then someone walking in the apartment above, their footsteps somehow permeating the six-inch-thick stressed-concrete floors. He looks at the Sony Dreamachine, then checks his Seiko, amazed that some poor bastard upstairs has to go to work at such an ungodly hour.

It's still pitch dark when he hails a black cab on the North Woolwich Road. The cabbie is vaguely pleased at the short trip and the minimal fare, knowing that he's fortunate to get any fare at all on his way from an East End home to a West End rank. Adam alights in Cabot Square and enters Mitchell's at 7.05. He's going to impress them on day one, knowing they will all remember his early arrival today for a long time and then he can gradually let his punctuality drift and safely get away with it.

He asks for Lloyd Weinbaum by name at reception. The solo receptionist on the early shift in her smart corporate uniform with the Mitchell's logo is puzzled by her screen display.

'We don't show a Lloyd Weinbaum in the internal phone directory.'

'You must. I met him here a few weeks ago.'

She's insistent. 'I said, we don't.'

'Is that a recent telephone list?'

'It was updated last week.'

'Lloyd's in FX.'

'It doesn't matter where he is, I still don't show him. So I can't contact him. Wait here.'

Adam sinks into a voluminous couch and waits. He's impervious to the expansive beech counters, the towering fountains of water and the glossy lighting. He wonders what's gone wrong here and how disastrous can a first day get when your new boss can't even be located? Already he's missing Beamer and the other guys at the Kapital desk. Adam's been away from the markets for too long. She returns.

'Any luck?' he asks.

'Not yet. It's too early. I'll make some enquiries. Wait here until then.'

The receptionist makes minimal further effort for the next thirty minutes as he watches unknown colleagues arrive. They in turn watch him as they run their ID cards past barriers and walk by uniformed security, all of them knowing he is an outsider on the wrong side of the divide. Everyone stares over at him. He doesn't much like their demeanour. They're far too sullen, determined and aggressive. Maybe Beamer was right about Mitchell's. The receptionist walks over to Adam nearer to eight o'clock.

'You've made a big mistake. Lloyd Weinbaum is in New York.'

Adam's incredulous. His agreed start date was in the offer letter sent weeks ago.

'He must have known I'd be here today. Did he leave me any message?'

'You don't understand. Lloyd Weinbaum has relocated permanently to New York.'

'Who's in charge of FX, then?'

'We have thousands of employees here. I don't know every one of them or who does what.'

It's now past eight and he's late even though he got here an hour ago. He seizes the moment and exerts some authority. 'Let me go up to the FX trading floor. I'll sort this out with the guys there.'

The receptionist shakes her head. She knows the in-house security rules.

'No one goes up without the name of whoever they're seeing.' The receptionist steps back, waving her hands in the air like she's losing interest in Adam's immediate plight. 'Why are you asking me all this? What's the nature of your visit today?'

Visit? He hasn't told her the single most important piece of information. 'I start work today. Call HR. Give them my name. They'll know what to do.'

Ten minutes later a blondie Sloaney horsy plummy thirty-something HR woman called Belinda Double-Barrelled something or other comes down. She takes Adam to an upstairs meeting room. First impressions of the inner workings of Mitchell's are not good.

'We didn't expect you so early.'

'All good FX traders start at seven,' he explains.

'Even on their first day?'

'Especially on their first day. What happened to Lloyd?'

'He went back home suddenly,' she explains, looking at some new-joiner file in her hands.

'Pity no one told me. Why did he go back?'

'I can't discuss that with you.'

Adam signs some pro formas on health cover and pensions, then papers on confidentiality, Chinese walls and personal share trading. Next up is a list of approved company cars. The Astra will soon be scrap.

'What car do I get?

'Not yet. You probably only get one when you pass probation in three months.'

Belinda needs a photograph for his ID card. He sits in a chair against a white wall while she takes an eternity to work the simple camera. When she finally takes the snapshot, he's sure that he looks like he's about to expire, the final photograph being almost as bad as his passport photograph. She has the nerve to give him a visitor ID card until his laminated employee ID card is printed. He follows her up to the trading floor where she adjusts her velvet hairband and long mane, pointing at the desk where the acting head of FX trading sits alone.

'Bruce is in charge of the FX desk since Lloyd left.'

Adam sees Bruce looking over at both of them. He's giving the Sloane more attention than his new hire. Bruce is looking puzzled as Adam approaches alone.

'What's going on? You back again for another interview?'

'I work here,' explains Adam.

'Where?'

'FX.'

There's no real welcome. Bruce is smiling, looking around like he's on *Candid Camera* or something.

'You serious?'

'I'm serious.'

'Here? FX? *My* FX?'

'I got an offer from Lloyd and signed up weeks ago.'

'But Lloyd is gone.'

'So I just found out.'

Bruce is shaking his head in disbelief. 'So Lloyd made you a job offer for FX after I spoke with him?'

'He signed the letter himself.'

Bruce is on his feet. He's looking past Adam towards the bank of elevators, like he wishes the Sloane would return to save him from this predicament.

'Lloyd and I were at cross purposes. Now he's gone. This is a bit of a surprise.'

Adam realises that his interview with Bruce was not a complete success. This can't get much worse.

'So what happens now?' he asks.

Another FX trader distracts Bruce. Bruce gets some message. He shouts back to Adam as he walks off.

'Take the spare seat by Samantha. I'll talk to you later on. First I gotta go and meet someone else who's starting here today. Someone who is far more important than any of us mere mortals.'

Diane has a bad night's sleep in Lloyd's former corporate penthouse. The alarm call from BT is on time. Her senses tell her it's only two a.m. back home in the Big Apple. It feels like the middle of the night. Hell, it *is* the middle of the night. A glance confirms that outside the heavens are pissing down on those who venture to work at this hour. She parts the curtains onto the vertical laminated glass. She has no intention of sleeping alone in Lloyd's bed in a foreign city for the next two years. She needs a foreign body.

She's already quite impressed by her unashamedly modern accommodation between Wandsworth and Battersea Bridges, perched on a north-south axis to maximise interior light. Montevetro is a slender diagonal wedge of a development, literally translated as 'glass mountain'. Her eighteenth-floor thousand square feet front the Thames and face both west towards Cheyne Walk, Chelsea, and east to the City. The two-bed apartment is one of 103 such within five connected blocks amidst an oasis of calm. She has a pretty view of St Mary's Church, a Grade I listed building which she thinks is quintessentially English.

She likes the solid façade of terracotta panels, the transparent glass walls, the security, the twenty-four-hour porterage, the landscaped river walks, the high-speed lifts, the gym, sauna, steam room and tennis court. She's heard that some models, jaded TV anchors and a celebrity hairdresser reside here. She likes to think it's an iconic building. Most of all she likes that Mitchell's picks up the tab of sixteen hundred quid a week.

Later she takes the waiting Audi A8 saloon, is met in reception at Cabot Square, has an introductory welcoming pitch with the suave yet married Mitchell's London CEO, devours the other management at a useless working breakfast, savages a demure girl from HR called Belinda, gets her new ID card on the spot and is walking down the main trading floor. Her first impression is that there is a serious amount of male talent and the hormones are running wild. A tall rangy thirty-something casually dressed guy approaches.

'You must be Diane.'

Her psychic powers are as good as his today.

'You must be Bruce.'

'Welcome to London.' She wishes she could show some genuine enthusiasm. He's walking alongside her like a puppy dog on a short lead, snapping at her Manolo Blahnik heels. She likes her men that way. Unfortunately he's no oil painting, more like a first stab at basic watercolours. 'You have Lloyd's old office. We had the cleaners in last week. It's all ready for you.'

Her first instincts tell her that Bruce doesn't seem to miss Lloyd much. She's unimpressed with the barren office space with its smoked-glass partition looking out on to the trading floor. Not as good as a seat on a New York trading desk. She finds his first basic error and points at the door.

'All you gotta do now is remove Lloyd's name.'

'Consider it done.' He's so keen. 'We're glad to see you here.' She's certain this is all an act. She's here from head office to cramp his style and space. They both know it. 'You and I should talk.'

'First we cover the more important matters.'

Bruce stares. 'Like what?'

'Like the only thing that matters on a trading desk.' Bruce is still blank. 'I wanna meet the traders.'

He returns in minutes with five other guys and a young girl.

Diane's puzzled because Horowitz in NYC told her the desk is Bruce plus five staff. There seems to be one extra person present. The first team meeting is her chance to stamp her authority on them. The guys are sitting in corner chairs and leaning against walls, joking privately, leaving lesser work matters back out on the floor, some with arms folded, eyeing her exterior glamour with some interest, wondering what sort of threat she presents. She's only initially attracted to a good-looking young guy who stands at the back. She stands up in the middle of the room and exudes pure one hundred per cent proof bottled confidence.

'I'm Diane Rubin. I've got twelve years in this firm. I ran the FX options desk in head office. Now I'm here to run the FX trading desk. We'll stick to our trading limits. We'll take our profits when we can. If you screw up you tell me first before I get to hear it from someone else. We will be the best FX desk in London.' There isn't any sort of acknowledgement from the team. This is hardball, it's the first game of a new season in a new league and she's the blow-in coach with a new game plan. 'You okay with that?' They nod silently. 'Your turn for the introductions. Tell me about yourselves. You first, Bruce.'

Bruce isn't prepared for this. He's momentarily speechless, conjuring up the right words.

'I'm the desk head. I've been here for five years. Came from Morgan's. I manage the desk day to day.'

It's a short speech. Too short. Everyone in the room knows Bruce should have done better. Already she's working her magic on the males, her predatory instincts rising to the surface, the power trip evident. Diane faces off to the next guy. He's older, fatter, shorter, paler, and the ugliest by a mile. She can see the remains of his dandruff-ridden hair matted down with sweat on his oily forehead. He wheezes.

'I trade the euro. I came from Chase four years ago. That's all there is on me.'

She's getting the impression they don't want to volunteer much information.

'You got a name?'

'Several, in fact. Most here call me Muppet.'

She doesn't see the need to ask why as she moves on down the line to a dark intense stubbled guy.

'I'm Bookie. Folks call me that 'cause I gamble a lot. Mostly horses and soccer. Sometimes FX. I was born in St John's Wood, went to local school, then Uni in Edinburgh, then two years in crap jobs, then a year in Morgan Grenfell before it was taken over, a year in Fleming's before it was taken over, a year in Dresdner before it was taken over, and three years here. Live in Hampstead, drive a silver Merc coupé and a black Land Rover, have a wife and one son, two cats and a Labrador. My favourite colour is aquamarine and my favourite Häagen-Dazs ice cream is Cookies and Cream. Did I leave out anything?'

She reckons their confidence is growing. Bookie is the one with the most lip. He's too cocky. She'll knock him back soon enough. Next is a small guy with a long nose and prematurely greying hair.

'I'm Cable Guy because I trade dollar/sterling. I can e-mail you my CV later. I gotta get back to trading.'

The next guy is slight and well-dressed, his fringe floppy, his voice clipped and upper-class.

'I'm Spoon. I'm trying to concentrate on FX these days but I get married in two weeks' time. You're invited. It's at Victoria's place in the country. You might enjoy a traditional English wedding.'

The atmosphere in the room is improving. They're making some effort for her, learning to meet her varied needs, slowly delivering, learning who's wearing the pinstripe trousers. Diane turns to the only girl.

'I'm Samantha. I'm the desk assistant. Position keeper. I've been here seven months. I don't trade. Yet.'

Next to the girl is the younger good-looking guy. He seems too hesitant to get the words out.

'I'm Adam. I joined from Kapital Bank.'

He doesn't seem to want to talk. He's tighter than an ocean-floor clam. She likes his vulnerability.

'How long have you been here?' she asks.

For some reason she sees the guy is looking at his watch, as if he's deciding exactly what to say.

'I've been here ... about an hour.'

'Don't get smart with me.' Amazingly this young guy could be the biggest challenge of all.

'I'm not being smart. I joined today. Honest.'

She looks at Bruce and sees from his reciprocal nod that it's the truth.

'So you're the seventh. No one told me we had a new hire.'

'It's a very recent new hire,' interjects Bruce. 'Lloyd did it all.'

She's seen enough. It could be worse. Though not much. 'Let's get to work and make some money.'

The team returns to the trading desk outside. Diane unpacks her bag, checks the contents of her office, shifts the two PC screens further away and repositions some desk items. She opens the desk drawers to check they're empty. There are a few folded pages at the back of the bottom drawer, almost out of view.

She unfolds the pages. She can see columns of dollar figures, one for each day of the week. She sees the page title and realises it's a spreadsheet of the desk's daily trading profit. One day each month is circled in pen. It might be Lloyd's handwriting. She can't be sure. There are comments scribbled in the margins. 'ECB. Thursday. Millions again!' It's the exclamation mark that grabs her immediate interest.

Gatwick a.m. is chaos. Henry loves this airport. There's a queue in the South Terminal international-departures area. Vacant BAA staff stand behind counters, checking hundreds of boarding cards, taking a covert digital image of each passenger and affixing a bar code to their boarding card. Henry stands in a line of anxious tourists and screaming brats, watching the suits overtake him on the left-hand side. The pre-pubescent expert examines his Club Europe boarding card, points and grunts back.

'You can use the Fasttrack, mate. It's quicker. It's much worse inside here.'

Henry looks past the glass partitions and into the smug Fasttrack area. The few solo Club suits are significantly out-numbered by six alert and focused BAA staff who search, frisk and examine the few passengers. He sees the staff member who eyes the images on the X-ray machines, watches him freeze-frame a briefcase or two until he selects one for examination. No one tells Henry what to do, least of all some BAA kid.

'I'm in no hurry.'

He ignores the obvious advice and walks past. The kid looks around.

'Suit yourself, mate. Your funeral.'

Henry stands in line in the security area and likes what he sees. Couples with much more than their six kg of carry-on. Parents with backpacks, karts, cameras, videos, food, Walkmans, Gameboys. And four kids. Indian women in bright saris with their life's possessions as cabin baggage. OAPs with BOAC holdalls from the fifties and M&S bags from the High Street. Late passengers running past the queues, blaming it on a delayed Gatwick Express. Wheelchair-bound travellers following their example to queue-jump.

The BAA staff in their nasty green uniforms can't cope. They're the few remaining shell-shocked troops in the trenches, on their feet all day, deprived of rest for hours, gasping for food and water, as wave after wave of relentless tourist cannon fodder rain down upon them. They've given up long ago trying to stem the tide. Instead they're happy to filter the flow of the refugees en masse. Henry sees their jaded eyes, their forearms folded in resignation, the hippies and oddballs they wave through, the distracted Asian girl on the X-ray machine, her eyes glazing over as vague images flash by at an impossible speed.

Henry's turn comes. He places his briefcase on the incessant conveyor belt and watches it disappear out of sight. He's taken the necessary precautions. It's serious needle-in-a-haystack time. The contents of his briefcase lie together with a few business papers and CVs. He waits and watches the BAA staff with interest. Individuals with personalities are more interesting and entertaining than boring backpacks and briefcases. The harassed staff exhibit the same inclinations as the last time.

They ask a gent to unroll an *FT* in case he's concealed a lethal weapon. They ask a Rastafarian to take off his woolly rainbow hat to check for any undeclared contents. A youth walks through the metal detector three times until they find his Metallica belt. They chat as they frisk people like they have some sort of formal training and qualification. Henry watches the Asian girl at the X-ray screen. It's a crap job. She's got long teased streaky-dyed blonde hair, bad skin and too much heavy red lipstick. Her expression is vacant.

Henry's turn comes to walk. He places his keys and coins in the plastic dish as required. He glances left to the conveyor belt. There's still no reaction from her. He waits and walks through the metal detector safely, turns to reclaim his personal effects, moves off to the left as his briefcase appears on the conveyor belt. He nonchalantly picks up the briefcase, avoiding eye contact with anyone in a BAA uniform. He walks off towards the seating area. He hears a lone male voice behind him.

'Excuse me, sir.'

Henry doesn't stop. It can't be him. This always works.

'Sir, one moment.'

It might be him. He stops and turns around slowly. One of the BAA guys is approaching. This is impossible. Henry's finally going to have to use those slick lines he's prepared for such an eventuality. He'll spin them a tale about what's in his briefcase, about how he got it, about how sorry he is and all that subservient stuff they expect from a compliant grey suit.

The BAA guy's left palm is open. Henry can see a single pound coin. The guy's smiling at him.

'You left this in the dish, sir. You don't want to be offering us bribes, now do you?'

CHAPTER ELEVEN

CANARY WHARF, LONDON E14: 10.10 A.M.

Adam sits at his new desk on the trading floor, wondering how it's all gone so wrong. There is no welcome. Samantha watches in silence alongside. He looks over at Bruce and waits for a quiet moment.

'Can you get me started here?'

Bruce rolls his head sideways and yells over, 'Pull up a chair.'

Adam slides his chair over on the carpet tiles. He feels privileged, as if his new boss is finally going to offer a welcome and share precious knowledge with the new hire. Bruce lowers his voice.

'Forget that damn' speech by Diane. That was bullshit. I set the ground rules.' Adam nods. 'We do things my way at this desk. In this firm ethics is a place to the east of London. Teamwork is lots of people doing what I say. If you're ever worried about something, then you tell me, not Diane. Otherwise we screw up, we lose money in the market and people get hurt. Innocent or otherwise. Understand?'

'I understand.' Adam tries to establish some credibility. 'I know how to trade FX.'

'It's not that simple. You need to understand how this desk operates. We take orders to buy and sell currency from the sales force, from the equities and bond guys, from syndicate and investment banking, from structured products and lending, from every Thomas, Richard and Harold in here. We quote them a price and if they like it, they take it. If they don't like it, then tough. They can't go outside to trade. We got them by the balls. We can run the position to make some money or we can close it out in the market with another bank at no risk. We make a few points of a spread on the difference in rates. You got it?'

'Yes,' risks Adam as his confidence grows. 'It's easy money.'

'You can tell me it's easy when, or if, you pass your three-month probationary period.'

'Sorry.'

Bruce leans closer, becoming more animated as he points.

'Never apologise to anyone. That's a sign of weakness.'

He is not talking to Adam. He's talking *at* Adam.

'Even if I'm wrong?'

'Especially if you're wrong. Ask Muppet here. You'll learn a lot from him. If someone complains about an error or a bad FX rate, you fight them tooth and nail for every last cent. If they give you serious grief, you deny everything. Eventually, they'll call me. I'll come looking to you for a damn' good explanation.'

'You get a lot of complaints?' Adam asks.

'No more so than at Kapital, I guess.' Bruce picks up a handset from the desk. 'You know what this is?'

Adam's staring back as if it's the stupidest question in the world, or else he's missing something.

'It's ... a telephone.'

'Wrong. It's something people can hang us by. It's recorded twenty-four-seven. Every word you say is on a tape and it can be played back by some smart-ass to haunt us. So what do you do?'

'Dunno.'

'You got a mobile?'

'Who hasn't?'

'Use it, then. If someone complains, hang up and call them on your mobile. Tell them your phone doesn't work or the dealerboard is bust. That way, we're safe. I use a mobile when I can. Watch me and learn.'

Adam nods and waits for the next gem of wisdom.

'That's the internal FX order flow. Secondly, we engage in principal FX trading, running a book, punting in the market, interbank trading, whatever you call it back in Kapital. We're a US investment bank so we run all the positions in dollars versus other currencies. We stick to trading in the four main liquid currency pairs: dollar / euro, dollar / sterling, dollar / Swiss and dollar / yen. We are not trying to corner the world market for Mexican pesos or the Kenyan pound. We do our research, we consider macro- and micro-economic fundamentals and government policies and shifts, we take a view on a major currency, we go long or short in decent size and we hope that the market moves in our favoured direction. We sell out to another bank and make the difference in realised P&L. That ain't easy either.'

'What sort of size do we trade?' Adam inquires.

'You don't need to know. You can take the internal order flow. You won't be punting in the market.'

Adam is aware that their conversation is audible to the others. Eyes are fixed on screens and desks but he knows they're all listening on the sly, smiling as Bruce exerts his authority.

'Why not? I got the experience.'

''Cause I know nothing about you.'

Adam's stunned. This isn't the job he accepted. He's wondering what the others make of the conversation, whether they already think he's history. He needs to make some sort of stand.

'I can't make any money for the desk if I can't trade.'

'And you can't lose any either. Maybe we'll review it after probation is up. And if you ever fuck up bad then I send you over to Daz there.' He points away at a tall guy with a crew-cut.

'He's in the Territorial Army. He keeps an old grenade launcher under his desk. I've seen it. Don't mess with him.'

Adam shifts in his seat, looking for some upside.

'I get the message.'

'Maybe you do, maybe not. Remember Lloyd hired you, I only inherited you.' Bruce sees the reaction. 'Is there anything else?' He is back looking at some Reuters screens. 'Good. So there endeth today's lesson.'

Adam rolls his seat back to the desk. The others look up and smirk. He hears Muppet mumble, 'Amen.'

Samantha monitors the others' intra-day trading positions on the in-house system but eavesdrops on the words of wisdom. Bruce gave her the same welcoming speech months ago. She already knows what the new guy is like because she knows the various types in the City. Fund managers will meet you, go out for a while, propose, get engaged, get married, have kids and stick by you long-term. Corporate financiers will say they love you, whisk you off to bed but won't remember your name in the morning. Salesmen will offer a quick kiss up an alleyway and won't ask your name first. Traders won't even look you in the eye.

The traders always hire their own sort. The new guy is just another face to her, although an attractive enough face at that. Soon he'll complain about everything at Mitchell's like the rest of them. There's the bloody chairs, the sucking air con, the damn' back-office staff, the crap systems, the colour of the carpet, their salary and bonus levels although she knows they earn many times her pay packet.

The new guy will borrow everything and return nothing. He'll take a phone call at her desk, sit in her chair with his feet up, hands behind his head like he's some mega global player and apologise without any sincerity. He'll bring curried junk food into the office and allow the smell to linger awhile. Last month she found a half-eaten weeks-old hairy green burger in one of Bookie's desk drawers. He'll chuck things around the open-plan office at the others. He'll never take her telephone messages when she's out. He'll boast about his sexual conquests or huge hangovers. He'll either stink or be awash with cheap pungent stick deodorant. He'll get up regularly to announce to the world at large he's taking a leak or a dump.

They're all the same. He'll rearrange his wedding tackle or stick an index finger up his nasal passage. He'll remove the accumulated molten wax from his ears with a large-size paper-clip. If she allows him, he'll ask her to collect his dry-cleaning, buy presents for his tacky girlfriends, pick up a sandwich or sushi, book a holiday break online because he can't surf the web, lie to a wife or mistress, or both. Sooner or later he'll make a move on her and she'll eventually tell him that he's wasting his time.

Muppet returns from his cigarette break. 'It's bloody brass monkeys outside.'

Samantha says nothing to encourage him. Last week Muppet went for a ciggy break with a visiting Jap options salesman from their Tokyo office. They shared the windswept concrete by the docks with a group of shivering teenage girls from Ops all dressed in dizzy heels and ridiculously short skirts, puffing away like they were on their last-ever cancer stick. Muppet told the Jap guy that the girls were all prostitutes openly touting for business with the loaded bankers. The Jap fell for it but failed to score with any of the fine young things despite offers of large monetary yen inducements to the girls who punch the keyboards.

Muppet sits down and exhales. 'Bun-run time, Sam. Let's go.'

'You've just been downstairs.'

'So what?'

She knows that today is different. 'It's not my turn, Muppet,' she confirms.

'Then who do you suggest?' he asks.

'I suggest that the new guy goes.'

'He does have a name, Sam.'

'So do I. And it's Samantha. I suggest Adam.'

'Thanks a lot.' Adam reluctantly rises and looks around. 'Where do I go? Starbucks downstairs?'

Muppet shouts over, 'Sit down. You're not going anywhere. Sam will do the honours for us.'

Samantha shakes her head. 'You said last month that if someone new joins the desk, they take over.'

'I said if someone else more junior joins, then they do the bun run.'

'Precisely. Adam is junior. So he goes.' She looks at Adam, racked with guilt. 'It's nothing personal, you understand. It's a work thing. A point of principle. A rare thing in investment banking, you'll find.'

Muppet is now on his feet too, looking more animated by the minute.

'Adam may be junior but there's a difference. He's a trader. You're a position keeper. Adam is higher up the food chain and always will be. I'll have the usual plus one of those chocolate chip cookies.'

Adam is still standing beside her. 'I'll give you a hand anyway.'

'Sit down, mate,' advises Muppet.

There's a pause. Samantha is resigned to her fate. She'll be on the bun run for life. Adam is still standing.

'I said I'll help and I will. I'm sure we take it in turns here,' he offers.

There's silence at the desk. Samantha takes the orders. 'You stay here. But thanks for the offer.' She walks off, mentally rehearsing the order, wondering if perhaps Adam is different from the others.

Henry takes a battered Nissan taxi along the airport motorway, through Drumcondra, past the quays and the potholed city streets to the five-star Meridien Shelbourne Hotel on St Stephen's Green. He checks in by two p.m., slumps onto the bed and turns on the TV. He hates CNN. An ethnically balanced anchor with stuck-on parted hair and a fake tan. Adverts for Marriott and GE. AT&T imploring guilty fathers to call their Shirley Temple daughters long-distance just to show they care. Smiling cuts to palatable news stories. Colours way too bright and luminous. After ten minutes the same news stories come around again.

He kills the two hours resting, unpacking his Samsonite, rearranging the room's fixtures and fittings correctly, playing with the radiators and air con and wondering why neither works, pacing the creaking floorboards that slope from left to right in the ancient bedroom, doing anything to kill the boredom and tension. He's been told if all goes well there'll be a few Guinnesses nearby before dinner at some posh steak place called Shanahan's on the Green.

At four p.m. he exits the hotel left and walks along Merrion Row under the shelter of a complimentary hotel umbrella. It's raining. The Irish National head office is on Fitzwilliam Street. He waits in a vast corner office with a decent view of the low-lying city. It's mostly half-built office blocks and towering construction cranes. Some administration and support staff nearby occupy nasty red cubicles in a similar floor space, their heads occasionally appearing like eager prairie dogs as they converse with colleagues.

'Thanks for flying over to discuss our requirements.'

The Managing Director of Asset Management is a stocky middle-aged gent in a dire brown suit and solid green tie, sporting a damp handshake, an unnecessary eager-to-please smile and more hair in a dodgy curling moustache than on his pate. Henry always makes the effort for a future client. It's business.

'Happy to come over. First time to Dublin. What can I do for you?'

'I need to hire two equity fund managers as a matter of urgency. We lost one to AIB, another is taking a career break. The job market here is small and tight. London is bigger and more liquid. Find me some London-based Irish fund managers who wish to return to the Old Sod and work for a big name like us.'

Henry smiles and nods enthusiastically. Irish National. Big name. He wonders.

'There could be some ex-pats in London. I can make enquiries. What sort of funds will they manage?'

'One is a small cap European fund that's getting smaller by the day. One is a technology fund.'

Henry starts scribbling some summary notes down on a pad.

'What about the candidate profile? Age, sex, marital status?'

The MD is frowning, his moustache hairs rising up and down on a tired face.

'We can't hire on that basis. That sort of discrimination is illegal too in the UK, isn't it?'

Henry's going to have to tread carefully.

'We can't *hire* on that basis, but we can certainly screen and interview on that basis.'

'Okay, then. Let's break all the rules. Under forty years old, male preferably.'

Henry knows that his lucrative fee, times two in this case, will be a percentage of the salary.

'What sort of package is on offer?'

'It's good. Seventy K plus a car and bank perks like cheap loans.'

Henry looks up from his random notes.

'Euros?' The MD nods. 'Are you serious?'

'Is it too much?'

'No one in London will move here for seventy K. Anyone good will be on a hundred K sterling minimum in London. They won't stomach a huge pay cut like that.'

The MD shifts in his swivel seat.

'You're missing the point. They'll come back for other reasons: the quality of life, the lack of hassle and stress, the fresh air, to be with family and friends again, to be a local amongst fellow countrymen. They'll move here for less money. They know the market always pays less here. They're homesick.'

Henry doesn't believe the Irish Tourist Board hype.

'I'm not so sure. I know their type. They grow used to the excesses of London, to huge annual bonuses, to flashy company cars and other perks. They prefer sterling to euros, prefer low taxes to Irish taxes.'

'I can't do anything about the Irish tax system.'

'Tell me why that guy left here for AIB. He wasn't homesick, was he?'

'No. He went for ... more money.'

Henry's insistent. 'You'll need to offer much more.'

'Seventy K per annum is the graded upper salary range for fund manager here. End of story.'

Graded upper salary range? What's the MD on about? This isn't the bureaucratic civil service.

'Don't you have any flexibility on the salary?'

'The board decides the upper salary ranges. It's cast in stone.'

'It will be difficult to complete this type of mandate with that level of remuneration.'

There's silence for a minute. The MD is contemplating developments, more aware by the minute that he might be wrong, that the London-based recruitment expert knows more, that the seventy K he had agreed with the CEO will have to be revised upwards somehow, that he will lose face. He is at a dead end.

'Then you will need to be creative and persuasive. Otherwise we will go elsewhere.'

The meeting's over. Henry walks down the long corridors of 1970s veneer wood panels and vomit-coloured carpet. He's unhappy that he's made the effort to fly to meet face to face, yet the day is still young. He approaches the Shelbourne in the rain, now even heavier, in the knowledge that there will be no Guinness and no eating-out tonight. He goes to his bedroom, repacks his overnight bag and returns downstairs.

There are four staff on duty at reception. The desk manager is on the telephone, avoiding eye contact with guests by staring out of the bay windows onto the street outside. Another youth speaks to a group of brightly clad Continental tourists who possess no English-language skills whatsoever. A third girl slowly guides a puzzled Scottish businessman around an open map of Dublin city with an index finger. The fourth staff member, a teenage girl with red hair and freckles, is dealing solo with a queue of seven guests and their lines of luggage and coats, all of them checking in for the night. Henry patiently waits fifteen minutes until the queue winds its way around the red ropes upon brass poles. He places his room key on the counter.

'412. I'm checking out.'

'Checking out?' she asks. 'Not checking in?'

'Correct. Checking out.'

She looks at a clock at the wall and then again at the glowing yet unseen monitor.

'You checked in a few hours ago.'

'I know I did.'

'We'll have to charge you.'

'Fine.'

'The day rate is half the overnight rate.'

He begins to take out his credit card but is stopped in the act. A Yank pushes in beside Henry.

'Sorry to cut in, but I'm real late. Couldn't find a damn' cab anywhere for ages.' He's too close. 'You don't mind, do you?' Henry says nothing, instead focusing on the American, his loud accent, his crooked nicotine teeth, the settled raindrops on his hair, his jowelled double chin and mean weasel features, his average frame and height. 'It's just I gotta meet someone real soon. I can't wait in this damn' line for ever.' The American turns to the girl. 'Check me in. I'll leave my bags here. Okay, hon?'

The American is bearing down on the girl. She's no match for his overt persuasion. She's looking at Henry for some sign of refusal or approval. He has no problems with the unwarranted intervention.

'Okay by me,' Henry says, smiling. He turns to the girl and decides. 'I'll be paying cash.'

CHAPTER TWELVE

CANARY WHARF, LONDON E14: 11.40 A.M.

Adam makes an effort to get to know the others at the desk but he's getting nowhere. Bruce is out of the office. No one says where he is and Adam doesn't ask. He yawns. He had a rubbish night's sleep. He worries that if someone at the desk talks loudly to him, he might wake up. The bastard upstairs had the TV in his bedroom on until all hours, loud enough to hear but muffled enough to make the programme indecipherable. The bastard had breakfast TV on first thing even before Adam's alarm boomed. He's going to kill the guy and get off at the Old Bailey murder trial on the grounds of justifiable homicide.

Muppet takes one look at Adam's smart-casual dress of open-necked shirt and khakis and gives him the party line.

'I'm the sartorial king. Here are a few tips. Chinos were fashionable in 1989 and that was it. Tight shirts only work if you're a member of a boy band. One open shirt button is professional, two open buttons is casual, three open buttons is for the Bee Gees. Medallions only suit Olympic champions. Sandals only look well on Germans. Donald Duck socks do not reflect your individuality or your wild personality; they just mean that your mother still dresses you. Ironing your jeans is evidence of an unsound mind. Got it? That's for men. And for women? Show more cleavage. Shorter skirts. Sling-back shoes, please. Sorted.'

Adam watches the others one by one and wonders how he can ever get on with people with names like Muppet, Spoon, Bookie and Cable Guy. Samantha has gone to some meeting on the executive floor. He worries about how they are going to christen him ceremonially in due course. Perish the thought. A salesman shouts over to Muppet. He's looking for a spot price on a small sterling/euro cross trade.

'How small is the trade?' yells Muppet with evident lack of interest.

'Fifty K,' comes the reply from the harassed salesman, telephone perched on his shoulder.

Muppet shouts back, 'Jesus Christ . . . fifty K? Tell your client to go to his fucking building society.'

The market is quiet. There's a lull until Spoon leans over to Adam.

'You're invited to my wedding and the afters. You can bring a partner. You got a girlfriend?' he asks.

'I'm in between girlfriends at the moment,' admits Adam, choosing his words carefully. 'But I think I'll have someone to bring along.' He glances at the draft e-mail in his saved mailbox.

'You can always accompany Diane. She's single and likes her men, so the guys in New York tell me.'

'I'll find someone else. I got a few weeks.' Adam has one possible date in mind.

Cable Guy looks at the others and smiles knowingly.

'You sure about that, sailor? You bat for the other team? You telephone your mother every day? You light on your feet or what?' Adam says nothing, refusing to lower the tone of conversation any further. 'Anyway, we'll sort you out this weekend.'

'What's on this weekend?'

'Spoon's stag. We got Ryanair flights booked out on Friday and back on Sunday afternoon. Forty-eight hours of drink and debauchery to come. Hope you can hold your alcohol like the rest of us can.'

Adam knows he has to attend. 'Where are we going?'

'We're going to the stag capital of Europe. Dublin. And don't argue with that. It was Bruce's choice. He likes it there.'

Bookie shouts over at Adam, 'Neville.'

'My name's Adam.'

'If you're on probation for three months, then you're Neville Newboy to us.' Adam has been christened. Bookie's rubbing his hands. 'Are you a betting man?'

The others at the desk fall silent. Gambling is a way of life in the City. When the markets are frantic, they sweat gallons and can't eat for the risk of throwing up. But when the markets go quiet and the screens are dead to the world, they need another outlet. Gambling becomes a physiological condition and they get withdrawal symptoms without a daily flutter. Adam knows there's only one answer.

'Sure I'm a betting man.'

'What do you bet on?'

'Sport.'

'We don't do boring sport here. Not since Lloyd took away the sports channels on the TVs.'

'What do you bet on?'

'Anything and everything.' Bookie smirks and looks around. 'Is it safe now?'

'Yeah, Bruce took a half-day. You know where,' advises Muppet. Then he grimaces. There's an uneasy silence, like he's said too much. 'And Samantha isn't here. Ready for a back-office flutter, guys?'

The others nod. A few of them call out times, like three minutes, five minutes, or not at all. Adam's lost. Bookie makes an irate telephone call. He shouts something at a distant back-office clerk about a problem FX trade ticket. He summons her up to the trading floor. Spoon stands up to adjust the air-con, which Adam knows is perfect. A teen soon appears, tall and slim and nervous, wearing a well-ironed pink blouse and black trousers. Bookie chats to her. The others, all smiles and sneers, watch as time slowly ticks by.

Adam sees Samantha walk back towards the desk, then stop. He watches her from afar. She must know what's going on but she doesn't want to join in. He's still lost. He watches her staring over from twenty feet. They others don't see her. Only Adam is facing the right way. She's fascinated by something. She waits.

In five minutes it's so cold at the FX desk that it's almost like a shopping trip to Iceland. Adam is shaking as he looks over at Bookie and the shivering teenage girl on twenty K p.a. The conversation seems pointless. Suddenly Bookie wraps it up and allows her to leave. Spoon immediately corrects the air-con. They all laugh and throw fivers over to him. He appears to have won some bet. Adam is still lost.

'What happened?'

'Spoon wins,' announces Bookie. 'It took exactly three minutes for the kid's nipples to become erect in the cold. Put it down to Spoon's experience. Next time we might invite you into the syndicate.'

Twenty minutes later Adam and Samantha sit alone on the lonely lunchtime shift. She's quiet.

'You okay?'

'I'm fine. You?' she asks.

'I take it you are excused from the stag weekend?' She nods. 'I'm not sure I'll survive a weekend's stag bingeing with those lunatics.'

''Course you will. Just pace yourself. Don't succumb to peer pressure. Tell them to get lost if you like.'

'And then there's Spoon's wedding and reception. I might be the only one there on my own.'

Samantha says nothing but turns back to the screens with a restrained smile.

Bruce hates making this damn' trip. He's certain that questions will be asked if he gets stopped. He hates the hassle, the day off work, the secrecy. Most of all he hates the risk of discovery. But the middle-aged pen-pushing civil servant insists on doing things this way, like he's got a morbid fear of wire transfers, bank drafts or cheques. He needs to see the colour of money. Bruce and the others have no choice. The worst part is putting his briefcase through the airport X-ray machines. There are lots of irrelevant papers, Mitchell's research reports and other crap inside. He wonders whether he could explain the contents if they were to stop him.

The afternoon flight departs Heathrow. In seventy minutes Bruce is on the ground and takes a taxi.

'*Die Hauptbahnhof, bitte.*'

It's a circuitous route but it gives him time to think. He alights and walks down the Kaiserstrasse, passing the seedy end first with its Dr Muller's, Dolly Buster video shop, and Arabs selling garments on rails for five euro each. Then the salubrious part with its mobile-phone outlets and street cafés. He can't fail to find the ECB. The Eurotower dominates the street. It still has the world's largest banknotes hanging from the side up high. Bruce avoids the ground-floor ECB souvenir shop. He wonders who the hell would ever shop inside. There's a giant euro sign and the twelve stars of Europe. Muppet hates this place.

Living Bar is a bizarre name but it's their usual rendezvous. The open-air location is a great idea for May but it sucks in November. In summertime Bruce sits by the Goethe statue and watches from afar but not today. He orders a neat shot of piping coffee to get his body temperature back to above freezing. At the appointed time the chrome chair creaks beside him under the weight of a stout middle-aged male.

'*Guten tag.*'

Karl has aged. His hair is greyer, his face more leathery. Last time Bruce was worried he'd have to retire soon from his desk job at the ECB. Now he's more worried that the guy will die before he gets his gold retirement clock. And then what will the stars on Mitchell Leonberg's FX desk do?

'Coffee?' he offers his host.

'*Danke.*'

Bruce nods to a waiter for two more shots. The waiter's keener to get back to the warmth inside.

'You had a good flight?'

'Fine.'

Bruce hates the way he makes small talk like they're best buddies or something. He never regrets making contact via people he knew who worked in the Bundesbank years ago but this is purely a business relationship. If the guy didn't work for the inner secretariat of the ECB council then Bruce wouldn't give him the time of day. More specifically, he wouldn't give him the contents of his briefcase. The local is looking around the plaza, lowering his voice like it's some movie and the eyes of the world rest upon him.

'You have it?'

Like Bruce comes over on a day trip to this soulless place just for the heck of it. He nods and decides to get this meeting over with as soon as possible. The briefcase by his feet is opened. They're on their own. The waiter's still inside, apparently sourcing coffee beans. The manila envelope is passed over.

'*Nein ... Nein.*'

The old guy is looking too animated.

'What's wrong?'

He's pointing at the envelope. Bruce sees it. There's a fancy corporate logo on the top corner.

'I can't take that. It's got your bank name on it. What if someone at work sees it?'

Bruce is losing it early today. He waits as the coffee arrives, tempering his response somewhat.

'Then don't take the fucking envelope back to work. Take it direct to the bank or stick it under the mattress.' Bruce sees him shut up. Now he's more curious. 'What do you do with the money?'

'I do what all other Germans do, the so-called money tourists.

I do what the self-employed Belgian dentists do with their tax-free cash earnings. I get into my car at the weekend and drive to the Luxembourg branch of Deutsche Bank. They don't ask questions there. All of us like that in a bank.'

'Easy drive?'

'Not quite. The *Zoll* at the border stop all middle-aged men in Mercedes, BMWs and Audis, especially those with registration plates from faraway cities like Frankfurt or Berlin. They're not looking for drugs, cigarettes or arms. They're looking for anyone crossing the border with more than the legal limit of fifteen thousand euro.'

'What's their problem?'

'There was a mad scramble before the conversion to the euro for all the illegal Deutschmarks to be lodged in banks before they became worthless, and the damn' *Zoll* haven't let up since. They want taxes to be paid on the money and they charge interest at twenty-five per cent. Now it's too dangerous to risk the drive in my A4. I take my wife's rusting ten-year-old Opel. It's not a comfortable drive, I can tell you. I have to stuff the notes into my underpants and hope for the best.'

Bruce is thinking about their business relationship. It's now in its third year. The desk hands over a hundred grand a year. Someday the junior clerk in Barclays in Canary Wharf will ask some questions.

'You got any cash left in Luxembourg? Or have you spent it all?'

'I still have it all.'

'You kidding me? You must have spent some? Like on a flash holiday or a new fur for the wife.'

'*Nein.* I don't want to draw attention to myself. People will ask questions. I haven't spent a cent. There's three hundred thousand dollars plus interest in the bank.'

Bruce is puzzled.

'What's the bloody point of that?'

'I like to know that it's there. It gives me security in my retirement. I have a nest egg.'

The guy's nuts, Bruce decides. He's had enough. The Lufthansa flight back to LHR leaves in a few hours time. He stands up, throws some euros at the waiter to settle the modest bill, takes his briefcase and looks at his watch to give his guest a definite signal.

'Same time again in two months? And you call me on Thursday at ten to eleven my time as usual. Make sure you call my mobile. This time I'll have it powered up.'

Bruce is turning to leave when the old guy grabs his arm.

'*Nein.* I don't want to do this any more.'

Bruce sits back down and waves at the waiter bringing the change to clear off back inside.

'What do you mean?'

'I have enough money now. I don't need to run the risk of being caught making those telephone calls. Greed is a terrible thing.'

'What are we supposed to do in London?'

This time it's the old guy who's on his feet, holding his manila envelope close to his chest.

'You're supposed to be the top FX traders. Why don't you trade like any other bank?'

Karl walks off. Bruce sits on alone, stunned at the sudden development. He's livid. Bloody livid.

He puts his briefcase down, puts on his black leather gloves, takes the weapon from the spine of the briefcase and carefully places it inside his left sleeve. One eye on the outside world confirms that the target is on the move. The target stands upon the pavement, silhouetted only by the welcoming lights of a nearby restaurant, looking like he's about to ask someone for a taxi. There is no taxi. The target crosses the three lanes of sporadic traffic, and walks away alone at speed, head bowed slightly into the slanting drizzle.

A stab with minimal force can still penetrate thicker skeletal bones such as the sternum and ribs. An incised wound, achieved by slicing, slashing or stabbing, is one where there is a clean division of the skin and tissues, leaving the surrounding margins almost free from damage. The more serious wounds are inflicted by a forceful thrust and involve the face, neck or upper abdomen.

He dodges oncoming traffic from the right and sees the target ahead take a right into a public park. This is promising. The streets are slippy underfoot. He follows the target inside the gates, past a Wolfe Tone memorial, past a sign announcing the public park closes at six p.m. sharp, past the by-laws prohibiting the riding of bicycles, the playing of football or the carrying of any weapon. He smiles.

Thirty minutes to go. Time to kill. They pass a set of life-size bronze figures from the Famine, emaciated matchstick people, all skin and bone, slumped on knees in despair, weak with hunger. He sees weeping trees, hedges and bushes, walls of wonderful foliage. It's almost deserted inside, mainly due to the inclement weather. He looks back at the entrance to the park. He's certain there are no CCTV cameras nearby.

The faster the movement, the easier it is to penetrate the skin. Very little force is needed to push a sharp object through the skin, especially where the latter is stretched across the ribs, as in the chest. The skin acts as a spring, indenting before penetration, and then springing back to assist with the movement. All this occurs effortlessly and smoothly even though an individual's skin is the most resistant tissue to an attack next to bone and cartilage.

He inhales and exhales, monitors his heartbeat and confirms that all is regular. His mental checks are complete. The Ten Commandments are buried deep within his subconscious. He hasn't been to Ireland in maybe ten years. He won't be back here in the foreseeable future. He knows no one here. There's a taxi rank nearby. It's thirty minutes by taxi to the airport. BA and others fly every hour to Heathrow, City or Gatwick.

The seriousness of the wound depends upon the blade, its length, width and thickness, whether it is a single or double-edged blade, the degree of taper from the tip to the hilt of the blade, whether the blade has a serrated or squared-off back edge, whether the face of the hilt guard lies adjacent to the blade, the extent of grooves, serration or forking of the blade, and lastly upon the sharpness of the edge and tip of blade.

The target seems to know where to go as he heads in an exact diagonal direction across the park, preferring a more direct route rather than walking two square sides of the park along the safer streets. An oncoming twenty-something girl with a toddler in a pushchair passes by them both. He looks away from her at the last minute. He's maybe ten yards behind the target. No one else is in sight. It's quiet. He looks behind and sees no one. The target is walking on a narrow tarmac path between bushes. He runs.

The larynx and great arterial vessels are often severed irreparably. The wound widens as the blade is actively moved and the body moves in relation to the blade in an attempt to avoid the attack, to bend or twist away from the blade.

'Excuse me.'

The target stops, then turns to face him, squinting his eyes through the rain.

He is closer, examining the target's coat. Thin enough. He joins his gloved hands together.

'You just pissed me off.'

The target smiles as if it's some sort of joke. Then realises there is no joke. Then some recognition. He stands firm.

'Hey, buddy, relax. You need to get a life.'

A stabbing incident is often dynamic and the target is rarely in a static anatomical position. Stab wounds will often be found on the trunk, neck, upper arms and head. Incised wounds of the palms and fingers are common features in stabbings and indicate an attempt to grab the weapon or to protect against it and show that the victim had time to react.

Rain falls upon the leaves overhead. He separates his hands in one swift movement and lunges forward towards the base of the heart. The blade easily cuts through the canvas of the raincoat.

The sharpness of the tip determines how easily the blade will penetrate. The sharpness of the rest of the weapon is less important because once the point is through the skin, the rest of the weapon will enter effortlessly.

'You are the one . . .'

The length of the wound is best measured when the edges are in apposition, with the edges being held together by a strip of transparent tape. However, wound contraction must be taken into consideration as this occurs after withdrawal of the blade, due to the elasticity of the skin.

'. . . who needs to get a fucking life.'

Transverse wounds across the lower portions of the heart give rise to punctures rather than lacerations and do not commonly cause cessation of life for a time, especially if the puncture is valvular in character and prevents the loss of much blood.

He cleans the blade on the grass, then drags the body off the tarmac and underneath the bushes. He pushes the body with his foot, until it's out of sight, then stands and watches the blood mingle with the raindrops and puddles, to run in crying streams into the anonymity of mother earth. He does an about-turn, walks for five minutes to a rank and takes a taxi to the airport.

Cardiac wounds are generally fatal. If the wound involves the base of the heart, with extensive laceration of the surrounding parts, death is inevitable. Serious irritation of the cardiac nervous mechanism produces instantaneous death from shock.

The trip back is the proverbial flight from hell. The last row in Club is next to six kids returning to London from some swimming competition. They spend the longest hour shouting at each other, knocking against his seat, chucking peanuts and sweets around, insulting staff, standing in the aisles and going to the toilet. There are a few parents allegedly in charge but they're either too weak or too fatigued to act. He has had enough. The plane stops at the Terminal I stand. He takes his briefcase down and turns to a parent.

'You're great,' he tells her. She's surprised. 'To work with all those retarded children.'

She stares back, slowly comprehending his words. 'But they're not retarded.'

He looks over at them before heading down the aisle. 'Really? You'd never know.'

CHAPTER THIRTEEN

COVENT GARDEN, LONDON WC2: 7.45 P.M.

Adam parks the Astra and exits the NCP car park. He wonders about this evening. If the restaurant is too romantic for a first time, if he's early or late, if she's inside waiting or if he'll sit alone in a room full of couples, what she'll be like outside an office environment, whether she'll turn up at such short notice.

The bar area by the door to Long Acre is heaving with singles, suits, wannabes, hot dates and blind dates. It's a blur. It's her choice. Adam is first. The maitre d' of Le Jardin leads him to a good corner table facing the full restaurant. Adam feels the eyes of the nation bearing down upon him. He takes too many sips from a glass of water, downs some pitted olives on a stick, plays with the bread and takes too many obvious glances at his Seiko, signalling to all that he's waiting. Then the vision approaches between the tables.

'Hi, Adam.'

He stands up to pull out her chair. She leans forward. It's an invitation. They kiss.

'Hi, Trish.'

She wears a loose top and perfectly worn denims with a wonderful belt. He can't be sure from where he sits, but judging by the male glances in their direction, he thinks her top may have an exposed back. They discuss the eclectic yet manageable menu. She fingers her glass of water until the New World red arrives.

'This is a bit unusual, isn't it?' She laughs.

'What do you mean?' he asks.

'No one's ever invited me out like this before.'

Some invite. Adam first thought about calling her at work but such conversations are difficult. If she's not there and calls back, then all the guys on the trading desk eavesdrop. They might even play back the call on the tapes, copy it onto a few cassettes and sell copies to others on the trading floor for a few quid. He crafted the wording of the e-mail over a day and edited and re-edited a draft in his saved mailbox.

'It's a thank-you. You handled all the paperwork for me so efficiently.'

'Henry did all the real work.'

Given a choice between the two, Adam's convinced that Trish is significantly better potential girlfriend material.

'I didn't fancy a quiet dinner with him so much.'

She smiles. 'How is Mitchell's so far?'

'Fine,' he lies. 'Great place.'

'You glad Henry hunted you down and got his man? He always does. He's like that.'

Adam's wondering how often Trish gets hers. Their waiter returns with starters. Adam mentally rehearses his list of conversation topics to avoid those dreaded lulls. The list is short. At the top of his list are people they both know. Just one name on it, to be specific. Trish has already broached the subject.

'Henry seem busy these days?' he asks.

He thinks he's doing well, feeding her open-ended one-liners by the time the starters are cleared away.

'He is. He's always disappearing to places for new vacancies.'

'Like to Mitchell's in wonderful tropical Docklands.'

'Sure, but he's got clients everywhere.'

'Really?'

Trish takes some wine to lubricate her vocal cords. Adam thinks she's so easy to talk to.

'Amsterdam. Brussels, too. A few weeks ago he was in Germany. It's all go with Henry.'

'So he has that stack of Air Miles to use.'

Trish nods at Adam's powers of recall. He's starting to get some positive vibes from across the table.

'You have the memory of a supergrass. Henry gives me a few free flights to go home to Dublin for my sanity.'

Adam's thinking that this is going well. There's lots of eye contact. The wine is working its charms on their inhibitions. He gives the waiter a nod for a second bottle as the main courses arrive. They eat as he asks Trish more about herself – her upbringing, family and friends and her move to London. People love to talk about themselves.

'I came to London for the money,' she admits.

'Who doesn't?'

'I'll go back to Dublin eventually to settle down.'

It's the first negative vibe of a great first date.

'You like Dublin?' he asks.

'Love it. Patrick lives there.'

Second negative vibe of the evening.

'Patrick?' as he puts down his knife and fork.

'My boyfriend.'

Third potentially fatal negative vibe of the evening. Maybe it's not as serious as it seems.

'Why doesn't he move to London?'

'He can't. He's in the Garda Siochana.' She sees his blank look. 'That's what we call the police. He can't easily transfer like some investment banker. But I think he'll propose this Christmas. I hope he does. I can't wait.'

It's the final and fatal negative vibe of the evening. It's a killer blow to the solar plexus. Adam fakes enthusiasm as the lush desserts arrive. His mind drifts. Suddenly he's self-conscious again. He wonders now how the evening will end, when it will end, and will he hold Trish, or kiss her, or do nothing?

'Patrick's a lucky guy.'

'Have you got someone special in your life, Adam?'

'I'm working on it.'

Trish leans over as she attacks the crème brûlée with assorted fruits of the forest piled on the side.

'You're a smart, successful, good-looking guy. You'll make someone happy soon.'

Adam pays the bill after coffees and mints. He sees Trish safely into a black cab as they part company, receiving a light kiss before the rear door closes. He waves to her as her cab speeds off down Long Acre. He's certain that Trish is not even aware that she's just been on a spectacularly unsuccessful first date.

Samantha sits in an office on sixteen behind a closed door. Across the desk is the thirty-something woman called Belinda who purports to run the human resources department for the trading team up on twenty-one. She's infamous for once sending a memo to all desk heads requesting a list of trading staff, broken down by age and sex. Bruce and the others replied that all the trading staff were broken down by age and sex. If this woman were ever accused in a court of law of managing the HR function, then Samantha is certain there wouldn't be enough evidence to convict her. Samantha already senses her unease.

'People don't often ask us for an appointment. Usually it's the other way around.' The accent of the HR guru is plummy and stilted, her inherited nasal tones enough to deter most, but not Samantha.

'I have to talk to someone.'

The office and its occupant are immaculate. There isn't a sheaf of paper out of place. The décor is as minimalist as the department. The guru sits in a smart black suit, with blow-dried hair and wheelbarrow loads of facial pancake. She looks at a desk clock as if she has better things to do mid-morning.

'Do you wish to discuss taking time off, your training needs, promotion or career development?'

'I wish it were that simple. This is more serious.'

'Oh, dear, it's about your pay and bonus?' she sighs. 'We get most of these complaints near year-end.' She writes Samantha's name down in block capitals on an A4 pad and sits poised to take notes.

'It's about sexism in this bank,' advises Samantha.

The guru rocks backwards in her seat, like Samantha has uttered some foul abusive language. She first examines her expertly manicured and warpainted nails, then repositions some expensive jewellery.

'Don't you mean *possible* sexism?'

'I mean sexism.'

'Is it serious sexism?'

'Is there any other sort? I've been on the receiving end for seven months. I know it when I suffer it.'

The guru writes nothing. Instead she lays down her pen on the desk and leans back with a smile.

'What exactly do you mean by sexism? Do you have any specific examples?'

'Dozens. We can walk up to the trading floor right now and look at the female staff. The men here all hire the same type. You don't see any overweight dowdy old battleaxes with bad dress sense sitting around, do you?'

'That's not an example. That's just a general perception.'

'Then take my job. My offer letter says that I am a junior FX trader yet Bruce won't let me trade. I am the position keeper instead. I have the worst job on the desk. I do the mundane number crunching and I also do all the admin and general gopher work. I have a damn' degree in maths and speak two languages. I'm working for men who don't have a degree or an iota of IQ, who are more interested in lewd e-mails, swearing and gambling, yet think they can treat me like some sort of menial skivvy. The other day one of them asked me to bring in a duster so I could clean the dust from their PC screens.'

'But you knew what the job entailed when you were interviewed here.'

'Whose side are you on?' Samantha recalls the interviews with Lloyd and Bruce. The guru remains tight-lipped. 'The interviews here were a joke. Bruce told me that it costs fifty K to train someone to be an FX trader. He wanted to know if I was planning to get married and have kids. Even told me I was a woman. I was vaguely flattered that he'd noticed. He asked if I was sure I wanted to work on a trading desk or whether I'd prefer to be in HR or research. I should have known then. I'm tired of being the only woman at the FX desk. I get invited to every damn' meal out with brokers and other banks . . .'

'Isn't that enjoyable?' the guru tentatively asks.

'You try it,' Samantha sighs. 'I sit at a table with a dozen men, most of them twice my age and bald. They leer over at me and make double entendres about Galicia melons for starters or fresh pears for dessert. I've had old men whispering their pathetic sex fantasies into my ear. Sometimes I'd like to scrape the main course over some bastard's toupee, but I daren't. None of the others at the desk ever intervene. I feel like I'm only eye candy, just one step away from prostitution. Bruce tells me that I add some sparkle to the social events. Says it shows this bank is keen on equal opportunities. Rubbish!'

The guru has written nothing yet, as if making notes will only lend credence to the discussion.

'So that's as bad as it gets?'

'I wish. Last month I went along to a late lunch with money brokers at a place in the East End. I was the only woman. The food was great and the company was okay. Then, at three in the afternoon, some busty Brazilian girl comes out, dances on the tables and slowly reveals all. I made my excuses and took a cab back here. That sort of thing is totally demeaning to everybody involved. We don't have to stand for it.'

'You could tell Bruce that you don't want to attend such functions.'

'Bruce doesn't take no for an answer. These meals are usually somewhere flashy, like Claridges or Le Gavroche. He can't see why anyone would turn the invitation down.'

'Anything else you want to say?' The guru is sounding even less interested.

'Then there's the sexist language. They swear all the time and it's all sexual. I constantly suffer what they think are jokes. Last week we all got an e-mail from Muppet, one of the most Neanderthal guys on the desk. I opened the attached file and it was a picture of a fluffy yellow chicken and a little kitten.'

'So what's wrong with that?' Obviously vaguely wishing she didn't have to ask the question, fearing the answer.

'The e-mail header said it was a Blonde Bird with a Nice Pussy.'

'You must remember that this is the City of London.'

'Does that make it all right?'

'No ... but I think you're overstating the problem. It's not that bad in Mitchell's.'

'That's because you don't work on the trading floor,' Samantha points. 'How come you're not writing this down?'

'Because I have a good memory. So what do you want me to do about it?'

'You tell me. I've come here for your expert advice.'

The guru looks around as if she has better things to do. She sighs under the burden of eleven years in HR.

'You aren't the first and you won't be the last. You have two choices. Firstly you can make a formal complaint quoting some of those examples. It will be reported up the line to management, probably to New York. Unfortunately, they may take a different view and may disagree. You will be seen as a difficult employee and your career here will be finished. No MD will want you to work for them.'

'So what's the other choice?'

The guru put her unused pad back into her top drawer, her desk once again devoid of any evident work.

'What do you really want to do in life? Not banking, I'm sure?'

Samantha knows. 'I want to make some money, maybe go back home, maybe teach there, enjoy life.'

'Me too. So be like the rest of us, Samantha. Say nothing about this, bite your lip, bank your cash and count the day to when you retire well or marry money. In the meantime, remember that sexism doesn't just exist at the FX desk on the twenty-first floor, or in Mitchell's. It's everywhere in the City. In London. In life.'

'I could go outside and take a sex discrimination case to an employment tribunal.'

'You could try. Some have done that in other banks and won damages. But it takes ages and you rack up huge legal costs. It's one little person against a giant American corporation with bottomless pockets and armies of lawyers. Your name will be all over the press. You will never work anywhere in the City again. Period.'

'Suits me.' Samantha stands by the door as she leaves. 'There is, of course, a third choice.' The guru stares back at her. 'I could always cocoon myself in a nice cosy job in HR.'

Henry runs through his voluminous Rolodex, wondering whom he'll call, focusing on his best clients. He sees Lloyd's business card. Henry hasn't spoken to him since Adam joined. It's time to call. Maybe he's returned from New York. He dials Lloyd, feeling the need to celebrate success. He'll ask Trish to courier over a magnum as per usual. Of the vintage Chateau, rather than the .45 calibre variety.

'Diane Rubin.'

Henry's puzzled. He thought he dialled Lloyd's direct line. Must some new unknown Yank PA.

'Lloyd, please. It's Henry Simpson here.'

'Lloyd's not here. Can I help you?'

Her American accent works for him. Lloyd has hired a good one this time.

'Sure you can. Are you new there?'

'I guess I am,' she replies.

'Then I won't rush you. Take a pad and pen and note this down. I'd like to buy Lloyd lunch on Friday.'

'Lloyd won't be able to make lunch.'

She sounds feisty on the phone. Henry looks forward to checking her out in person next time.

'Don't you want to clear that with him first, dear?'

'No need. He's returned to the States. Dear.'

'Isn't he back?'

'It's permanent.'

Henry's aghast. Another key contact gone. He'll have to cultivate a whole new relationship.

'So who's in charge, then?'

'I suppose I am.'

He's beginning to wonder what illegal substance this new PA is on and if he can source some.

'Sorry. I mean, who is the person managing the foreign exchange team in London?'

'Well, I wonder who it can be? I mean, I'm sitting at Lloyd's desk right now.'

'So you're not his PA?'

'Correct. Maybe that makes me the FVP for FX?'

Henry's speechless, almost paralysed, as he holds the handset in his left hand.

'I've made a terrible mistake here. You see ... I work with Lloyd on his staffing requirements.'

'You mean, you used to work with Lloyd?'

She's good. 'Precisely.' He's trying to recover the situation. Somehow. 'We must ... meet up soon?'

'Friday, isn't it?'

'What?' he stutters.

'Lunch. Lloyd can't make it – I'll be there instead. I

could do with a free lunch from a recruitment consultant. And I'll use the opportunity to tell you in person that I'll break your balls if you ever try to tempt one of my team away. You call my PA with the details when you've made a reservation. 'Bye.'

Henry's in shock, stung, wondering why Lloyd got the big push and why he never called? It must have been deadly quick. A glowing Trish arrives and stands beside his desk. She's holding a few pages of a fax.

'You look exceptionally well today, Trish,' he observes.

'I had a pleasant night out.'

He hazards a guess. 'Anyone I know?'

'Adam Lewis.'

'What? Him?'

'It was just dinner. That's all. You know I'm spoken for.' Trish seems excited. 'Good news, Henry.'

'Don't tell me someone's accepted a job offer we made to them?'

Trish holds up some paper. 'These faxed CVs came in today from a husband and wife who both work overseas. They're Irish, have been away for ten years and want to move to London or return to Dublin. They work for SocGen and Paribas, both good-name equity fund managers.'

'So?'

'Remember your two Irish National jobs in Dublin. This might kill two birds with the one stone.'

Henry scans the CVs. Trish is as right as ever. The candidates both look perfect, at least on paper.

'Maybe those Irish National jobs are gone?'

'I just checked with the MD you met in Dublin. He hasn't filled the roles yet.'

'Then you know the next step?'

'You wanna meet them. Here or over there?'

'Where exactly are they based?'

'Luxembourg.'

Henry's thinking on his feet about Luxembourg. He's never been there.

'Seems like the middle of nowhere. How easy it is to get there? Can I get over and back in a day?'

Trish has already done the necessary research on the BA website.

'BA fly from Gatwick twice a day. The last flight back is at eight p.m. on weekdays.'

'Give the two a call and set it up. I could do with a change of scenery.'

CHAPTER FOURTEEN

CANARY WHARF, LONDON E14: 9.20 A.M.

It's Thursday. It's ECB rates day. It's still his first week at Mitchell's and Adam's about to lose it. The job is the least of his worries. Each morning the bastard in the apartment upstairs rises at 5.30 or earlier and makes as much noise as possible. Adam attributes the noise to one of three possibilities. Either the guy has a well-used mini-gym in the bedroom, he's training circus elephants for the big top, or he's got someone locked away who is trying to summon help from the outside world. One evening there is blaring Dido music so he also doubts the guy's musical taste. Adam's not getting enough quality sleep. Today he looks out of his bedroom window. The yellow VW Beetle speeds off. At least he knows the bastard drives that car.

Work is getting better. He's done a few internal euro trades for the equity and bond desks and made the sure-thing small-fry trading spread. He's had lunch with Bruce in a nearby wine bar where his boss picked up the gargantuan tab for beers and pasta. He's had a few vaguely social chats with Muppet, Bookie, Spoon and Cable Guy, but they're on different planets. They don't offer much information and Adam doesn't push the conversation. He's even had a voluntary hello from Diane one morning in the lifts. She knows that he exists.

Samantha is the only problem. He's increasingly attracted to her but it seems unreciprocated. She sits three feet away but it feels like there's a chasm between them. She's major league. He lives in hope.

'Big day today,' as he decides to open a conversation.

'Is it?' she replies disinterestedly.

It's one of those adrenalin-loaded Thursdays where every FX desk waits on the news from Frankfurt. It's Adam's first chance to see how the experts in Mitchell's do it, rather than the rank amateurs in Kapital.

'ECB.'

She looks up and he watches her eyes sparkle. 'So it is.' Seeming suddenly more interested.

Adam's waiting for some insight from the team but with forty minutes to go to the rates announcement, Bruce gives the four others the eye. The gang of them head off for a chat behind the closed doors of a spare meeting room. Adam reckons they're discussing strategy. He wishes he had been invited to join them. Adam and Samantha man the FX desk of the biggest global investment bank in London. But she's a position keeper, he's a trader, so he must be in charge. This is the way it's meant to be. But he's still not convinced that he's the right person in the right job. He needs her reassurance. He tries again.

'How am I doing so far?' he asks.

'No worse than the others,' Samantha opines.

He sits back in his chair, watches the screens, feels the power, enjoys the illusion, debating about whether to risk putting his feet up on the desk. If there is a sudden international crisis of epic proportions, like the US president is taken out by an assassin, or China swoops on Taiwan, or there's a bloody coup in Moscow, he'll make the right calls and make millions. Then their colleagues emerge and cut into the conversation.

'Twenty minutes to go to the ECB. What do you think, Adam?' asks Bruce.

He knew that someone would ask him eventually. He's done the research today. No *FT*, no comment.

'I say no rate change today. Rates didn't move last time. Conditions are the same as last month.'

Bruce shakes his head.

'Not so sure myself. We'll see.'

A mobile phone rings. They all look around. It's Bruce's mobile phone. Samantha touches Adam.

'See that.'

She's pointing at Bruce. He looks over. The wall clock says it's 9.45 GMT. Bruce is taking a call but he's turned around and looking away. His voice has dropped to a murmur. He's inaudible.

'Who's he on to?' asks Adam.

'I'd love to know,' she replies.

Bruce hangs up quickly and looks at the others. Adam sees a vague nod to them before Bruce looks at Diane's empty office, then he speaks.

'Like I said . . . I'm not so sure. There were hopes for a rate cut last time. This could be it. We just decided inside that we're going to risk it and take a punt today. We're going long the dollar and short the euro. If euro interest rates fall, then the euro falls and we buy it back and make some fast bucks.'

There's five minutes of frantic trading as they all sell a few hundred million euro. Bruce deals with Deutsche. Muppet deals with Citibank. Spoon deals with HSBC. Cable Guy deals with ABN Amro. Bookie deals with UBS. Even Adam does his bit with a whopper trade with BBV. Samantha runs the position sheet and gives them a shout at 9.50 GMT.

'We're now short three hundred million euro.'

Bruce calls a halt to the trading. Otherwise they'll bust their limits and Diane will be all over them like a rash. They sit at the desk as the wall clocks slowly drag towards 11 a.m. CET.

/Adam watches the others. They're laughing at each other now, looking around the office, surfing the web, writing e-mails and the like. The calm before the storm continues. At 11 CET the news from Frankfurt appears on the Reuters screens. It bloody happens! It's a shock. Interest rates are down twenty-five basis points. The euro falls fast. The trading desk is making serious money. They're all on the edge of their seats, hammering the keyboards, crystallising profits, making a million. The carnage is over in minutes. It was an inspired trading decision.

'Fucking hell!' yells Bruce, with his fist clenched in the air. 'This is like a crap shoot.'

Adam's wondering about what happened. It seemed ... so easy. So much easier than his days in Kapital. He used to think that Beamer was a great trader and role model. Now he knows that Bruce is a killer trader. The five are up on their feet and off for a smoke and fresh air. Bruce turns to the newer hires.

'You guys are in charge. Don't screw up.'

Adam is left evaluating the events. He loves their overt oozing confidence. There is no sense of panic here. They were always in complete charge of their own destiny. He's still puzzled about what's happened, though. The words just come of their own accord.

'Something's not right here.'

'What do you mean?' Samantha asks, spinning around on her chair. She is so close.

Now he knows why it's different from Kapital. He speaks slowly.

'It was too quiet. It's like ...'

'Like what?' she asks.

He's almost laughing before he gets the words out. It's such a ridiculous assumption.

'... Like they knew this rate cut was gonna happen.'

Samantha turns and honours him with the biggest smile he's seen in days of sitting beside her.

'You and me are going for an early lunch together. We need to talk.'

Samantha leads the way. Adam follows in her wake. They pass the water fountains of Cabot Square, dodge a London City Airport bus doing forty or more in the wholly artificial city suburb that is Canary Wharf, and into the sanctuary of number ten, Corney & Barrow. It's early yet heaving, a sea of affluent faces everywhere he looks. She stands inside the swing door, waiting for him to make the first move, but he doesn't. She thinks he looks stunned by something. The ECB? Or seeing so many people?

'You okay?'

'Sure. It's busy in here.'

She makes the decision for both of them and finds two bar stools near the counter. They sit in the shadow of a wall of shelved bottles of champagne lit by spotlights, there more for effect than to buy. She waits.

'Well?' He is distracted, like there's too much happening in here. 'You want to order, Adam?'

He takes a wine list, takes ages to grab anyone's attention behind the bar, but eventually orders a mid-range white with two glasses. He goes to pay. Samantha stops him, her warm hand touching his.

'We want to eat too,' she advises. 'There's no hurry. You can run a tab.'

She watches him checking out the bar's interior, then peering through the plate glass. There's an outside sandpit set amidst sleepers for boules in the summer, giant urns with year-round plants, tiered steps down to Wren's Landing, old warehouses on the far side of the dock with her favourite restaurants. Up close and side on she hopes Adam's going to be different. He's human, has a softer side, not like the other arrogant bastards at the desk. He's drinking the white wine too fast, like it's an excuse not to have to converse.

'So I hear you know Henry too?' she asks.

'I have him to thank for getting me into Mitchell's.'

She lets it lie. He's still enthusiastic. 'Lloyd too?'

'It's a hell of a shock to arrive on day one and find the guy who hired you has gone back to New York.'

'Did he hire you as a spy too?'

'A spy?' he laughs.

'When I joined Lloyd told me I would be a trader soon. Then after a few weeks he told me about my other role. He wanted me to sit at the desk and tell him exactly what the traders did each day. He and I spoke about it on and off. I gave him some of the desk printouts. We were close. He said he'd look after me at year end. Then Lloyd left us suddenly, I don't know why. I do know that he suspected that the FX desk has some trading scam.'

Adam puts his near-empty glass down. His expression has changed. He looks tense.

'A scam? You're joking?'

'You saw the desk in action today. You saw something odd happen this morning. You said as much, and what you said to me was unprompted.'

'You must be wrong.'

'You saw Bruce on his mobile. He gets a phone call just before each ECB announcement.'

'It could be anyone. It could be his wife . . .'

'I don't think his ex-wife follows interest rates that closely. The telephone call matters. I heard a tape recording of one last month. Someone calling from overseas, I think, said to him "no change".'

'That could mean anything.'

'Rates didn't change that day despite expectations that they might. Some other banks lost a lot.'

'Tell me about it! I was one of them.'

She watches his despair. He's finding all this impossible to believe. Mitchell's must be better than Kapital.

'I don't think there can be a scam at a name like Mitchell's. The guys are bad but they can't be *that* bad.'

Samantha turns on him immediately.

'You really think so? After a week, you know it all? I've been here months. I'll tell you about them.' She draws her stool nearer. 'Take Muppet. He claims that his job is ruining his life and that he's too stressed. When I joined, he corners me in a bar when he has a few too many. Tells me that he and his wife were trying to have kids for years but this trading job gives him a low sperm count. So he settles for two Porsches and his wife settles for two cats. That same night as we leave the bar he asks me if I want to shag him back at my place. His exact words. Much like the *News of the World*, I made my excuses and left. He's a sleazeball. He scares me sometimes. I'd never go to a bar with him like you and me are doing now.'

Adam's speechless. There's no stopping her. It's like she's bleeding from an open wound.

'Then there's Bookie. He's a compulsive gambler. I mean, he has it bad. He shouldn't be holding down a day job anywhere, least of all on a trading desk. Since I've been here I've seen him take bets on what colour shirts guys wear to work, how many dumps they take each day … He needs medical help.'

Adam's worried. She's on a roll.

'Spoon thinks he's lining up the wedding of the year. He has such an inflated opinion of himself just because he has some distant title in his family. I'm surprised he hasn't sold the wedding rights to *Hello!* magazine, that's if they'd want them. He's the most condescending snobbish person I've met in the City of London, and that's saying something. And he's thick as a plank, too.'

'I get the drift.'

'Cable Guy is a Jewish Cockney git and he's the most homophobic person I have met, which can only mean one thing – he must be gay himself. He still lives at home with his lovely mum and the guy is thirty-something going on fifty so I rest my case. If anyone phones for you and they don't talk like a Cockney, then he assumes they're gay. He once asked me if I thought Lloyd was a closet gay.'

'So you and me are the only two normal people at the desk?' he asks.

She holds his gaze before choosing her words carefully. 'Depends what you mean by normal.'

'And you know what's the worst part? I'm going on a stag trip to Dublin with them. I'll die there.' She watches him search for some upside, clutching at non-existent straws, wondering what he has done. 'I wish I'd never left Kapital. I can't believe I left there for a place like this. It's hell. What do we do?'

'We hang in there,' she offers.

'Not so easy. If there is a scam, and word leaks out to the market, then we will be tainted along with the rest of them. Working at Mitchell's in FX will be a black mark on anyone's CV. So, you and me will stick it out for a while longer, learn what we can and gather enough evidence to protect ourselves.'

Samantha raises a glass in some sort of bonding ritual. He does the same. She makes a toast of sorts.

'You know more about FX trading than I do. It's up to you to find out what's going on, Adam.'

Henry is last to leave the office. As he steps into the lift, a lone male figure emerges from the shadows.

'Henry, fancy meeting you here.'

Lionel Roberts allows the doors to close. They are alone. The lift starts to descend. Roberts opens the safety box on the wall, finds a turnkey and shifts it to the left. The lift shudders to a sudden halt.

'What are you bloody doing, Lionel?'

'My offer to buy you out is still good. I am a man of considerable means. What do you say?'

'I said no.'

'My offer was an opening gambit.'

'I know.'

'What if I offered another million on top?'

Henry is beginning to like what he hears.

'I'm still not interested.'

'You'll get half when we sign the sale contract. The other half a year later. To make sure you stay with us for the transition period.' Henry says nothing. Roberts is an insurance policy on which he doesn't need to make a claim yet. But Roberts is insistent. 'So have you decided?'

'Yes, I have decided.'

'Good.'

Henry moves forward and takes control of the turnkey. 'Ground floor, please.'

They part company downstairs. Outside on the cobbled Covent Garden streets it's dark and depressing. Henry knows why he always feels so manic in these long seasons. A keen doctor in the army spotted the first symptoms years ago on a punishing winter training exercise in the Norwegian fjords. Henry had three or four check-ups before the shrink finally diagnosed Seasonal Affective Disorder.

Henry found SAD in the index of a medical book. It said that ten million Americans have it, but then again ten million Americans have everything. It was listed as a mental health disorder, under 'moods and depression'. He experiences fatigue, inability to concentrate, hypersomnia, depressed moods, and cravings for carbohydrates that often lead to wintertime weight gains through no fault of Amanda's.

Henry's symptoms appear in autumn, triggered by a decrease in daylight hours, are aggravated by time spent inside auto-mobiles and offices, worsen through the holiday months, poss-ibly aggravated by the Christmas celebrations of those around them, and lessen when the springtime sunshine reappears. The only cure is sitting in front of a fluorescent light box for hours at a time to simulate sunlight. Henry hasn't the patience for such endeavours. One week with Amanda at their holiday place in the Canaries is never enough light to regulate his serotonin levels and the circadian rhythms in his brain. Sometimes he feels like running off to some hot and sunny climate and leaving the English winter behind for ever.

He walks alone along the Strand, avoiding vacant oncomers and the cracked pavements, stepping over the strewn urban rubbish and circumnavigating pools of stagnant rainwater. He passes the awakening West End theatres, stinking burger and pizza joints, shuttered shop windows and alleyways full of steel bins and black plastic liners, all contrasting with the glowing opulence of the Savoy on the other side of the road. There's a new community moving into their residences in the early evening.

Cardboard boxes and grubby sleeping bags appear from the shadows as vagrants settle down to sleep and beg. Henry almost collides with a young guy with dank dreadlocks, a bad mullet haircut and two days' acned stubble. The guy's got a can of Tennants in one hand and a bald emaciated mongrel on a piece of string on the other. Henry is standing in a pool and it's impossible to tell whether it's rainwater, beer or urine. He moves towards the edge of the pavement but the waster makes a sudden plea.

'Any change, mister?' Spoken in some sort of guttural northern accent.

The smell of life on the streets hits him full on. Henry can make out the bad breath, then the stench of raw body odour. It could be attributable to man or beast. It's hard to tell. The smell is overpowering.

'What?'

Up close, Henry sees the guy's eyes have receded into his face. He can only make out two dark hollows.

'Any change?'

The guy is standing in his way, blocking his path towards

the Tube station, almost forcing him to make a contribution of sorts. Henry steps off the pavement and replies as he walks past the puzzled freeloader. 'I find life is full of constant change.'

CHAPTER FIFTEEN

BARRIER POINT, LONDON E16: 7.15 P.M.

Adam takes a detour on foot into the underground car park of his apartment complex. It's pissing down again. He got soaked commuting home from work. The forecast is for the same tomorrow. He's left his only usable umbrella in the boot of the Astra. He's standing by his car when the purring engine of another vehicle comes down the ramp at speed. The brakes squeal as it pulls into the next space. Rivulets of rainwater run down the shiny yellow bodywork. Pools form by the painted number of space 1305. It's the Beetle.

A girl sits alone inside the car. He should have guessed a long time ago. No bloke would ever drive a cute VW Beetle. She swings open the door and emerges, wearing a pair of perfectly faded figure-hugging Levis. She's tall, slim and maybe mid-twenties. She too has been caught in the rain. The ends of her long strands of hair are seductively wet, while other curled strands by her fringe have settled on her forehead. Adam thinks he's seen her before. She takes out four bulging Tesco carrier bags. Adam wonders when she visits the local Tesco and why he's never seen her there late on a weekday evening when he shops for life's culinary essentials. Adam thinks she'll ignore him but she doesn't. She smiles encouragingly.

'Hello.'

'Hello,' is the only possible reply.

They walk towards the door to the ground-floor elevator, both unsure who's following whom. He wonders if she is the sole cause of all the manic activity upstairs or whether she shares with a guy. Four Tesco bags seems like a lot of food for one unless she hates shopping and only shops annually. He doesn't know her name and they both missed the chance they had to do the introductions and shake hands. He carries a somewhat redundant brolly. She carries the four heavy bags. He has the solution.

'Can I carry some of those for you?'

She smiles again. It's almost infectious.

'Thanks a lot.'

He opens the door and holds it ajar for her like any decent gentleman would. Instinctively he walks towards the nearby bank of letter boxes to check his mail. It's a subconscious action, force of habit. As soon as he's made the move to the left he knows it's a mistake. She stands alone by the elevator. She pushes the call button. He can hear the lift doors open. There's a moment of indecision. She walks inside. The doors are about to close. He is so near. The doors stay open. She's holding the open-doors button. He's in.

'Thanks for holding it.'

'Well, you have got half of my shopping.'

'So I have.' He puts the bags down. The lift hums. She presses thirteen and looks back at him. 'I'm on twelve,' he offers.

She moves closer. The elevator seems smaller than before. She is only a foot away. There is a sweet aroma. 'I'm Lisa.' Her hand is warm to his touch, with long elegant fingers and gleaming nails.

'I'm Adam. Good to meet you.'

'I'm in 1305.' She is making all the running. The interest might be mutual.

'I'm 1205.'

Suddenly he can see her face in the full light, rather than that of the darkened car park. She sees him too.

'I've seen you before. Briefly. In the local shop,' she says.

He recognises her. The girl in the jogging gear. His mad exit that day. It was a disaster.

'Yeah, you're right ... I was in a hurry that day.'

He watches the numbers rise to floor twelve. The lift is way too fast. It's all over in twenty seconds.

'Thanks again,' she says. 'It's good to know someone else here. In case of an emergency, you know.'

He steps outside. 'Likewise. Drop down if you ever need anything.'

An hour later he's had a microwaved pizza de luxe and oven chips when the music starts. He can make out the smooth R&B voice of Craig David. She's playing the melodic track three on the CD. He wonders how she feels tonight and if this is her song. It's romantic. Maybe she's playing it for him or maybe Adam has too vivid an imagination. The same song plays again. She must have the CD player on auto repeat. Her heels are audible. Adam realises that he has only ever heard one pair at a time. She must live alone.

He can hear a window or something opening above, then heels upon wood. He thinks she might have her balcony door ajar because the decibels are booming. It's a great song. It's his invite to commune. He looks out towards the river. The rain has stopped, evidently saving itself until morning. It's the calm after the storm. His curiosity is aroused. He steps out onto his own balcony, peers up through the wooden sleepers and tries to glean some insight. She leans over the edge of the rail, with a glass of something in one hand, running her other through her hair as she faces into the soft wind.

'It's me,' she announces enthusiastically, raising the glass as the track recommences.

He can see her face smiling down. The moonlight plays on her face. 'So I see.'

She takes a drink. He's hooked. She turns to go inside. 'Like they say in the movies, come up and see me sometime.'

Diane carefully pushes her lime-green Lambertson Truex Box Car bag under the table and looks out of the window. Rain speckles against the glass of La Cantina but for an American a long way from home the vista is impressive. Tower Bridge rises from the mist, to the left the Tower of London and the eastern outskirts of the City, to the right the regenerated docklands of St Katherine's Dock and Butlers Wharf. A solo man in his late thirties approaches her at ten minutes before one.

'Ms Rubin, I'm Henry Simpson. Apologies. I'm not usually late.'

He's got presence, a firm handshake, impeccable dress sense and clear diction. He stands with his shoulders held back and head erect. His posture, height and so much more immediately impress her.

'Don't apologise. I never do. You're not that late,' she advises. 'I got here early.'

He glances at a watch as he flexes his wrist. A Brylcreemed asexual waiter approaches with two menus, minimalist works of Brit Art on pastel cards, holding them as a priest would his Sunday sermon.

'Hello, I'm Randy and I'm going to be your waiter today. Enjoy.'

The waiter is an American. Diane hates the way he lisps and minces about, almost embarrassed that she shares the same nationality. She wonders how to counter Randy. Henry catches her eye and smiles.

'I'm Henry and this is Diane and we're going to be your customers today. Enjoy.'

Randy knows he's met his match and goes off to wait in the wings to be summoned as and when required.

She likes the way Henry orders quickly and decisively, then turns to give her his undivided attention.

'Sorry about my dreadful telephone call. I didn't know Lloyd was back in the States.'

It's his second apology. Diane likes a man who knows his place in the world. She's the corporate customer and the customer is always right. His only role is to service the many and varied needs of the customer. He's not wearing a wedding ring but she thinks she can see an indentation where a band might be worn. Her initial instincts were right. He might be the one. She hasn't had a guy in weeks. She needs one.

'Lloyd didn't know either.'

'What happened?'

'Politics. If you want to do any future business with Mitchell's, then you deal directly with me.'

He purses his lips over a glass of white, so chilled that the condensation rests on the side of the glass.

'Suits me . . . Diane.'

Randy tries to interest them in the dish of the day, some pigeon with shiitake mushrooms, his voice bursting with gourmet pronunciation. Instead they both order the crab, à la carte. She wonders if it's a deliberate move by her host. Maybe he's very good. Randy closes his notebook with a snap and flees.

'I need to know more about you, Henry.'

'Before we do business?' he asks.

'*If* we do business.'

'I'll tell you about my firm, the associate staff, the services we provide and what we do for clients.'

She shakes her head across the table.

'I'm not interested in your associates. I'll only be trading with you. I'm interested in you. Tell me about you.' She pauses in her search for more background information. 'Have you always been a headhunter?'

'Yes, and no.' He reflects momentarily. 'After college I joined the army – the Paras. Didn't like it much. All those early starts, following orders, people less intelligent telling me what to do every day.'

She puts down her knife and fork, suddenly excited to find that Henry has a less polished edge. She examines his hands up close, notices the well-cut cuticles and wonders what sort of action he's seen.

'It sounds more like life in Mitchell's, not the army.' He nods slowly. 'Tell me about it.'

Henry spent two years in the drab Hyderabad Barracks in Colchester. Two years in a NATO base near Hamburg where he learnt German and honed his skills with weapons. Then two grim tours of duty in Northern Ireland. After his thirtieth birthday Lionel Roberts approached him in person. He had long appreciated the finely honed talents of soldiers moving into the recruitment business. They were organised, professional, committed, driven, motivated, ruthless, and always keen to get the body.

'I spent seven years in 3 Para. You don't want to hear about it. It wasn't pleasant at times.'

'You have any chance to get married and have kids with all these army manoeuvres?'

'I got married. No kids.'

'You forget your wedding band today?'

'I've a loose arrangement with my wife. I don't wear my ring any more. But she wears hers.'

'Meaning what, exactly?' Diane asks, staring into his eyes.

'Meaning that we live in a free world.' He stares back. He's got a great set of polished teeth.

Diane finishes her main course, pats her rouged lips with her linen napkin and leans forward. She takes his left hand in hers. He is wonderfully warm to her touch, his hand alone enough to excite her imagination.

'Tell me, did you ever kill anyone with these?'

The first person Henry killed was a seventeen-year-old youth who was asking for it. It was a summer Saturday night in his first tour of duty with the 3rd Battalion The Parachute Regiment. They swapped maroon berets for helmets. The squad was summoned to attend the usual petty rioting in West Belfast during the Loyalist marching season when temperatures and emotions run equally high. Henry and the others stood behind rows of Land Rovers and RUC plods, sheltering from incoming bricks, stones, Molotov cocktails and fireworks. After midnight, random shots came from a block of Republican flats. It was a lone sniper but the brass in charge wanted an example made that night. Henry had won the Army Sniper Trophy at Bisley and was selected. His Enfield picked off a solo vacant youth with a shaven head wearing a Celtic FC home strip. The youth went down immediately, like he'd just evaporated out of the soccer shirt. The platoon closed ranks as per usual and attributed the incident to a loose ricochet. No harm done.

'That sort of information is classified. If I told you, I'd have to kill you,' he tells Diane.

Henry is knotting his regimental tie for the third time in front of the full-length mirror in the bedroom when Amanda sweeps into the room. She's in a black evening number, a gold chain around her neck, ready for another PR function. Anyone would think they're about to take London by storm together.

'So this is your one social outing of the year?' she inquires sarcastically.

His knot is now perfect. His regimental cap badge lies on the chair with its set of wings either side of a parachute above the crown of the reigning monarch. Underneath the cap badge is the regimental motto: 'Utrinque Paratus'. Ready for Anything. He places it in his pocket, swivels around and grabs a navy Hackett blazer with gold buttons off a rail.

'I'll be back late.'

She fusses over her brimming jewellery case in the corner. He decides to broach the topic.

'I met Lionel Roberts yesterday. We had a chat.'

She pivots on her heel, simultaneously inserting glittering diamante earrings into her lobes.

'Steer clear of him. I don't trust him. He tried to ruin you when you first went solo.'

'He's mellowed over the years.'

'Sharks don't mellow. They just sharpen their teeth and get better at hunting. He's bad news.'

Amanda is ready. The doorbell rings. Her minicab is here. Henry decides to test the water.

'Roberts wants to buy the firm from me. He's offering good money.'

'Much?'

'Millions. He seems genuinely interested in it.'

'He'll run it into the ground.'

'Do we care, if we have his money?'

Amanda looks out of the upstairs window and signals to the driver down on the steps.

'Are you seriously considering his offer?'

'Might be.'

'Why are you telling me this now?'

'I can't sell the firm without you. You remember when we set it up? I own ninety-nine of the shares but you own the other one. We'd have to agree to sell together.'

'How much would I get?'

'One per cent.'

'I know that. One per cent of what?'

'Of maybe three million quid.'

Amanda nods. 'Sounds to me like you're seriously considering. If you sell up and retire under forty, then please God don't hang about here at home all day. Go and do something useful. Get out from under my feet.'

'I won't be here. That's a promise.' He lingers on his exact choice of words. 'Enjoy your evening.'

'I don't know why you enjoy raking over the past like you do.' And she's gone. He follows soon after in a black cab.

Their annual reunion is at The Guinea in Mayfair. Henry knows the routine. The management never advertises the event on noticeboards below in case it encourages lefties, loonies and pro-Argies to show up. He alights from a cab and climbs the stairs to the upstairs floor. Already the room is at close to maximum capacity, most wearing maroon berets and medal collections, a few seeming too young to be part of his peer group, all in blazers and well-pressed grey trousers. There are the usual speeches, then the food. They don't need to order. The meal is identical every year. Sides of rare pampas beef washed down with a vat of throaty Argentinian reds. Some of the guys hark back to good times spent in the Falklands, Operation Corporate in the South Atlantic, task force capers, Darwin Hill, Wireless Ridge, Goose Green, the yomping, the conscript opposition, the lost comrades and comment on the irony of it all.

After the port, they adjourn to the low-ceilinged smoky back bar. The red still flows with ease. Henry circulates and mingles amongst the crowd, glass in hand, occasionally finding one-to-one conversations difficult as others enquire about his home life, his current occupation and Amanda. Suddenly he's approached by a fellow ex-serviceman, tall and with good posture. It looks like Jimmy but maybe not. Jimmy was never this muscular yet so gaunt around the face, his eyes so vacant and far away.

'Henry, it's been a long time.'

It is Jimmy. Henry knows that Glaswegian accent. They shake hands, the mutual grip almost bone-breaking. Jimmy made his name in the night assault on Mount Longdon.

'Jimmy, haven't seen you here for years. Where you been?'

'Away.' He looks down towards the carpet.

Henry is jealous. 'Anywhere nice? Somewhere sunny?'

'I mean, away.' Jimmy sees Henry's puzzled stare. 'Inside. Locked up. Bird. D'ye ken?'

'Shit, I never knew. You look ... different.'

'Aye, lost a few stone picking cockroaches out of cold porridge. Gained a few pounds up top pumping iron in the gym. Safer spending my time there than hanging around the shower stalls looking for the soap on a rope, I can tell ye.'

'What happened after you left the regiment?'

'I didnae bloody leave, they threw me out. Cashiered me for punching that NCO. I couldnae get a job, no one would touch me. I was desperate so I started delivering wreaths for a bookmaker in the East End.'

'Sounds like an okay job,' observes Henry.

Jimmy moves closer. 'If the client didn't settle his account when he got the flowers, I went around with a baseball bat and introduced it to his fibula. Easy money but I only did the driving on some other jobs. Got arrested when the Flying Squad turned out to know more about a job in Barnes than we did. Still, what can ye expect from a bunch of thieving English villains, eh?'

Henry is keen to move on. 'What do you now?'

Jimmy smiles. Henry can see that he's lost a few front teeth through bookmaking. 'I'm a broker.'

'Excellent. A stockbroker? Moneybroker? In the City? Maybe we can do business some time.'

'I doubt it. I'm an identity broker.'

Henry is lost. 'What the hell is that?'

'I find new IDs for people who want tae disappear.'

'You serious?' Henry can see that he is. Jimmy hands over a smart business card. There's a name and a mobile number, but no home address or landline. Henry is puzzled. 'Who would want to disappear?'

'You'd be surprised. It's a growth industry. I'm doing okay.'

'What do you charge?'

'Interested?'

'Never know when some client will come gunning for me.'

'You still in headhunting?' Henry nods. There's a brief silence. Jimmy finally reminisces. 'We shared some good times. Bunked together for years in those barracks all over the place, yet I never really knew you.'

'Nothing to know, Jimmy. I was as normal as any other guy in the forces.'

'Dinnae know about that, pal.' Jimmy searches his memory bank. 'You still a diehard Chelsea fan?'

'Sort of. Not as keen as I was years ago. You still following Rangers?' Henry asks.

'Ye know my best moment in the regiment?' Henry nods in anticipation. 'The time you dropped that kid in Belfast from a hundred yards. When I go to home games in Ibrox, I still tell the guys on the terraces about the day ye took out the Fenian bastard in the Celtic strip. They like that story.'

CHAPTER SIXTEEN

MERRION STREET, DUBLIN 2: 10.20 A.M.

Adam sits at a table in the Mornington Room of the Merrion Hotel. He's not sure if it's a self-service buffet or whether it's menu-driven. Today is a haze. If the Ryanair flight back to Stansted weren't in a few hours' time, he would still be in the king-size upstairs, dead to the world. A teenage waitress approaches.

'Good morning, sir.'

'Not quite. I'm suffering. Bad head.'

It was some night. First a few pints of the black stuff in the Cellar Bar of the hotel. Then a pub crawl along the Golden Mile of Merrion Row, into O'Donoghue's for one, then Toner's, Doheny & Nesbitt's, and back again to O'Donoghue's because their live craic agus ceol is the best. Much later the entire desk took a cab to Temple Bar and sat in a draughty dive of an Italian restaurant because no one else would serve a party of six drunken-yob FX traders. Then more creamy pints in The Porterhouse and Thomas Read's. Muppet and Bookie pulled two teenagers from the northside and left early. Cable Guy joined a party in Club M in the small hours and wasn't seen again. It was the mother of all stag nights.

'Tea or coffee, sir?' the waitress perseveres.

'Coffee, please. Lots of it. Thanks.'

The life-giving caffeine is decanted from a polished silver pot. Croissants and assorted preserves arrive on the table, and then a complimentary *Irish Times*. Again Adam looks around at the others and sees that no one else has a newspaper at their table. He deduces that the young waitress is making a special effort for him. She knows he's on his own and needs some distraction in the absence of social conversation.

He lazily grazes the bold headlines about incestuous local politics, financial scandals, high-tech job losses, new motorways and fatal road accidents. His eyes rest on a short paragraph about developments in a murder case, an American tourist found in St Stephen's Green. Turn to page eight. They all walked by that park last night. He never knew that this tranquil and welcoming city could be so dangerous.

'I've got a head like someone took a fucking sledgehammer to it!'

Adam puts down the newspaper. Muppet arrives down at twenty minutes past the hour. He has showered but hasn't bothered to use either a comb or a razor. His loose yellow RL shirt hangs out over his ample belly and faded jeans and is badly creased. He hollers at the same waitress who reluctantly ambles over.

'I need food, I'm starving. Get me a fry-up. Everything. I need to line my stomach.'

She hesitates, looks at the swinging pendulum over the antique marble fireplace, and shakes her head.

'Sir is too late for the hot breakfast. We finished serving twenty minutes ago.'

'Sir didn't damn' well know that!'

'It says so on the room-service menus.'

Muppet leans closer to her. Adam knows that the trader smells like the inside of St James' Gate brewery.

'Sir has paid a hundred and fifty of your euros for a room and that includes breakfast,' Muppet advises.

'I'll speak to the chef and see what he can do.'

'You do that, dear.' He mutters to himself as she disappears, 'Fucking five-star hotels.'

Muppet sits in a daze, his eyes bloodshot beyond hope. Adam makes the effort.

'What happened to you last night?'

'I got her back to my room.'

'Who?'

'Some girl. Great sex, too. She likes the ceiling.'

'Does she have a name?'

'I expect she does but I'm damned if I can remember it.'

'Is she up there now?'

'You think I'd be down here if she were upstairs? I'd do her again. She had to go to work.'

'On a weekend morning?'

'She works in some hairdresser's.'

The waitress arrives with the works. Bacon, egg, sausage, tomato, mushrooms, potato and much more.

'I don't want this stuff.' Muppet points at the crammed plate.

'That's black pudding. It's a hotel speciality from Clonakilty in Cork,' she advises.

'I don't eat that sort of muck.' The waitress turns to leave. 'Hey, I need some toast.'

Adam shakes his head as the waitress disappears.

'Go easy on the girl. She's done you one favour already.'

'No, she hasn't. She's paid to work here. I'm a guest so she does what I tell her. If she wants a tip.'

'Are you gonna tip her?'

'Read your newspaper and let me eat in peace.'

Adam is on the home news page as Muppet stuffs calories, grease and fat down his ample gullet. Adam is now on page eight. He sees the more prominent headline. 'St Stepher's Green Murder Baffles Detectives'. He reads the salient details, sighs and shrugs, and folds the open page carefully onto the table.

'What's up?' asks Muppet through a mouthful of food.

'An American was murdered in that park we walked by last night.'

'You know him?'

'No.'

'So who cares?'

Adam reads on. The facts of the case slowly become clear. The dead man was a forty-three-year-old IT consultant from Boston, working for an Irish telecommunications company. He was last seen in the Shelbourne Hotel on the evening of his death. An early-morning walker found his body hidden from view in bushes. The State Pathologist estimated the time of death as early evening. She confirmed that he was stabbed several times in the main chambers of the heart with a small narrow blade. The police said that the dead man's wallet, traveller's cheques and credit cards were all found on his person. Robbery was not the motive. They were appealing for any witnesses.

Muppet looks up, bleary-eyed.

'I need some toast to mop up the grease. Where has she gone? Hey, over here!'

Adam's thinking the news account seems vaguely familiar. The manner of death . . . In the early evening, in the undergrowth. A blade in a heart. No robbery. No motive. He's unable to decide why but it interests him. It bugs him. He needs to know more. He tears the article from the paper. Muppet looks up.

'Hey! I might want to read that. Is there a page three in Ireland?'

The waitress appears and ignores Muppet. 'Would you sign for breakfast, sir?' Adam takes the check and signs for two.

Muppet cuts in. 'Sir here needs more toast.'

The waitress with two months' silver service experience and an hourly rate of six euros plus tips leans closer to the stinking Vice President of Global Foreign Exchange on six figures p.a. plus cash bonus, stock options, mortgage subsidy and car at the world's largest investment bank. She whispers within earshot of Adam: 'Sir is very close to outstaying his welcome at this fine hotel.'

Adam smiles at her, adds a five euro tip and places the torn press clipping in his trouser pocket. He's sure he'll eventually remember why the details of this particular murder seem so familiar. He stands to leave but Muppet grabs him by the arm.

'I need some euros. You got a hundred to see me through the day?'

'You had plenty of cash yesterday,' notes Adam.

'Of course I did. But I had to pay the bloody hairdresser, didn't I?'

Samantha wakes in their Elephant & Castle two-bedroomed flat, peers at the alarm clock and decides she urgently needs hot liquid caffeine. She shrugs on her old pink bathrobe while walking along the narrow hallway to the kitchen, brews up, finds her favourite mug in the sink but no fresh milk, and sits slumped at the table. The view from their rented home is limited. They always leave the window in the kitchen a few inches ajar but only can because it has ugly wrought-iron bars on the outside. The lead oxide and incessant noise from the traffic on the A2 seep into her consciousness. She feels she lives on the asphalt, not just beside it. She hears a key in the hall door, footsteps coming closer and the rustling of shopping bags.

'Morning. You look well.'

Her flatmate has returned. Fortunately there are no mirrors in the kitchen. She offers a welcome hug.

'Thanks. Good day?' asks Samantha.

'Yes and no. I got paid. But it's never enough. I'm still so broke that I couldn't even pay attention. There are more deductions in this payslip than in a Sherlock Holmes novel.'

Working the antisocial night shift on alternate weekends at Guy's is no joke but somehow Kerys finds the energy and enthusiasm to keep going at all hours. Kerys's rosy cheeks glow, her long wild hair tousled by the elements. She throws off her coat and unpacks the bulging Safeway's bags.

'I got milk and croissants. Bacon, eggs. Newspapers too. Ready for some breakfast?'

'Aren't you going to bed for some sleep?' Samantha asks.

'I slept yesterday evening. I'm wired now,' Kerys answers as the frying pan starts to smoke. 'Anyway, cheer up, today's the big day.' Samantha looks blank. 'We're going up West to buy your outfit for that wedding at work.'

Memories of a bad week at Mitchell's and those bastards on the FX desk come flooding back.

'I wish I hadn't accepted the invitation.'

''Course you don't.' Kerys smiles knowingly. 'Weddings are great places for people to meet future partners. If you're looking, that is. Pity I can't go as well, I love weddings.'

'I mean, I don't even like the groom. I don't like any of the bloody guys at work.'

'They can't all be that bad, surely? They must at least be intelligent, educated and successful?'

'You would think. They're sexist pigs who don't want me at the desk except to look at.'

'Then complain.'

'HR doesn't want to know about it.'

'What if the guys saw you now in that robe?'

'They wouldn't want me near them. They hire women purely based on legs and looks.'

'If only they knew the real you! Give 'em a fright.'

'Now that *would* shock them.'

'Every morning you leave here looking great. Make-up on, hair done, smart clothes, heels. So, one day, don't bother. Go to work looking like you do now, as you rise and shine. See how they handle that.'

'They'd fire me on the spot.'

Kerys swivels at the cooker, spatula in hand, and smiles knowingly.

'So when do I get to meet your hot wedding date?'

Samantha smiles. 'You know he's not a date, just the least objectionable guy on the desk. It suits us both. He's quiet, polite and harmless.' She runs her hands over her face, then through her dank hair, knowing she needs a power shower but she's presently lacking any motivation. 'God, what am I doing, going to this wedding with him? I'm leading him on 'cos it suits me to be seen with him. What's the point of it all?'

'Point of what?' asks Kerys as the bacon and eggs hit the pan.

'Being here.'

'We're here because I chose here a year ago. Elephant & Castle might not be the most glamorous or safest place in London but the rent was all I could afford when I moved here. Then you moved in. If you don't like it then I am sure you could move to High Street Ken on your salary, but then we'd be apart.'

Samantha watches the articulated trucks, white vans and black cabs pass by outside at blurring speed. She's wondering why she traded the open spaces of the South-West for the concrete and grime of SE12.

'No, I mean what's the point of even being in London . . . why do we all move here?'

'For the jobs, of course, and the money,' advises Kerys as she expertly cracks eggs with one hand. 'Everyone says if you have half a mind to, then come to London. Because let's face it, that's all you need to live here.'

'There's got to be more to life.'

'Sure there's more, but money gives you a wider choice. Helps buy breakfast, too.'

Samantha gets the hint. 'Take what that shopping cost from the jam jar. I'll put another twenty in later.' Then a long pause as Kerys assembles two plates of food. 'I'm going to resign from Mitchell's,' Samantha says into the silence.

Kery's eyes widen. 'Are you mad? Think how much you earn there. And what do City people do, exactly? Sit at a desk and look at screens and TVs, go to lunch in wine bars, and get the company to pay for it all? I'd kill for a job like that, and what do I have? Twenty thousand a year, I work late nights emptying bed pans. If I had a brain like yours I'd swap jobs this minute, believe me.'

'I didn't mean it like that. I'm not ungrateful. It's just not for me. I'm not a city person.'

'You'll adjust over time.'

'No, I mean I'm not a city person. I don't like big cities like London or Birmingham or anywhere. Even going up to Bristol years ago put me off. I need space, trees, wildlife and nature. I'll go mad here.'

Kerys sits down beside her and takes her hand, like they're making some agreement, a personal bond.

'Don't make any rash decision without discussing it with me first. When is that big bonus day you mentioned?'

'Last week in January.'

'How much do you get?'

'I don't know. It's my first year. Maybe nothing. It's all down to Bruce and Diane.'

'Wait at least until then. Then take the money and put it all into our jam jar. I know you're unhappy but there's no point going off half-mad, is there? Stick with it, mate!'

They look at each other for a moment, then burst out laughing together. Kerys has that effect on her.

Henry wakes in the king-size in the master bedroom. He's certain that Amanda is still sleeping so he rolls over the other way and sees daylight under the curtains. It's early on Sunday morning, the best time for a walk in dozy Islington.

He gets a clean shirt and a fleece but stumbles when it comes to finding socks and shoes in the semi-dark.

'What's up?' She's suddenly awake.

He pulls on his shoes and hobbles towards the door.

'Nothing's up. I'm getting the papers.'

She rubs her eyes, lifting herself up onto the pillows, adjusting to the red neon of the clock radio.

'It's not even nine yet. What's the hurry?' He ignores her. 'You expecting to see something? Another advert?'

Henry pulls the front door closed and crosses the road between her Z4 and his Saab convertible, both safe in their Zone E residents' spaces from the ever-present threat of clampers and council hired hands. There's no need to take the car now. He walks around the square and down Theberton Street to Upper Street. His usual Asian shop on the corner is a minute away but he's not going there. Prakash knows him too well.

He strides past the steamed-up cafés where the locals queue for a fry-up, past junkies and hippies opening up second-hand record shops as if people still buy old vinyl, past the stale stench of beer from O'Neill's fake Irish pub, past Hampton's estate agent's with a window of inflated prices and four international clocks as if people fly in from all over the world to buy property in Islington, past the collectors' antique market selling tat to everyone with more money than sense, past the rubbish strewn in the gutter of the red route, past every fucking flyer and smear of anarchic graffiti pasted to every fucking pole and boarded-up hoarding, past several other newsagents until he stops outside Islington Tube station.

The vendor's newspapers and mags are well displayed. Henry picks a *Sunday Times* for himself and a *Mail on Sunday* for her, but he's looking elsewhere for another. Then he sees the *Sunday Independent*. He pulls out a copy, pays for the rags and turns without saying one word to the vendor, who likewise hardly even registers a sale in his jaded eyes.

The black iron gates to Gibson Square are already open. He walks in, past the stupid sign about a Greenspace Ranger who tends the small communal park, with a mobile number in the event of an emergency. He wonders who would want to have such a useless day job. There's no one else in the park. He sits on a bench near the single stone edifice, shielded by trees and high bushes from the second-floor bedroom window with the closed curtains where Amanda sleeps on. He likes this park, likes the signs saying No Dogs, likes the signs saying No Ball Games. No fun here. No nothing in fact.

He finds what he's looking for in a small paragraph on an inside page. The details are committed to memory. He's engrossed in the small type, blissfully enjoying the sound of silence so rare in London, when he's suddenly conscious of a creak from the nearby gate.

'Morning.'

Henry looks up. A guy with a spaniel on a lead is standing there. He thinks he vaguely knows him, then realises it's the prat from a few doors down with the tarty younger wife and the OTT Audi TT.

'Morning.'

The prat's staring back, like the park belongs to him and him alone, like he can't grasp the concept of another person being here today, like he can't see the point of reading a Sunday newspaper outdoors on a chilly November morning. The prat is still staring. Henry wishes momentarily that he could do something about the situation, then decides to ignore the neighbour. The spaniel feels the need to take a leak near the No Dogs sign so they move off and leave him alone. Henry has read what he wanted to so he tosses the newspaper deep inside a black rubbish bin.

Back inside he rushes upstairs as if every second is part of a vital alibi and throws the two remaining newspapers onto the bed. He opens the curtains slightly to let in some semblance of natural light. He thinks about getting back into bed, wondering if his side is warmer than the rest of the bedroom because he knows there isn't any mutual body warmth to be shared. Amanda turns on him.

'Where did you go?'

He's definitely not getting back into bed this morning.

'For the papers. Like I said.'

'You've been gone twenty minutes. Where did you go? The printing press in Wapping?'

He bites his lower lip, knowing that he doesn't need this inquisitorial conversation. He thinks about offering to make her a cup of coffee downstairs, like model couples in love do in the movies or on TV.

'I stopped to have a read in the park on the way.'

She's sitting up in bed, holding the two newspapers, closely examining the edges of the paper.

'In the cold? Doesn't look like either of these papers has been opened.' He says nothing. 'Where's the magazine?'

'Which magazine?'

'The *You* magazine inside the *Mail*. Didn't you ask Prakash for it?'

He's definitely not making her a cup of coffee.

'I forgot to ask him.' He pre-empts her objections. 'And I'm not going back for it, either.'

'I'll get them off him later on when I get up.'

'Suit yourself.'

'So?' she asks.

'So what?'

'So is there any news in the papers today?'

'Nothing you'd be interested in.'

CHAPTER SEVENTEEN

CANARY WHARF, LONDON E14: 11.45 A.M.

Adam's standing near the water cooler at midday with Samantha, hands deep in his pockets of his fave ironed chinos, when he wonders, *What's this junk?* He produces the contents of his pockets. There's a few receipts from Dublin restaurants, huge bar-till rolls, utterly useless euro notes and coins, and more.

'Want some euros?' he asks Samantha.

'Sure,' she replies. 'For my holiday.'

'Going somewhere soon?' He's wondering who she'll go away with. Other girlies? Boyfriend, maybe?

Samantha takes the proffered cash.

'I'll go somewhere next year. France, Spain, Italy, wherever.'

'But that's months away.'

'So? You asked, I said yes. And you're supposed to be the expert on foreign currency.'

'Don't tell Bruce I lost a load of euros so easily. It might hit his beloved monthly P&L.'

He's distracted, having found a creased press clipping in his pocket. They're walking back to the desk with cups of still mineral water. They are alone. Adam unfolds the page as they sit down.

'What's that?' She peers over at him.

'It's about a murder in Dublin.' He rereads the fine print slowly.

'You are some morbid character! Why are you interested in that?'

He sits down and racks his brain. The mist of a weekend of smoky pubs and clubs slowly melts away.

'I don't know. I kept it because —' he struggles to articulate his thoughts '— because it's like another murder. Look, I was high on Guinness and Smithwick's. I didn't know what I was doing.' He drops the clipping into the bin.

Samantha leans down and retrieves it, reading it quickly. It's a quiet day at the desk. A public holiday in the US. New York sleeps. London dozes.

'What other murder is it like?'

Adam's thinking back to the good old days.

'Oh, nothing, I dunno. Yes ... Hang on. One a month ago, of an ex-colleague in Kapital. Dusseldorf.'

'I never heard about that.'

'Well, you wouldn't, would you? No one in London would know it. Forget about it.'

'So how did you hear about it?'

'Guys at work. It was all on Reuters, under Kapital Bank. Somewhere.'

Samantha immediately works the keyboard, finds the story, reads the press clipping again and grows more excited.

'They *are* similar.' She pins both items up on the edge of her desk. 'They have exactly the same MO.'

'You're watching too many police shows on TV.'

'Maybe it's a coincidence, maybe it's not. But what's the logical deduction, Adam?'

'You tell me, Spock.'

'Two similar deaths mean one likely killer.'

'If you say so, Inspector.'

Samantha sighs and sits back, still intent on the two articles. 'So the killer, if one exists, is someone who's been in two places, who maybe travels a bit to European countries. Bruce does that, doesn't he?'

'What do you mean?'

'He was in Germany recently, wasn't he? And he was in Dublin before that because that's why he chose it for Spoon's stag weekend. And I know he likes going on those FX conferences held in five-star hotels.'

Adam looks over at Samantha. 'Do you seriously see our dear Bruce as a killer?'

Then they both think and speak in unison. 'Definitely.' They laugh and sit there smiling for a few minutes until another idea occurs to Samantha.

'Let's make an agreement. You solve my trading scam here, I'll solve your murder inquiry. Whoever gets an answer first is taken out for a slap-up meal and the other pays.' She holds out her hand. 'You on?'

It's the closest thing to a date she's offered him so far. He doesn't mind who pays. 'Sure thing.'

'What's happening here?' Diane is suddenly standing behind them, puzzled by their handshake.

'Nothing,' Samantha answers quickly.

'Doesn't look like nothing to me. Why don't you two go out to lunch much?'

'Bruce makes us cover the desk most days. The others get to go out.' Samantha looks over at Adam and winks. 'We are on the graveyard shift, so to speak.'

'Isn't there a rota?' asks their boss.

'No. It's us every day. I haven't seen daylight since August.'

'I guess that's life as a new hire. Tough. We've all been there.' Diane is about to walk out to her own lunch. Then she sees the two pages they seem to be studying, a printout and the press clipping on the desk. 'What are these?'

'Nothing,' answers Samantha again.

'Let me see,' Diane says, picking them up over her shoulder. They don't dare protest. She reads fast and concisely. 'A Kapital banker murdered in Dusseldorf. A guy stabbed in Dublin. What's the point of this?'

'Adam saw them.' Samantha almost stammers in her haste to speak. 'It's just research.'

'Research the euro and the dollar instead of wasting your precious time on this sort of stuff.' Diane halts near the desk. 'Are you guys going to Spoon's wedding this weekend?' Samantha nods. So does Adam. 'You bringing along a partner? Is that the done thing in these parts?'

'I sure am,' replies Samantha. 'And so is Adam. See you there with yours.'

Diane walks back to the quiet Mitchell's trading floor after a disappointing yet wholly satisfying lunch. Henry made the effort to commute to Canary Wharf and they never discussed work, recruitment, staffing, resourcing or headcount. The oriental food was dire but there was enough loaded innuendo on his part to confirm that he too is interested. She needs an orgasm. Henry might be the one she selects to provide it, as and when she's ready. She's sure he won't say no. They never do.

She sits inside her office, wondering what sort of staff she's inherited from Lloyd, whether hiring Samantha and Adam in the past few months was some sort of parting shot from an old man on the way out. She checks the screens. FX market is dead today. She opens the top drawer and sees that spreadsheet of daily trading profits. She's still puzzled by its contents. She looks out and sees Bruce swagger back to work alone. The time is right. It'll be fun to unsettle him. She calls him over.

'Bruce. A minute.'

He obliges and slouches across the desk from her. She first makes for her in-tray and the envelope.

'I got these in the internal mail from Finance today. They're your last few expenses claims.'

'What's the problem?'

'I need to approve them first before they'll pay. Were these trips sanctioned?'

'Lloyd gave me the okay.'

'Then I'll sign them, but it's the last time. The bank does not encourage unnecessary expenditure. You seem to be some sort of serial junket junkie. Do you have to attend every IFR and Euromoney Conference on every trading topic? I make it three jollies to Zurich, Frankfurt and Madrid in six weeks.'

'I need to stay in touch with the market. That's how we make so much money at the desk.'

'I'm coming to that. In the meantime you go nowhere without my prior approval. Got it?' He nods as she signs the pages. 'And a man of your means doesn't need to claim Tube fare to Paddington for the Heathrow Express. That's just petty.' She lays another page in front of him. 'What do you make of this?'

'What do you mean?' he asks slowly, refusing to lean forward and look closely, yet his composure seems shaken. She can see his dark pupils dilate and he's avoiding direct eye contact of any sort.

'It's a simple enough question. You recognise this page?'

'Where did you get that?' he asks. 'Who gave it to you?'

'No one did. I found it.'

He's incredulous. Overacting. 'Where?'

'In this bottom desk drawer. So what does this page show?'

She watches him consider the earlier question, then sees his confidence slowly return.

'It's an Excel file of the daily trading profit at the desk.'

'You keep the file on your PC?'

'It's saved on the C drive of Samantha's. She keeps it up to date. It's password-protected.'

Diane points at the scribbles in the margins.

'Do you recognise this handwriting?'

He looks uninterestedly. 'Not really.'

'It looks like Lloyd's handwriting to me. This is Lloyd's old desk. Makes sense.'

'You'd better ask him.'

'I might do that.' She points again. 'What does he mean by writing "Millions again!"'

'Like I said, you'd better ask him.'

Diane runs her hand along the daily profits and comes to the same conclusion.

'We always seem to make the most money on the days of the ECB interest-rates announcement.'

'Nothing wrong with that. We take a view and take big positions and trade it out.'

'Suits me. But on some of those days we only break even.'

'They're the days when we don't take a view on the announcement.'

'I've been through all the months year to date. You never seem to lose big money on any ECB day.'

'That's because we're damn' good at our job.'

Diane folds the page, confident that Bruce is shattered behind his calm exterior.

'I've run trading desks in New York for twelve years. I've never seen any desk that avoids losses.'

She's making real progress. He shifts in his seat. There is more to this. She will call Lloyd.

'Like I said, we're good,' he bluffs.

Diane's telephone console rings. She sees the number displayed on the caller ID facility. It's a mobile number. She wants to ignore the call and carry on with this fruitful inquisition. She sees Bruce looking over at the console for any welcome distraction. She thinks she recognises the number on the screen.

'You can take it,' he offers.

She picks up the handset. 'Diane Rubin.'

'Henry here.'

'Yes?'

'Did you enjoy today?'

'Sure.'

'I didn't go back to the office after our lunch. I had another client meeting at HSBC here ...'

She chooses her words carefully. Bruce is glancing away but she knows he's listening. 'So?'

'So I'm downstairs in a black cab in Cabot Square. My meter's running.'

'I'll say it is.'

There's a long pause while he considers his next step, while she lets her imagination run riot.

'Do you wanna come for a ride?'

Diane sits in the black cab, allowing her long black skirt with the left side split to ride up so that she sits almost naked against the plastic. She permits Henry to move closer as they pass along the Embankment. They both study the driver, tuned to Capital Gold, miles away. She allows Henry to place his right hand on her left thigh as they pass through Westminster. She makes no protests, no eye contact. Nearer Chelsea she takes his hand in her leather-gloved one and places it higher up her thigh. He tries to take some initiative but she decides that enough is enough and anticipation is often better than the event.

When they reach Battersea the cab jolts over unfinished roadworks, the sensation providing extra stimulation to her. He dares again to move his hand further up. She moves away, knowing that she's as wet as the Thames below. She takes him past the curious Montevetro concierge and leans against him in the high-speed lift up to eighteen.

He tries to take her in the hallway but she walks away. She hangs up her coat. Then a scarf. She keeps her black leather gloves in her hand. He's amazed by her apartment, partly because of the stunning views of London but mainly by the interior of her home. All he can see are unpacked cardboard boxes and little or no furniture.

'Someone actually lives in here?' asks Henry as he walks into the kitchen. 'You don't seem to eat.'

'I eat but I don't cook. In Manhattan you can buy lofts without a kitchen. Who needs one? Eat on the way to work. Eat at work. Order in or eat out later. The most important thing in my kitchen is the telephone.'

Henry walks around the living room to the window. 'So when does the furniture arrive?'

'You really wanna talk about furniture?' she asks.

'You got a bed?'

'Are you sure we need one?' She opens the double doors to a master bedroom. There's a huge bed but few bedclothes. 'The comforter is in one of the boxes. You want to unpack it first?'

He moves nearer to her, runs his hand under her skirt, but she recoils.

'I'm taking a shower first. Then you. I can still smell the City.' She uncoils his tie. 'And please don't wear that tie with that shirt again. They say to never wear checks and stripes unless you want a job in a circus.'

He's still trying to wrest control of the situation from her. 'So there will be another time?'

'Maybe. You okay with that?'

He's puzzled but eventually smiles. 'Why not? Let's see how it goes. A change might do me good.'

Her shower is a huge tiled walk-in, big enough for two or more. Henry hears the water power up. He waits until the water is steaming up the full-length mirrors and the atmosphere is heady before joining her. He watches the incessant rivulets fall off her sheer breasts, marvelling as the water diverts around her erect nipples. He tries to move closer, knowing that this is to be their moment. She has other ideas.

'Please wait until I'm finished.'

He wonders what game she's playing. This is so different to being with Amanda. It vaguely amuses him. She watches him, seeing his interest aroused. She steps out and takes a towel, leaving the water running inside.

'Your turn.' He's barely wet when she moves nearer. 'Can you lean back against the tiles and face me?'

She lathers up her hands with perfumed soap. Henry wonders why she needs so much. She moves lower, takes his member and rhythmically washes it from base to tip. He reacts almost uncontrollably.

'I'm very impressed. Who's a big boy?' she advises, engrossed in her work.

'Oh my God. That is so good. You have great hands.'

Diane uses more soap, cupping his sac below, feeling his testicles one by one, then running her nails up and down his shaft. He closes his eyes and perseveres, slowly acknowledging that he's literally in expert hands. His steady exhalations become more pronounced as the hot water continues to rain down. 'I hope you don't do anything premature, Henry.'

He tries his utmost but after five more minutes, it's becoming impossible. She knows when to stop.

'Let's go to the bedroom. My oh my.'

He's still wet as he lies on the bed. For some reason she's putting her black leather gloves back on. He wonders why? The gloves are fascinating to him, a symbol of her power. It's a new sort of rush for Henry. He makes the mistake of trying to move on top of her. She rolls over and reverses places.

'I'd like to be on top.' He'd sensed as much. 'Can you cross your arms behind your back?' He hesitates. 'Henry, trust me. I want to get as much pleasure from this as you do. We can both be happy, you know.'

She must think he's some sort of contortionist. He folds his arms out of sight. She sits astride his chest, hands pressing down on him until he can hardly move. He can't touch her breast or her still-erect nipples. She takes his member again in her gloved hands and manipulates every last red bulging inch.

She avoids any eye contact, instead closing her own eyes and rolling her head in ever-widening circles, her wet hair flailing around her face. When she deems the time is right she raises herself up and then down, effecting a perfect communion of corporate client and those who service. He thinks that she orgasms maybe twice. He is long spent, yet she won't allow him to withdraw for an eternity. He's used to being on top. Next time he'll make the running and she'll do what he says. Like Amanda does.

They lie side by side looking up at the ceiling, each recovering from climaxes of differing durations. Somehow it all happened too fast for him. Diane takes a packet of Marlboros off the bedside table, lights one and takes a drag. 'Only afternoon sex beats morning sex. I only smoke after great sex. I can get through a box in a day sometimes.' He believes her. She sighs and shudders. 'I so needed that.' He says nothing. 'You did well, Henry. Very well. Nine out of ten. Best I ever had in London. What do you think?'

She's scoring him? He rolls sideways. Henry's thoughts are slowly turning to Amanda in Gibson Square. He can see her sleeping with her back to him at home. He needs to avoid the guilt trip.

'We are not discussing my sexual performance.'

'Let's discuss work.'

'No.'

She moves on to work matters, still inhaling. 'So you're the one who brought us Adam and Samantha?'

'Jesus! What's that supposed to mean? Is there some problem with them?'

'I don't know about Adam's trading acumen yet.' Diane rolls nearer, slowly coming down from her orgasmic high. 'And Samantha seems to be more interested in other matters than she is in trading.'

'Like what?'

She takes three or four drags in quick succession, then stubs out the butt and kneels up on the bed.

'Today at the trading desk she was wasting time talking to Adam about some murders.'

She lights a second Marlboro and makes him wait until the tip of the cancer stick is burning bright red. Henry says nothing but she doesn't expand. He feels obliged to express some nominal interest.

'What murders?'

'Oh . . . Adam was in Dublin at this guy's stag weekend and he read some press article about a visitor who was stabbed. Some other guy in Germany too. I dunno. Who cares?'

'Really? Tell me more. Sounds interesting.'

'Not. If you had a choice between having sex again or hearing about these murders, which would it be?'

He realises that she's deadly serious. There is only one answer. 'Sex with you, of course.'

'So you don't want to hear about a guy killed in Dublin and another stabbed in Dusseldorf?'

'Of course I bloody well don't.' He begins to show signs of definite arousal. 'So what about sex?'

She stubs out the second cigarette and walks to the shower. 'It was a rhetorical question. I'm through.'

DECEMBER

CHAPTER EIGHTEEN

ROYAL TUNBRIDGE WELLS, KENT:
12.05 A.M.

Adam is up early for a Saturday morning. He's had a great night's sleep thanks to Lisa upstairs. For once there's not a sound from the apartment above. He thinks about running his shower for twenty minutes or blaring some CD at maximum volume while he gets into his formal clobber. But there's nothing to be gained from sheer spite. He reckons she's sleeping late, perhaps suffering a hangover from Friday-night excesses. Maybe some lucky bloke is curled up beside her in her bed as Adam downs his Cornflakes. He wonders if great sex is audible through six inches of pre-stressed concrete slabs.

He drives along the Thames, crosses via the Rotherhithe Tunnel and finds the agreed pick-up point near the Elephant & Castle roundabout. He's late. Samantha is there already, waving at him. She sits alongside. There's a fragrant scent wafting through the car. She seems so alive, excited at the trip. She looks wonderful, wearing a cream linen suit with a hat held in her hand for later. No one like her has ever graced the interior of his Astra. Her leg is close to his hand as he works the gear stick.

Samantha looks around the car's worn plastic fascia, perhaps worried that her new suit will suffer. 'Is this your Mitchell's car?' she asks, somewhat bewildered.

'Not unless they're cutting back. HR says I have to pass probation before I get a new motor.'

'I'm sure you will. You're doing fine so far.'

Adam isn't convinced. 'Where's your bank car?'

'None was ever mentioned in my contract. I guess I'm just the desk junior who gets the coffees in on the bun run.' Samantha takes the liberty of trying to revive the ancient heater on the dashboard. 'Why on earth is Spoon getting married at this time of the year?'

'He told me in Dublin that his wife-to-be will be delivering their first offspring in May.'

'I'll watch out for the shotgun, then.' She looks ahead at the road. 'You know the rest of the way?'

'I'm relying on you.'

Samantha demonstrates excellent map-reading skills over the next two hours. They head south on the A23, through Croydon, east along the M25 orbital and finally down the A21. She calls out obscure village names as she directs him with ease. They pass huge mansions set well back from rural roads.

'Do you think it became Royal Tunbridge Wells before or after the family moved here?' he asks.

The church is a solid grey-stone building surrounded by fading gravestones, all leaning slightly to one side as time demands. There are people everywhere.

'How come we get invited both to the wedding and the reception?' he asks.

'Because this is a Big Wedding.'

They enter the nave together. Adam hangs back. Samantha pulls him along.

'Let's sit near the front so we can see more.'

They're so close to the altar that Adam worries others will think that they are family.

'I can't see anyone else from work,' she observes.

'That's because they're all behind us. One more pew nearer the front and we'd be at the top table.'

The wedding passes with only one unscripted incident. Towards the end of the ceremony, Spoon kneels down for the first time on the step near the altar. He's wearing new black leather shoes with tan-coloured soles. Everyone in the front of the church can see them clearly. On his left sole is written the word 'Ass'. On his right the word 'Sole'. Adam thinks he recognises Muppet's feeble handwriting. Samantha can hear Bruce and the others in a pew somewhere further back sniggering as only they can.

Later they drive to the reception at their ultimate destination. Adam hangs a right, shows his invitation to a guy in tails and top hat at the manor lodge. Spoon's wife's ancestral home hoves into view at the end of the gravel drive. It's huge, with more front than a page three model. They are directed to park with other arriving guests on frosted sloping lawns to either side of the driveway. It's wall-to-wall gleaming machines. Adam reverses his motor between a fifty-grand Carrera and a CLK 320 Kompressor. They get out.

'I'll probably be towed away for making the car park look untidy,' he observes.

They walk through a great hallway, then a side drawing room and via French doors into the cavernous heated marquee outside. Samantha leads, looking for their table. Adam follows. Bruce approaches them.

'Have you two come on your own today?' he asks.

'No. I came with a partner,' Samantha replies.

'So did I,' volunteers Adam.

'Who?' asks Bruce, looking around the marquee for the significant others.

'We came with each other,' Samantha confirms.

'Bloody hell.' Bruce scratches his head.

'What's the problem?' Samantha asks him.

'Looks like I owe Bookie fifty quid. He reckons you two have been shagging for weeks.'

The optimally placed Mitchell's table seats ten. Muppet is there on his own as per usual, a flute of decent Bolly already in hand. Cable Guy is on his own too and didn't bring a boyfriend. Bookie chats with his present wife who seems far too pleasant and normal to be married to an FX trader. Bruce has a long-time girlfriend of three months who looks like some prepubescent Latin American pop star but after some brief conversation the others at the table are convinced that while the light may be on, there is no one at home.

Adam and Samantha feel the need to sit together for mutual solidarity. Adam looks around with confidence. He is here with possibly the most attractive girl to be seen. There are still two empty seats.

'Who else is at our table?' asks Adam, exerting some burgeoning assertiveness.

'Diane and her new man.' Bruce looks up. 'And here they come now.'

Diane sits down, again dressed in black, hardly appropriate for the day. Conversation stops as she seizes the spotlight. Her other half wears immaculate tails he evidently owns, not hires.

'Everyone, this is Henry,' she announces. 'Henry's a headhunter. I think he knows some of you.'

Henry shakes hands, making a major effort with his former clients, Adam and Samantha. 'Great to see both you guys again.' The speeches begin, then the meal. The others knock back bottles of decent red but Henry is on the Italian still mineral water. Adam is aware that a sober Henry is not interested in making conversation with him or Samantha, showing a clear preference to network with the senior traders and not with junior desk staff. Then a change of heart. Henry is hunting.

'Heard you went to Dublin. How was it?' he asks.

'Bit of an endurance test,' replies Adam. 'You ever been there?'

'Last month,' interjects Diane. 'So I'm told.'

'How's Mitchell's going so far?' Henry shouts to Adam above the din of earnest conversation.

It's an impossible question with his boss sitting one foot away. 'Fine,' he lies for the millionth time.

Henry holds his knife and fork poised above his plate. 'We must do lunch sometime.' He points the blade directly at Adam and then Samantha. 'I'll give you both a call next week. Trish will set it up.'

Samantha gives directions to Adam when they hit the clogged traffic on the outskirts of South London in the early evening. They negotiate the nightmare neon and pink hues of the Elephant & Castle roundabout, then drive down an A-road full of aggressive red buses, sixties council flats, takeaways, filled skips and used-car forecourts. Adam stops under a row of sodium lights in a residential one-way street, near a converted three-storeyed Victorian schoolhouse on the corner. Samantha points ahead, gathering her bag from the floor of the passenger seat, her left hand already on the door handle.

'I'm on the ground floor at the back.'

This is the difficult part. There's a black metal gate leading to a car park at the rear. Adam's wondering if he'll leave Samantha at the kerb or if he'll get past the gates. Part of him is still recovering from the day out and the drive, but the rest of him wants to be inside with Samantha. She's in no doubt.

'I'll open the gates so you can park the car.'

It's a functional apartment. Adam sees that there is a chaotic double bedroom and a tidy single one. He assumes, even hopes, that the former belongs to Samantha. She runs around the rooms, turning on lights, pulling curtains together, powering up heating, lighting a small but real coal fire. Adam is curious.

'You live on your own?'

'I share with Kerys. She's a nurse. Works crazy hours, like

nights and weekends. That's where she is today. I don't know what time she gets off. Until then we're on our own.'

Adam resists the temptation to comment further. 'What about your parents?'

'My mother lives in Cornwall. That's where I'm from. Rather a long commute to the City, unfortunately.' Samantha makes for the kitchen. 'All that nouvelle bird food left me ravenous. You hungry?' He nods, glad that it's not just an offer of token tea or coffee, glad it's an implicit invitation to stay a while longer. He follows her into the kitchen.

Samantha opens the stainless steel fridge. Inside it's wall-to-wall chocolate — mousses and desserts. She sees his reaction. 'Relax, these aren't mine. They're Kerys's comfort food. I know what we need on a winter's day like this. Can you watch the fire for me? Put on some music if you like.'

He returns to the living room, pokes a few encouraging red coals, checks out her modest CD and book collection, impressed by her taste. She returns from the kitchen, sits on the only sofa and puts down on earthenware teapot and two huge mugs on the low table. He notices she's changed out of her suit and into a loose-ribbed polo-neck jumper. 'Eats will be in twenty minutes. Until then there's steaming Earl Grey.'

He sits close beside her, holding the warm mug in his hands, watching her stare at the welcoming fire in silence for a while, wondering what she's thinking about. Her face glows in the firelight. She slips off her shoes and stretches her long legs out to the edge of the hearth, jiggling her toes up and down.

'I enjoyed today. It's funny how weddings make me go all sentimental. Guess they have that effect on us all.'

There isn't much conversation after that. They chill out after the exertions of the day. He's conscious that now and again their bodies brush against each other as they shift on the sofa. She seems content, then starts humming some vaguely recognisable tune off the Capital FM Pepsi chart. 'I need some music.' She finds the remote control for the CD. Soul appears. She lowers the volume to mere background status, since full-on mega-decibels don't seem right for the moment.

'You like soul?' he asks.

'I listen to it. Never on MTV. If you watch too much of it, you begin to wonder why your life isn't like one long glossy video with flash sports cars, muscled beefcake with strong jawlines, lithe girls with exposed midriffs and navel piercings, and one big happy ending. Real life is a bit more complex than that.' She jumps up. 'Time to eat.'

She brings in two warm plates. Adam's taste buds are already working overtime. Grilled herbed sausages, maple back rashers, baked plum tomatoes, halved mushrooms and a suspicion of baked beans are perfectly presented with slices of well-buttered brown toast on the side.

'It's not much but at least it's not nouvelle cuisine.'

They eat in silence, the food sating their appetite and sapping their energy. Samantha finishes first and slides off the sofa onto the rug by the blazing coals. He waits, watching the flickering light reflect off her perfect face, feeling the mutual heat, wondering at the way it seems so natural and easy. She curls up on her side. He sits down on the rug and lies next to her, cradling her from behind.

'Thanks for a wonderful meal.'

She turns around, their lips inches apart.

'No trouble.'

'Are there afters?'

'You bet. What do you want? One of Kerys's chocolate mousses?'

It's not what he meant. He's about to try another angle as he instinctively yawns. She catches his drift.

'I think you've done enough travelling today. It's late enough. Do you want to stay the night?'

He's in. He's about to reply positively when there is the sound of keys in the hall door. The door swings open and a sturdy girl in a nurse's uniform beams at them both.

'Well then, what do we have here? The happy couple. Are you being unfaithful to me?'

Adam's not too sure how to take the comment. Samantha rises and introduces Kerys. The girls kiss.

'So you're the famous Adam? I've heard a lot about you. Great to meet you at last.'

'Adam's staying over,' announces Samantha. 'You don't mind, do you? The other room is okay.'

Adam is way ahead of the game. 'Thanks for moving for us, Kerys.'

She smiles at Samantha. 'He doesn't know, does he? They never do. Men are so one-track, I find.'

'Know what?' he asks.

'Can I tell him?'

She doesn't give it much thought. 'Why not? I trust Adam. We get on. He'll keep it to himself.'

Kerys holds Samantha closer. 'We're a couple. We're in the double room, you're in the single.'

Henry is in Gatwick departures when he encounters a new procedure with the BAA jobsworth.

'Look up at the camera, sir.'

'What?' he asks, like he's been picked out in an identity parade.

'The camera above me, sir. It's for ID purposes at the boarding gate.'

Henry sees his polished face appear on a flat screen. A sticker is attached to the back of his BA boarding card. Now he's a bad mugshot and a striped bar code. This security lark is way over the top.

'You're in business class, sir.'

'I know.'

'You can use Fasttrack.'

It's the same old line that Henry's well used to.

'I'm in no hurry.'

The BAA guy looks up from his screen, glares at him and speaks firmly.

'It's too busy this way. I'm telling you, use Fasttrack. Over there to the right.'

There's a moment of indecision. The BAA guy points decisively to the right, making brief eye contact with a cop who stands inside. The cop wears an earpiece, bulletproof flak jacket, chequered peaked cap pulled low over unseen eyes chunky black boots, and carries the latest lethal assault weapon from the mail-order Heckler and Koch winter catalogue. Henry doesn't need a scene and so hangs a right to the quieter confines of Fasttrack.

A young girl mans a single X-ray machine inside. She's a bright young thing, maybe an enthusiastic new hire. Her eyes are glued to the monitor like she's watching her favourite BBC1 soap opera of an evening. Henry places his briefcase on the conveyor belt, walks through the metal detector with confidence. The belt stops. There's no sign of his briefcase. The bright young thing views a freeze-frame. He can see the rectangular shape. Other suits wait in the queue. She peers at the screen. What is her damn' problem?

The belt kicks into action again. His briefcase appears. A red light flashes over it. An elderly BAA guy wakes from his morning slumber and pulls the briefcase along metal rollers to the side.

'Is this your case, sir?' They are alone. It's a stupid question. Henry nods. 'Can you open it?'

'It's not locked,' he advises, wondering where all this is going.

'I said, can you open it?'

Henry obliges. The OAP moves a few papers and CVs around, looks at the Casio calculator, eyes a few pens and the silver magnifying glass that Henry always carries. He runs a hand in vain along the edges of the lining. He seems satisfied about something and is about to hand the briefcase back to

Henry when the bright young thing comes over and whispers. He returns to the edges of the lining and immediately finds something sharp. He carefully extracts a letter opener.

'What's this, sir?' he asks, getting more excited, holding the item vertically like it's some sort of evidence.

Henry sees the cop with the piece looking over. He moves a few steps closer and keeps his voice steady.

'It's a letter opener. I always take it with me on trips.'

'You ever been stopped before?'

'No.'

'Why is it hidden in here?'

Henry watches the cop speaking discreetly into a handset hanging from his flak jacket. Henry's wondering whom he's advising. He can see a distinct possibility of this incident getting out of hand.

'It slipped down the side, I guess. I never had a problem with it before.'

'You have a problem with it now. Don't you know the significance of this? Don't you know that things have changed? Permanently. A blade like this one is now classified as a very dangerous weapon. Didn't you read the signs at check-in about what you can take on board in your hand luggage?'

Henry's now conscious that other passengers are passing and looking over at the suspect. Him.

'I did, but I didn't think . . . Sorry. It's only a letter opener.'

The OAP is deliberating his next move, debating whether he's trading with a genuine businessman or a madman on day release from some institution.

'I need your passport and boarding card.' Henry hands them over without protest, keener than he has ever been to comply. The cop still watches from afar. 'Wait here. I have to escalate this.'

He disappears up a few steps to a room with a window with one-way reflective glass. Henry wonders where to look, whether to stare confidently back into the glass because there must be pairs of eyes staring back at him, or whether nonchalantly to gaze around with his hands in his pockets. He tries a bit of both but to no avail. He's trapped in a situation that's completely outside his control. He'd like to run but dares not.

The OAP brings a middle-aged man down the steps. The latter is wearing a nasty grey tweed sports jacket and an almost matching tie, with a too-tidy haircut and parting. He doesn't feel the need to introduce himself because he has a police tag with crest hanging from the breast pocket of the jacket.

'Is this yours, sir?'

How many times do these idiots have to ask him about the bleeding obvious?

'Yes.'

'Are you aware that it's a dangerous weapon?'

'I am now. Sorry.'

The plain-clothes officer places his finger on the tip of the letter opener, then runs it along the edge.

'It's very sharp.'

'It's new. I just got them.'

'Them?'

Henry produces the matching magnifying glass.

'This is the other half of the gift.'

'Who bought you these items?'

'My PA bought them. We bought lots of them. I give them as gifts to my clients.'

'What sort of business are you in?'

'I run a recruitment company in the City.' Henry produces a business card, like it's all the proof needed.

The officer examines the small print and seems as convinced as he'll ever be. He picks up the magnifying glass. 'Do you use this?'

'I might sometimes.'

The officer examines his face closely, seemingly looking at the bridge of Henry's nose.

'Do you wear glasses, sir?'

'No.'

'Contact lenses, perhaps?'

'No.'

'Then why do you need a magnifying glass?'

Henry's stumped.

'I guess ... I don't need it. It's just a nice thing to have. It's like the letter opener. It's useful.'

The officer shakes his head but has reached a dead end.

'I'm going to bag this item and tag it as luggage for the hold. It'll be placed in the aircraft by the airline staff here. You can pick it up at your destination with the rest of the hold luggage.'

'Fine by me.'

Henry gets his briefcase, passport and boarding card back. He's about to walk away.

'Next time, sir, pack that item in your luggage for the hold. Don't put it in your carry-on baggage.'

Henry nods. He doesn't carry luggage usually because he prefers convenient day trips to unnecessary overnight stays. He could put the briefcase through in the hold next time but no one else in Club does that. And think of all the hanging around at the conveyor belt at the other end when he could be in a taxi to the next rendezvous. He can never take the letter opener through Gatwick again. They will remember him.

CHAPTER NINETEEN

BARRIER POINT, LONDON, E16: 7.50 P.M.

Sunday drags for Adam. He wonders how he never deduced Samantha's sexual orientation. He feels foolish and more than a little let-down. The expectations of the past weeks disappear after a bad night's solo sleep in that single bed in Elephant & Castle. Yet part of him is glad that Samantha confided in him, that she felt confident enough to do so. Bruce and the others will never hear the truth from him.

He feels like he's leading a double life, like he's slowly subconsciously merging into someone else's daily routine, as if he's been cast for an unwanted bit part in a movie. Lisa's apartment is directly above his place. The two floor plans are identical. At first she annoyed him. Now that he has seen her in the flesh, spoken with her, it's a whole new ball game. He likes the fact that Lisa is on top.

He sits in his living room and hears her upstairs, her heels staccato on the wooden floors. He hears her balcony doors or windows opening and closing. She prefers cool fresh air. He hears her telephone ringing in the evening and wonders who calls her and what her friends are like. He hears her run up and down the hallway and doesn't know how she has the energy of an Olympic sprinter.

Sometimes he hears her television set in the corner of the living room. Often he can decipher what channel she watches. She prefers Sky News, it seems. On weekdays it goes deadly quiet at 8 p.m. so he assumes she is a big *EastEnders* fan. He enjoys her extensive CD collection apart from Dido. She likes loud bass music, dance tracks, fast R&B, but Lisa plays sad songs sometimes.

Nowhere in his home is he safe. In his kitchen he hears water run, then the tumbler and spin-dryer on full blast above. He hears her traverse the floor tiles in the kitchen. He listens to her preparing evening meals, whizzing a food processor to death, chopping on a wooden board, eventually turning on a dishwasher. Her only known vice seems to be a secret fetish for some late-night hoovering.

He sees her Beetle come and go irregularly. She disappears into the underground car park, the fated scene of their one and only meeting. When he gets into his own car, sometimes she's parked so close beside his space it's impossible to open his door. Her parking is wonderfully inaccurate but her Beetle is always clean inside. There are no obvious clues within as to her mysterious livelihood or lifestyle.

Weekends are different. She rarely gets up before midday on Saturday or Sunday. He wonders why she prefers to lie on in bed with perhaps a coffee and her colour portable, why she doesn't have somewhere to go. On some Saturday evenings he hears music pump before she heads up West but she's always back next morning. Adam never knows where she goes, who she sees, who she invites back to her E16 pad.

He's never seen her with a guy in the car park or in the communal areas of the apartment tower. He's never heard a male voice raised in anger or adoration upstairs. Sometimes he thinks that she too is alone upstairs on an evening when it seems every other young Londoner is out on a hot date in the West End.

Sometimes in the evening he hears a bath run in the rear of the apartment. He tries not to think about what happens next upstairs, as she submerges herself into the piping water, to immerse her consciousness below the waterline, to empty her pores of the stinking grime of London life. He imagines she might light scented candles by the bath, or douse it with aromatic oils. Then he pinches himself and thinks about a cold shower.

Last thing at night is the worst. He usually hears her bedroom door close as all goes quiet around eleven p.m. He tries to sleep but it's difficult sometimes, knowing that she's lying directly above him in her bed, only eight feet away. As he drifts off to sleep he doubts that he exists in her life as much as she does in his.

Once it goes quiet for an entire seven days. He deduces that she's gone on holiday. He wonders where she goes and who she goes with. Girlfriends, boyfriends, friends, parents, family? Impossible to tell. In that solitary week Adam sits alone in his apartment and realises that he misses her presence. Sometimes she disappears and there isn't a sound for a few days. He doesn't know what she does for a living or why it requires her to remove herself so completely from his life without any notice. He thinks she might travel often.

Samantha wakes and realises that today is the day she will take Kerys's recent advice. She enjoys her usual power shower but deliberately avoids washing her hair, preferring instead to brush it loosely. She eschews any make-up, eyeliner, perfume or lipstick and leaves her favourite jewellery on the table in the bedroom. She ignores the various pairs of heels on the floor of the wardrobe and chooses a flat Bally pair. Her favourite garments remain on the row of hangers. She selects an old shapeless skirt that falls well below the knee and a loose top that has faded as much as has her enthusiasm for working in Mitchell Leonberg.

Her arrival at the ground-floor reception of Mitchell's is novel. Usually the spotty greaseball security guard with the bad fringe and the ill-fitting uniform smiles at her, almost leers. On occasion she's seen him in the reflection of the aluminium doors to the elevator, watching her from behind as she passes. Today there's no recognition whatsoever from him. He stares blankly through her like she doesn't exist.

Upstairs the opening comments from the guys on the FX desk are unprecedented.

'What happened to you?' asks Bruce. 'You look like something that the cat dragged in.'

'You've been out all night at some party. Just come straight in to work,' observes Muppet.

'What will Adam think when he sees you today?' asks Cable Guy. Samantha ignores him.

'Leave her alone. It's probably just that time of the month, guys,' advises Bookie.

Adam fumes silently in the background but gives her as much support as he can in the circumstances. The others ignore Samantha for the rest of the morning. She knows that Kerys is right. It's all about the image she projects. The City is like the armed forces, with generals and privates, marines and paratroopers. The uniforms vary by rank. There's the Territorial Army, or the back-office operations people. Back-office girls wear polyester numbers, nasty perfume and not much else, and the guys wear Mickey Mouse socks, shiny suits, and leave caked Brylcreem stains on the headrests of their swivel chairs.

There is a pecking order in Mitchell's. People in the open-outcry trading pits on the exchanges are the lowest of the low, brokers are one notch higher, then spot FX traders, then other traders, with sales people further up still. Finally, originators and corporate financiers are at the top of the food chain.

Samantha sussed out the range of males on the floor in her first week. She knows the distinction between sales and trading. The salesmen wash and shave most days, are broadly familiar with deodorant and aftershave and possess matching socks. Traders are more forgetful and have a simple attitude. If they see nobody all day, then why should they bother to look good, and who cares if they fart and burp?

Samantha recognises them by the suits they sometimes wear. There are the in-house gigolos in their unconventionally cut Moschinos and bright single-colour ties. There are the 'I haven't had sex for years' types who wear something bought before the '87 Crash. There are the 'I made a fortune and spent it all on a suit' types. Lastly there are the 'I've made so much money, I don't give a fuck how I look' Alpha Males. She places all of the guys on the FX desk in the latter category – except Adam, of course. She quite likes his latest smart casual gear.

She knows too that women can get away with anything as long as the men nearby are able to concentrate on work – just. Today she can see that girl called Justine Somebody in equity sales wearing that almost transparent camisole under her jacket and nothing else. On busy days Justine takes the jacket off and chats to clients, pretending not to notice the sudden silence. Samantha has seen her receive six coffees from male colleagues over the course of one morning. She wonders if the choice of clothes is her way of asking for a drink. Another salesgirl once complained but got shot down because the clients love Justine and she sells deals to salivating clients.

Samantha goes on the bun run because it's still her turn. As she walks the long mile past the rows of beefcake, their eyes don't wander as usual but remain fixed on neon screens, the *FT* and Mitchell's research department reports. She returns with the goods but only Muppet manages an effort at conversation.

'Are you ill or something, dear?'

Lunchtime is different too. Samantha goes to her favourite Aran deli in the underground shopping mall. Today the swarthy Italian guys in their white shirts and navy waistcoats aren't interested in serving her up a BLT on rye to go. She stands on her toes to make eye contact over the glass counter with the dreamboy who's heating up the bacon. He hands her the finished article without comment, preferring to eyeball the burgeoning queue with his lusty colleagues, all of the Romeos wondering who's going to serve that American brunette in the Gucci from the CSFB fixed-income sales desk. She's a favoured regular.

In the afternoon, it's quiet at the FX desk. Samantha feels ostracised, like a leper on day release. No one has spoken to her in hours. Adam does his best. The guys don't walk around to her side of the desk or shout over for information or assistance. Instead they stare towards the suite of corner offices. One of the Managing Directors has a new temp PA who has turned up in a skirt that might properly be described as a large belt. There's a nod and a wink to each other, like a private joke shared by all the males on the floor.

Samantha knows Bruce only hired her because of her looks. Lloyd too must have been of the same mould although he did seem genuinely interested in the information he requested she compile on the desk trading profits. She can't take this much longer. HR won't help her at all. She'll talk to Diane soon, if she dares. As she puts on her coat after the worst working day at Mitchell's, Muppet ambles over, like some reluctant UN diplomat sent against his better judgement to the war zone to keep the peace.

'Whatever you do, don't come to the damn' Christmas party looking like that.'

Henry's scheduled Luxair flight leaves on time. He wanted to fly with BA for the Air Miles but Trish said the flight was fully booked. The fifty-seater Fokker 50 covers the three hundred nautical miles in one hour, its cramped interior feeling much like the interior of a polished cigar tube hurtling through outer space. Henry reads an *FT* in Business Class, then the imaginatively titled in-flight magazine, *Flydoscope*. He dismisses both the embarrassingly basic 'Beginner's Guide to London' and a limited article entitled 'Culinary Delights of Luxembourg', focusing instead on the relevant details of an inadequate map of the city centre.

'*Le centre ville*,' he instructs the first driver at the rank at the tiny Aeroport du Findel on the AI.

He alights near the bus terminus on Boulevard Royale and heads by default towards the network of narrow pedestrianised shopping streets. He ignores the Villeroy and Boch, Hermes and Prada boutiques, and follows those in the know who gravitate towards the Place d'Armes. It's a pleasant leafy square with a central bandstand surrounded by cafés, restaurants and municipal buildings. There's a tourist information office on the corner of the Place where Henry sources a significantly better complimentary street map.

There's just over an hour to kill before his appointment. A few elegant locals in cashmere coats and furs brave the elements by sitting outside under canopies at the Café de Paris. He joins them, takes a good sheltered table and orders successive mineral waters. The map shows him the location of the gare, the Grand Ducal Palace, the museums and statues and the old underground ruins of the Casemates, but he's not interested in the usual tourist trail. Soon he memorises his optimal route, identifies a few alternative exits, the agreed rendezvous and the closest taxi ranks.

At a quarter to five he settles the tab and carries his briefcase along slippery cobbled streets past the town hall and the royal palace. He stands upon the battlements of the old brick-walled city. There's a panoramic vista of the Alzette gushing down a winding valley, with huge road bridges spanning the gullies. He uses the tiered steps to descend towards parkland by the river and joins a road to the Grund. Their agreed rendezvous is a four-storeyed bar called Scott's adjacent to a narrow one-way stone bridge. He sits in an upholstered corner snug at the appointed time, their two CVs folded on the table, his briefcase by his feet.

At twenty past the hour a thirty-something couple arrive. He's a short pasty guy with receding hair, wearing a grey suit, a limp white shirt and a stupid shapeless green woollen coat of the sort much loved by the Belgians at large. She's in a voluminous dark suit and appears to be at least six months pregnant. Henry is immediately thrown at this irrefutable familial evidence. They approach him. The husband stands back. Wifey does the introductions, immediately displaying that she has not lost her soft native Irish accent.

'Hello, I'm Angela Hennessy. This is my husband Frank. Thanks for coming over to meet us.'

Henry tries his best but already he's worried about exactly where and when the baby will be born.

'It's not often I get to meet two such excellent candidates together. You okay with meeting here?'

'Sure. We work nearby on Boulevard Royale. That's where we met. In a bar there. The other fund managers don't drink around here after hours. They're boring locals, go straight home after work.'

'What will you drink?' he asks.

She decided for both. 'I'll have a glass of Riesling. Frank will have a beer.'

He wonders if Frank has the use of his own vocal cords. The couple sit in the snug while Henry approaches the bar. He's got a prominent twenty-euro note in his hand and has immediate eye contact with the only barman when a guy in a shirt and tie suddenly backs into him, turns and shouts some exaggerated and seemingly complicated order at the barman in a heavy French accent. Henry wonders if perhaps the guy is a Luxembourger, and if so, whether fries come with that.

It is a huge drinks order. Henry stands tapping his foot and glares at the local but there's no hint of an apology being forthcoming. The guy is all arms, his pug face ruddy and sweaty, speech overly loud and slurred. He looks like he's been here since opening time and is substantially hammered. The local is more interested in pivoting on his feet and playing to a crowd of equally hammered colleagues. Henry eventually collects his modest order and returns to the warm snug, the raucous pointless laughter still ringing in his ear.

'Are you okay time-wise?' he asks as he places a Mousel beer, a glass of wine and a Perrier on the small table.

'We need to be home by six,' she advises. 'That's when the au pair leaves.'

Henry's wondering if they're serious. They've allotted less than thirty minutes to discuss their future.

'Then let's cut to the issues. You really want to leave Luxembourg and move back?'

They both nod decisively. 'Dublin would be best. London at least would be nearer home.'

'You want to leave Luxembourg salaries and taxes behind and move back to Irish salaries and taxes?'

They nod again. The wife volunteers more.

'Money doesn't matter as much to us. We want quality of life for our children.'

The guy in Irish National was bloody right. Henry is distracted. He can still see that queue-jumping local through the smoke of the bar. He's trying in vain to be the centre of attraction with his colleagues, puffing relentlessly on a slim cigarillo, slapping the backs of others nearby, ordering more drinks on his tab and being just plain objectionable. Henry's rapidly losing count of the kids. The time is now right. He nods towards the wife.

'Can I take it that the baby is due soon?'

'Due in eleven weeks.'

The local is an asshole. Simple as that. Definitely excess to the world's requirements. Henry refocuses as the wife slowly puts down her wineglass.

'So you want to move back to Dublin before the birth?' He asks hesitantly.

'Goodness, no,' she advises. 'We want to move back home in about six months' time. Didn't I mention that to Trish in your office? I'm sure I did . . .' she muses. 'Then again, maybe I didn't.'

Henry knows that no one, not even Irish National, will wait six months. He doesn't dare to think about the ridiculous maternity and paternity leave implemented by the EC of late. This move will not happen.

'That's a showstopper. If you need to wait six months we should maybe talk again after the arrival.'

It's so over. They're looking at their watches in unison like the au pair is about to do an early runner tonight. Henry reads the signs in the bar. He needs to get rid of them as soon as possible. He stands up.

'If you need to go now, that's fine. I'll be in touch again. Thanks for contacting me.'

The couple are on their feet too, the wife not as embarrassed as she should be.

'Sorry for all the trouble. Will you be okay here on your own?'

He can see the local in the bar. A glance at his watch confirms he has sufficient flexibility in his itinerary.

'My flight back is in a few hours' time. I'll be fine here. I have to deal with someone else.'

CHAPTER TWENTY

CANARY WHARF, LONDON, E14: 12.25 A.M.

Adam sits with Samantha in the same seats in Corney & Barrow. He's settled into the wine bar well. It's now his local, he knows the lunchtime menu and can order effortlessly from one of the waitresses who know him by sight. They down a seafood pasta and share a garden salad. The weekend revelation is still recent.

'I'm sorry about what happened. It wasn't fair.' Samantha grins and rolls her eyes at him. 'I should have told you before.'

'It's okay. It was a surprise but it's not the end of a friendship. I like you whoever you are. We can still be mates.'

She nods. 'Mates it is. Who knows? Maybe best mates in time. Kerys likes you too, she says.'

'At least I know there's no point in chasing after her. Thanks for the heads-up.'

They finish eating. Samantha puts down her napkin. 'How are you doing on your research?'

Adam pushes his plate aside. 'Those euro trading profits are too much of a coincidence. Our best chance will come on the next ECB rates day. We'll be watching closely. There's little more we can do until then. Just pray that no one else in the City has the same suspicions.'

'I've been doing some of my own research,' Samantha tells him.

'What sort of research? FX cross-rates, like Diane told you to do?'

'Not exactly. I went to Books Etc.' Samantha delves into her handbag, the contents of which would likely frighten any male. She holds up a well-thumbed paperback. It's not Chick Lit or an Aga Saga. Instead it's called *Serial Killers: The Beginner's Guide*. 'I've been doing some research on our man.'

Adam raises his eyes towards the ceiling. 'Hold on a minute. You're getting carried away with this theory of yours. There's an incredibly tenuous connection between the murders in Dusseldorf and Dublin. It's probably complete pie in the sky. There is no man, as you say.'

'Hear me out, we have a deal. You solve the ECB, I'll find out what's behind your press cuttings. This will help.' She holds up the book. 'It's all in here, all about the profile and method of serial killers.'

'We don't know there is a serial killer.'

'We think someone was in both places so he travels a lot. Hear me out on the facts. See what you think. Then judge me.'

Adam sits back, one eye on the others in the bar, resigned to his immediate fate. He nods. 'Shoot.'

Samantha thumbs through the pages. Adam sees that some of the text has been marked up in red pen.

'Serial killers leave tidy crime scenes behind. They always hide bodies after the killing, never leave a weapon around. That sounds like the two crime scenes in Dusseldorf and Dublin, doesn't it?'

'Maybe,' Adam admits reluctantly.

Samantha reads on. 'Victims are generally selected at random. They're usually in the wrong place at the wrong time. But the individual victim is carefully selected, often based on physical characteristics, maybe even by showing some vulnerability.

Sometimes the serial killer is trying to eliminate a group of people based on a common trait ... race, sex. The victim is never known to the serial killer.'

'That doesn't help your theory much.'

'Give me time. There's more on the means of death. The two you read about were stabbed?' Adam agrees. 'If there are lots of heavy repetitive wounds with a weapon, then the chances are that the killer knew the victim and it was personal. Real personal. It's called "overkill" in here. If there are a lesser number of wounds, like there were in these two cases, then the victim is most likely to be a stranger.'

'Go on.' Adam is growing more impressed with her research.

'The most important part is the killer's profile. Most serial killer are male.'

'Well, that eliminates half of London's population,' Adam confirms.

'Most serial killers are in the 25 to 40 age bracket.'

'That's a few million more eliminated. We're getting closer.'

'Most are white.'

'Another million knocked off.'

'Most are married with children.'

'So are many of the adult inhabitants of Western Europe.'

'Most are sane, not insane,' she continues.

'Now we're in a grey area. I've seen Londoners going to work on the Tube in the rush hour. It's a fine line.'

'Most have issues with significant female figures, women in authority. Think of Bruce.'

'Based on what I see, I'd say Bruce is pissed off with the bitchiest woman we know. Diane.'

'Most are of average or above-average intelligence.'

'Agreed. Bruce is intelligent, I'll give you that.'

Samantha sighs and reads on. 'You're not helping much. Serial killers are unique, they're different from mass murderers who go on random spree shootings, like Dunblane years ago. When a mass murderer is caught or kills himself in some shoot-out, all his neighbours say he was a weirdo, that he was antisocial and a loner, that they always had grave doubts about him. But when a serial killer is caught, neighbours reacts differently. They're in shock and say he was the last person they would suspect of being a killer. So the more you think that Bruce is not a serial killer, the more likely a possibility he becomes. You agree?'

'Not really,' admits Adam.

Samantha reads aloud. '"Serial killers have personality traits. They have a feeling of superiority, grandiosity, that society's norms are not meant for them, that they're too smart and clever to have to start at the bottom and work their way up. That they can do whatever they want." Is Bruce like that, do you think?'

'He's a supremely confident guy. Assertive, pushy even, at times. But so are most people in Mitchell's, even in the City. On that basis most of the FX dealers in Canary Wharf are serial killers.'

'What about the ECB scam? Doesn't that prove he wants to get one over on everyone else?'

'Yeah. Maybe. If we can ever uncover what it is they do.'

'What do you know about Bruce's home life?'

'Nothing. Apart from seeing his vacant girlfriend at the wedding. How does that fit?'

'Serial killers don't feel they have to live by the normal rules, those governing social relationships. Many serial killers suffered some sort of abuse or neglect as a child. Beaten by their father, ignored by their mother, sent away to school, some sort of abandonment when young. They have dysfunctional backgrounds, inconsistent parental discipline, an absence of love or attention. Some of them resort to petty theft, fire-starting or exhibit cruelty to other children or animals. See, Bruce isn't a family man.'

'That hardly makes him a murderer. And it doesn't matter to us.' Adam gets up and leaves a twenty on the table, knowing that it's enough. 'We can't get diverted from our main problem. We're both convinced that something is going on at this desk on the day of the ECB announcement. Serial killers won't help us, don't concern us, but if there's a scandal at Mitchell's, then we're finished in the City.'

Diane has seen enough. She's been in the business too many years to ignore a scam when she sees one. She needs further confirmation before the final confrontation. She closes her door, sits down, dials NYC and asks for a specific FVP. He picks up the call immediately, evidently with zilch to do.

'Lloyd. It's Diane in London.'

He can't resist a sarcastic jibe at his successor.

'Congrats on your new ex-pat assignment courtesy of Horowitz. It's richly deserved. I thought it was only a matter of time before you contacted me. Are you calling to seek my expert advice or just to gloat?'

'The former, Lloyd. You know all about FX here.'

'Are you sitting in my old office?' he enquires with growing interest.

'Sure am. I'm calling to thank you for the gift you left me.'

'What gift?'

'The gift you left hidden in your bottom drawer.' Diane has the page on her desk. She's tracked the monthly P&L down to the last cent. She's seen the spikes and knows that no one such as Bruce can be that consistently good. She's added two and two together and got about eighteen million bucks, year to date. She pauses. 'That page.'

'I dunno what you mean.'

'The page with the monthly profits and your comments written in the margin. It was very useful. Gave me all the right leads, saved me a lot of guesswork. Does Horowitz know you left this here?'

''Course he doesn't.'

So Lloyd doesn't deny the page. She's making inroads. She looks outside. 'I'm about to confront Bruce.'

Lloyd is slower to respond, like he's choosing his words in a court of law. 'You've lost me, Diane.'

'Cut the bullshit, Lloyd. You and I both know there's a scam going on. You didn't like what you uncovered. You told Horowitz what you thought. You got difficult. You cut a deal with him for a cosy desk job.'

'It's not a desk job.'

Lloyd only denies the desk job. He still doesn't deny the scam. He has already said too much.

'Lloyd, I'm listening to the background noise there. It's too quiet. You're in an office on thirty, locked away from sales and trading, away from all the hassle. You have done well with Horowitz. A trip home and an office on thirty was the price. That says it all for me. So what's the scam?'

'Diane, I can't spell it out for you. Horowitz would have my balls before year-end bonus day. You work it out for yourself if you're so goddamn' smart on the uptake.'

He hangs up abruptly. So there is a scam. She's ready for Bruce. She'll risk it. Diane motions him inside.

'I got a problem, Bruce.' He looks interested. 'What's the story with the ECB rates announcement?'

'What story?'

'You suffering from memory loss? There seems to be a lot of it about these days, even in head office.' She pushes a piece of paper over. 'We didn't get to finish this discussion last time.'

'I remember,' he says. 'You got a phone call which seemed to be more important at the time.'

'I want the answer now.'

He refuses to look at the page. Instead he reclines further.

'There's no answer, no story. We just trade well on the right days.'

'Bullshit! I spoke with Lloyd. He told me everything. Says you know all about it.'

'You serious?'

'One hundred per cent,' Diane bluffs. 'Call him if you like.'

'If Lloyd told you all about it, then you don't need to hear it from me.'

'I wanna make sure we're watertight on it.'

His eyes widen. 'Say what? Watertight? You mean, you're not pissed about it?'

'Why should I be? You found a way to make some money for Mitchell's. That's what we're here to do.'

Bruce relaxes for the first time and looks up straight at her. Suddenly he's smiling.

'Thank Christ for that! Quite a change in attitude.' He shakes his head. 'Lloyd never gave me any support on this. He just wanted outta here. I made all the running, found the guy in the ECB. Lloyd did nuthin'.'

'He said the ECB guy is good,' she bluffed, going with the flow, picking up on his every nuance.

'Karl is an old banker in the ECB who likes getting cash in envelopes. He calls me with the rates decision ten minutes before it's official, then we go long or short the euro in size.' Bruce is running his hands through his hair. 'There was no hassle until Lloyd hired those two bastards to spy on me.'

'Which two?'

'Samantha and Adam. She's the worst. She gave that page to Lloyd. He never even knew about the file before that. It was our internal record at the desk. All he ever saw was a monthly number from Finance. Pity we can't fire her for that. If we did, HR would never buy it. We'd be found out. Word would spread in the bank.' Bruce sees Diane's look. 'Don't worry. We're going to lose Samantha soon, I reckon. She won't stick it much longer. I told the guys to hassle her good and proper. Muppet is giving her a hell of time and enjoys doing it. I'd give her until bonus day in January at the latest. Then she'll be history.'

'What about Adam?' asks Diane.

'He's a waste of space too. I told Lloyd not to hire him but he did out of spite. Lloyd knew that Samantha wouldn't stick the pace in the City, Adam was his alternative choice.

He hired someone impressionable, malleable. He's too polite, too goddamn' civilised for us. He'll never make a serious FX trader.'

'When we sack him, we'll need a reason.'

'We don't. He's still in his three months' probation. We'll fail him and then he's out. Problem solved.'

'You sure Adam and Samantha know nothing substantive?'

'She asked Muppet a few questions a while ago but not lately. Adam can't know anything. He's too new. Anyway, there's nothing for them to find. All there is is a telephone call to my mobile once a month.'

'Is everyone else on the desk on board with this scam?' she hazards an educated guess.

'Sure. We all club together to pay off the guy and take our share of the profits in our year-end bonus.'

'So you got it all sorted out?'

'That's why I run the desk.' Bruce is beaming back at her until his demeanour changes. 'There is a problem, though. The guy in Frankfurt is quitting the scam. Says it's too risky for him.'

'Then we get someone else involved there,' suggests Diane. 'Ask him for the name of someone else who needs cash.'

'I'm working on it,' Bruce tells her as he stands up to leave. 'Thanks for your support. It makes a big difference. All the subterfuge with Lloyd was driving me mental. It's good to know we want the same thing.'

Diane lets him leave and immediately dials her boss's number in the WFC. His PA puts her through.

'Jerry, I'm about to go talk to the Financial Services Authority in London. I just found a big scam at the desk. Bruce and the others are using illegal inside info from the ECB to make huge euro-trading profits.'

There's a sharp inhalation of breath at the other end of the line.

'Have you lost your fucking mind, Diane?'

There's no denial. No expression of surprise. Just raw naked confrontation.

'So you already know about it? Then I won't go to the FSA. You'll advise them, won't you? It's probably best that it comes from someone at your level in the firm since it's such a serious matter.'

'Are you on some sort of medication?' Horowitz asks.

'I'm on the drug called greed. Have been for years. So do we have a deal, Jerry?'

'What sort of deal, Diane?'

'I want ten per cent of the gross trading profits in my bonus check in January, and every January while I'm in London running this desk, running the risk of being caught and being picked up by the authorities here.'

'How about five per cent?'

'Let's not fight over a few percentage points. Seven point five per cent it is.'

Horowitz waits an eternity. He regrets these transatlantic telephone calls are taped like all the others. There's no way out. She's smarter than Lloyd ever was. Diane has him over a barrel. 'You got a deal.'

He's rapidly running out of time. The last BA flight leaves in ninety minutes. He reckons it's twenty minutes maximum to the airport and thirty minutes minimum to check-in. The target is on his fifth or sixth local beer. There's no sign of an imminent departure. He sits, watches and waits. If he is successful, then this will be front-page news tomorrow.

He estimates the target to be five foot ten, early forties, married, judging by his wedding ring, French by the sound of it, of above average build but sufficiently intoxicated from early afternoon as not to represent any threat. He settles for a last solitary drink. Fate will decide, as ever. He orders a final water, certain that if one of them has to be sober for what may follow, it had better be himself. He's idly playing with the remnants of a slice of lemon and molten ice cubes in the bottom of his glass fifteen minutes later.

Suddenly the target looks at his watch, slapping the backs of colleagues, and hands over a gold card to the barman to settle the tab. The target spends an eternity looking for a dark coat under a pile of other equally dark coats.

He downs the last contents of his glass. He places his briefcase up on his knees, opens it, puts on his gloves, looks around, removes the letter opener and places it up his left sleeve. He takes the handle of his briefcase in his right hand and gets ready. The target waves goodbye to everyone as he walks out onto Rue Saint Ulric. He waits thirty polite seconds, then rises and follows the target.

Outside it's much darker than it was earlier. A crisp chill wind gusts down the narrow streets. There's a brief moment of anxiety until he spies the target off to his left, crossing the bridge in an erratic zigzag fashion, then walking up a steep street called Rue Large. He follows a short distance behind, noting that the street is one-way upwards, with the incline being maybe thirty degrees. Unlike the target ahead, he has no trouble keeping his footing on the angled cobbles and damp winter leaves.

The right-hand side of the street looks out over the river and the valley but the left-hand side is lined with terraced houses with dimly lit windows revealing the exposed beams and stone walls of smart regenerated urban homes of distinction. This street doesn't meet his usual criteria. The risk of being overlooked is too great. Now there's less than twenty feet between them. He's close enough to the target to smell the alcohol. He hears the target play with some keys in his pocket, then in his hand. He's wondering if they're house keys, if he lives right here, and whether the window of opportunity came and went before he even knew it.

The target passes the last house and slows near the bricked-up underpass of what looks like an old viaduct. Overhead there are dark trees swaying in the wind, the occasional late leaf gliding downwards. To the left are bushes and maybe ten rain-soaked local-reg cars parked sideways on the narrow incline.

There is little street lighting and neither car nor human has passed him recently. Others will read about this over breakfast and know that they were nearby but no one has seen him here on this street and he has no connection to the target. The target stops halfway up and presses his key ring. The hazard lights of a maroon Audi A4 blink back. He knows the target is too drunk to drive. Either way the man's not getting home alive this evening.

He is thinking that right here and now will work. He places the briefcase on the ground, up against the wheels of a nearby car. He can take the target by the car door, push him back into the bushes and onto the unforgiving earth. He takes one last eyeball of the vicinity. There's no one about. He's thinking that if the worst comes to pass then he'll take him sitting in the driver's seat in the left-hand-drive car, have to settle first for a few jabs into the side ribs before going directly for the heart. He moves closer. Ten feet away. All quiet. A telephone suddenly rings. The target takes out a Nokia mobile.

'*Allo? ... oui ... oui ... cinq minutes ... ma cherie.*'

The target's not hanging up, tilting his head sideways with the mobile under his right ear so he can carry on the conversation while opening the car door. Maybe the call is a positive development. The target's attention span is miles away at home with the wife.

'*Oui ... Scott's ... dans le Grund ... à la voiture ... oui ... dix minutes ...*'

If he strikes now, then the mobile will drop to the ground with his first decisive lunge and the last drunken gasp, the wife at home will hear everything and panic. She knows roughly where they are, she'll call the cops and the BA flight home is too distant. He stalls. The target turns and faces him.

'*Oui?*'

He knows the moment is lost. The target sits into his car and closes the door. He hears the central locking being activated. He turns away back down the treacherous incline to gather his briefcase and drops the blade into the fast-flowing river as he crosses the bridge. Without a murder, no one will be looking for a weapon. He's never known failure before and he doesn't care for the taste of it.

CHAPTER TWENTY-ONE

CANARY WHARF, LONDON, E14: 12.35 A.M.

Adam and Samantha work their usual lonely lunchtime vigil. The closer it gets to Christmas, the less active the global foreign exchange market becomes. Any wise trader holds onto his profits for the year to date and avoids any losses. No one takes unnecessary risks. Many of their peer investment banks have effectively closed their trading books by early December.

Today is one of those rare ECB interest-rate announcement days but nothing happened. The FX desk didn't build a position, there was no surprise, interest rates didn't move and the desk broke even. Bruce still took a hushed phone call on his mobile at ten minutes to the hour. Adam and Samantha watched closely but learnt nothing new. His thoughts wander from the Reuters screens to more trivial matters.

'How's your hunt for the phantom serial killer going? Don't tell me Bruce is still a prime suspect.'

'Hah hah. I'm stuck,' admits Samantha. 'It's too difficult to pin down the facts. I know the dates the two murders happened but I don't know the dates on which Bruce travelled overseas. Dead end. That's the only way I can eliminate him.'

Adam thinks laterally. 'Someone must know. You could ask the travel department here in the bank.'

'I thought of that but I don't think all of Bruce's travel is for work. The vibe I got from the guys at the desk before you joined was that a few of the German trips were his own. He pays for the flights himself and takes half-day holidays.'

'Wonder why he does that?' Adam sits back with his feet up on the desk. 'So you need a record of his movements. Does he record anything on his PC? How about checking his Outlook diary? Maybe he logs his travel itinerary there.'

'And just as I break his password and log in, Bruce will amble back from lunch and I'm an ex-position keeper. But you're on the right track. There must be some record of flights taken. I wonder if he books online?'

Adam is thinking about people who take frequent flights. Someone made a comment to him like that before. He remembers something that was said. Something about Trish and her free flights to Dublin. It's worth a try.

'How about an Air Miles statement? That shows all the flights taken by someone.'

Samantha shakes her head. 'Nope. It only shows one airline. Like BA or BMI or whatever.'

'Gimme a break. It's the best idea we've had so far. No, it's the *only* idea so far.'

Samantha considers it for a moment. 'What made you think of that?'

'I saw someone's free ticket recently. Someone else travels a bit in Europe on business. See, there you go.' He throws his hands in the air. 'I can think of someone other than Bruce who flies frequently. This is crazy. There must be millions of suits who fly around Europe on expenses every few weeks.'

'Agreed, but how many of them will have been in Dusseldorf and Dublin?'

'Hundreds. Even my guy was in Germany and Dublin. There you go.'

She looks up, suddenly excited. 'Was he?' She's intrigued. 'Who is it?'

'Doesn't matter who it is, you'll only go off on one of your wild-goose chases again.' Then Adam has second thoughts. A smile plays on his lips. He can make her guess. 'You know him too.'

'So we're still talking about Bruce here?'

'No. Someone else. Male. Late thirties. Married. Lives in London. Works in the City. Go on, guess.'

Samantha leans closer, looks around at the empty seats, regaining her excitement at the thrill of detection.

'I haven't worked in the City long enough. I don't know anyone else. Is it someone at Kapital?' Adam shakes his head. Samantha is frustrated. 'I'll never guess. Tell me! I'll go mad otherwise.'

'Henry.'

'Which Henry?' she asks.

'Henry Simpson.'

'No way. Our Henry? He's far too civilised to kill anyone. Are you sure?'

'Trish in his office told me that he was in Germany a while ago. And he was in Dublin last month per Diane at the wedding.'

'It's a wind-up.'

'Yep. It's a crazy coincidence. Bin those press articles and let's get back to work.'

There're a few moments of uncertain silence. Samantha's about to follow his instructions but has second thoughts. 'So now we've got two suspects. We need to eliminate Henry from our inquiries.'

'We're not making any inquiries. We haven't got the time.'

'Aren't you even curious? This is far more interesting than trading euros for Bruce.'

Damn it, she's right. Adam moves closer to her chair. They're still alone and getting hungrier by the minute.

'So, Detective Inspector Samantha Perry of the CID, what evidence do you have on the second suspect?'

'None, but we'll get the evidence. We'll find out the exact dates that Henry was in Germany and Dublin. When they don't match with the murder dates, we'll eliminate him as a suspect. Easy.'

'How do we do that?'

'We talk to the only person who has the exact information we need. You ring Trish and ask. She'll make all his flight reservations if she's his PA.'

Adam's not keen to call Trish. He's already been blown out once before. They haven't spoken since.

'So I'll call her and ask her to tell me where Henry goes in Europe 'cause I think he's a serial killer?'

'Be more creative.' Samantha pauses. 'Say you have a bet with Bookie. Say the two of you think you saw Henry in the airport one day and you need to find out if it was him. Make up whatever you like.'

Adam wonders about the conversation, whether Trish will mention their meal in the West End.

'I'll do it later.'

'Do it now before the others get back from lunch. Then this will still be our secret. And we don't want the first suspect to know we now have a second suspect to check out. Bruce will get jealous.'

Adam reluctantly dials Trish on his handset. There's no way to avoid the call. Samantha leans over.

'I'll put her on the speaker so I can hear too.'

She's already hit the speakerphone. Trish is loud and clear to the world.

'Simpson and Associates.'

'Trish, Adam Lewis here.' He's keen to avoid the risk of small talk. 'I've got a quick question for you . . .'

'Another invitation?' she asks.

Adam throws a puzzled glance towards Samantha. She gives him a reproving look and wags a finger at him.

'That question . . . we have a bet here in Mitchell's. One of the other guys says he saw Henry on a flight to Dublin last month. I thought Henry was in London that day. I need to prove to this guy that he's wrong.'

'You lose,' she advises. 'He *did* go to Dublin last month.'

'Do you know what day?'

'Does it matter?'

'Yeah, that's the whole point of the bet.'

'He went over and back on –' she's ruffling some pages '– the seventeenth, a Thursday.'

'You sure of that?'

'Positive. I can see it here in my desk diary.'

'Have you got proof? The guy here won't pay up otherwise.'

'Like what?'

Adam chooses the words carefully. 'How about a copy of his Air Miles statement?'

'Strange request, but what's the harm? One came in this week. Gimme your fax number. It's a fair exchange for a meal for two.'

'Thanks, Trish. See you.'

Adam hangs up. Samantha raises her eyebrow.

'What did Trish mean, another invitation? Did you go out with her, Adam? You did, didn't you? You dark horse . . . I'd ask her myself if I wasn't spoken for but I don't think she'd accept. What happened? Are you seeing her again on the quiet?'

'Dunno about that. She's got a boyfriend hidden away in Ireland.' He waits by the fax, hoping for a page and that the conversation will move on. Their vigil is suddenly broken. Bruce returns from the deli.

'What are you two up to?' he asks.

'Nothing,' advises Samantha by the fax.

Bruce throws his lunch onto the desk, with his mobile, and heads off to the water cooler with a parting shot. 'No one tell you that the fax is dead? E-mail took over. You'll be waiting a long time for a fax.'

Samantha perseveres. Adam looks over at Bruce's desk. He has an idea. 'Watch out for Bruce.' He stands by Bruce's desk, eyes the trading floor, sits down quickly and picks up the chrome Nokia. The screen is active, the phone is not locked with a password. He selects the calls option and then selects received calls. The first received call is a London 207 number, then there's a 208 number. The third received call number is a +49 prefix with a long row of digits. Probably another mobile, he reckons. It definitely came from overseas. He knows from his days at Kapital that it's the dialing code for Germany. He scribbles the number down.

'What are you doing?' asks Samantha.

'Finding out who called Bruce this morning.'

'Clever boy!'

'Speak of the devil, here he comes now. Act normal.'

They do their best. The fax whirrs into life. A single page with a BA logo appears. Samantha grabs the fax. Bruce is in sight but he's talking to a colleague in an office way down the floor. He's out of earshot.

'It's Henry's Air Miles statement.' She reads out the dates of the two flights to Dusseldorf and Dublin. 'Wow! Isn't that odd? The dates match exactly. Henry was there on both of the days.'

Henry picks up a call made to his direct line.

'Henry, what are you doing today?' Diane rasps.

He recognises her voice immediately but it sounds too quiet in the background. She must have her office door closed.

'Working,' he says. 'What else?'

'I'm not. I've got a day off. I'm home alone, going to have lunch here soon. Wanna come?'

Henry isn't exactly sure how he should decipher that last one-liner.

'Right now?' he wonders.

'Yeah, right now. I need you here because I want great sex during lunch.'

Henry prays that Trish isn't listening in to the call. He has no choice. Already he's reacting to the invitation. And he is feeling somewhat peckish.

'I'll be there by one.'

Henry tells Trish that he has a meeting and will be on the mobile. He hails a cab on the Strand and gives directions across the river. He sits in the back, marvelling at the sort of hold that Diane thinks she has over him, to believe she can summon him so easily without the slightest hint of any protest. Power is a wonderful gift. He of all people should know. He will play her little game as long as it suits him.

Montevetro is deserted at midday. Diane opens the door. She's dressed only in a loose bathrobe. She looks like she's just woken up, her hair tousled, no make-up, flash City uniform or high heels. She doesn't seem to have made any special effort for his visit, doesn't seem to feel the need to impress him. He's shocked but nevertheless drawn inside her web, knowing he cannot leave without some sort of conclusion. He walks inside and looks around, still amazed at the lack of personal effects on display.

'You hungry?' she asks.

'Starving.' He nods. 'What are we having?'

He follows her into the chrome designer kitchen. She opens the refrigerator. Henry sees it's barren inside except for a litre of milk and six bottles of champagne lying side by side on the shelving.

'We're having a liquid lunch today.' She sees his reaction. 'Is that a problem?'

'I might need my energy.' He shakes his head. 'You want me to open the bottle?'

'I can manage. I'm a big girl.'

She takes two surprisingly cheap glasses from a cupboard and motions. 'Lunch is in the bedroom. Shower first, then wash your mouth out with the bottle of Listerine on the top shelf.'

He wants to ask her what the plan is but likes the sense of

the unknown. Instead he throws his suit over the only chair and takes a short yet steamy shower. This time she doesn't join him under the water. He's disappointed. As he gargles enthusiastically and towels down, a cork pops in the bedroom. He appears with a towel around his midriff. She places two glasses on a bedside table. He makes to remove his towel.

'Leave it on,' she instructs him and points to the bed. 'Lie down on your back, hands under your butt.'

He thinks that she wants the same as last time, wants to be in total control. He doesn't object. It's a role change for him. Last time was climactic. He tries to seize the initiative.

'So how are Adam and Samantha these days? What are they up to?'

She takes a huge gulp of Bolly and sits astride him, still wearing the loose bathrobe. She runs her hand along his chin and appears satisfied with her initial inspection.

'No work conversation, please. Did you get a good close shave this morning, Henry?'

'Sure did.'

'Electric or blade?'

'I always prefer a blade.'

She shifts her weight on his chest. She seems heavier. He can't move much at all.

'It *is* close. What sort of blade did you use?

'I used an unprotected Wilkinson.'

She's still stroking his chin and running her finger around his mouth, then along his lips.

'I'm going to see how psychic you are, Henry. Do you know what to do?'

'I think so.'

She moves further up his heaving chest, so far along that her robe covers his face. It's almost suffocating him. Henry is inhaling fragrant scents, maybe talcum powder, maybe aromatic oils of some sort.

'Any ideas?'

'A few.'

'Show me one.' He is still bewildered at the role reversal. 'Now close your eyes,' she instructs.

She lifts her robe over his entire head. Suddenly his chin is touching her crotch. It's raw skin upon raw skin. There's a whole new raft of overpowering aromas. To his surprise, Diane also has a perfect close shave. His tongue explores. She is wet. He tastes the juices, recoils instinctively, yet probes deeper as she shifts her weight onto his perspiring face. Her instructions are explicit. He does what she wants.

'Yes, Henry. Slower ... faster ... deeper. Easy. Yes, that's better. You learn well. Very good.'

He feels her move off to the left as she takes another gulp of champagne. Five minutes pass, then maybe ten or more but she has no desire to vary this intense foreplay. He grows more puzzled. He still wears his towel. Her breathing is rhythmic and more audible. He thinks she's reaching some sort of sexual plateau.

'You want some champagne too?'

He moans. Diane takes a huge gulp and leans over his face. He opens his mouth, then she hers. The liquid cascades into his mouth, but overflows onto the pillows and sheets, almost drowning him in its wake.

'Jeeee ... sussss.'

Henry tries to speak, then tries to move away but it's impossible. She's taken his head in her hands, pulled him even closer towards her aroused genitalia until he's almost expiring. Suddenly the doorbell goes in the hall. Someone is at the door. She roars aloud in ecstasy. There seems to be no end. The doorbell rings again. The bed will never recover. There's someone at the bloody door and they're not taking no for an answer. Now they're knocking on the wood. Finally she rolls off him and exhales loudly.

'I needed that.'

'Who the hell is that?' he asks.

'Oh, don't worry.'

Henry can hear someone outside calling out loud. They must have heard all of Diane's sound effects.

'Who can it be?' he wonders.

'Relax. They're early.' Diane finishes the remnants in the glass, looks at a clock on the table, pulls on the bathrobe and wipes the beads of sweat off her forehead. 'I know who it is. It's the removal men.'

'What?' Henry exclaims.

'That's why I'm at home today. They're delivering my stuff from the States. About time, too.'

Henry lies on the bed, deflated. His glass of champagne by the bed is similarly flat. The bottle is almost empty. She downed it all alone. He's still wearing the towel. She never touched him. 'What about me?'

'Do you want to unpack the boxes?'

'Not particularly.'

'Then you'd better go. Hope you enjoyed that lunch, Henry.'

Henry has a last-minute rush, as happens every year on this day. He is in Prakash's newsagent shop on Islington High Street but this time with a different objective. He eyes up the middle shelf of the international newspapers absently but there's no point in looking. Instead he takes a *Times* and then walks around the shop a few times to find the optimal greeting card.

He thumbs through the row of stock, most of it being nasty shrink-wrapped crap priced at £2.99. The banal dedications inside are too personal and way over the top. Eventually he settles on one with a bland vase of flowers on the front. The greeting is a modest four-line verse. He takes a box of chocs and pays at the till. Prakash puts the card into a paper bag as Henry reads the words again. *Happy Birthday to a Dear Wife.*

He signs the card in the kitchen, writes her name on the outside, deliberates and leaves it propped up against the matching beech salt and pepper mills. He's too unmotivated to deliver it in person. Time to head off for the office, to flee the scene and leave her to discover his token gesture. Amanda has a day off work because she never works on her birthday. But she is up already and sweeps into the kitchen in a robe.

He offers the envelope to her. Then the chocs. There's never any other present. 'Happy Birthday.'

One kiss. It's a hollow yet necessary sentiment. Henry feels no emotions about birthdays, anniversaries, engagements, marriages and births. News of separations, divorces, accidents and car smashes excite him. Of late he doesn't even feel much genuine emotion about involuntary death. He feigns modest interest and exterior happiness today but Amanda knows him too well. She accepts the envelope reluctantly.

'Thanks.' She touches her name on the front with a finger. 'Ink still dry?' He thinks she's not even going to open the envelope, rather she holds it like it might explode if handled incorrectly. She extracts the card, doesn't bother to read the verse and places it with others on a ledge. She is more interested in the newspaper headlines. 'Any news this morning?' Henry shakes his head.

Amanda wears subtle make-up. She's had a shower and her hair dries au naturel as she powers up the kettle and takes out a cinnamon bagel. Then she reaches for a knife from the block of lethal blades.

'You going out later?' he asks.

'The girls are taking me out for lunch. We've got a table at The Ivy. They booked it months ago.'

The girls are mainly PR and media gurus. One owns a hair salon. Another does dried flowers.

'Am I invited?' he asks.

She is about to slice the bagel in two, holding the glistening nine-inch serrated blade upright. Instead she looks over at him incredulously.

'I'll invite you out when you ask *me* somewhere.'

'Meaning what, exactly?' he retorts.

'Where were you last Saturday?'

'At a wedding in the country.'

'Did you go on your own?' He nods reluctantly. 'Did you enjoy it?'

They'd had sex in an upstairs room after the Baked Alaska but before the coffee and petits fours.

'It was ... adequate.'

'Was it anyone I know?'

He hopes not. Shakes his head. 'You don't know her.'

'What?'

The words just came out. 'I mean, you don't know the bride,' he restates explicitly.

'Don't they invite spouses to weddings any more?'

He leaves the rhetorical question unanswered. This fucking birthday, this crap gift, this bloody lunch, this damn' inquisition. It's all so irrelevant. This week is a watershed. He has failed for the first time ever and there is no one to talk to about it.

She replaces the blade in the block and takes a steaming mug of coffee plus the thickly buttered bagel back upstairs. She has his *Times* under her arm. Henry feels the urge welling up inside. For the first time ever he'd like to run that blade through his wife.

CHAPTER TWENTY-TWO

BARRIER POINT, LONDON, E16: 7.20 P.M.

Adam is doing a last-minute frantic clean-up, hiding used dishes, lone socks and films of dust. His apartment is tidy but not yet clean enough and girls know the subtle difference. The doorbell rings. In the hallway the monochrome videophone instantly comes to life. TV never lies. Samantha looks wonderful on screen, albeit in black and white. She focuses towards the unseen eyehole-camera lens, then peers through the glass door, as if expecting him to appear in person.

'It's me,' she says.

'Just push. I'm on twelve,' he advises.

He hears the lift swing into operation, hears the taut cables wind upwards and she's at his door.

'Nice place.' She points to the thick carpets and wall lights. 'Nicer than mine.'

'I can't take any credit, I'm only renting.'

She sees the videophone and runs a forefinger along the top. There's dust. Already he's undone.

'You have a videophone to see callers.'

'It comes with the place. It doesn't get used much, unfortunately.'

'Well, thanks for asking me around. Yours was a good idea.

Far better than doing this at work.'

Like every other first-timer visiting a high-rise, she instinctively makes for the doors to the balcony. The door opens to her touch. There's no need for a lock on twelve. 'I wanna see the view outside.'

It's too cold to loiter for long. The gusting wind drowns out the ebb of the Thames. Samantha is silent as she looks down and around, lost in her own thoughts. He feels the need to explain the disappointing vista.

'It's better in daytime. And summertime, I guess – if I'm still here by then.'

Her curiosity is soon sated. They sit together in the living room with Molsons in their hands.

'Where's your PC? Let's get started.'

Too bad she's only here for the World Wide Web. He takes an extra chair from the kitchen and they sit together in front of a Dell mini-tower in the spare back bedroom. He logs on, still sceptical.

'This'll never work.'

'Trust me. We'll find something, if it's there.'

'There are a billion-plus web pages.'

'And one of them is the one we want.'

'But what page is it?' he wonders as he moves the mouse.

'If there's a murder in a city, then the local newspaper will have it. Every good newspaper has a website.'

Adam opens the web on Yahoo!, his usual default search engine. Samantha's not convinced.

'Let's Google.' She commandeers mouse and keyboard, pulling her chair closer to his.

'We need the right keywords for this search to work. You got that statement?' Adam hands over the faxed BA Executive Club statement. 'The first place Henry went, according to this, is Madrid.'

Samantha types in 'Madrid' and then 'newspaper' without even looking at the keyboard. She hits return.

'We got a few Spanish newspapers in Madrid. I like *El Pais.* That's a big national daily. That will do us.' She opens the newspaper's home page. There's a site search facility in the right hand margin. She pauses.

'Think about those two deaths in Dusseldorf and Dublin. What are the common circumstances?'

Adam recalls the Reuters screen printout and the *Irish Times* press clipping.

'Death? Murder? Something like that?'

'The words are correct but the language is wrong. If it's a death in Spain, we want it in Spanish.'

Adam leans back and opens his palms towards the ceiling.

'Well, that's the end of that, because I haven't got a single word of Spanish.'

'I spent six months with a backpack in South America. Without Spanish, I would have starved.' Samantha types in *muerte.* Then *asesino.* 'We need more. Wasn't a stabbing common to both? Knife.' She types *cuchillo*, then hits a 'go' icon. There are many news stories in the search result. Adam eyes them quickly. They're still in Spanish.

'This is going to take us all night,' he observes. 'We'll need a dictionary!'

'Gimme time.' She's already opening up the first story and scanning the screen. 'More beers?'

Adam feels surplus to requirements and disappears into the kitchen in search of two more ice-cold Molsons. He's opening two long necks as she calls excitedly, 'Come here! Quickly! Look at this.'

He sits down to examine a busy PC screen. There's too much Spanish text but there are two photos. One is a bad passport photo of a pasty middle-aged male with glasses. The other is a shot of layers of bright orange sheeting over a box frame near a lake in a park. Samantha translates slowly as she points.

'A businessman was stabbed in the evening in Parque del

Retiro in the centre of Madrid. Police have no known motive for the killing.' She turns to Adam. 'But look at the date on Henry's BA statement.'

He sees why Samantha is excited.

'The statement says Henry went out on BA on the twenty-second and came back on BA on the twenty-third.' Samantha is pointing to the top corner of the screen. Even Adam can read the date of a press article.

'Jesus,' he exclaims. 'The twenty-fourth. The very day after he flew back to London. Does it say what time the murder happened?'

Samantha is reading the small print, running her finger down the screen, paragraph by paragraph.

'Says here the deceased was last seen going into the park yesterday – the day before the date of this story, that is – at six-thirty in the evening.'

'And Henry's flight left at eight-thirty p.m.' Adam pauses. 'Some coincidence.'

Samantha sits back and looks at the screen with satisfaction.

'So Henry was in three different European cities on the days of three similar murders. That's even more relevant than Bruce's movements. You're right. Lots of people must travel as much as Henry does but still it's unbelievable, really ...'

'What next?'

'You knew the guy who died in Dusseldorf, didn't you? He worked with you?'

'Not really. But I know some people on the FX desk there. Natalia knows everyone in head office.'

'Who's she?'

'A completely unattainable German blonde.'

'Don't get me interested! But it might be worth a trip out there.'

'What's the point?'

'Maybe get a description of the murderer if there were any

witnesses. Find out more about the scene. Don't instantly dismiss it. Let's sleep on it. Kerys was on afternoon shift today. I said I'd get back early so we can go out to a club together. We'd ask you too but I'm not sure Miss-Shapes is your scene.'

She places the empty bottles in the kitchen, then walks with her coat to the hall. He opens the door and calls the lift for her. The doors open. Samantha leans closer to him and gives him a kiss on the cheek.

'Thanks for satisfying my curiosity. See you tomorrow.'

He's not listening. He's staring into the open lift. Lisa from upstairs stands inside. She's going down too and has a couple of bulging plastic refuse bags. She stares out at Adam, both of them uncomfortable with the mutual silence, both of them failing to take any notice of Samantha, who still grins broadly.

'Hi,' says Lisa from inside the lift.

Samantha winks at Adam and steps inside. The doors close and the only women in his life disappear. Adam is rooted to the spot, unsure whether he's just ended another potential relationship before it ever started.

Samantha watches Muppet throwing up on the far side of the desk and tries to stay upwind. The others nearby are more worried than the last time he gave such a performance. There's not only vomit splayed over the flush grey carpet tiles, there are specks of blood too.

'Bad pint last night?' inquires Cable Guy.

'Not sure. First six were okay. Must have been the seventh,' replies Muppet.

Bookie obliges with a wad of toilet paper from the gents' and mops up the mess, then swaps the spattered carpet tiles with others from further under the desk. All looks well. The others carry on trading like nothing's happened. Samantha often wonders about the smell at the FX desk. Bruce tells

Muppet to go see the bank Doc on thirty-two. Muppet is not keen.

'Doctors are useless. They only ever tell you half of what you need to know.'

Spoon discusses last night on BBC2. 'Why is it you never see a girl on University Challenge? Last night there were four blokes from Hull University and four from Durham. Can't the women make any of the teams? Or would they burst into tears at the first question?'

Muppet lumbers queasily back to the desk. Samantha is fielding another query from an irate salesman regarding one of Muppet's misbooked FX trades. She asks him for an explanation of what happened with the ticket.

'Don't worry, dear, I'll fill you in. Any time,' he smirks back at her.

Samantha's had enough. She has already postponed this confrontation on several occasions. Now is the time. She plucks up her courage, walks over to Diane's office and steps inside. 'Can we talk?'

Diane turns away from a glowing PC screen. 'I'm busy, have a meeting to go to in five, but pull up a seat. What's the matter?'

Samantha exhales. 'I can't take much more of it here.'

'I know. It's tough. I guess we all feel it gets too much sometimes.'

Samantha sighs. 'Thank God for that! I thought I was the only one here who feels this way.'

Diane cracks a smile. 'Stress is part of the job. It comes in waves. Next month will be better. Hang on in there.'

Samantha knows that next month will not be any better. Diane has no idea what she's talking about.

'Stress I can live with. It's being a woman on the FX desk that bugs me. Discrimination. Sexism.'

'Really?'

She's rehearsed the words. 'I know I'm paid less and have

less responsibility than male peers. I can live with that, for a while, but I can't take the constant sexual harassment and innuendo any longer.'

Diane's expression hardens. 'So you're still bothered by that?'

Samantha picks up on the nuance. 'Belinda in HR told you about my visit to her last month?'

Diane nods. 'I was hoping you'd let it lie.' She looks out of the glass-walled office at the motley crew manning, in every sense of the word, the FX desk. 'The guys out there are no worse that the ones I worked with at head office in New York.'

'And that makes it okay, does it? Do you want me to tell you the sordid details of exactly what happens to me out there, day after day?'

'HR told me enough. It's regrettable but endemic. They're just men. Pigs, the lot of them. Ignore them.' Diane looks for some upside. 'What's your life plan?' She sees Samantha's confusion. 'I'm talking about your endgame. What do you want out of the City?'

'I want a job, a salary and a future. But most of all I want some respect from the others.'

Diane waves her left hand. 'Look outside. There are no old people. We're all here to get rich quick and get out while we can hang on to our sanity. Do you think I'm staying here until my retirement date? Damn right. I'm not! I own my own place in New York. I'm liquid after ten years in the firm, I can retire to a beach in ten more. If you can stick it here, Samantha, that could be you.'

'I'm not sure I want that.'

'We have one secret weapon in our arsenal.' Diane improves her posture, checks her reflection in the PC screen, tilts her head provocatively. 'I use it. And someone who looks like you most certainly should. You could have every guy out there dangling from the end of your little finger if you made the effort.'

'I'm not interested in that sort of shallow approach. I'm gonna have to take some official action on this.'

'Don't do anything rash,' her boss advises.

'I've done my research. There's a bond analyst with a US bank who claimed she was harassed, humiliated and undermined, despite her consistently good performance. She claimed her bonus was slashed because she was a woman. She went to an employment tribunal and won her case. Maybe I could too.'

'Is that your research? She got lucky. I wouldn't take too much from a one-off like that.'

'There's another girl who received a million quid in damages after an employment tribunal found that she was forced to resign from her job at a German bank. She suffered sexist remarks by colleagues and her managers' allegation that she had an affair with a bank client. Her boss referred to women as "top totty" in the bank's offices. Sounds a bit like the guys here, doesn't it?'

'So you managed to dredge up two examples. Are you done?'

'Not quite. Another girl won an unfair dismissal award from a US bank, saying she had been sacked during her fourth pregnancy after asking for more flexible working hours to spend time with her children. Her boss described having children as a lifestyle choice similar to playing squash. Need I go on? Women like me are refusing to put up and shut up any longer. I have a legitimate grievance and if I don't get any help from you or from HR then I'll have no choice but to go official.'

'Often I find claims of sexual discrimination are just an easy cop-out. I prefer someone to work hard.' Diane shifts in her seat as she gathers some papers in her hand. 'Take my advice. Chill. Go with the flow.'

'I can't do that any longer.'

Diane stands up. 'As I said, I'm busy and have a management meeting to attend so let's leave it there for today. Unless there is anything else of a more practical nature that you wish to discuss with me?'

Samantha stands up, enraged at her lack of interest and her apathy. She needs to make an impression. She stops by the door and turns with a vaguely puzzled look. 'Oh, and I'm concerned about a euro interest-rate trading scam at the FX desk but since you're so busy today, maybe we can discuss that some other time.'

Henry sits in the front row of a premier corporate box at Stamford Bridge. A steady drizzle falls upon the lads on million-quid annual pay packets who are in between court appearances in the media spotlight. The pitch is heavy and there's more mud than grass. It's a derby game with real edge. Chelsea play from left to right in their royal blue home strip. The away team is in white. To Henry's right are tables laden with complimentary drinks and hot food served in silver tureens. To his left an overdressed dizzy Essex blonde asks her husband if Tottenham and Spurs are two different teams. He in turn tries in vain to explain the aggregate scoring system of a Worthington Cup quarter-final second leg.

Lionel Roberts, his host for the evening, approaches Henry. 'Another drink, old chap?'

'A Ramlosa, please. From the fridge. Thanks.'

His host does the needful. 'I seem to remember you as a keen Chelsea fan.'

'I was, but I haven't been here for years.'

'Why didn't you bring Amanda along to the game?'

'I asked her,' Henry lies and then shakes his head. 'She's not interested in soccer.'

Roberts nods towards the blonde. 'They're best left at home. Though I would have liked to impress her too.'

'Don't worry, Lionel, I'm impressed enough for both of us and that's what matters. And I have the majority shareholding.

I'll make the decision. She'll follow suit. She does what she's told.'

Roberts looks momentarily disconcerted by Henry's assertion, then rallies.

'If you do sell, you'll be part of the management team. You can use our box here whenever you want. This is the only way to watch your team. In style, rather than stuck down there in the stands.'

One of the Tottenham players displays some exquisite silky dribbling skills near the centre circle, evading several lunging tackles from over-eager Chelsea players. He is black. The home fans roar.

'You black bastard! You black bastard! You black bastard!'

'So much for kicking racism out of football,' observes Roberts. 'They should be ashamed.'

'Yeah,' replies Henry. He recalls the old days as he looks down on the home fans on the terraced seating in the Harding stand, searching for any familiar face. Some of them must still be there, ten years on, fatter and greyer, older and wiser. Henry gave up coming here when the cops got heavy. Too many body searches, too many stewards, too many video cameras inside the ground, too many arrests outside, way too much grief. The association wasn't worth the risk, even for someone like Henry who eagerly watched the others, eavesdropped on the stories, but never mingled with them.

The black guy places a twenty-yard right-footed drive into the top left-hand corner of the virginal Chelsea net. The Italian keeper on megabucks per week watches the ball pass him by more in admiration than with any hope of preventing a local seismic disaster. Over-the-top celebrations are held near the corner flag by the home fans. Some are on their feet, giving lewd hand signals and a few Nazi salutes.

'Disgusting reaction,' observes Roberts. 'It was a fine goal.'

'Yes, splendid,' replies Henry again. Suddenly he sees them. They are there. He can see Eddie, then Razor. Sparky and

Chubby, too. And Jed, Darren and Chas. They're in their check Burberry baseball caps, their Rockport, Stone Island, Lacoste and Aquascutum match-day clobber, always better dressed that the opposition like it's some sort of competition, never seen dead in a give-away home strip.

They did it all. Some days. Getting well tanked up on the King's Road before the game. Steaming into the away fans at the agreed rendezvous. Away weekends on BR against Sunderland, Leeds and Middlesboro. Cutting up immigrants with Stanley blades. Stabbing an off-duty policeman on the Tube for the heck of it. Snorting lines of coke inside the Finborough Arms. Mounting a vicious campaign against the Chelsea Independent Supporters Association for their lily-livered views. Reading *The Stormer* magazine. Spitting at elderly Pakis waiting at a bus stop. 'You get out of my shop.' Being the Chelsea firm. Receiving respect.

There's a bad tackle near the sideline below Henry. The referee lets it go but the two players are on their feet in an instant. The Spurs hard man fakes a mock head-butt at the Chelsea Under-21 England star who slumps to the ground in simulated pain. The referee offers two yellow cards. The home fans roar in unison.

'Off! Off! Off! Off! Off!'

Henry remembers the pitched battles against Dutch supporters at Rotterdam train station. Meeting up with Combat 18, the KKK, the BNP and the NF. Getting stuck into the Paddies at the annual Bloody Sunday memorial march in the West End. Supporting BNP candidates in general elections. Sparky and some of his mad mates once went on holiday to Auschwitz and got a photograph of one of the guys doing a Nazi salute outside the ovens with an old Polish geezer crying in the background.

The home fans sing to the away fans. 'Going home in a body bag, going home in a body bag.'

One of the elite Chelsea back four knocks a lazy back pass

in the direction of the keeper who is still largely an observer in the game. The ball sticks in the worst mud outside the area. A Spurs centre forward latches onto it and slides it under the lethargic Italian into the open net. A few foolhardy away fans cheer in celebration. Henry knows the others will give them a good kicking on their way out to the Tube. The referee puts the home team out of their misery with a shrill half-time whistle.

Roberts moves closer to Henry and seizes the moment. 'So are you still interested?'

'Sure I am. It's only two-nil. We can come back. It's a game of two halves and all that.'

'I mean, are you interested in selling up?'

'I wouldn't have accepted your invitation otherwise. We need to discuss the exact terms.'

'Excellent. I'll put my people in touch with yours. We can close this in a few weeks.' Roberts slaps Henry on the back and raises his glass. 'Here's to more nights like this at Stamford Bridge.'

'Indeed,' replies Henry, absently. Roberts see him glance down at the great unwashed below in their Fly Emirates replica shirts. More lewd and racist chanting comes from the direction of the Harding stand.

'Pity about some of the so-called soccer fans here,' Roberts feels the need to apologise.

'It's disgusting,' replies Henry on cue. 'I was once stuck on a Central Line Tube with a bunch of Man United fans. They spent twenty minutes chanting; Ryan Giggs, Ryan Giggs. He's got speed, he's got flair. And he's shagging Dani Behr. That's all most of these players are good for these days. Fast cars and faster women, and a bit of designer modelling and TV work on the side. They make me sick.'

'It's improving here,' explains Roberts. Henry looks blank. 'You'll remember the worst of the Chelsea fans years ago? Called themselves the Chelsea Headhunters. They were a bloody evil bunch. I was embarrassed to support the same team. All skinhead right-wingers and neo-Nazis. Thankfully, times have changed. The police infiltrated them. Now they don't even get inside the ground. The real headhunters sit in corporate boxes and sip fine champagne. Which is how it should be, don't you think?'

Henry nods in agreement, remembering the thrill of the old days, a part of him wishing even now he was down in the drizzle in the stands with a bloody raw beefburger in his hand, waiting for the final whistle and the real business of the day to begin.

CHAPTER TWENTY-THREE

PARK LANE, LONDON, WI: 8.15 P.M.

Adam alights from the black cab, passes the doorman, enters the swing doors, descends a few steps, follows the signs to the Great Room of the Grosvenor House Hotel and immediately hears the excited buzz of his colleagues. There must be hundreds, no, thousands, of loud laughing traders, salesmen and bankers. The vista ahead of him is a sea of wealth.

He worries that his rented monkey suit from Moss Bros. is too large and hangs awkwardly, that the size 16 dress shirt is too tight around his neck and should be a 16½, that his bow tie came pre-assembled, isn't the real knotted thing and is crooked. He worries about who he will talk to tonight since he knows so few people in the firm. He looks forward to being with Samantha but not to being with her colleagues.

'You made it, Adam,' observes Bruce from a chair in the wings.

His eyes adjust to the light. His desk colleagues sit at a corner table. He hasn't seen them since they all took a half-day and left him alone on the afternoon morgue shift. They are unrecognisable from their usual selves. Their alter egos have recent haircuts, decent shaves, maybe even facials. Their dazzling formal wear looks like their best clobber. Muppet wears a red cummerbund that reduces his beer gut to a more manageable size. Cable Guy's cufflinks look like the Crown Jewels. Bookie comes over.

'Nice bib and tucker.' He feels the lapel. 'Is that your suit?'

Adam knows they know that it's rented. They've sussed him out already.

'Mine for the night at least,' he replies.

'Here comes your hot date,' advises Bruce.

All eyes turn to stare and leer. Samantha looks like a million bucks of FX trading P&L. It's one of many long black numbers at the party but it's the best dress in the room. She sits beside Adam and ignores the loaded comments around her. The meal begins with the usual festive choice. Turkey or beef. Beef or turkey. There's unlimited red and white on tap. Conversation is desultory as they eat.

Bookie breaks the silence. 'Thanks for the great advice on Christmas shopping for my kids, Muppet.'

Earlier Muppet had sent Bookie to a new place in the East End, called Lapland, known only to a few.

'Did you get what you wanted?'

'The girls were peeling off red Santa bikinis for twenty quid. It's not a shop, it's a bloody lap-dancing club.'

'I know,' replies Muppet, without looking up from his plate. 'Beats fucking Toys R Us, though.'

After the main course, Bruce points over to Adam. 'Guys, it's official. Adam is a wash-out. Guess what? He's taking tomorrow off work. No doubt to get over his massive hangover. What a wuss, eh?'

Samantha gives Adam a knowing look that's also tinged with guilt. Tomorrow's planned trip is her idea. Adam says nothing, preferring to let the matter rest. Where he goes tomorrow is between the two of them.

The party drags on. Muppet seizes centre stage as the loud music pumps. He stands up on his chair and sings something unintelligible. 'I come from a musical family. Even the sewing machine was a Singer.'

Later he's walking to the bar, weaving his way past the other freeloaders with hands around clutches of glasses, when a girl steps into his path.

'Hi, Adam.'

He faces a thirty-something with well-groomed hair, sparkling body paint upon exposed shoulders and plunging neckline. He's sure he's never seen her before. She offers no assistance to ease his recognition of her.

'Hi, how are you?' he bluffs.

'A bit tipsy, actually.' She must be someone on the sales floor who's seen him from afar. He's vaguely impressed that an alluring girl is making a move on him. He's beginning to hope that everything they told him about last year's debauchery might be true. She leans closer and places her hand on his arm, maybe for support. 'I haven't seen you since your first day.'

It's the clue he needs. He does know her. She's someone in HR, that apologetic girl on day one.

'Oh, I remember . . .' By some divine inspiration, he suddenly remembers her name. '. . . Belinda.'

'Adam . . . when I first met you I thought you were very nice.'

She's more than tipsy, she's completely hammered and it's not even eleven o'clock. She places her two hands on his right arm. He looks around, hoping that the others are nowhere in sight. He tries to make his excuses when the DJ determines his immediate fate. The next song booms out from the wall speakers. It's the one they're all waiting for at the party. Belinda grabs him and screams.

'It's "Dancing Queen". C'mon, I need a partner.'

Belinda drags him through the crowd, throws her clutch bag on a table and suddenly they're on the dance floor under the neon strobe lighting, the pulsing beat inviting them to sway closer together. The place is heaving. Some of the trading guys are standing up on the tables with glasses, bottles and magnums in hand. Adam can only see a sea of unknown faces. Jackets are discarded, sleeves are rolled up, bow ties hang loose, mammaries ditto. Mutual groping is all the rage, perspiration everywhere.

A pal of Belinda's screams at her, gives her the thumbs-up sign, produces a throwaway Kodak and takes a flash photo of the two of them. The print will surely appear at the FX desk. Adam turns away from the paparazzi. Belinda collides with everyone around while he tries to keep a safe distance. He looks back towards Samantha but he can't even see their table. He grabs Belinda as she's about to keel over.

'You need a rest,' he shouts unnecessarily.

The Abba anthem is suddenly over. It's gone quiet. It's a slow set. The dance floor starts to empty as entwined couples avoid further public embarrassment and make for the bar. Others make for the floor. Adam has to get away, mainly because the lecherous teenage DJ is playing that crap love song from the mid-eighties by Jennifer Rush. Belinda is not keen to leave the scene of the crime and remains insistent.

'Don't go. You can't leave me alone. A gentleman never leaves a lady.'

She has hold of him again. They're much closer this time. Adam is conscious that there are fewer couples on the floor, that he can be seen from the pitch-dark recesses of the Great Room. Belinda is moving in for the kill as the first chorus grates. She goes for the first kiss and is successful. Adam backs away. She goes for the second. This time her tongue explores deep within his mouth. He looks around but he can't see anyone else, can't even see their table, can't see any sign of Samantha anywhere.

Samantha's tired of the low lights and the low life. She has the best corner seat but she's trapped up against the wall. Muppet sits beside her. He's hung around her all night like some unwanted puppy in search of his next dog biscuit. He keeps hollering at equally pissed mates from other floors in Mitchell's to stagger over to take a look at Samantha, like she's some work of art on public display.

It's too dark. It's too smoky. It's late enough. She can finally leave. She stands up and squeezes past Muppet, wondering why he doesn't move, why he brushes his open legs and crotch up against her legs.

'Where you going, dear?' His speech is slurred. Too many Bud long-necks mixed with shorts.

'Home.'

She can see Adam in a one-way conversation with a girl near the bar. Adam's listening, not speaking. She gets her long black coat from the coat check. Outside on Park Lane the heavens are teeming down at right angles. There's a rank for taxis but there's only one vehicle with its light on. She runs across the wet oily tarmac.

'Elephant & Castle, please.'

She relaxes into the warmth and security of the rear seat. Before the cabbie can even start the engine, the side door is reopened.

'Can I have a ride?'

Muppet stands there in the rain, no coat, just water running down his matted hair and jowelled cheeks.

'Get another taxi,' she says.

'This is the only one.'

'I said, get another one.'

'It's fucking pissing down! I lost my coat.'

'I'm not going your way.'

''Course you are, dear.'

She enjoys a brief moment of hope as the cabbie turns around in annoyance at the delay. Then she sees his tired pensioner's face and knows he'll be no help. Muppet lurches into the rear seat and collapses.

'Get out,' she says.

'Where are we going?'

'I'm going home.'

'Suits me. Where do you live?'

She doesn't know exactly where he lives. Fulham? She hopes against hope. 'South of the river.'

'Me too. Let's go. Drive on.'

Muppet sits too near the centre of the seat. He's much too close to her. She looks away but sees nothing through the misted windows. Lights flash by outside at blurred speed. She's aware that they have crossed the Thames and are southside but she doesn't recognise the bridge. The back of the cab reeks of beer and BO. At a set of red lights the cabbie shouts at her but doesn't bother to look around.

'Where exactly, love?'

She doesn't want to utter the words, to tell Muppet where she lives, but there's little choice.

'The top of Mason Street.'

Muppet stirs alongside, places his hand on her coat-tails, firmly pressing her right thigh.

'I can get a minicab home from there.'

'Damn' right you will.'

They stop. Samantha alights by the gates to the block and hands over the fare. She has an idea.

'Here's a twenty. Take this guy home. He lives somewhere near Fulham, I think.'

Muppet's suddenly awake and is out of the cab before he can be stopped.

'No fucking way! I said, I'm getting a minicab. These fucking black cabs are a rip-off.'

The cabbie is sufficiently insulted to start up his engine and leave.

'This clown's your responsibility, love, not mine. Sorry.'

The cab is gone. They're alone, rain still falling. The street is deserted. A dog barks somewhere.

'Call me a minicab from inside.'

Samantha's not going inside her home with Muppet.

'I'll use my mobile.'

She's about to dial the local firm she uses for shopping trips when he grabs the phone from her.

'I said, let's call from inside. It's pissing down out here.'

He grips her hand, guides her to the security gates, expecting her to key in the magic code. Suddenly she sees a saviour. Someone is on the other side of the metal gate and they're on foot. The gates open from the inside. She looks over to the stranger in the crash helmet but in vain. He's a pizza delivery guy going back to his Five Star moped with the L-plates. He's not interested at all. Muppet's hustling her along.

'Which one is your place?'

She's feeling the rain now. She opens her front door and leaves it ajar in the hope that he'll take the hint. She reaches for the phone on the wall. Muppet slams the front door closed and places his hand over the phone.

'There's no rush. Let's get a drink first. What have you got?'

'Nothing. You gotta go. Otherwise—'

He leans against her, his excessive body weight pinning her against the wall in the narrow hallway.

'Otherwise what? What are you gonna do?'

She's knows she's safe. Kerys must be at home. It's her night off, isn't it? Or is it? Did she swap with someone else on the ward this week? Maybe. Samantha screams as loud as she can down the hall.

'Kerys . . . come here.'

There is no reply. She must have swapped, Samantha realises, her heart sinking, fear growing.

'Seems your mystery friend isn't here. It's just you and me.'

'Get off me, Muppet! You're drunk. Get outta here. I'll call the police, I mean it . . .'

He reaches behind her and yanks the handset off the wall, then holds up the loose dangling wires.

'Call them on this. Will you? I don't think so.' He tightens his grip on her arms. She's seizing up, real fear coursing through her veins. 'You and me know each other quite well, don't we? We're already friends. We need to get to know each other even better.' He pulls off her coat and throws it behind him on the floor. 'Ain't that so?' He places one hand on her leg and runs it up to her crotch. 'You know you want this as much as I do.' He rubs his hand back and forth across the warm cotton fabric covering her mound, aware that it's the closest he's ever been to the object of his desire. 'It's raining and you're so wet.'

He drags her into the living room and forces her down on the rug by the fire, next to the dead embers and dry ash. Up close she inhales the smell of beer and wine and lust as raindrops fall from his hair onto her face, mingling with her tears. She's about to scream when he places a huge sweaty hand over her mouth.

'Shut the fuck up! It'll be better for you that way. Dear.'

Henry stands on the Northern Line platform. He hates the fucking Tube. All the wasters and lowlives, the flotsam and jetsam, the rats that run under sleepers ahead of the trains, the human hair that blows from tunnels, the dirt that invades his nasal passages, the poisonous carcinogenic air, the waves of body odour, the latent aggression and the vacant stares. Some asshole belatedly alights as he boards the train.

Henry feels the urge. At moments like this it's always useful mentally to rehearse the Ten Commandments. As the carriage doors close a lanky youth bounds on and sits in the ripped seat directly opposite. He has the white tracksuit top like he's sponsored by Nike, has the baggy jeans with hundreds of pockets, has the swagger back on his heels like he's out to impress someone. Only Henry's not impressed.

First Commandment. Thou shalt not kill in the UK. Henry's a people person. He's in the people business and knows too many faces and names here. The UK is too small for him to take the chance, to run an unnecessary risk, to be seen by someone who knows him. London's eight million inhabitants are an even worse proposition. Doing anything in the Square Mile is unthinkable. The youth has cropped dyed gelled hair, wears monster Nike Airs on his feet, and carries a DAT with headphones and a bulging Burger King paper bag.

Second Commandant. Thou shalt not kill in the USA. The downside of discovery and capture there is beyond contemplation. Either a life-stretch in a six-by-ten cell with a huge bisexual muthafucka or a short sharp shock tied to a gurney in the execution block of some private correctional facility waiting for a lethal chemical cocktail. The youth opens his legs wide, displays his crotch to the watching world, stakes his claim to his territory and deters other passengers from sitting on either side.

Third Commandment. Thou shalt not kill twice in the same country. Police forces are stupid and incompetent, but not *that* stupid and incompetent. Regional police forces share common data about gruesome murders and bizarre deaths, but rarely do so with overseas forces. The risk that Interpol is actually an effective cross-border supranational police force is omnipresent, although the evidence to date indicates they're useless. The youth repeatedly picks his nose, then proceeds to scratch his balls.

Fourth Commandment. Thou shalt not kill in spring and summer. Winter and autumn are better. Evenings are cold. Nights are dark. Storms and rain sap energy and enthusiasm. People stay inside, run in haste from the safety of doorways to waiting cabs, stride with heads bowed and vision obscured by umbrellas and hats. People don't wait to watch others who loiter with a more morbid fatal interest. The youth places a pair of chrome Sony headphones on his head and switches on the music.

Fifth Commandment. Thou shalt not kill the wrong target. The target must be of a lesser or similar build, alone, harassed, no one bulky or more threatening, in case of practical difficulties. The youth listens to music of sorts, like there's a hissing snake high on speed escaping from inside the DAT.

Sixth Commandment. Thou shalt not kill in the wrong location. It must be quiet, depopulated, private, never overlooked. He prefers woods and forests, bushes and undergrowth, trees and parks. The youth sways his head. Heavy repetitive So Solid Crew bass lines pass through the vacant space between his protruding ears.

Seventh Commandment. Thou shalt not kill with undue complications. Use a simple blade and avoid a piece that produces noise to burst the eardrums, that can jam at the crucial moment or that shows up on airport X-ray machines. Finish the job and never allow a target to recover and become a witness. Clean up and leave no evidence behind. The youth rips open the Burger King bag and stuffs fries into his gaping mouth at excessive speed. The smell of grease and cooking oils permeates the carriage.

Eighth Commandment. Thou shalt not kill without an exit route. He will never be stopped at an airport if the target is not as yet missing, the body unnoticed, the crime unreported. He enjoys day trips to Paris, Madrid, Brussels, Amsterdam and Milan. Dusseldorf and Dublin, too. There's something very comforting about an imminent short flight back home on BA. He worries if he might run out of suitable cities. But he's never been to Scandinavia or the new emerging countries of Eastern Europe. The expansion process within the European Community is a positive step. The youth takes out a slice of gherkin and lets it drop to the ground, then mashes it into the floor with the heel of his Nikes.

Ninth Commandment. Thou shalt not kill anyone you know. Familiarity comes later when newspaper articles and names can be researched at home in complete safety, a mineral water to hand. The youth rolls the bag with its remains of fries and burger into a tight ball, plays with it in his hands and tosses it up and down.

Tenth Commandment. Thou shalt not kill with a motive. Because who needs a motive to kill? The youth drops the Burger

King bag on the floor. Henry's had enough. He leans forward and makes direct eye contact.

'Do you mind?' The youth slowly acknowledges the unheard words. Henry speaks louder. 'I said, do you mind?'

Other passengers shift. The youth takes off the headphones. The music's suddenly much louder.

'Wha'?' he grunts in an accent from the high-rise council blocks of Walthamstow or Dagenham.

Henry points at the rubbish rolling along the floor to the end of the rocking carriage.

'I said, do you mind?'

The youth looks blankly, some vague recognition dawning, then a lairy grin replaces it.

'No, I don't mind. Looks like you do, innit?'

The carriage rocks to a halt at Angel station. Henry rises slowly and stands closer. The youth looks less certain, wondering what will happen next. Henry wishes he's in Europe, wishes he's somewhere less brightly lit, wishes the carriage was empty, wishes he had a BA ticket in his pocket, wishes he had a blade to run through this guy's aorta. He steps off the carriage at his station in the knowledge that the Ten Commandments are never to be transgressed. The youth replaces the headphones and lives.

CHAPTER TWENTY-FOUR

TRINKHAUS STRASSE, DUSSELDORF:
11.50 A.M.

Adam has a hangover but it doesn't deter him from waking early. An hour later he's at City Airport. He touches down at sunny Dusseldorf Flughafen at midday and takes a taxi directly to Kapital Landesbank's HQ. He waits in reception until Natalia appears from upstairs. It's all true. She makes a great first impression, with her long blonde hair, a ski-tan and black leather trousers. It's a well-known fact amongst the London FX market that her lucky husband is Russian, six foot three, and not to be tangled with. She's welcoming and smiling, oozing natural charisma. Adam wishes he could bottle it and sell it.

'I shouldn't even be talking to you. Someone might see us,' she jokes in perfect English. 'Seeing as you went and jumped ship and left us for a competitor. So how is life in Mitchell's?'

'Fine,' he lies once again, wishing he could be genuinely enthusiastic about his current employer.

'You seem like the euro of late — a bit bearish, perhaps?' She's seen straight through him without any difficulty. 'Have you had lunch yet?' He shakes his head. 'Me neither. Let's go to the canteen first.'

They join a queue of polite German bankers who move effortlessly through various hyper-organised counters. They sit at a table on the mezzanine level with a view of the Konigsallee. Natalia charges the food.

'Are you sure I can still eat here?' he asks.

'You're honorary Kapital staff today. I'm sure Beamer and the others would want it that way.'

He's seen more genuine hospitality today from Natalia and Kapital than he has from Mitchell's in two months.

'So why call me out of the blue?' she asks.

'You're the only person I know in Dusseldorf who is so well connected.'

She recalls their brief conversation. 'Why exactly do you want to meet Ulrich's wife?'

He gives the matter some thought over his soup and a stuffed baguette, recalling Samantha's input.

'I have a friend who's on the trail of a serial killer . . .'

'Funny!' she laughs. He doesn't react. Natalia sees his steady stare. 'Are you serious?'

'I don't know. I need to learn more about Ulrich's death. There are similarities to another death I read about. It was in a newspaper in Dublin.'

'Why don't you talk to the police in London? Or here?'

'I have nothing to tell them yet. All I have is some coincidence. It could be nothing. I want to retrace Ulrich's last steps, to see where he died, to talk to his wife and get any information I can on the killer and the circumstances.'

Natalia is finished and on her feet, looking at her watch.

'We're due to meet Brigitte in half an hour at her home. I'll get the car. Wait for me by the taxi rank out front. That's where Ulrich caught his last taxi. It's the best place for you to start.'

Adam waits below in a small queue of locals, wondering

how Ulrich would have felt leaving work to go home to his wife and kids, recalling the brief time they spent together while they had both been working for Kapital. He has a moment's doubt when the queue begins to shorten and it could be his turn for an unwanted taxi. Then a set of metal gates opens nearby and a vision approaches.

Natalia sits in the driver's seat of a blue metallic Porsche Boxster, soft-top rolled back, sporting cool shades and an upturned coat collar, her hair blowing over the headrest as she brakes by the rank. Adam hops into the single passenger seat of a completely impractical car. Other guys in the queue look on enviously. Adam wishes that reality bore some vague resemblance to the appearance.

'Nice car,' he observes.

'German cars are cheap here. Anyway, the bank pays. You probably have one of these from Mitchell's.'

'I have a Vauxhall Astra.'

'Sorry to hear about the cutbacks,' she laughs.

They drive through the city streets. Adam's conscious that others stare over at them.

'If Ulrich had taken a lift home with you, more people would have remembered his last movements.'

'If Ulrich had taken a lift home with me, then I'd have ensured no harm came to him in his own front garden.'

They cross the span of a huge bridge over the Rhine, drift into quiet residential streets and pull up outside high gates that are closed to the outside world. Natalia gets out and points up and down the road.

'This is where the two taxis stopped, apparently. Ulrich's taxi driver, a local, dropped him here by the gates. The second driver, a Turk, parked thirty metres away, waited about five minutes until his fare, the killer, returned.' Natalia walks to an intercom by the gate. 'Brigitte has since had this installed for security.' She speaks some fast German into the speaker and the heavy gates creak open. 'This way.'

They walk up a winding gravel path and stop by a mailbox set upon a small post to the right. Adam notices the overhanging trees rustling above and the high hedges sheltering them. It's a peaceful location but he knows it shouldn't feel so calm. Someone died here. Natalia points to the grass.

'This is where Ulrich was killed. Everything now is the same, only it was raining heavily that night, not like the soft-top weather today. He was found over there, face up. His house keys and some letters were by his side. Brigitte knows a little more but she won't tell me and I don't want to ask. The police have some photos of the crime scene. I haven't seen them. I don't want to. It's too depressing.

The door is opened by a pale thirty-something woman who tries her best to smile. She speaks moderately good English as she shows them into a living room with a log fire. Two freckled children suddenly appear, looking curious, and disappear just as fast, from shyness or fear. The trio sit close together. Brigitte leans towards Adam.

'Why are you visiting us from London?'

Adam's not sure what Natalia has told her widowed friend.

'I'd like to help in some small way, if I can. I came here to get the best information.'

'Why?' Brigitte asks.

'I think I may know about another very similar death.'

She reacts with immediate disbelief, looks at Natalia who nods encouragingly, then speaks again.

'An old woman saw the killer first at the taxi rank but remembers nothing. She suffers from dementia. The taxi had hundreds of fingerprints. It was useless. The taxi driver said that his fare was in his thirties, six foot, well dressed, clean-shaven and American, we think.'

'American?' Adam asks. 'Are you sure?'

Brigitte nods. 'He spoke like an American, so I'm told. The police looked for him in the train station and in Bonn and all stations in between but he disappeared that evening. Do you know where he is now?'

Adam tries to be realistic. He can see her hopes rising. It's all been in vain.

'I know of someone from London who was in Dusseldorf that day. He is sort of similar to your description but he's not an American. I fear he's a different person. I think I'm wasting your time.'

Brigitte leans forward and takes Adam's hand.

'I need to know what happened. Who killed Ulrich?'

Adam is thinking on his feet.

'I wish I knew. I should speak directly to the taxi driver. He'll have a better description.'

'That's impossible now,' advises Brigitte. 'The driver is an illegal immigrant. Once the police spoke to him he disappeared.' She thinks in silence while Adam wishes he had never come here to raise her hopes. He blames Samantha for sending him out here to waste the time of someone still grieving. 'So you want a good description of the man.' He nods. 'Then please have a look at the police photofit.'

'You have one?' he exclaims.

She rises to her feet and rummages in a drawer in a side room, talking wildly as she searches.

'The police compiled it after talking to the taxi driver on the next day. It was difficult. The driver said that the man sat out of sight of his rear-view mirror. He only saw him as he paid and gave him a receipt.'

She returns with a folded A4 page. Adam accepts it slowly, opens it and turns it around to face him.

'What do you think?' she perseveres. 'Is it like the person you know?'

Adam examines the computer-generated face. His heartbeat begins to quicken, then slows. A pair of bold eyeglasses dominate the picture. He tries to blot them out of his vision, focusing instead on the facial features and jawline. It's sort of like Henry. It's sort of like Bruce. It could, in truth, be anyone, any clean-shaven white male in his late thirties. He shakes his head with indecision. The jury is still out.

Diane sits in her office. The others wait, lost for words. Bruce paces. Muppet sits awkwardly, like he's in some sort of pain but can't tell where it emanates from. Spoon has a puzzled look on his face. Bookie has stopped taking bets on what's happened since it's now considered to be in bad taste. It's the second day with no word. Yesterday was excusable, given it was the day after. Today is inexcusable. Suddenly Diane sees Adam walking along the corridor towards them, standing puzzled at the deserted FX desk, wondering where all his colleagues are today. She stands up and shouts over at him to join them.

'Where were you yesterday?' she asks as he enters the crowded office. The others stare at him.

He looks somewhat bewildered. 'I was on a day off.' He looks at his colleagues. 'Bruce knew that.'

'Were you out all day? We tried calling you at home,' she insists. 'Even your mobile didn't work.'

'I didn't take it with me.'

'With you where?' she perseveres. 'Where were you?'

The others stare back like he's some sort of suspect. 'In Germany.'

'Where?' Diane asks.

'I was in Dusseldorf.'

Bruce glares at him. 'That's where bloody Kapital have their HQ! Are you job-hunting?'

'No.' He feels the need to explain and turns to Diane. 'It's that murder thing in the paper we spoke about. Samantha wanted to know more, so I was the one who went over. I vaguely knew the guy who died.'

Diane gives a grin and folds her arms. 'At last we're getting somewhere. So where is she?'

Adam is lost. 'Who?'

'Don't give me "Who?" You know who. Samantha.'

Adam tenses, suddenly excited. 'What about Samantha? What's up with her?'

'She's disappeared,' Diane advises.

'No, she hasn't.'

'How do you know that?'

'I don't know. It's just ... she isn't the type. She must be around somewhere.'

Adam looks at the others in puzzlement, increasingly baffled by events and worried at their hostile stares and defiantly folded arms. Bruce is the first to voice the apparent opinion of many.

'You of all people must know where Samantha is.'

'Why me?' replies Adam.

Spoon points over. 'You two are close. You went to my wedding with her. You're an item.'

Adam wishes he could tell them more. 'No, we're not. We're just good friends. That's all.'

Bruce moves closer to him. 'When did you last see Samantha?'

Adam refuses to answer such pointed questions. He ignores Bruce and instead faces Diane.

'What exactly is happening here?'

Diane composes her thoughts as she places her hands together on the desk.

'You tell us. We had a wild bank party and it went on until very late. I didn't mind if people came in late yesterday as long as they got in at a reasonable hour and made an effort to do some work. We all showed up by mid-morning. One of us even managed to take a day off to sort out our career prospects. Only Samantha never made it in.'

'Have you telephoned her?' asks Adam.

'Give us some credit. We called her on her mobile phone all day. It's switched off, powered down, whatever. We called the home telephone number that we got from HR. There's no answer there either.'

Adam thinks on his feet, remembering his visit to her home and her easy amiable conversation. 'I know her mother lives in Cornwall. Has anyone called her and asked her if she's heard from Samantha?'

Diane nods. 'HR have been calling her mother all today. She's the only next-of-kin that we show in our records. There's no reply. They don't think anyone is home. Short of driving to Cornwall, we're lost.'

'Did you go round to her place in Elephant & Castle?' asks Adam.

'So you know where Sam lives?' asks Muppet, belatedly joining in the conversation. Adam looks at him. Muppet shifts awkwardly in his seat. He seems subdued, less animated than usual.

'What the hell is that supposed to mean?' asks Adam.

'Leave it,' advises Diane. 'Bruce went round to her place. He met Samantha's flatmate, a nurse coming home from night shift. They looked in Samantha's bedroom. Her bed wasn't slept in. It's like Samantha never made it home. But her telephone was trashed. Bruce figured maybe she might have stayed with you at your place.'

'Did he now?' All eyes again turn towards Adam. He shakes his head. 'Samantha didn't stay with me.'

'Tough luck,' Muppet pipes up again. 'What time did you leave the party?'

'What's the point of all these questions?' Adam turns back to Diane. 'Do I really need to answer that?'

'Unless you feel you will be compromised.'

'I left after midnight. I walked up to Marble Arch and got a black cab after I'd spent ten minutes looking.'

Muppet perseveres. 'When did you last see Samantha?'

Adam sighs but feels obliged to answer. 'I don't know. It was close to midnight. I saw her sitting at our table with most of you guys. Next time I looked, she was gone.' He faces Muppet. 'You were there too.'

'Don't get personal. You're the boyfriend.' Muppet shrugs. 'Is there anything else you want to admit?'

Adam feels the urge to whack him in his beer belly. 'I've admitted nothing. If I knew any more, then I'd tell you.' He shakes his head. 'So what happens next?'

'We call the police and tell them that Samantha is officially missing,' Diane advises.

'The police will especially want to talk to boyfriends,' interjects Muppet.

'That's enough.' Diane asserts her authority. 'Get back to the desk and man the telephones.'

They file out of the office and resume their seats in lonely silence, each of them throwing furtive glances at Samantha's empty chair. Trading volumes at the desk are minuscule. The City does sleep after all. Adam is thinking the worst, recalling how much his colleague really knew about the deaths, whether she might have taken some risky sort of initiative. His thoughts race towards the most sinister scenario. He wonders about Henry.

Muppet shouts across. 'There was a call from Trish, Henry Simpson's PA yesterday when you were on your holidays to Dusseldorf. She says you and Samantha and Henry agreed to do lunch when you were at Spoon's wedding. She suggested a time and place. I said no problem. So you're on. Twelve-thirty. West End. Today. Don't be late. Table for three booked but somehow I don't think Samantha will be there.'

Henry is delayed by an appointment at Goldman's and so takes a cab from the Strand. He clock-watches and simultaneously marvels at the cabbie's spatial awareness. They are on the move, down one-ways and mews lanes, tailgating at forty-five m.p.h. with a foot of space on either wing, never conceding an inch of tarmac except to a fellow cabbie, always two streets ahead of the game thanks to the Knowledge. He walks into the Criterion near Eros on cue. His hopes are partly confirmed. He will not be stood up or have to eat alone. This is his opportunity to learn more about the people who may present a latent threat. One target is already sitting alone at a table near the rear of the room and rises to greet him.

'Hi, Henry.'

'Hi. How are you? Glad you could make it. Trish told me she could only leave a message yesterday. Someone said you were on holiday. You away somewhere?'

'Something came up at short notice.'

Henry looks around the room. 'Is Samantha with you? I invited her too.'

'None of us has seen Samantha since the bank's Christmas party two days ago.'

Henry looks concerned, then laughs it off. 'Must have been some party.'

'I was hoping you might know where she was,' his guest challenges him.

Henry's amazed that Adam has the front. He's changed in two months in Mitchell's. He is more confident – aggressive, even. American investment banks have that nasty side-effect. Henry holds his hands up in mock amazement. 'What sort of a question is that? I haven't seen her since the wedding. But if she calls me up looking for a new job, you'll be the first to know.'

'So much for client confidentiality.'

'Let's order. You choose a good wine. It's on me today. We're celebrating. Congratulations.'

'It's a bit premature. I believe you don't get the rest of your recruitment fee until I pass probation.'

'Adam, it's only a matter of time.' Henry peruses the menu. 'So can you give me your impression of Mitchell Leonberg?'

Adam risks all.

'I'm sorry. I don't do impressions.'

Henry stares back, then perseveres.

'I meant, how is work going?'

'You tell me.' Henry looks blank. 'Ask Diane. You see more of her than I do, according to the guys at the desk. She's the one doing my probation review in January.'

Henry smiles. Adam *has* changed. 'I never discuss people with Diane. That would be unprofessional.'

Their food takes an eternity to arrive. Henry is conscious that the restaurant is emptying as other diners settle up and leave. The hands of an Art Deco clock approach two as the main courses arrive. Adam chose the monkfish, Henry the filet mignon. It's so rare that a good vet could revive it. Henry looks up from the blue beef as he chooses his words carefully. 'So what are you doing these days?'

'Like what?' Adam is still confrontational.

'Have you been anywhere interesting recently?' Henry asks.

'I was at a flashy wedding at Royal Tunbridge Wells.'

Henry resists the jibe as he holds his knife in a deliberate manner, with a firm grip and at a precise angle. He's meeting unexpected resistance. 'I was there too. I meant, have there been any work trips. Head office in New York, maybe?'

'I don't think Diane would let me loose in head office.'

Henry's looking at the knife, examining the blade up close, staring around the room to see who's watching. He puts his fork down and surreptitiously runs his right index finger along the knife blade and frowns. He thinks it's not sharp enough for his liking, nor for the meat. He sees Adam staring at him.

'What's the problem?'

'You seem to be taking that meat very seriously.'

Henry is tucking into his filet mignon. Adam watches him carve each thin slice of beef with real precision. The meat is so rare. Henry seems to like it like that, enjoys the flow of blood on the plate as he slices, likes to mop up the blood with the meat before devouring the flesh.

Adam deliberates. 'I was in Dublin. Some weekend.'

He's made the first admission. Time to pursue this. 'The stag. Where did you stay?' asks Henry.

'Merrion Hotel. On Merrion Street.'

'Good location. Right near St Stephen's Green.' Henry watches Adam closely. 'Did you go for a walk outside at all?' He can see some reaction. His guest's appetite for the monkfish wanes before his eyes.

'I spent most of the time in pubs with the rest of the guys.'

It's close to three. The restaurant is almost empty. Adam has downed a bottle of Merlot. They skip dessert. Adam has a coffee. Henry drinks more still mineral water. There is no such thing as a free lunch. Henry waits for the waiter to depart before talking shop. 'You know why I asked you here? I wanna pick your brains. I want you to tell me all about the guys you left behind at Kapital. I want to know which of them needs to move on. Who should I call next?'

'I'm not breaking confidences like that. You'd better cold call them direct, like you cold called me.'

A waiter arrives with a bill on a silver tray. Henry hands over some plastic.

Suddenly Adam volunteers some information. 'Actually, there *is* a vacancy at Kapital now. I heard they're looking for replacement hire for a syndicate banker. Only problem, it's not in London.'

'I do recruitment work elsewhere. Where is the vacancy?'

'Dusseldorf. Ever been there?' Henry nods slowly. 'Terrible tragedy. A guy was murdered.'

'Sorry to hear that. You must have known him well?' asks Henry, treading carefully on the emotions.

'Why do you say that?'

'That's where you went yesterday, wasn't it?'

Adam is stunned. He wonders what else Henry knows – like where Samantha is. 'How do you know that?'

'I know everything about my clients. And I spoke with Diane an hour ago. She told me you were away.' Henry leans forward. He's only a foot away from Adam. 'So what happened in Dusseldorf yesterday?'

'I met the widow. She told me about the murder. And the killer.'

Henry holds Adam's gaze. Stares back in sheer amazement. 'And what did she tell you?'

'Enough.'

CHAPTER TWENTY-FIVE

ST MAWGAN, CORNWALL: 12.15 A.M.

Adam gets the telephone call in the early hours. He's already awake, doing enough worrying for two, when the mobile rings beside his bed. It's a huge relief. He can't sleep afterwards but waits until first light to leave Bruce a voicemail to say he's got food poisoning. He leaves London at the crack of dawn to beat the traffic but encounters tailbacks on the M25, a three-car RTA on the M4 westbound, then successive contra-flows on the M5 southbound near Bristol. He drives at excessive speed on occasion.

He breaks the two hundred-mile-plus trip with five minutes at a BP services out of sheer necessity. He avoids the booming sound systems of yobs in the car park, the company reps in their Omegas and Mondeos, the pervasive smell of fried food and the Formica table tops of the Little Chef. He's back on the road almost immediately, drawing ever closer. On the A30 past Exeter he sits with others in a single lane of cones for thirty minutes, wishing he could be there sooner, watching gangs of Mowlem contractors and foremen admiring their virginal and stationary resurfacing equipment. He sits in the car and fumes at the delay.

He thinks about Samantha as he crosses frosted Bodmin

Moor. She volunteered nothing on the telephone but she's got out of London, miles away from Henry and from Adam's worst fears. Henry has their home addresses on their CVs filed away in his office, but he couldn't possibly know her mother's address.

Samantha never told him how to get to Newquay Airport but he's got an AA map. He passes ominous government hilltop radar installations, then an RAF base, and takes a right after a low railway bridge. He pulls into the car park of the parochial airport terminal and calls Samantha as agreed hours earlier. This time her mobile is powered up. She evidently recognises his mobile number on caller ID.

'I'm here,' he announces. 'Your mobile works this time.'

'Only for you. I'll come and get you.'

Soon he sees a blue Freelander. Samantha sits alone in the front. She jumps out and gives him a huge kiss. They hug for minutes, each feeling immense relief. Samantha wears a green Barbour jacket and faded torn denims and blends into the surrounding tranquillity. She seems fine, at least on the exterior.

'Thank God you're okay,' he says. 'I was so worried about you.'

'Who told you about what happened? Was it the guys at work?'

Adam is surprised. 'They don't know about Henry. How could they? It's our secret.' Samantha doesn't seem to understand. 'The Dusseldorf trip was scary. I thought it would prove that we're wasting our time, but it didn't. Quite the opposite. Henry looks somewhat, a bit, like the suspect. Then yesterday I had lunch with him in the West End and he asked me some leading questions about where I went. I didn't think it could be him, but when I heard you'd disappeared . . . Jesus, I even thought at one stage that he had . . .'

'You mean, the killer might *be* Henry?'

'Yeah, that's why I was so worried. But it can't be him. Can it?'

Samantha slips into her 4WD without offering an answer. Adam follows her down a series of impossible one-way roads and dirt tracks until they both pull up outside a low stone cottage.

'This is where I grew up,' she announces with obvious pride. 'Home.'

'It's wonderful.' He is genuinely impressed. 'Quite a change from a flat in Elephant & Castle.'

'Mum still lives here. And before you ask, she knows about Kerys and is fine with it.'

A kindly sixty-something lady emerges from the front door and crosses the paving stones. She wears several layers of woollen clothing, and is genuinely interested in him and welcoming. Adam is sure Samantha will age as beautifully as her mother. He wonders how much her mother knows about her daughter's life at Mitchell's. The telephone rings inside the cottage. No one moves.

'Shall I get it this time?' her mother asks, turning to Samantha for guidance.

They walk inside. Adam ducks his head below the low exposed wooden cross-beams. Samantha's mother is a serial car-boot bric-a-brac collector. The house has blue delft, copper utensils, earthenware storage jars, wooden carvings, green plants, table lamps, musty books and travel mementoes. She is trying to corner the global market in plump cushions and sofa throws.

'It might be them again,' Samantha advises. 'Listen to it first.'

The three of them stand in the living room, watching an ancient BT answering machine finally kick in with a standard welcoming message. Then a smarmy female voice is audible.

'Mrs Perry, sorry to bother you. This is Belinda from Mitchell Leonberg's HR department. We're trying to locate your daughter who hasn't been at work. Please call me if you get this message. Thanks. Bye.'

'That bloody woman,' retorts her mother.

Adam recognises the voice from the Christmas party. There's

no reaction from Samantha. He reckons she saw nothing of the antics that night. They wait until the line goes dead.

Samantha turns to Adam. 'What are they saying about me in the office?'

'Diane is worried. Bruce too. Muppet seems ... anxious,' he offers, choosing his words carefully.

'You won't tell them that Samantha is here?' asks her mother.

Samantha pulls Adam closer by the arm, urgency in her voice.

'Mum, I want to show our guest around. We'll be back in time for lunch.'

They walk down the garden at the rear of the cottage. Samantha is in wellies but Adam's city shoes are soaked by settled dew in the long grass. The hedges are overgrown, the beds full of weeds and the trees in need of some aggressive pruning. Whatever Samantha thinks, they need a man about the house to fight Mother Nature. A Scottie and a cat gambol ahead, evidently at ease with each other. There's a stone bird bath, a small fountain and a circular granite seat for two at the end of the garden.

'I always come here to think,' Samantha says into the silence.

Adam listens to the sound of nature and takes her hand in his. Conversation seems so much more difficult here. He wonders what has changed.

'Think about what?'

'Danger. Fear. Disappointment.'

Samantha looks back towards the cottage. He uses his intuition.

'What's wrong?' he asks. 'If it's not Henry, then what is it?'

He watches her expression slowly change. She wears a coat but is shaking from the cold. She looks away, past a stable, and out to the open fields. A horse neighs in the distance. Samantha looks at Adam. 'We have a horse. I ride her every day when I'm here. I used to jump at gymkhanas when I was younger.'

'Samantha, I need to know.'

Her mother appears at the doorway. 'Lunch is ready.'

Samantha looks at Adam, kisses him and gets up, her energy renewed. 'Later.'

Lunch is so substantial that it runs late and merges seamlessly into a long afternoon spent by a roaring log fire. Adam desperately wants to talk to Samantha one on one but she crashes out beside him on the sofa and soon slumps onto his shoulder. Her mother stays in the room, one eye on an old Channel 4 black and white movie and another eye on Adam and her daughter. He is too polite to disturb Samantha and also to refuse her mother's second invitation. He stays for tea that appears on cue at seven as the evening news beams in. Samantha's mother stands up, draws the curtains and makes an official announcement.

'It's too late to start a long drive back to London. I'll make up the spare room.'

Samantha is awake and takes the chance to squeeze closer to Adam on the sofa. At last they are alone.

'Samantha, I need to know. What's wrong?' he asks. 'Is it work? Is it Bruce or Diane? Or Henry?'

'It's Muppet.'

'Muppet! What about him?'

'At the party.'

'What about the party?' Adam watches Samantha's face up close. She runs a finger under one eyelid. There's a single tear about to run down her face. She looks away into the embers. Suddenly he sees the light. 'Muppet? You and he were sitting together. You left all of a sudden. He must have gone soon after. He didn't ... you know ... hassle you afterwards, did he?'

Samantha wipes away the tear and regains some composure.

'You're the first person I've told. Not even Mum. I left the hotel before midnight. Got a black cab. Muppet got in too. I told him not to but he came to my house, forced me onto the floor of the living room. I was that close to being raped ... so bloody close ... I was so scared. Never, ever again.'

'Jesus, I should have known. The bastard! I'm so sorry I left you at the party. How did you ...?'

'Tell me. Was he limping in Mitchell's?' Adam nods. 'Good. I gave him an almighty kick in the balls. I sat up all night alone and took the first 6 a.m. train to here.'

'Jesus, you gotta do something about this. Tell Diane. Tell the police.'

She stares into the hearth. 'I can't do that. It'll be his word against mine. The cabbie saw me let him into the cab. I have nightmare visions of investigations, medical examinations, testimony, even a court case.'

'But you have to do *something*.'

'I'm not going after Muppet. I wouldn't bother with such a lowlife. He's so insignificant, so nothing. I'm going after Mitchell's. I'm going after the whole stinking rotten-to-the-core City.'

Adam shakes his head, shocked at her vehemence.

'You'll never beat the system. You'll never work there again.'

'That's okay. I'm not going back to London, except to see Kerys.' Samantha is excited. 'I'm going to teach. I'm going to do an H. Dip. in Bristol. I'll get a temp post in a school or a college near home. Come home for the weekend to Mum. Have Kerys down to stay for long weekends or visit her at her parents' place in Cardiff. It's less money but I'll be happy. So will you help me?'

He nods. 'If I can. How?'

'I'll need someone on the inside in Mitchell's to tell me what's happening there.'

'Like what?'

'I need everything on that scam. It'll be great ammunition for me. What have you found?'

'Not much progress to report. Sorry. I'm half thinking of phoning that German number.'

'You'd better find out more soon. Diane annoyed me so much that I had to tell her of my suspicions.'

'Jesus! What did you do that for? She'll tell Bruce and the others. Now the clock is ticking.'

'I didn't mention you at all. She won't know you suspect too. Adam, hang in there. For me.'

'What about Henry? The evidence is circumstantial but it's there nevertheless. What do I do?'

Samantha rolls her head. 'I was just playing around. I was so bloody bored and upset at work it gave me something to do. But it's ridiculous. Has to be. You and I cannot have been recruited by a serial killer.'

'Sure.' But Adam's not so sure. He's seen that photofit, watched Henry carve rare beef, fielded the loaded questions. Adam already knows where his next trip will be after Christmas. But Samantha's been through too much to give her any more worries. 'Okay. I'll stay clear of Henry.'

'Promise.'

'Promise.'

After more *News At Ten*, Samantha's mother shows Adam upstairs. His room is in the attic, with a small window and a low ceiling. There's a single radiator but it's cold. Adam tests the world's narrowest single bed, with more plump pillows and a bright yellow floral duvet. It's been a long day with too many miles covered and too many words unspoken. He's angry at what Samantha has endured and sad that the only person he can talk freely to at Mitchell's is gone for ever. He's lost a colleague and fears losing a friend.

His mobile on the bedside table hums into action. It's a text message.

'THKS 4 LISTENING. LV SAM!'

Henry is in Selfridges. It's early evening, directly after seasonal drinks for Trish and the other employees of Henry Simpson Associates in a Covent Garden pub. He only downed a succession of disgusting mineral waters so has a clear head and remains completely focused. He is irresistibly drawn to the elevators to Lower Ground and then along the aisles towards the silverware department.

He hates this time of the year. Incessant advice on what to wear to the office party and why not to copy your backside on the photocopier. Branches of Comet and Dixons, Asda and John Lewis, open morning, noon and night. Year-on-year like-for-like retail sales up by miraculous percentages according to the high-street pundits. Endless weekend newspaper supplements on what gifts to buy for sons and daughters, nieces and nephews. If you have any.

There are people everywhere, pushing their way against him en masse. He inhales a tangible sense of communal panic and fear in the tepid air-conditioned atmosphere. The lemmings are impervious to the vicious glances he throws in their direction. He sees the fear in their wide white eyes. They're terrified. They all know that there are only five shopping days left to Christmas. He passes the food hall, seething. Everyone panic-buying food the proletariat never seems to eat during the rest of the year: Norwegian prawns, smoked salmon roulades, asparagus tips and broccoli spears, cheese boards, Belgian pâté – the lot.

It's almost impossible to get through to silverware. He struggles to the counter, enjoying only a lingering glance at the row of letter openers. He knows what he wants. He's seen it here before. Perfect for the well-dressed lady about town. Henry waits to be served, his patience running lower by the minute. Five minutes later an assistant catches his eye.

'Can I help, sir?'

Henry points to the glittering trinkets on display. 'I want to see those ladies' cufflinks.'

The guy insists on opening the cabinet, which takes an age. This fucking shop, at this time of year. It's all gone mad.

Royal Mail announcing their last posting dates sometime in early November like they're going to down tools for December. Extra fluorescent cops on the streets as they enforce parking regulations for three weeks of the year. Incompetent traffic wardens herding shoppers like sheep across zebra crossings on Regent's Street. People who have obviously never heard of plastic or Switch who actually enjoy standing at bank ATMs.

Henry points again. 'I'll take a pair with the dollar and pound signs on them.'

Assholes in the neat suburbs who decorate their home like it's some fucking lighthouse perched upon Land's End or John O'Groats. Queues of Range Rovers and MPVs outside NCP car parks. Adults in Hamley's asking for 'inoffensive' gifts for distantly related children, as if such gifts even exist.

The assistant holds the proffered item. 'A nice choice, sir.' They move off to a cash desk. 'A gift for the lady in your life?' The guy gift wraps them. Henry doesn't object. It adds value. 'Anything else today?'

He's tempted. He could use a letter opener on any one of a number of shoppers inside the store.

'Nope.'

Outside on Oxford Street he hails a black cab with some difficulty.

'Where to, guv?'

'Gimme a minute. Just drive slowly.'

Henry dials on his mobile. Diane answers on the first ring. They speak. She's at home. He hangs up.

'Battersea, please. The Montevetro building. You know it?'

'Who doesn't?'

The cab pulls up at eight o'clock on the south side of the Thames. He gains entry via the videophone and takes the lift. The hall door is open. As he walks in, Diane approaches him. She's wearing a low black silk robe, drawn loosely around her waist. There's a deep v-shaped plunge and as she walks he catches glimpses of her thighs. The lights are down. The only illumination comes from several huge eccelesiastical candles on mantelpieces and side tables. There's a soft smell of incense in the air. He is so ready for sex.

'Happy Christmas. I got you this.' He kisses her and hands over the small gift. She places it unopened on a side table. He moves closer to her. 'You can open it now, if you like.'

'Later.' She raises her eyebrows. 'I didn't think we were exchanging gifts.'

She sits down and crosses her legs, the material sliding off her curves. She's still wearing one of his favourite pairs of heels. They may be unnecessary, yet are essential to the pose. He hopes she wears nothing else.

'It's okay,' he replies. 'You've got time to get me something. There are a few days left to go.'

'I mean, I've done my shopping weeks ago. Everything is packed away. I'm not venturing back out.'

He throws his coat on a chair and sits alongside her. He catches the nuance. 'Packed away for what?'

'I fly tomorrow.'

'Where?'

'Back home, of course. I'm not staying in this damn' city for the next two weeks. I'm back on the sixth.'

'How will I manage?'

'Talk to your wife.'

'I'll have no choice. We're away for a week.' Henry is still transfixed. 'So what's the plan?'

Diane inhales, her breasts rising above the silk. 'A long hot bath, a nightcap and then to bed.'

'Sounds great, shall I run the water?' he asks, once again enjoying this reverse power trip.

'You misunderstand me. My flight is at nine a.m. tomorrow. I'm taking an early night.'

Henry is definitely not catching her drift. 'I find you irresistible tonight.'

'Who wouldn't?' Diane stands up. 'This isn't the time. I'm not in the mood. You should go.'

She leads him back to the hall door like he's on a leash, his coat in her arms. She places a finger on his lips in a bad attempt at a bad kiss. His emotions churn. He wants her now, to throw her up against the wall and take her in that robe. He is sorely tempted but it would be too much. He'd never see her again. The more unobtainable and elusive she is, the more desirable she becomes.

'See you in January, Diane.'

'We'll see. Have a good one. Don't do anything silly.'

CHAPTER TWENTY-SIX

WEST HAMPSTEAD, LONDON NW6:
8.15 P.M.

Adam reverses into a minuscule parking space that was never meant for a Vauxhall Astra. He kills the wheezing engine with minimal bumper damage to the cars on either side as Brian appears from the house.

'Welcome back.' He exclaims and points in horror. 'What's with the motor?'

Adam alights and shakes hands with his ex-flatmate. 'It's the same car.'

'You're still driving this MOT wreck? Where's the flashy bank car you were promised?'

'It's on its way in a few weeks' time.' Adam hesitates. 'I need to pass probation first.'

'But that's a foregone conclusion?'

'I hope.'

Cheryl emerges from the steamy kitchen, wooden spoon and oven glove in hand. She greets Adam like long-lost family, with an enveloping hug and a hearty kiss.

'You look tired. You okay?' she observes.

'Sure. Work is busy. There's so much happening.' Euro scams. Harassment. Insecurity. Murders.

He inhales the wonderful aroma of basted turkey, rich gravy, crisp roast potatoes and green vegetables, all the trimmings as per usual. It's their traditional pre-Christmas feast but different from last year's festivities. Adam is a blow-in visitor from the East End, not a resident who can crash out upstairs afterwards with a full stomach and a sore head before a long lazy day at Kapital. Easy times.

'It's good to be back,' he says as he hands over a decent Chianti from one of Thresher's top shelves. Adam produces his presents as is the custom, plus some Harrods crackers and reliable After Eights for later.

'Great to see you,' Cheryl enthuses. 'Everything's ready. Let's eat.'

Adam and Brian sit at the seasonally decorated candlelit dining table in the one and only living room, waiting for the food to arrive, as only blokes do in such situations. Brian uncorks the red.

'When I called you, I half thought you might bring someone else along. Any joy of late on that front?'

Adam thinks about his meal with Trish, about Samantha, and his illusory hopes. Most of all he thinks about Lisa upstairs.

'I was trying to see someone at work for a while. But she's leaving, moving away.'

'Sorry to hear that.' Brian looks around excitedly, like he's about to break some news. 'Let me tell you something ...' The door swings open. Cheryl has outdone last year's banquet. Brian carves with ease. They eat until Adam turns to Cheryl.

'So what are you doing for Christmas this year?'

She looks over at Brian who appears non-committal.

'We're going to Brian's parents in Edinburgh. It'll be quiet. That's all, I think. And you?'

'Same as usual,' Adam replies. 'Take the train to my parent's place, have a family meal on Christmas Day, my father will make some speech about how I should visit more during the year, how well I am doing so far in my career, although he'll probably choke on the words. He'll say I'm some genius whizz-kid trading billions every day, when in fact I get the coffees in. We'll go for the same tramp in the hills on Boxing Day except that the tramp is getting a bit sick and tired of us at this stage. Then too much cold turkey and reheated pud for a few days, and back to sanity and London by New Year.'

Brian picks up on Adam's voluntary admission. 'So work isn't going that well?'

'It sucks! It's like a demotion. In Kapital, I traded for the bank. In Mitchell's, I only handle client orders. There's also some trading scam at the desk on ECB announcement days. Sorry for the jargon.'

He's not sure they understand. There's an uneasy silence as his hosts look for some upside.

'So how's your new apartment, Adam? We drove by the tower one day. It looks really ... impressive.'

He wishes he could be more optimistic. 'It's fine, but soulless. The place is deserted in the evening. Local transport is non-existent. I have to almost drive to the shops to buy a newspaper.' Then he remembers, as he sits in these tranquill surroundings. 'And I have a neighbour living upstairs who is driving me mad.'

'Go up and complain to him,' advises Brian.

'Trouble is, she's a fit, tall brunette who seems available and eligible.'

'Go up and ask her out, then.'

'I'm waiting for the right moment.'

'Get stuck in, my son.' Brian stands up. 'Who's for some dessert?'

A flaming intoxicating pudding arrives. They eat on, all increasingly aware that there is a pervading silence and that Adam is not the same hopeful person he was three months ago. Cheryl places her hand upon his arm.

'Something else is up, isn't it?' Adam shakes his head. 'If you can't tell us, then who can you tell?'

'Nothing . . .' He stumbles on the word. 'It's too weird, too bizarre. I must be losing it.'

'Tell us?' Cheryl puts down a dessert spoon piled with pudding and brandy butter and leans closer.

'I think . . . I might know a serial killer.' He knows it sounds ridiculous.

'There's no serial killer at large in London.'

'These deaths happen overseas.'

'Jesus!' exclaims Brian. 'Are you serious?' Adam nods. 'Who is it?'

'It might be the guy who got me the job at Mitchell's. And the worst thing about it is I think he knows that I suspect.'

Adam tells them the full unexpurgated details, speaking at speed for ten minutes, exorcising the fear and uncertainty yet feeling guilty to be sharing his burdens with his friends. Cheryl's natural instincts shine through.

'You're in real danger. Go to the police right away.'

'They'll think I'm mad. These deaths happened outside the UK. They won't be bothered about them. I don't want to make a fool of myself and waste their time. I'll go when I'm sure.'

'But how can you be sure?' asks Brian, his appetite apparently diminishing.

'I'm going back to Dublin in the New Year. I want to check out the murder there, somehow.'

'You better take care. Steer clear of this guy at all costs,' advises Cheryl. 'If you need help, ask us.'

Brian has an idea. 'You'd be better off moving back in with us. That way you'll be safer. You don't want to be caught at home alone if you are right about this guy and he gets scared.'

'I'm safer where I am. This address was on my old CV. He doesn't know where I live now. We have security gates and a guard. Thanks, anyway.'

Just before midnight, after the presents have been opened at speed and the last wafer mint has disappeared, Adam says his farewells on the doorstep. It's close to freezing outside. Brian helps him clear the frost from the windscreen using the edge of a credit card to scrape off the icy layers.

'One piece of news I've got to tell you.' Brian looks back inside and knows it's safe. 'We're not staying in Edinburgh over New Year. I've booked a week for two in Dubai. I got time off work for Cheryl. She doesn't know yet. I'm proposing to her on Christmas Eve. I hope and pray she'll say yes. What do you think?'

'She'll say yes,' confirms Adam, shaking his hand. 'Because she loves you. Congratulations, both of you.'

Adam starts his car third time around. He looks at Brian in the rear-view mirror as he waves goodbye. Brian has an average job, a modest income, a car loan, credit-card debts, a rented home and a worsening waistline. But Brian has it all, everything a man can hope for in life. Brian has Cheryl.

Adam doesn't notice the convertible Saab 93 on his tail, its lights dimmed, its solo male driver wondering why he doesn't live at this old address yet confident his new address is just a short drive away.

The five men sit behind a row of pillars in the discreet private dining room of their favourite restaurant off Sloane Square. Bruce booked the table this time last year and reconfirmed twenty-four hours ago to hold the table. Normally *le patron* refuses bookings more than one month in advance but Bruce likes breaking the house rules. The food is Michelin-starred haute cuisine, the cooking done with an ease, grace and simplicity that is immensely attractive to him, like a beautiful girl without make-up. They're wearing their DJs, proper bib and tucker for their annual FX desk Christmas party.

The restaurant interior has an off-white natural wallpaper-weave, dark timber trim, a rust carpet, and an energised, almost fatal-accident-with-a-paint-set wall mural. Among the tables of globe-trotting food lovers and chefs nicking new ideas are several parties of lithe young women who dine. The five traders enjoy this added feature. The room is bathed in a soft white light that bounces off the silver vases, gleaming cutlery and sparkling crystal *objets d'art*. It's spotless, pristine and professional. Waiters go about setting up like eager stagehands before the curtain rises. The maitre d' speaks to them all in fluent French.

There's a rumour tonight that the obsequious *patron*, a former BBC celebrity chef who has since seen sense and lowered his public profile, is in the house. He's an alchemist who turns raw ingredients into pure gold. If they're lucky, he'll visit their select party before the evening is over. He did last year.

Impeccably mannered staff dance around the other tables, explaining everything and constantly pouring wine. A small cup of hot vichyssoise topped with a chive cream is presented on cue, a totally appropriate winter warmer. The large bread basket offers a diverse choice of warm rolls such as malty walnut, olive and raisin. The sommelier brings over the extensive wine list and ceremoniously hands it to Bruce who's seated at the head of the table. He runs an eye over it. The others watch him decide.

'Still quite a good list,' he observes. 'A few new bottles, too.'

'What did we have last year?' asks Muppet.

'I think it was some bottle of red. Decent enough, I recall.'

They all laugh, recalling the red. The sommelier smiles. He remembers the exact vintage. Bruce points.

'We'll start with this.'

The wine waiter returns with a bottle suitably covered in dust. A cobweb wouldn't be out of place. They sit in silence as the bottle is expertly uncorked, allowed to breathe and slowly decanted. Bruce nods in approval. The other glasses are filled and they are left alone as Bruce stands up and clears his throat unnecessarily.

'Gentlemen, here's to another very successful year. How much exactly is it?'

'Twenty point three million bucks in trading revenue as of yesterday,' advises Muppet.

'Excellent. And so much more achieved. We lost that dead weight Lloyd, got a sexy Yank broad instead, and haven't seen Samantha since the night of the Grosvenor party. Thanks to Muppet.'

'And Adam won't be around for much longer,' confirms Bookie. 'I'm offering odds of ten to one.'

'You don't need to offer odds. I'm going to tell Diane to fire him. He'll never get past probation. Then we're rid of him. The only downer was that Kraut Karl losing his nerve and bottling out of providing assistance.' Bruce raises his glass. 'Don't worry, guys, we'll find someone else on the inside of the ECB soon enough.'

'Perfect. Here's to the Gang of Five. Long may we reign.' Cable Guy raises his full glass.

'Why didn't we invite Diane?' asks Bookie.

Muppet glares back. 'A bloody woman at our annual dinner? Leave it out.'

The first bottle is emptied before the five starters arrive. It's nothing extravagant, just the Scottish lobster poached in bouillon with creamed guacamole, the carpaccio of pigeon, the layered terrine of foie gras and ham knuckle with aspic, the warm salad of pig's trotters and sweetbreads, and the crispy scallops, grilled asparagus with a sweet-and-sour vinaigrette. Basic fare, really. Much like Mitchell's staff canteen.

They order two more bottles for the main courses. They're nothing fancy, just the roasted monkfish tail cooked with baby spinach, the shining silver fillet of sea bass with basil leaves, steamed new potatoes, celeriac purée, baby pak choi, crème fraiche and caviar sauce, the grilled fillet of red mullet on an eggplant and ratatouille base, the slowly braised pork belly with spices, and the fillet of Aberdeen Angus with baby artichokes, new season girolles, and a gratin mix made from bone marrow. Best to stick to what they know.

They order a dessert wine well before the desserts arrive. They're still nothing fancy, just the caramel ice cream rolled in chocolate with a demerara gauze wafer, the caramelised pineapple, the unmoulded crème brûlée surrounded by slices of candled apple, the orange tarte Tatin and the raspberry souffle.

The coffees come with a dozen coloured meringues served in quaint pottery bowls. It's well past midnight as the maitre d' arrives with the bill. They like the way he carries the piece of paper folded upon a silver tray at the end of an extended right arm. Bruce watches the tray for a while, unfolds the paper slowly, eyes it casually and smiles.

'What's the damage?' asks Muppet. 'Give us a clue.'

'Cheaper than last year.' Bruce invites the maitre d' to return within earshot. 'There's been some mistake.'

The maitre d's about to go into spasm, as if his entire culinary career is on the line. His face reddens.

'A mistake, sir?'

'You forgot to charge us for the damn' food.' They all laugh around the table, puffing on cigars.

Le patron suddenly hoves into view, looking much older in person than on his last TV series for the Beeb.

'No mistake, gentlemen. My compliments. I appreciate the repeat visit. Could I interest you in a reservation for next year?'

Bruce is enjoying the fawning attention as the pseudo-celebrity turns eager commercial weasel.

'We'll be back. Free food, eh? What a wonderful find this place is.'

His platinum card is on the tray. *Le patron* is happy. They laugh and chat until the maitre d's return. Bruce adds one per cent service and signs with his customary flourish much loved by American Express.

They imbibe amid the accumulating cloud of cigar smoke, enjoying the heady decadent atmosphere and the memories of another stellar year of global foreign exchange trading. The bow ties that took an age to knot properly are slowly unravelled. Top dress-shirt buttons are loosened. Taxis are ordered but no one dares to ask the party to leave. It's well past two a.m. as they stumble out to the row of five black cabs waiting with the meters already running for an hour on the kerbside. Bruce shouts to Muppet.

'Now keep your hands off Samantha tonight, if you can find her. 'Cause none of us can find her.'

Muppet is completely pissed. 'Call me a cab. Call me a cab,' he shouts at the others.

'You're a cab. You're a cab,' the others insist in unison.

Muppet opens the door of the first cab but can no longer stand the tension.

'Come on, Bruce, tell me the fucking damage. I need to know.'

Bruce clambers inside his own cab and turns to them all before he closes the rear door.

'The first bottle of Chateau Petrus '45 was twelve grand. The second bottle of '46 was ten grand. The '47 was twelve. The dessert wine nine. All quite good years, I thought. Much like this year, in fact. Roll on a most excellent bonus day in January, gentlemen.'

Henry and Amanda sit on the small patio overlooking the resort. It should be idyllic but it's not. The temperature is in the low sixties. There's a cool onshore breeze they don't need. They haven't seen the sun for two days and the overhead canopy is unnecessary. The crescent beach at the foot of the hill is almost deserted save for the reliable Germans. The grey sea offshore is choppy and unwelcoming.

Off to the left the diesel engines of jaded trucks rev as they carry rubble and topsoil up the steep inclines. Irregular blasts emanate from the next valley as builders dynamite sheer cliffs to knock up another cheap sun-kissed apartment block to be flogged by aggressive timeshare touts on commission to vulnerable OAPs taking their daily constitutional along the burger, eggs and chip butty-infested 1970s promenade.

'What's wrong with you?' Amanda asks, peering over at his plate.

Henry pushes his knife and fork around another damp lifeless salad that she unfortunately threw together. It's turkey and ham but it's cold. It's not the same as oven-roasted turkey and crumbed ham, roast potatoes, braised celery and broccoli, gravy, cranberry sauce, English mustard and all the trimmings. His serotonin levels are still low. He needs more sunshine.

'You know I don't eat much in a hot climate.'

'It's not that hot,' she observes.

He hasn't enjoyed a Christmas meal since they bought this desirable one-bedroomed apartment with kitchenette in an exclusive Gran Canaria enclave; ten minutes' walk up a then sparsely populated hill. Others in the complex moved on to bigger and better things. Their holiday home is now unmistakably downmarket. Two ugly kids from a few apartments away run around the pool semi-naked as their lobster-red parents yell and swear at them in harsh Glaswegian accents. They scream at the top of their voices. Henry sighs.

'Jesus ... some of the fucking people around here ...'

'Relax, Henry,' his wife advises.

Puerto Rico is unable to stem the tide of the charter yobs with their Man Utd away strips, Adidas baseball caps, shaven heads, tattooed muscles, large wives, larger kids, boxes of wine and six-packs of lager. Air 2000, Britannia and the others ruined the island by flying them over weekly in their thousands. Henry sat beside a huge prison offi-cer and his wife plus three teenage brats on the way out last weekend. By the end of the four-hour flight to hell, he reckoned the guy worked on the wrong side of the prison bars.

'How can I relax with all this noise?'

He sees Amanda looking at the street urchins, perhaps wistfully.

'They're only children.'

She's broken the golden rule. They never mention children. He thinks about what he could do if he had his briefcase, his black leather gloves and his nine-inch blade, how he could shut them up permanently and how he's sorely tempted to seek closure. Henry likes children. Only he couldn't eat a whole one.

'We gotta sell up soon. This place is going downhill every year.'

'I like it here. It's a home from home.'

'I'm not coming here next Christmas,' he states defiantly, putting down his fork for the last time.

'You say that every year.'

He downs his glass. Even the local mineral water sucks. 'This year, I mean it.'

'And what are you going to do? Sit at home in Islington on your own with a Tesco takeaway?'

'Suits me.'

They finish lunch, the conversation rapidly dwindling. Christmas is for children. It says so on the television. Without children, they get out of London and pretend that Christmas doesn't happen.

'I'm taking a siesta for a few hours,' Amanda says as she unnecessarily stacks the two plates inside. 'Why don't you get out for a while? Go for a walk. See a few new faces. Make some friends.'

Years ago he used to walk to the town centre and the beach. Now he hates the place, hates the commercial centre with its crap souvenir shops, hates the top-tier open-air restaurants with four courses for a tenner, hates the smell of grease and fat, hates the sight of Lineker's Bar and Molly Malone's, hates the African women who accost tourists for money, hates the concrete minigolf, hates every fucking thing about this fucking place that he just happens to have sunk a hundred grand into more than a decade ago.

'I'm going to do some reading,' he advises.

'You have anything left to read?'

'Don't worry about me. I'll be fine on my own. I could do with some peace.'

He sits alone in the uncomfortable plastic seat until he hears the bedroom and bathroom doors closing inside the apartment. Then it goes quiet. The kids go inside their apartment. There's no else around. It's safe. He walks to the edge of the patio, to where the cracked uneven flagstones meet the dying cacti plants and parched grass patches. There's a small unkempt rockery. The biggest granite stone in the middle eases sideways to his touch. He takes the plastic wallet with the red hexagonal logo from underneath the rock, wipes grains of dirt off the cover, looks back inside the apartment and sits down.

The wallet is credit-card size and comes from some freebie customer promotion in the HSBC Bedford Street branch three years ago. There are four clear plastic double-sided holders inside. It's big enough to hold eight credit cards, if you want it to use it like that or are sad enough to possess eight credit cards.

The contents are in strict chronological order. He runs through the plastic. It's better than thumbing the pages of any book. There's a BA boarding card from a flight to Helsinki three years ago. Then a card from Sabena from a trip to Brussels months later. There's a stub from a flight two years ago to Amsterdam with KLM. Then a stub from last year's trip to Madrid with BA. He looks at the cards, remembering the circumstances, visualising the scenes, sensing the atmosphere, reliving the climax.

He takes out his wallet from his back pocket, extracts two pristine boarding cards from the wad of tawdry euro notes. There's a BA stub from Dusseldorf and one stub from Dublin. He remembers the names gleaned from the newspapers. He inserts the cards but his satisfaction is tinged with regret. He didn't bring the boarding card from Luxembourg because events there didn't work out as planned. That failed night still weighs on his mind. And the fact that someone working at an FX trading desk in the City might know too much. It's a risk too far. Henry dislikes risk. He prefers the cut and thrust of the City.

JANUARY

CHAPTER TWENTY-SEVEN

CANARY WHARF, LONDON, E14: 1.15 P.M.

It's the New Year, a clear crisp dawn in the City of London, maybe even a new beginning at Mitchell Leonberg. The FX desk is back in business. The others drift out for a long lunch. Samantha has telephoned HR to say that she is ill in Cornwall and a doctor's cert to prove it is already in the post. Muppet says there is an unconfirmed rumour that she has tendered her resignation and she's on some sort of gardening leave, that is paid leave at home. Adam recalls the state of her mother's garden. Samantha will be busy.

Adam sits alone, pondering much over a lazy holiday period spent in Faversham. He worries about his job security, the upcoming bonus, the next ECB interest rates announcement day. Most of all he worries about the photofit from Dusseldorf and Henry's Air Miles statement. Muppet ambles up to him.

'Natalia in Dusseldorf sends her fondest personal regards to you,' he mocks. 'She wants to know how your top-secret investigation is going. What sort of investigation is she talking about, do you reckon?'

'I don't know. When did you see her?'

'I spoke to her on a big euro / dollar trade yesterday. She sounds damn' hot on the phone. Is she?'

'Too hot for you.' Adam kills the conversation.

They know all about Adam at the desk. Jesus! His New Year's resolution is to be proactive, seize some sort of initiative in the myriad issues. He knows what has to be done. First he makes a telephone call to Dublin for his upcoming trip.

Next he has to tell Diane what makes the desk tick. Samantha dropped the hint to her. He has to pursue the matter. Diane's only been in London for a few months. It's a risk but there is something to uncover and if he's right, then it will make him. Now is the optimal time. He walks over to her office.

'Can we talk?'

She looks up from a half-eaten sandwich. He thinks it's a crayfish and rocket salad from Pret-à-Manger. Bad timing on his part. 'Why not?'

He closes her door and sits down opposite. She wipes her full lips carefully with a paper napkin. It's vaguely seductive until the residue of red lip-gloss marks the napkin like blood on white cotton.

'Did you have a good break back in the US?' he asks.

'You haven't come in here and closed the door to ask me a question like that?' she replies.

He's already regretting his new resolution – he's in uncharted territory, unsure about the immediate impact that his knowledge will have on his boss. He searches in vain for the right words to break the news. 'There's no easy way to say this ... but I have to tell you. What I mean to say is—'

Diane interjects, her hand held upwards. 'I know what this is about.'

'You do?' Such relief.

She nods and smiles back unnervingly. 'You want to resign. I saw it coming. I understand.'

He stares back, stunned, completely nonplussed. 'What makes you think that?'

'Because you're struggling here.'

'I'm still learning the job. I'm here to stay at Mitchell's. I'm not resigning.'

'Oh.' Her eyes linger on the sandwich, then on Adam. He senses that she wants to eat, to do anything else but engage in this conversation. 'So what do you want to tell me?'

'Like I said, this is not easy, but like Samantha mentioned, there's a scam going on at the FX desk.'

There's silence. Diane takes a leisurely bite of fresh crayfish and mayo, pushing a trailing rocket leaf past her lips, killing time that now drags eternally. She swallows a full mouthful very slowly, then stares back. 'A scam. You too? Are you sure? That's a brave thing to say.'

Adam wishes now he hadn't walked into the lions' den. She has turned the tables on him in an instant. He worries about his future. That's why she's a First Vice-President and why he's a junior gofer still on probation. He nods reluctantly. 'I'm ninety-nine per cent certain.'

'Have you spoken to Bruce about this?'

Adam looks outside. Bruce is still on lunch. She can't call him in. Adam has timed this well.

'He's part of the problem. I think he's the guilty party.'

'That's a hell of a serious allegation to make.' Diane is no longer eating. She pushes the curling sandwich crusts aside. 'Why wait until now to tell me?'

'I wanted to be sure first. Otherwise I'd feel stupid.' Diane stays silent. Adam is puzzled. She's not really that interested. 'Don't you wanna know about the scam?'

It's as if she already knows the details. But she couldn't possibly. She nods slowly. 'Go ahead.'

Adam points at a printout of the monthly desk profits. 'These are the spikes in the profits on the days of any ECB interest rate changes. These big spikes of several million dollars' profit don't happen in other banks. It's all so different to when I was in Kapital. They only happen here because Bruce knows the outcome of the rate decision before it's officially announced.'

'Where did you get this?' Diane asks, touching the page momentarily, soiling it with mayonnaise.

'From Samantha. She helped me uncover it. She had the first suspicions when Lloyd was here.'

Diane sits back in her desk and wipes her long dagger-like fingers with the napkin.

'How is Samantha these days? You met her recently?'

'I saw her at Christmas time in her mother's place in Cornwall.'

'Is she well?'

'Not really.'

'So you and Samantha are our two little detectives at the desk? You two are as thick as thieves. First it's some murders, then this wild idea. What else did you imagine out there?'

It's not the best metaphor. Diane hasn't reacted positively to his news. Adam is disappointed. 'Don't you want to know how the scam works?' he perseveres.

'Go on.'

'A guy in Germany calls Bruce on his mobile phone ten minutes before the interest rates announcement. He must work in the ECB. The desk then goes long or short the euro in size depending on the inside information. They can't lose.' Adam sees her reaction. She's half-thinking about returning to the remains of the sandwich. 'Aren't you shocked?'

'Is there any evidence of this telephone call?' she asks.

'One day the guy called Bruce on a desk line. That call is on our trading tapes. And I even know the telephone number of the guy in Germany.'

'You've listened to the tapes?' she asks sharply.

'Samantha did.'

'That requires management authorisation. I never signed for that. How did she manage it?'

'She conned Bruce into it. He let her go down to ITS with Muppet. She says the call is damning.'

'Who else knows about this alleged scam?'

'Just me, Samantha and you. And Bruce, of course. He's known since day one.' Adam points. 'I think that some of the others out there know too. Probably Muppet. What do we do?'

'Leave it with me.' Diane takes the sandwich and dumps it into the bin under her desk, instantly regretting the action since her office will stink of rancid crayfish by late afternoon. 'I'll decide how we handle this in order to minimise any possible damage to the firm.'

'That's a weight off my mind.' Adam gets to his feet. 'You'll tell someone about it today?'

'Sure.' She catches his drift. 'I'll tell Horowitz in head office.'

Lisa Taylor deliberately yawns twice from experience to regain her hearing as the British European BAE 146 whisper jet descends to Mother Earth. Outside the starboard porthole she can see the gleaming towers of Canary Wharf, the old wharves and rows of pointing dockside cranes, the new red-brick Wimpey and Barratt mass housing estates, the calm waters of the Royal Docks, her Barrier Point home, and finally City Airport. After a firm landing she breaks the rules of international air travel and rises out of her front seat while the jet is still in motion. She grabs the PA.

'Ladies and gentlemen, welcome to London City where the local time is twenty past three. Please remain in your seats with your seat belts fastened until the captain has brought the plane to a complete standstill. Thank you for flying with us today. We hope to see you again soon.'

She has it verbatim. Angie, a mother of three from Chiswick and the cabin supervisor with eight years' service, stands up and also watches the rows of subdued solo suits and tetchy timid tourists.

'Any talent out there today?' she asks her colleague.

Lisa recalls the short flight. Serving the tea and coffee along the aisle is like walking down a catwalk of leering males. She hates those who lean into the aisle and brush up against her hips.

'Nope,' she replies without any hesitation.

Angie looks down the aisles of groomed heads to the very far end of the fifty-seater jet.

'What about 3D?'

'Too old.'

'7C?' she asks optimistically.

'Too fat.'

'9B?' she asks encouragingly.

'Too married.'

'12A?' she asks despairingly.

'Too much like a criminal.'

There is no welcoming airbridge. The engaged captain performs the required U-turn to position the plane for the outward journey back to Europe. Angie perseveres with her endeavours.

'Some of the girls are meeting up near Piccadilly at eight tonight. Are you going?'

'God, no. I'm shattered. These six o'clock pitch-black winter departures are wearing me down. Anyway, I have a guest to look after. Maybe next time.'

'You gotta make more of an effort,' Angie sighs. 'How else will I find Mr Right for you?'

'All in good time, Angie. And I'm making progress of my own.'

They rock to a sudden stop. The suits rush to power up their mobiles and to deplane first.

'Of course ... you have your mystery man. The one that none of us have met yet.'

'*I* haven't even met him yet. Not properly.'

They drift into automatic farewell mode, smiling successive goodbyes at the alighting passengers, most of them too busy to utter a civil acknowledgement in reply. The half-full airplane,

320

a blessing for any aircrew, empties in a few minutes. They're alone at the top of the steps to the jet.

'So is Mystery Man also interested?' asks Angie.

'Might be. Hard to tell.'

'Does he have a name?'

'Adam. He introduced himself in the lift.'

'What's Adam like?'

'Nice. Young. Smart. Interesting. Polite. Reserved.'

'Looks like you'll have to make the first move.'

'Isn't that always the way with men?'

'Is Adam available?'

'Not sure. I think he lives on his own like me. But I saw him with a girl one night. Maybe he's taken.'

'Pity. Where's he from? Any accent?'

'Hard to tell. Maybe London. South-East, at least.'

'Is Adam a man of means? Could he keep you in the style you wish to become accustomed to?'

'If he owns an apartment like that, then yes. But I doubt he does. I've seen his Vauxhall Astra.'

'Would Adam make a good father?'

'Gimme a break. All I know is that we have compatible body parts.'

'But you must remember the downside. It says in the Bible, Adam came first.'

Lisa exits the plane with the rest of the crew. Inside the terminal they go their separate ways. She walks to the short-term car park, wondering if male eyes would linger on her less if she didn't have a smart sky-blue stewardess's uniform, high heels, black stockings and all-round careful grooming.

The drive home takes less than ten minutes off-peak. The location is perfect. She could never endure a long commute from the suburbs to somewhere like Heathrow or Gatwick. His Vauxhall is parked in his space. He must be still at work, wherever that is, at this time of the day. She makes for the lifts but can't resist a look inside his car. It's clean inside. No bags or rubbish. Just a brolly on the back seat and a UK road map on a seat, open on a page for the south-west. There are no leads to sate her growing curiosity. She wonders what her next move is in the relationship that simply doesn't exist.

Henry sits alone at his desk in his office. He's thinking about damage, the sort of damage he can inflict on people, Diane. Maybe Adam. Even Amanda. But Trish suddenly barges in, evidently excited.

'I'm back,' she announces.

'So I see. How was Dublin?'

'Best time ever. Better than my wildest dreams.' She's surely overdoing it. 'And you?'

'The Canaries was the same as ever. But it beats London. I feel more energised.'

She can hardly contain herself. 'I got some news,' she advises. 'Big news.'

Henry looks up from the remnants of junk post and rubbish CVs received over the Christmas period. Trish beams as she takes her left hand from behind her back and holds it out.

'This is it.' There's a gold engagement ring on her index finger. It's a decent sparkler, with at least a few diamonds. 'Patrick proposed to me on Christmas Eve. I accepted. Of course.'

Henry stands up and gives her a hug and a kiss on the cheek, wondering about the implications.

'Congratulations.'

'We'll be as happy as you and Amanda. Married! And I'm moving back to Ireland.'

He is aghast at the prospect. 'You're leaving me all alone? How will I manage?'

'You'll manage. You'll get another good temp.'

Henry knows he won't. He doesn't like unscripted change. He dares to inquire further.

'So when are you leaving London?'

She looks guilty. 'Patrick says, why wait? He's got an apartment for two in Christchurch in the heart of the city. It's perfect. I can't wait to move in with him. I'm going back this weekend.'

It's way too sudden. 'You can't leave me with that sort of notice.'

'I checked with the agency this morning. I'm still on a week's notice. So that's what I'm doing.'

Henry has to start recruiting a replacement this week. He hates being on the receiving end of those fucking amateur recruitment agencies. But Trish has done a great job over the past two years. It was good while it lasted. Maybe it's for the best. He's doing some lateral thinking.

'Have you booked a flight to Dublin?' She shakes her head. 'How about I get you your last-ever flight home on my Air Miles, for old time's sake. But one-way this time. How's that?'

'Henry.' She leans forward and reciprocates his earlier kiss. 'You're the best boss anyone ever could have. I'll take the BA flight from Gatwick this Saturday evening. Because on Friday evening you, me and the others will be having the best ever night out in London.'

Trish leaves to tell the associates outside the news. Henry tries to make the call immediately before he forgets. His BA gold card is somewhere at home in his luggage so the number is not to hand. He quickly sifts through his in-tray and finds the most recent statement from Air Miles. He dials the number shown and waits in a queue of calls. He hates bloody waiting like this.

The tape plays on. Thank you for calling Air Miles. Please hold. Estimated waiting time five minutes. Your call is important to us. Like hell it is. If his call were important then they'd fucking answer it first time. He is distracted by the statement. He surveys the list of flights he took. Madrid, Dusseldorf. Dublin. Happy memories. His thoughts drift away.

He's about to hang up and try later when a limp male voice comes on the line from some godforsaken warehouse in some exotic suburb like Hatfield or Hounslow.

'I want to book a flight from Gatwick to Dublin,' Henry advises. He reads out his membership number, gives the departure date as this Saturday and Patricia Sweeney as the passenger name.

'So you are making a reservation for another passenger, sir?' the limp voice asks.

'Is that a problem?'

Henry holds the statement page in his hand, admiring the font, style and clarity of its content.

'We have rules to prevent abuse, sir. The passenger has to be either you, a relation or a spouse.'

'Patricia is my partner,' he lies. 'She still uses her maiden name.'

Henry examines the creases in the A4 page, allowing the page to fold like it's in an envelope.

'When is the return date, sir?'

'It's one-way.'

The top of the page folds over. Henry sees the reverse side. He sees a handwritten 208 telephone number.

'How do you want to pay for the taxes?'

Henry doesn't hear the question. He recognises the handwriting and the black pen. The telephone number is in Trish's hand. His attention span is waning.

'Hello?'

'Amex.'

He wonders if she scribbled it on the back in a rush, but the writing looks unhurried. He thinks that he recognises the number. The first four digits of 7080 are somehow familiar.

'That's all booked, sir. We'll send it to your office address. Have a nice day.'

'Bye.' Henry is miles away. Literally. He's uneasy. There's one sure way to check out the telephone number. He dials it. It rings once. He waits for an answer. He'll hang up immediately. There's a high-pitched whine. It's not a telephone number, it's a fax number. Of course. He's seen Trish send faxes before, seen how she writes the destination number on the reverse of the page, places it face down on the tray, reads it aloud, keys in the number simultaneously and hits send. Suddenly he wonders if she has faxed this page.

He's certain that he calls someone with a 7080 in their number. Sure that it has to be a client. He mentally rehearses his blue-chip client list. Goldman's, UBS, SBC, HSBC, Morgan, Citi, BOA, Paribas, Deutsche, Mitchell's. Yes, it's bloody Mitchell's! But who . . .

There's no need to revert to the Rolodex. He takes out Diane's business card from his wallet. The first four digits of her direct line are 7080. He reads the fax number at the foot of the card. Then again to make sure. It's the same damn' fax number. Trish has faxed his Air Miles statement to Diane Rubin at Mitchell's.

Henry debates the merits of calling Trish into his office and grilling her, then decides there's nothing to be lost. What's the worst that she can do at the questioning? Resign on the spot? Hardly. She appears immediately when summoned. He holds up the single page as evidence.

'Did you fax my Air Miles statement to Mitchell's?'

She takes the page, sees the number on the back and nods slowly.

'Yeah, I did. You're not mad at me, are you? It was my idea to send it. They needed it.'

'Why did Diane Rubin need to see my Air Miles statement?' he asks.

Trish stands in front of him, growing more puzzled at the line of questioning.

'Diane Rubin? It wasn't her. It was the guy we placed there who requested it. Adam Lewis.'

It's the FX desk's shared fax. Henry grips the statement and tries to remain calm.

'Why did Adam want to see it?'

'He needed to know if you flew out of London on a certain day. The statement proved you did.'

Henry's trying not to lose it but it's not easy. He can see huge ramifications here. Massive downside.

'Why the hell did he need to know that?'

'It was for a bet at the desk. Someone thought they saw you in an airport, I think. Don't get so excited about it. What's the harm?' She turns to leave him. 'Is that all?'

'Yeah. That's all,' he says slowly, knowing she's seen another side of her boss today. It's just as well that she's leaving.

Henry sits alone, staring at the incriminating statement, wondering how much Adam knows about his recent travels to European capitals, increasingly certain that he already knows too much.

CHAPTER TWENTY-EIGHT

BARRIER POINT, LONDON, E16: 6.40 P.M.

Adam is in the ground-floor entrance lobby, cleaning out the letter box for 1205, when he sees it in his hand. Amongst the Vodafone bill, the Barclays account statement and some junk mail from NTL and Sky, there's an envelope addressed to another apartment. It's the sort of error easily made by an early-morning Royal Mail employee with a poor attention span and thousands of letters to deliver. It's a plain white envelope with her address neatly typed in the centre. He knows her surname now. It's Ms Lisa Taylor. Not Mrs. Progress.

He waits for the elevator. The simplest option is to push the envelope into the letter box for 1305. But this is his excuse to make a move. He'll deliver it in person and must do it now or he'll bottle out of the task. She'll take the envelope and thank him and they'll exchange a few more words. She'll think that it's odd if he delivers the letter but he'll say that he only saw her envelope when he got out at twelve and it was easier to go up one floor than back to the ground. He selects thirteen in the elevator and rehearses the conversation. He can't remember whether her VW Beetle was in the car park. He wonders if she'll be there as he knocks on her door.

'Yes?' from inside.

'Lisa ... I've got some post for you – I think.'

It's not what he rehearsed. She'll be expecting a postman in a uniform when she opens up.

'Hang on a minute.'

He hears the door being unlocked. He's amazed she doesn't want to ask him more questions from the safety of the apartment. He wonders if she is alone inside or if she has protection. Suddenly she's standing in front of him. He's never had such eye contact before. She seems smaller standing on the carpet, but he looks down and sees that she's barefoot, maybe about to put on a pair of shoes. She looks well, her hair gathered back, some light make-up, dark trousers and loose top, some gold jewellery. It's as if she's about to go out somewhere on a hot date.

'Hi, Adam.' She holds out a hand. 'That for me?'

He feels the overpowering need to explain.

'It was in my box.' She watches him up close, smiling. 'I noticed it among my mail when I was coming up in the elevator.'

'That's good of you.' He thinks it's all over. 'Come in for a moment,' she invites.

Hers is an apartment identical in its layout to his but nonetheless very different. His is barren, without character, untouched since the day his pushy landlord gave him the key. Hers has ochre walls, cream curtains, soft table lamps, houseplants that live, cushions on a burgundy three-piece. On the wall there are modern prints and gilt-framed mirrors. She has taste. These are freshly cut flowers. She's a girl.

'Nice place.'

'Thanks.'

'You own or rent?' he asks.

He regrets the material question. Lisa sits down on the sofa. Another invitation of sorts.

'Rent. My landlady did all the work. Who can afford to buy these days? And you?'

'I'm renting, too.'

She holds the envelope, wondering whether it's important enough to open. He's on the sofa.

'It's good of you to visit. Neighbours in London usually never talk to each other.'

'I know the feeling.'

He hears heavy footsteps on the beech floor outside. Adam turns as a guy enters the room.

'Who's our visitor?' the guy asks.

Lisa gets to her feet and stands beside the twenty-something guy. He's in a smart jacket and open-necked shirt, stands six-foot plus, has jet-black gelled hair and a great shave on sallow skin. He exudes confidence and presence. She takes the guy's hand in hers.

'It's Adam from downstairs. This is Mike.'

They shake hands. An awkward pause. Adam is shattered. He knows it's time to go.

'Looks like you're off out somewhere. I won't delay you.' He wants to ask her to drop down sometime but worries that Mike might not take too kindly to the impromptu invitation.

'We're only going out for a meal,' says Lisa looking at the watch on her slim wrist. 'Don't worry. If I ever have any post for you, I'll bring it down.'

The happy couple ride the elevator down to ground level. Adam trails down one flight using the emergency stairs. His hopes and aspirations sink as fast as the plunging elevator.

Samantha negotiates midday tailbacks and broken traffic lights at Elephant & Castle and reverses her mother's Freelander into the empty space nearest to the main door. Kerys hears the diesel engine and appears from inside their basement flat. She wipes away a tear.

'I've missed you so much,' she says as she offers a huge welcoming embrace.

'Me too,' admits Samantha as she reciprocates. They kiss meaningfully.

'Thanks for all those long telephone calls. It helped me make up my mind.'

'My mobile bill will be a world record this month. How is your job application going?'

'Early days. I put in for the transfer to a hospital back home. It's closer to Cornwall. It'll be fine.'

'You're always welcome in Cornwall. But you and me, we've both had enough of London.'

Inside the flat, her bedroom is exactly as she left it on that fateful night. Kerys remembers.

'It seems ages since you were here. What happened on the night of that party?'

'You don't want to know. It wasn't the turning point. I wanted to leave London long before.'

It takes them an hour to pack cardboard boxes with artefacts and black plastic bags with clothes. Samantha stops suddenly. That last party dress hangs in the wardrobe. She removes everything else and leaves the one remaining garment, a long black number. Kerys looks over as Samantha closes the door.

'You've forgotten one dress inside.'

'I haven't,' advises Samantha. 'Throw it out.'

They break for mugs of coffee and Jaffa cakes but finish the job by early afternoon. Samantha closes the swing door of the Freelander with difficulty. 'That's it. All done. Thanks for the help.'

'Stay a while longer. You've got plenty of time to drive back to Cornwall,' implores Kerys.

'I have to make one more stop before I can hit the M4 west. I gotta go.' She sees Kerys wipe away another tear. 'See you next weekend at home. Good luck with the move. I'll call later when I get home. Miss you loads.'

Samantha drives east along the river, breezes past the security guards at Canary Wharf with an easy smile and parks in the Mitchell's staff car park, courtesy of an advance telephone call to HR. She walks through reception in jeans, sure that no one will recognise her. She rides the glass elevator and avoids looking across at her old desk before she alights on the deep-pile executive floor. The same plummy-voiced HR manager ·takes her to the same office for her official exit interview.

'I'm so sorry that you've resigned. I guess it happens to us all eventually,' Belinda empathises. Samantha restrains herself, certain that this faithful corporate employee will be at Mitchell's until they carry her out in a box. The HR guru continues, 'There are forms to sign. Then we're done.'

'Fine by me. The quicker the better.'

First to come across the desk is a letter of resignation dated today. Samantha signs. The HR guru produces another official form and scribbles some details on the front. 'This is a questionnaire. I need to know why you have resigned from Mitchell's. You choose a reason. I tick a box.' ·

'What are the choices?' asks Samantha.

'There are a few. To join a competitor, to join a non-competitor, to move overseas, family reasons, to pursue a career break. And then there's Other.'

'So, I guess I'm Other.'

'Excellent.' The guru ticks the last box. 'I need some narrative. What sort of Other is it?'

'Do you have a box there for sexual harassment and dis-crimination?'

The HR guru stares back. 'This is a form for head office. I need a proper reason.'

'I told you. Write it down.'

'I can't write that down.'

'I'd say no one in New York ever reads these forms. Write it badly, if you're so afraid.'

'Sexual harassment and discrimination is a very serious alle-gation.'

'You've changed your tune,' notes Samantha. 'Why didn't you listen to me last year?'

'Harassment is a matter of perception and discrimination is notoriously difficult to prove in the workplace.'

'I was subjected to a barrage of lewd and obscene comments and jokes. That's harassment. I had the same job title as Adam Lewis yet I was paid ten thousand less than he was. That's discrimination.'

'How do you know how much he was paid?'

'I asked him. We're good friends.'

'Take my advice and forget about it. Move on in your life. Do you have any career plans?'

'Only one. I'm never going to work in an investment bank again.'

The guru sighs, writes something illegible, signs the form with a jaded flourish and stands up defiantly. 'Sorry it didn't work out for you. Goodbye.'

'It won't be that easy for you. Or Mitchell's. We'll be meeting again soon.'

'I doubt it very much.'

'I'll see you in an employment appeals tribunal. I'm taking an action. I have legal advice.'

The guru fakes a smile. 'You can try. Many have failed before. We won't meet again.'

Samantha turns as she reaches the door and clenches a fist. 'See you in court.'

Henry sits in Lionel Roberts' plush CEO's office on the top floor in Bedford Street. It's their third such recent meeting but this time they are not alone amongst the faux-Impressionists bought by the yard. Alongside is Henry's legal adviser, an experienced American securities lawyer called Brent, as in crude oil. Henry found Brent a mega-role in UBS years ago. He has since offered ad hoc legal advice, despite his expertise being in ISDA swap agreements and Eurobond documentation rather than the finer nuances of English jurisprudence. Henry hopes Brent knows enough about the sale of owner enterprises.

'I knew you'd eventually see sense, Henry,' chimes Roberts, chomping at the bit to close the deal.

'It's true what they say, Lionel. Time is money. The longer I waited, the more you offered.'

He shifts in his seat. 'And now I am at my limit. This is the very final offer.'

'An offer which we are pleased to accept.' Henry's smile is not reciprocated.

There's an uneasy lull in the proceedings. Alongside Roberts is the head of his plc legal department, some thirty-year-old legal eagle with an aggressive pair of glasses and a sharp dark suit. Henry has already forgotten his name, as if it matters. The eager eagle offers up a set of legal contracts.

'Gentlemen, this is the sale agreement that we intend to execute here today.' Henry stares over at the eagle. He thinks 'execute' is a nice word and just what he'd like to do with a sharpened letter opener today. 'We will sign the documents now that both sides are happy with the content.'

Brent takes a copy of the sale contract and thumbs through the voluminous pages.

'Are those minor wording changes okay now?' Henry asks him, knowing that in any negotiation that involves lawyers on hourly rates, it's essential that both sides exercise their muscle by insisting on completely irrelevant and perfunctory wording changes just for the goddamn' heck of it.

'Yeah, it looks fine. The amended clauses are to my satisfaction. We can sign this, Henry.'

'Excellent, excellent,' confirms Roberts, producing an exquisite Mont Blanc silver pen. 'Let's use this to sign. It's one I've used for other deals. My lucky pen, never fails me.'

Henry is thinking that Roberts's luck is about to run out. The deal is here in black and white, but he knows that the two parties are contemplating a different endgame. Roberts thinks that he has Henry by the balls for the next year, like the bad old days. Henry knows he'll be gone in weeks. Maybe days.

He takes the pen, nods to Brent and is about to sign when Amanda leans forward and touches him on the arm. He wishes he had never given her one per cent of the company.

'Are you sure we want to sign this?' she asks.

'We have discussed this at length at home,' he sighs.

'What are you going to do for a livelihood?'

He glares over at her. 'I'm going to work with Lionel for one more year. I'll have a salary.'

'What do we live off after that?'

'Maybe your PR business will be commercially viable by then.' He sees her hostile reaction. 'And if not, then it doesn't bloody matter. We will have enough cash in the bank to live off.'

'Precisely,' soothes Roberts. Why do wives always get in the way?

'And what then?' she asks. 'Are you going to start another recruitment company?'

Roberts's eagle is quick off the mark. 'Most definitely not. There is a non-compete clause in the contract. Henry cannot set up in the same business in London for two years. We don't want him stealing all his old clients back from Lionel Roberts plc, do we? Not like last time.'

Amanda knows the jargon and seems resigned. 'So what is the final sale consideration?'

The eagle knows the crunched numbers off by heart. 'Three point three million sterling.'

'I get one per cent?' The eagle nods. Henry needs the deal to close today. She's wasting his time. Amanda looks around the room. 'I wish I'd got more shares all those years ago, Henry.'

He doesn't agree. 'Don't worry,' he assures her. 'It's *our* money.'

She doesn't look so convinced and turns to the advisers. 'When is the money to be paid?'

'Half now, and half in a year's time if all goes as per the terms of the contract,' advises Brent. 'There's one outstanding issue.' They all look up. 'The exact method of payment is not yet determined. We can choose to accept a cheque, a banker's draft, a wire transfer to a bank account, or even cash if you like.'

The eagle turns to Henry. 'How do you want it paid?'

'A bank transfer. Here is our joint bank account number at HSBC.'

'Fine.' There's much nodding of heads. Amanda seems to have run out of pointless loaded questions. Henry hasn't yet finished.

'I want to brief my staff this week about the sale of the business. Until I do that then this deal is to be kept under wraps. I don't want them to hear this from some Lionel Roberts junior staffer in the lift.'

'Agreed.' Roberts nods.

The contracts are passed around the table. Henry signs. Amanda signs. Roberts signs. The two lawyers sign as witnesses. Roberts stands up, beaming. There's much shaking of hands.

'I look forward to a successful transition of your business from Henry Simpson & Associates to Lionel Roberts plc over the course of the next twelve months. It's great to have you back.'

'My sentiments exactly,' confirms Henry, lying through his teeth with a practised ease.

The trio of visitors files out of the office. They part company at the door to the street. Brent heads back to his office in Broadgate. Amanda loiters on the pavement, maybe looking for an invitation from Henry to some celebratory lunch. Dream on. He hails a cab and pushes her into it.

'I've got to meet some bankers in the City. Another time.'

She's gone. It's safe. He walks back into the building and directly up to Lionel Roberts plc, breezes past the girl in reception and into Roberts's personal fiefdom. Roberts and his lawyer looks surprised.

'We've changed our mind,' advises Henry.

'You've what? What the hell—?'

'Relax. We've changed our mind about the payment. No bank account transfers, please, we now want that first half in cash.'

'You must be joking! Cash? Funny guy. You want a suitcase stuffed full of tenners or what?'

'Fifties will do.'

'We can't get one and a half million quid plus in cash from an ATM. It'll take us days to assemble.'

'Fine. You've got three days. Call me when you have it. Just don't send it downstairs to me in a plastic bag and leave it at the reception with my new temp. I'll come up here to collect it in person.'

Roberts nods. Henry makes to leave.

'What about your wife's share of the money? Shall I give that to you in cash as well?'

'Yes.' Henry smiles. 'I'll make sure she gets what's coming to her.'

CHAPTER TWENTY-NINE

GRAFTON STREET, DUBLIN 2: 4.05 P.M.

Adam flies from City Airport to Dublin on an Aer Lingus Commuter and touches down on the wet asphalt ten minutes ahead of schedule. He catches a battered Nissan cab at the queue by the rank and heads into town along the MI airport motorway. The driver is as keen to chat as the rest of his nation.

'So what brings you to Dublin?' he asks in the vague direction of the rear-view mirror.

Adam gives the question some careful thought before replying, 'I'm here about a serial killer.'

'You'll get on fine,' comes the reply up front. 'We like people with a sense of humour.'

Adam alights at the top of pedestrianised Grafton Street. He avoids the huge oncoming crowds of January sale shoppers, recalls the salient details from the *Irish Times* clipping read in the cab, then crosses the road into St Stephen's Green. He has timed the trip to perfection. It's late afternoon and dark already. Close to the approximate time of the victim's death.

He walks along narrow winding tarmac paths, past a deserted bandstand and pond, recalling that the newspaper reported that the American was killed somewhere near the centre, adjacent to one of several diagonal paths that traverse the park. He thinks he's chosen the right one but there's too much damn' space to cover without any local knowledge and his hopes fade. He'll never find the exact place of death. He's passed the halfway mark. He's completely lost. Then he sees the impromptu memorial.

One withered wreath of weathered roses is attached at eye level to a single tree off to his left. It looks recent enough. The death occurred months ago yet someone still remembers. He leaves the path for the mud and stops to read the rain-stained message attached to the plastic wrapping. There's a handwritten note with the Stars and Stripes from the American Embassy in Ballsbridge. Other walkers pass nearby, staring at Adam, wondering what he's doing. An elderly lady stops.

'I remember it too,' she says. 'Terrible, wasn't it? Sure you're safe nowhere these days.'

He nods in silent agreement but his thoughts are far away. Miles away. Somewhere else. There's something about this darkened corner where life ceased to ebb – the dense bushes and hedges, the trees rustling overhead. There is complete silence again as the woman's faltering footsteps recede into the quiet. Adam recognises this feeling of privacy and security. He's been here before. Suddenly he is standing in a dark Dusseldorf garden in the evening. There are definite parallels.

He's late for his rendezvous so he strides back to the crammed streets, down Grafton Street, past the invading giants of the UK high street, first right like she told him. Kehoe's is down a paved street of restaurants, cafés, diners and other public houses. Inside it's like stepping back a few generations, with old wooden panels, faded prints, creaking floorboards and barmen as stout and reliable as the pints they decant from a row of impressive taps. At first he can't see her.

'Hi, Adam, we're in here.'

Trish sits alone in a small snug by the window. Adam deduces that maybe she's been here since opening time since she has the best seat in the pub. Other envious eyes glance over at the couple. Adam knows why. It's not the seating arrangements.

Trish is wearing mostly black, some worn leather, some faded denim. She's positively glowing, her eyes shining through the smoky haze, looking better than behind the sterile reception desk of Henry Simpson & Associates, better even than on that phantom date in the West End. They kiss briefly.

'Great to see you again,' he begins. 'So how is Dublin?'

'Magic,' she laughs. 'I don't know why I didn't come back here sooner. How's London?'

He's thinking about the guys at work, Diane in her office, Lisa upstairs, Samantha long gone.

'Manic.' There are two empty pint glasses upon the table in the snug. 'Who else is here?'

'Paddy's here too. I asked him along.'

Adam has a flashback. He's about to meet the boyfriend. He hopes he can restrain himself.

'Great.' He's distracted. There's a solo guy approaching with two pints of Guinness. Something is not right. He's six foot two with wavy grey hair, a moustache, a navy sports jacket, belly protruding over dark trousers. He's forty-five years old minimum. It's a huge age gap. This can't be her other half, can it? Paddy puts the pints down on their table. It might be him. Bloody hell.

'Adam, good to meet you. I'll get another.' He's gone. Jesus, it *is* him. Trish watches Adam.

'There's no easy way to say it,' he stammers. 'That's Paddy?'

She's quick on the uptake. 'You are funny! Yes, that's Paddy. He's a friend of Patrick's. My Patrick is on the evening shift in Bray station now. This Paddy here works in Garda HQ in Harcourt Street. He's Paddy Doyle, attached to the murder squad. I told him everything you told me in that email. It all sounds a bit weird. I still don't understand why you're interested in some murder here.'

'All in good time.'

'Tell me more.'

'I don't want to alarm you.'

Doyle returns with the extra pint, going on the long-standing assumption that every visitor to Dublin prefers a pint of Arthur's plain, brewed two miles up the Liffey, to some imported barrelled fizzy lager. Paddy doesn't hang about. He downs almost half his pint in one smooth gulp. So much for not drinking on duty.

'Trish tells me you're a London banker.' Adam nods. There's an embarrassed pause. 'And she tells me you think you can help us find who killed the American in de Green last month.'

Adam has trouble deciphering his gruff accent. It's rural, he deduces, very different from the taxi driver's.

'I'm not sure I can but I have a hunch.'

'Many's the hunch tha' solved a crime. Go on,' Paddy advises.

'You tell me first what you know about the murder.'

Doyle sighs, downs the rest of his pint, gives a barman the eye for another, and refocuses.

'We don't know much. The victim was seen leaving the Shelbourne Hotel by the doorman. Then he walked into de Green. It was rainin' hard that night. The place was almost empty. A mother with a child in a pushchair saw the victim walking alone, quite fast. She says that another man was walking close behind. The body of de American was found at seven a.m. next morning when de Green opened up for the day. He'd been stabbed several times in the heart. Clinical, like.'

Adam looks at the black stuff as he leans forward.

'Was any knife or blade found?'

'No.'

'Was anything taken from the victim? Wallet, credit cards?'

'No.'

Adam's pint remains untouched.

'Anything known about the man seen in the park? What did the mother see?'

Doyle takes a folded page from an inside pocket and places it in the pool of Guinness.

'Sure wouldn't we all like to know that? She didn't see much. We have a photofit. It's not great.'

Adam looks at the picture. It's an amateurish effort. The burgeoning beer stains don't help either. It's not as well drawn as the Dusseldorf picture. There's a strong similarity but he thinks it's not enough to get Doyle excited. Adam says nothing. Is it Henry or not? Trish takes the picture in her hand.

'Funny . . . Paddy, this looks like someone I knew in London. It's someone Adam knows, too.'

Adam bites his tongue. He doesn't want to voice his opinion. Best to let Trish decide alone.

'Who is it?' asks Doyle.

'What do you think, Adam?' she asks.

He watches her face turn pale. Her usual smile disappears. 'I want to hear you first,' he says.

She's having difficulty. 'It looks like Henry, doesn't it?' She turns to Doyle. 'It's my old boss in London.' She laughs nervously. 'It can't be . . . can it?'

Diane looks forward to another bout at her place. Henry faithfully arrives at the appointed hour. He carries some ready-to-eat food in a bulging Cullen's plastic carrier bag.

'You're not here to eat, Henry,' she says, looking past him at the view of Battersea.

'You look addled.' He stands beside her by the sheer plate-glass windows. 'What's up?'

'Problems at work.' She turns to face him. 'Problems with the guy you brought us. Adam.'

'I didn't hire him. You did. Or rather Lloyd. What's the problem?'

'He's not up to working in a place like Mitchell's. Should have stayed in Kapital. He's going to fail probation. We're going to fire him, then hire a replacement. Sorry about your fee.'

Henry senses that she's not telling him everything. 'There's more to it, isn't there?'

She reacts instantly. 'There isn't. It's only work stuff. Adam might be the difficult sort. You know, I'd gladly see the back of him. If he were to disappear overnight, I wouldn't give a damn or shed a tear.'

'You serious?'

'Deadly,' she replies. 'A nice accident would do.' She laughs. 'I should be so lucky.'

Henry kisses her and smiles. 'I'll see what can be arranged.'

She steps away from him. 'Enough of this work talk. Leave the food for later. Let's play.'

Inside the sparsely furnished room, Diane sits on the edge of the king-size and points. 'Can you kneel in front of me in the centre of the bed.' Henry does as instructed. 'You need a raincoat.' She reaches inside the bedside table drawer and produces a Durex Featherlite, opens the foil expertly and holds the rubber with her long red fingernails. 'Allow me.'

'Why this?' asks Henry. 'I never needed one before.'

'This is for hygienic reasons.' She pauses. 'Make an effort for me. It's easier if you're erect.'

'Make it easy for me.'

'Think about what you and I are going to do today. Think about how we will play my game. Think about the pleasure you are going to provide to me. Think about the pleasure you might receive too. Think, Henry, think.' It has the desired effect. She watches him inhaling her musky scent. 'That's better.' She slips on the rubber, allowing her nails to run like daggers down his shaft, raking his skin back and forth.

'Jesus,' he exclaims. 'Go easy.'

She reaches into the drawer and produces three wide-gauge rubber bands, the sort easily purloined from the Mitchell's stationery room on the trading floor. 'So you're pleased to see me. Let's do our best to keep you that way.' She wraps one of the bands around his base, then doubles it up so that it's tighter. Another band goes around his sac. The last is wound twice around the glans. She sits back and admires her handiwork. 'How does that feel?'

'Tight,' he exclaims, hardly daring to look down, preferring instead to imagine the effect.

'I'll tell you how you look.' She runs her nails up and down. This time the sensation is more pronounced. 'You are completely hard, your veins stand out, your blood rushes to the head, your skin tone is dark red. No, it's close to purple. We are nearly ready. Are you worried?'

'I'm in good hands.'

She takes his manhood again and allows one nail visibly to indent his taut foreskin. 'You are.' She reaches into the drawer and produces a half-used tube of KY. 'Be careful with this. I don't want you smearing these new sheets unnecessarily.' She applies a liberal amount, taking care not to excite him with any unnecessary movement.

He stares back at her. He's naked. She wears her banking gear – a pink cotton check blouse and a medium-length black skirt, plus a pair of black heels. 'What about you? Are you peeling off?'

'No need.' She hitches up her skirt around her waist. She wears nothing underneath. 'I am ready.'

He moves closer to her, wondering how she wants to play this unprecedented scenario. She places a hand on his chest and points. 'I have some advice. That may grow quite painful for you. It will be even worse when you orgasm, if you can with those bands. So take your time. I prefer long slow comfortable strokes, rather than uncontrolled thrusting. The food isn't going anywhere. I'm in no hurry.'

'Me neither. I took the afternoon off work.'

She looks at the clock radio and stares at him. 'Don't be too confident. This stamina record to date is about twenty minutes. It's twelve-thirty now. See if you can contain yourself until quarter to one.'

Diane takes three plump pillows and places them in the centre of the bed, near the headboard. She lies face down over the pillows. Suddenly he sees what is required of him. He inches forward until he is positioned optimally. She looks to her right. He realises she can see the scene in the full-length dressing mirror on the wall. He touches her from behind.

'Not yet,' she instructs. She reaches into the drawer and carefully takes out a small glass bottle, unscrews the cap and inhales deeply three or four times, enjoying an odorous heady rush. Henry can smell something heady too in the room. She screws back the cap tightly 'It relaxes my muscles. It's easier for both of us. But you don't get any. I never want you to relax.'

Henry leaves Battersea in the late afternoon for the HSBC branch on Bedford Street. He wastes time in the queue, unwilling to draw undue attention to himself, until a diminutive girl behind a bulletproof glass screen serves him. She looks like she left comprehensive school yesterday.

'I want to make a withdrawal from my current account. Henry Simpson is the name.'

'You have to fill out a form,' she advises.

'I called earlier. The assistant manager said you'd have it ready. The funds are in my account.'

She looks at him blankly, then thumbs through an open drawer and finds a chunky envelope.

'Simpson,' Henry nods. 'Five thousand, isn't it?' She's too loud. Henry nods again. She counts the fifty-pound notes. She's about to hand it all over. 'People rarely take this much cash. It's dangerous, you know.' Henry bites his lip. 'Are you doing what everyone does with it?'

'What's that?' he asks. The queue behind is lengthening. He could do without the chit-chat.

'You're buying a new car,' she prompts, like Henry would be seen dead in any car worth five K.

'That's right. It's for a new motor.' Now he knows why the queues in banks move so slowly.

He escapes with the bundle of notes and heads to his favourite local haunt. He's late. Jimmy is already sitting on the nominated bench in St Peter's churchyard, the collar of his Timberland fleece turned up against the evening chill, his eyes darting around the scene yet his bulky frame remaining still, his controlled breathing causing minimal disturbance in the cold air.

'Why didnae we meet in your office? It's bloody freezing out here,' he asks.

Up close, Jimmy's eyes are bloodshot, his stubble is two days old and his skin discoloured.

'Because everyone would ask me who you are, Jimmy.'

'Then why pick some old graveyard like this? All these fucking gravestones give me the willies.' Henry remains silent. 'Are you still serious about all this? There's no going back, ye ken.'

'I've given it a lot of thought. It's the only solution to my problem. How do we do it?'

'I need tae see your money first.'

'I have half of it in my pocket. You get it when you tell me what you're going to do.'

Jimmy looks ahead, waits until a couple of old dears pass, then speaks without turning his head.

'First you pick a new name. The best thing tae do is borrow someone else's. Someone from an obituaries column or who emigrated to Canada or Oz forty years back. That's the easy part. You got a name, Henry? If I can still call you Henry?'

'I got a name. You'll hear it later. Go on.'

'I have a pile of change-of-name deeds that I got from a legal stationer. We'll fill out a deed changing your name to the new one. The bent solicitor I know will stamp it. The deed costs £1.50 and the solicitor charges me a tenner to stamp it. It's legit. You're supposed to register it with the High Court, but what the hell? No one ever does and it's up to you.'

Henry is reminded of the five-grand fee. 'Sounds like you have quite a mark-up.'

Jimmy ignores the jibe and relaxes into his sales patter.

'Next I have some accommodation addresses that I use. Good ones, mind, nae rubbish. They're easy and cheap to acquire, listed in *Exchange & Mart* and in *Private Eye*. I got one in Brompton Road, one in Marylebone High Street, even one in New Bond Street. Posh, eh? It's only a room with a bunch of mailboxes inside but who the hell else knows that?'

Henry is beginning to be impressed. It looks like Jimmy didn't waste his four years inside.

'Go on.'

'So you have a new name and address. Now you're ready to apply for a new photo driving licence. You send the deed and proof of address tae the DVLA in Swansea, get a new licence back.'

'I have a licence. Won't they record my name-change on their computer?' wonders Henry.

'Sure they will, but they only have the new accommodation address. Soon you won't be at your old address any more. They can check their records but they'll never find you. The only risk is that the person whose name you choose had a licence, but we can allow for that. Someone who died aged ten or emigrated when they were fifteen never had one.'

'Okay. Next?'

'I'll go tae the Family Record Office in Clerkenwell, not a million miles from here. I'll buy a copy of the birth certificate of the man whose identity you're stealing. It costs £6.50. No one will ask me any questions. The authorities see it as a record of an event, not as proof of identity.'

Henry is nodding silently, encouraging Jimmy to continue.

'We gotta decide if you're staying in the UK or going overseas. Take my advice, the UK is too risky. You can bump into someone you know when you're just out buying a newspaper. Someone like you could never stay in London or the Home Counties. Best go overseas for your refuge.'

Henry has decided already. He even remembers the advert in the Tube. 'Overseas it is.'

'So you need a passport. We'll apply for a replacement passport in your new name. Tell them you lost the original. Do all this at Petty France. We'll need photographs of you signed by what they call a person of good standing who has known you for two years, like a priest or a copper or a justice of the peace. I know a few crooked ones. They'd sign their mother's death warrant for a few hundred quid. That's where some of your money goes.'

'That sounds risky.'

'Nae worries. That's the normal procedure. If we follow that, no one will suspect a thing. The passport office require two forms of identity. One will be the driving licence. They also accept a bank statement as proof of ID.' Jimmy points over to HSBC. 'You'll be opening a new bank account. Not in that damn' branch, mind you. Miles away in the suburbs.'

'But we can't fool banks so easily.'

'The bank need to be happy that you are who you say you are and that your new address exists, so we call the local BT customer-service division and ask for a new phone line to be set up at your accommodation address. You don't actually want the new line. The letter confirming the request from a utility company like BT will suffice for the bank. They'll open a current account. Then we have the passport. With a new passport under a new name, you're a new person.'

'I need this done quickly. How long will it take?'

'Maybe a week. I move fast when I have to. How about the cash?'

Henry passes the cash from his pocket directly into the side pocket of Jimmy's fleece.

'Better all be there, pal. It's too fucking cold tae take off these gloves and count the stuff.'

The two men stand up, about to go their separate ways. Jimmy stops.

'I need your new name.'

'This way,' advises Henry.

They walk past the imposing façade, then hang a left along a wall. The gravestones are sparser in this sheltered alcove. Newer, too — more vertical, with clearer engraving on white stone.

'This one.' Henry points. 'Graham Edward Berisford. Died 1965, aged three months. Influenza. Sadly missed by a loving mother and father. That's the name I will use. That's me.'

'Fine. I've got all I need.' Jimmy confirms. 'I'll be in touch —' he pauses as he turns away '— Graham.'

CHAPTER THIRTY

HARCOURT STREET, DUBLIN 2: 5.15 P.M.

Adam and Trish follow Doyle around one side of the Green, up a street lined with Georgian houses now primarily populated by solicitors and accountants, past rows of double-parked white Garda Siochana Isuzu Trooper 4WDs and leaning fluorescent Yamaha bikes, into the gates of Garda HQ at Harcourt Square, through a small landscaped area with barren trees and mulched leaves underfoot, past benevolent yet efficient security, through an unnecessary X-ray machine, down long dim corridors and into a small room with a table, four chairs and no view of the outside world to break the tension.

'This is not an interview,' explains Doyle as he pulls back two chairs for his guests. 'It's only a friendly chat.' He turns to Adam. 'You'll catch your flight back tonight. I guarantee it.' Another younger plain-clothes officer arrives with a notepad and pen. 'Des here will take some notes. We won't use the tapes. Okay?'

Trish and Adam nod in unison. Doyle sits across the table and leans forward.

'So who wants to start? Which of you two knows Simpson best?'

'I do,' admits Trish. 'I worked for him for two years.'

'You see him regularly?'

'Not any more. I left his office a week ago.'

'Won't he suspect something?'

'It's not like that. I moved back to Dublin. But I can't help you. Only Adam knows what's happening.'

Doyle turns, showing some frustration. 'Tell me everything you know about Henry Simpson.'

Adam explains in fifteen minutes. Des writes fast. Adam mentions the various European cities.

'How do you know that Simpson was there at the time of these murders?' Adam produces the fax of Henry's Air Miles statement. Doyle isn't convinced. 'This is only a fax. Is it the same as the real thing?'

'It sure is,' interjects Trish. 'I faxed it to Adam. Henry went there. I know. I booked those flights. Only problem is that Henry knows what I did. He found the fax number. I told him I sent it to Adam. Sorry.' She turns to Adam. 'But that was last year. You've suspected for ages. Why did you wait?'

'I never knew for sure. It was sort of a bet I had with Samantha. We both thought there must be hundreds of businessmen who travel around Europe. Henry is just one.' Adam recalls his recent trip. 'It was only when I went to Dusseldorf that I first began to think that maybe he killed that banker.'

'What changed your mind?' asks Doyle.

Adam reaches into his pocket and unfolds a sheet of paper. 'The victim's wife gave me this police-computer photofit made by a taxi driver.' Adam places the page on the table. Doyle examines it closely.

'Jesus!' exclaims Trish. She's shaking, pointing down. 'It's definitely Henry too. Even with the glasses.'

'Hold on a minute, love,' cautions Doyle. 'Let's not jump to any conclusions.' He takes out his own crumpled photofit and places the pages side by side. He examines the features and profile.

'So what are you thinking?' asks Adam after an interminable wait.

'I'm thinking the German police have better technology than we have.' Doyle looks up. 'This could indeed be the same man. It's definitely worth pursuing. And it's the only lead I have. So we will.'

'What next?'

Doyle gets up and paces the room, stroking his moustache, deep in procedural thought.

'I'll talk to our overseas colleagues tomorrow morning. We've got contacts in Bonn who can speak to someone local in Dusseldorf. And we've got long-established contacts in New Scotland Yard. They'll have to pick up Simpson if we ask for an arrest. They can hold him on our behalf, Des and I will travel over to check him out in person, see if he fits the bill, then we'll look for extradition back here.'

'Can't you arrest him right now?' asks Adam, feeling some relief.

'As soon as we can, we will.'

'How long will all this take?'

'Hard to say. It could be a few days. We have to do this right, follow the proper procedures. We only get one chance to make an arrest like this, especially across other jurisdictions. We don't want some judge in the UK throwing out an extradition request 'cos I didn't dot the i's and cross the t's. You okay with that?

Adam shakes his head. 'No, I'm not. I think I'm in danger. Don't I have a say in this?'

'Not really. You're not a witness to either death. Trish knows Simpson better than you do. Even the mother with the child in the park matters more to me. Sorry.'

'I'm scared. He might suspect something. He might come after me,' admits Adam. 'I might meet him.'

Doyle looks interested. 'Is there a risk you could meet Simpson accidentally?'

'There could be a social event. He might come into the bank where I work.'

Doyle looks directly at them, slowly alternating between Adam and Trish. 'If you spook Simpson, then he may do something unprovoked. Might even kill again, if he is our man. Or worse still, he might disappear on us. So I'll give you some important advice. If you meet him, don't tip this guy off. Act like you normally would. Be cool.'

'Easy to say,' observes Adam. 'We had lunch together before Christmas. What if he wants to have lunch again?'

'If that happens, then stall him. Do whatever you have to do. If you're worried in the next few days, then let me know and I'll try to get the Met to give you some cover. Spin by your home.' Doyle hands over his Garda card with phone numbers on it where he can be reached night and day. 'Use this if you have to. Is there anyone else in London who knows about this and might tip him off?'

Adam doesn't need to give the question much thought. 'I'm sure my boss is dating Simpson.'

Trish turns around. 'What about Amanda, his wife?'

Doyle shrugs. 'It happens. Moon world. Does your boss suspect anything?'

'Not that I'm aware of.'

'You talk to her much about Simpson?' Adam shakes his head. 'Keep it that way. Tell no one about our chat.'

Doyle looks over his colleague's notes. Adam and Trish are shown outside. Adam's return flight leaves in fifty minutes' time. He's definitely going to miss it. He stands in Harcourt Street, wondering where he can hail a cab, if he can change his economy ticket to another airline, wondering about the best way to say goodbye to Trish, or if he'll ever see her again. A uniformed Garda approaches from out of the darkness.

'Mr Lewis?' Adam nods. 'Ready when you are.' Adam's lost. 'Airport, isn't it?'

The exhaust of one of the Isuzu Troopers pumps lead oxide into the cold air. Adam holds Trish closer.

'It's great to see you again,' he says. 'Keep in touch. You're safer here than in London.'

'Will do,' she says. 'You keep safe, too.'

They kiss briefly, her lips so much warmer than the chill of the night air. He clambers up into the front seat and watches her through the condensation as the 4WD veers into the rush-hour commuter traffic.

'Doyle says you're in a hurry,' the unknown driver says.

Adam looks at the clock on the dashboard. 'My flight leaves at seven-ten.'

'Then let's not stand upon ceremony.'

The roof lights overhead swing into action and a siren roars painfully loud as the driver pulls left into an elitist bus lane. The huge wheels pound the pitted city streets. Adam lapses into silence, admiring the evasive driving technique, watching the blue flashes merge into the wet tarmac, looking at blurred street names, along Gardiner Street and Dorset Street, wondering how he got so deep into a multiple-murder investigation. He is safe inside in the warm Garda 4WD. He wonders how safe he will be back in London.

Lisa's flight touches down again at City Airport. 'Please remain in your seats.' It feels like her millionth flight. 'No smoking until you are inside the terminal building.' Angie gives her the nod after the cabin announcement. 'Doors to manual.' She swivels and pushes the door. The wind propels sleeting rain into the cabin interior. She sees the twinkling lights of Canary Wharf. Legend has it that the truly eligible single guys all work in investment banks. Lisa travels thousands of miles in search of something special but the true object of her desire lives only eight feet below in her apartment block. 'Welcome to London City.'

There's a short delay as an Aer Lingus Commuter BAE whisper jet pulls alongside on the sodden apron. Its turbine blades slowly whirl to a halt. Some of the overweight suits in the front premium rows huff and puff like they have a critical business meeting at this time of the night. Lisa knows the truth. Their true bosses, their wives, want them home for the evening meal. Their expectant children want the duty-free gifts.

Lisa smiles a trade-mark goodbye at her passengers as they deplane and board a bus for the short trip to the terminal. In contrast the Aer Lingus passengers are near enough to the terminal to walk. She watches some of them huddle, looking for the shelter of the terminal, shielding themselves from the rain. Her cabin is soon empty. Angie has observed Lisa closely on the day return from Europe.

'Why the long face? Love life getting you down?'

'You're forgetting, I don't have a love life,' replies Lisa.

They walk together on the leeward side of the terminal building, merging with the scrum of passengers from Aer Lingus. Lisa ignores the glances from the males who stare at air stewardesses like they're from another planet. She looks down and tries to avoid their eyes when someone up ahead suddenly looks familiar. She first recognises his build, then sees some of his side profile as he turns to face the terminal.

'I think it's him.'

'Who?' asks Angie.

'The guy downstairs. The guy I told you about. Adam. It *is* him,' she exclaims.

'Which one?'

The passengers ahead stall as they are shepherded through a small door to file past the ever-anxious Metropolitan Police guard on immigration control. He is ahead of them in the queue, far enough ahead that Lisa can talk aloud to her colleague.

'He's the tall guy in the dark coat at the door now. The one with a Dublin duty-free bag in his hand.'

Angie squints her eyes through the glass window. 'Hmmmnn. Nice. Very nice. It's fate.'

'What do you mean, fate?'

'Fate brought you to the same apartment block. Fate brought you to the same airport tonight. Fate is bloody working overtime to get you two together. Fate might just chuck it all in if you blow this.'

'What do I do next?'

'You both live in the same apartment block,' explains Angie.

'So?' Lisa wonders.

'You *are* dreadful. Catch him up. Engage him in conversation. Get a lift with him to your place.'

'I have my car parked in staff parking.'

Angie raises her gaze to heaven. 'He doesn't need to know that. Leave it here. Grab a ride.'

The queue moves on. They are in the tiny baggage hall. He's walking very fast, looking around like he's on the hunt for someone or something. Neither of them has any luggage. They're in the arrivals hall. There are people milling about. Lisa almost loses sight of her quarry. He stops momentarily near a Barclay's cash machine, checks his pocket and moves on immediately. They stand near Bewleys café and watch from afar. The three-storey atrium is well lit with adverts. Angie sees his face in the light and prods Lisa.

'He is well worth the effort. Now or never, dear. Go for it.'

They're near the passenger lounges. Lisa always avoids this place. It's all Euro suits and well-heeled blondes. Some girls, too. It's mobile mania, Samsonite carry-ons and Toshiba laptop penis envy. It's *FTs*, *Le Monde*, *City to Cities* and The Wharf rags. It's Travel Shopping, Thornton's Chocs, the Caviar House and Bally tax-free. It's Bar Trattoria with chain smokers and frothy cappuccinos. It's Bloomberg TV and rolling NYSE stock prices. It's a world of delays, pushy corporate customers and gold-card freeloaders.

'Won't I seem a bit forward?' Lisa asks.

'Make it look like a coincidence. Bump into him outside. Go! Otherwise you'll lose him.'

Adam walks to the revolving exit door, below the sign for taxis. Lisa follows him, unsure whether to run to catch him or to slow down so it looks natural, unsure of how to open the conversation, rehearsing the vital first words. He's in the taxi queue. Only there is no queue today. He's first in line and gets into an open door. The cab revs and moves off. Lisa stops on the pavement, next in line, but it's too late. A driver in the next cab calls out as his right hand opens his door with an ease practised over the years.

'Over here, love. Where are you going?'

She's miles away, watching the first taxi disappear out of view around the bend in the road.

'I've ... I've got my car in the car park,' she explains.

'Then you shouldn't be looking for a taxi, darlin'. Stop wasting my bleedin' time.'

Ten minutes later she's taken the Beetle out of the staff car park and is heading for Barrier Point, wondering how she managed to miss him, wondering what she has to do to show her interest.

Henry is home alone. It's almost eight o'clock and it's dark and wet outside. No one will be out and about in London this evening. He feels that urge, to have a look, to do some reconnaissance like in the old army days, to check out the lie of the land before a covert mission. First a telephone call is required.

Caller ID from BT makes a telephone call from home or his mobile too risky. He leaves the house and walks to the public telephone box on the corner. He stands inside the box, vaguely conscious that someone might have urinated inside it recently. He dials the residential number written on a Post-it note in his wallet, garnered from a call to Directory Enquiries. The call rings several times, he's ready to hang up, then a click as an answering machine cuts in.

'Hi, this is Adam. I can't take your call right now. Please leave—'

Henry hangs up immediately. His next target is not at home tonight. He debates the relative merits, the upside and downside, and decides it's good news. There's no risk of bumping into the target in the grounds of his own apartment block. Henry guns the Saab down Islington High Street, watching the windscreen wipers arc back and forth in the drizzle in some hypnotic trance.

The *A to Z* in the glove box is essential when he reaches the murky twilight of half-built Docklands. He's lost for five minutes until he sees the tower of Barrier Point rising off to the right. He slows along the deserted Woolwich road and stops opposite a formidable set of security gates. There's a lanky guy in a peaked cap sitting inside a well-lit gatelodge, more interested in the contents of what looks like the *Standard* than in a serial killer stalking one of the residents in his care. Henry reverses the Saab for a few feet so that he's out of the line of direct vision from the gatelodge and watches from afar.

Five minutes later an Audi A4 leaves the complex. The security guard doesn't raise his gaze from the newsprint. The gates swing open immediately. A Merc coupé arrives. Henry sees the middle-aged driver point a remote control at the gates. The gates swing open again. He wonders how to get inside without such technology or engaging in unnecessary conversation with the security guard.

Suddenly the guard is on his feet, folding away his news-paper, looking at a wall clock and then his own wristwatch, scribbling something on a pad of paper, picking up a flash-light. He opens the side door and slowly walks off along a cobblelock path in the direction of the river and behind the complex, aimlessly scouring the trees and undergrowth with random beams of light. Henry looks at his own wristwatch instinctively. It's precisely nine o'clock. On the nail. The guard is doing his rounds. Maybe hourly? The complex is big enough. He'll be gone for five minutes minimum, maybe even ten.

There's another car coming along the Woolwich Road towards Henry. The previous cars all came into Barrier Point. He gets out of the Saab and slowly walks towards the gates. A Volvo estate swings into the complex and stops on the incline, the gates opening as red brake lights light up. He quickens his gait, times it to perfection and nonchalantly walks inside as the gates begin to close.

He makes straight for the same footpath as the security guard, aware that the latter is walking around anticlockwise and probably won't return by the same route. There are beautifully landscaped gardens, with dense bushes and water features. It reminds Henry of the peace and tranquillity of a garden in Dusseldorf or a city-centre park in Madrid or Dublin.

He looks up as he ambles. There are drawn curtains, darkened apartments and deserted balconies. He stares upwards. There are small bedroom and bathroom windows, lift doors and communal areas on the one side of the tower that faces towards the road. There are three balconies on each of the other three sides of the tower. He knows from the telephone enquiry that Adam lives in 1205. He reckons that the apartments are numbered sequentially from either side so Adam must live in the centre apartment facing the river.

Henry melts into the undergrowth and begins to count off the floors. The curtains to the main room in 1205 are open. The room is in darkness. He deduces that Adam is not yet at home. He wonders where he might be at this hour, if perhaps there is a more optimal location for an untimely death. He inhales the atmosphere and feels rejuvenated by the fresh air of the Thames, the leeward shelter offered by the huge tower and the wonderful security and anonymity in the centre of a heaving metropolis.

Suddenly there's a car horn honking at the main gates. Henry's seen enough here. The horn honks again. Someone's stuck inside or outside and this is his ticket back to the Saab.

He runs back along the path and sees a black cab close to the gates, a solo male passenger hunched in the rear. The security guard is waving back at the pushy cabbie, telling him to ease off on the horn, shouting back in frustration.

'Gimme a minute, I's is on my rounds, mon.'

Once the guard is back inside his gatelodge, the gates swing open. Henry steps back into the darkness. The cab stops at the ground-floor communal entrance. The male passenger gets out and stands by the driver's open window, taking notes out of his wallet. The passenger is in his mid-twenties, tall, lean, and looks familiar. The light is not so good. Henry peers forward. It might be him. It *is* him. Adam accepts the change. Henry is taking in the scene, slowly comprehending the full ramifications of the details.

Adam holds a duty-free bag in his left hand. Henry reckons he's been away somewhere. Maybe for work. He might even have flown back via nearby City Airport. The cabbie must have spent an hour in a taxi rank and is pissed off with the whole world because he got stiffed with a crap fare to local Docklands. Henry is still looking over. He can read the words emblazoned on the duty-free bag. *Dublin Duty Free.*

Henry is in shock. He must leave now by following the taxi out on foot. The gates are open. He walks briskly through the gap. He's in a hurry as he steps off the pavement to his Saab. A car horn sounds in the rain. He looks up. Some mad young woman driver in a lurid canary-yellow VW Beetle almost runs him over. She stares back and drives past him at speed. He glares at her, anger welling up inside.

CHAPTER THIRTY-ONE

CANARY WHARF, LONDON, E14: 7.05 A.M.

Adam fears the worst. He opens the front door of his apartment to the threat posed by the outside world and wonders how much Diane tells Henry. He walks through the already ajar security gates of the apartment complex and wonders at the lack of physical security when he needs it most. He hails a black cab and wonders if Henry fears imminent discovery. He looks out the window of the cab in the early morning and wonders if there's a car following him to work. He passes through Mitchell's reception and wonders if the security guards would be able to stop Henry if he came calling for a spot of recreational headhunting.

'Where were you yesterday?' asks Bruce.

'I had a day off. Holiday.'

'You still got a lot to learn about US investment banking. We don't do holidays. We do vacations. Did you do anything exciting? More job hunting?'

'I did some research.'

The trading floor is obsessed by the pre-bonus seasonal wave of greed and expectancy. At lunchtime Adam is eventually left alone to man the desk. It's safe. He pulls out a business card from his wallet and dials +353 for Dublin. He's immediately through on a direct line.

'Doyle speaking.' It's him all right. Adam knows that gruff accent.

'Adam Lewis here.' There's no immediate reaction. 'You remember me from my trip.'

'Sure I do.'

'Tell me what you're doing about Simpson?'

'I've sent our file to our contacts in the Met. They'll review it. All in good time. We'll get him.'

'You need to move fast. What's next?'

'I'm on the red-eye to Heathrow tomorrow morning. Is that fast enough for you?'

'Hope so.'

He cuts off Doyle and immediately dials a number he knows off by heart. She answers promptly.

'Samantha, how are you?'

'Not so good.'

'What do you mean?' Adam's voice rises. 'Are you in danger?'

'I hope not. I'm just a bit down with all the change, the move and the hassle. Do you have news for me?'

'Sure do.'

'Well done. You nailed the scam. Tell me more.'

'Not quite. That doesn't matter any more. Have you heard from Henry?' he asks.

'I told you I'm not going back to the City.'

'I didn't mean it like that. Has he called you about anything?'

'Should he have?'

'Trust me, you don't want to hear from him. Stay clear of him.'

'What do you know?'

Adam has to break the news. 'I went to Dublin and saw another photofit. I'm almost sure Henry is a killer. Trish thinks so too. So do the police in Dublin. It's not just you and me now.' He hears her gasp. 'There's too much evidence. All the travel to those cities on the right days. The two photofits. Even the way he handles a steak knife.'

'Jesus! What are you doing about it?'

'The police are onto Henry. They'll pick him up in days. Until then, stay in Cornwall and stay safe.'

'Does he know any of this?'

'I don't know what Diane tells him but she knows we have those press cuttings. She knows that I was in Dusseldorf before Christmas. The rest of the desk know that too. Trish says he knows I have his Air Miles statement. But he doesn't know that I was in Dublin again.'

'Take care. Let me know if I can help.' Samantha sighs. 'Sometimes I wish I'd never made you investigate the connections in the murders. If anything happens to you, I'll never forgive myself.'

Adam hangs up. In the early afternoon he watches Diane pick up her coat and head off. He hopes that some day he'll have the sort of job where he can confidently down tools for the day and leave early.

'Shall I give Henry your best wishes?' She smiles unnervingly.

He nods hopelessly and wonders if she wants him to go job-hunting or if there is more to it. Today, however, he sits on at the desk, long after the others have all left, snacking from the vending machine, knowing that he is safer at a Reuters screen in Mitchell's offices than alone in front of a TV screen at home in E16.

Henry is summoned at short notice on his mobile telephone to Diane's apartment. She immediately directs him into the bedroom and asks him to undress. He reluctantly lies face up on the bed sheets. She examines the immediate vicinity like she's lost something of value. He wonders what is planned for today.

'Do you ever run out of ideas?' he asks.

She shakes her head before walking out of the bedroom with some unknown purpose.

'Not yet. Don't move. I'll be back. Lie down. Close your eyes and anticipate ecstasy.'

He wonders what she means. Does she pop pick-me-up pills or do recreational drugs or will it be merely orgasmic? He worries about her increasingly bizarre sexual props. He looks around the bedroom but there are no clues. The bedside table is bare. He opens the drawer. Empty. He looks over to a low table by the window. There are only glossy women's magazines, an ashtray, a wax candle and a pack of Marlboro. But there's also an elongated burgundy box half-wrapped in gold gift paper. He's seen something like it before.

There is still silence beyond the bedroom door so it's safe to wander. He's intrigued, so he dares to roll off the bed and pick up the box. The designer logo is familiar. He carefully opens the lid. The polished contents glint back, sitting perfectly flush under two clasps into the recessed velvet, still apparently untouched by human hand. It's a gleaming nine-inch silver-plated letter opener. Diane breezes back into the room. She steps closer, still fully clothed.

'I told you to lie on the bed. What part of that instruction did you not understand?'

He fingers the blade. 'How do you have this? I mean ... I have one just like it.'

She brushes a single index finger against his lips. 'How stupid can you be? You gave it to me.'

He stares back incredulously, oblivious to the fact he is standing naked in the bedroom. 'I did?'

'Sure you did. It was another present from you.'

Henry is losing the plot, memories of other blades flooding back and adding to the confusion. 'Did I?'

Diane sees the reality. 'You're far too important to buy the gifts yourself. So you get your PA Trish to do it for you like any lazy guy. You sign the gift cards and she dispatches them to your clients.' She grabs the box, removes the blade and juggles it about in her hand. 'I like this. It's a wicked implement.'

Henry disagrees because it came direct from Selfridges mail order. 'It's not sharp enough.'

She stares back intently. 'Sharp enough for what?'

'Nothing. It's just an expression.' He looks around. 'Didn't you get a magnifying glass too?'

'I didn't, you cheapskate,' she sneers.

'How about a thank-you for the gift?'

She places her hand on his chest and pushes him backwards until his knees fold at the edge of the bed.

'You're about to get it now. Lie down. Stop complaining. We can start. I have what I need.'

'What do you need?' he asks naively.

She holds up a lit chrome cigarette lighter, her smile wicked. 'Do you enjoy playing with fire? I do.' He watches her gather the candle and the pack of cigarettes and place them on the bedside table. 'We'll start with the molten wax and then we'll try a cigarette.'

'I don't smoke,' he tells her.

'Tough.' She runs her fingers around his mouth at a lazy languid pace, over and over while she leans closer to him. 'Do you think I'll need an ashtray?'

He understands vaguely what she intends to do. 'Damn' right you will! I've had enough.' He gets up off the bed. In one movement he grabs her and swings her onto it. He sits on top of her.

'Get the hell off me,' she screams, arms flailing about near his head.

He's had enough of her assertiveness. He grabs the letter opener off the bedside table. 'I'm tired of playing your silly games. Today we're going to play *my* games. You'll do as I say this time.'

'The hell I will.' She shakes her body violently but his weight is overpowering. 'Get the fuck off me.'

He holds the blade in his right hand, his left hand progressively popping open the buttons of her cream blouse. The lace of an expensive bra and a cleft of pink flesh suddenly excite him. He kneads her breasts. 'You like it edgy. This time you're going to get what you like.' He pulls down her bra and brings the blade closer to her hardening nipples. It's a good sign. She too is aroused.

'You bastard!' she screams. Her left hand comes up. The surging naked flame of the cigarette lighter is suddenly in his face. He feels the heat, inhales the acrid fumes and smells singed hair. He lurches backwards. She scrambles up and pushes him off the bed onto the unforgiving hardwood floor where she stands over him and swings a pointed stiletto shoe into his balls. He crumples up and moans.

'Get out, you bastard. Get out now.' She pushes him along the floor with her feet. 'Get out.'

'Wait.' He's by the bedroom door, on his knees. 'Wait.' She has his suit and shirt in her arms. The hall door opens as she pushes him again. He slumps outside, clothes falling around him.

'Don't ever come back here. Don't ever call me again. And that's the last fucking recruitment job you'll ever do for Mitchell's in London!' She holds the letter opener in her hands as she stands over him. Henry lies on the floor, his balls aching, staring up at the glint of silver flashing before his eyes, wanting so much to have that blade in his own hand, to slide the edge into her chest. She slams the door. Henry needs a blade.

Henry checks the barren cabinets in his office and afterwards enters Selfridges from one of the Oxford Street entrances in the early afternoon. He ignores the expensive talent buying equally expensive gifts at the Louis Vuitton, Fendi and Loewe in-store concessions, and takes the escalator down to LG. He walks briskly through the books department where every single copy seems to be personally signed by the author. The silverware department is halfway down on the right-hand side.

He undertakes some reconnaissance from afar, standing by

the glass displays that border the stock, pretending to examine the christening presents, napkin rings, bridge pencils and photo frames. He stands beside the long mahogany table with the six silver-plate place settings and the rip-off candelabra at three grand a shot. Up on the wall to the right is a CCTV camera. Henry sees that the lens remains fixed on the tall glass case with the most expensive trinkets.

Bass music booms in LG. Henry waits. There are two male staff. One's a middle-aged assistant in a dark suit who cleans a display cabinet with a cloth and thus is available to serve customers. He's got nasty ginger gelled hair that climaxes in a geometric cranial point as sharp as his suit. Henry hears his affected lisp, smells his cheap aftershave and sees that he's all touchy-feely. He's hamming it up like he's on some Christmas Day menu. A younger tall black assistant in a crisp maroon shirt works the tills. Two bored-looking women dripping silks and winter furs enter and seize the attention of the middle-aged assistant. Henry approaches the vacant till and is greeted by the younger member of staff.

'Can I help you, sir?'

'I'm looking for a gift. I thought a silver letter opener might be a good idea, if you have them?'

Of course they have them. Selfridges have everything on five floors. They even sell refrigerators.

'Certainly. This way, sir.'

Henry follows. He sees the glass case in the corner, sees the third shelf down, sees the row of polished items. He sees what he wants but prefers to play the charade of the curious customer. The assistant opens the glass case with a key and runs his hands along the array of letter openers.

'We have a nice selection, sir. Is the gift for a gentleman or for a lady?'

Primarily for a gentleman. The overly inquisitive FX sort of gentleman. Henry guesses.

'A gentleman.'

'Do you prefer something small and discreet or large and substantial, sir?'

It will be exactly nine inches long, comprising a solid five-inch handle and a finely tapered four-inch blade. It will weigh ten ounces like the first one he weighed on Amanda's unused kitchen scales at home.

'Large and substantial.'

'What sort of price range are you considering, sir?'

£90 exactly. It says so in the Selfridges corporate gift catalogue.

'I'm prepared to pay for the best.'

'Excellent, sir.'

He's getting sick of all this 'sir' business. The assistant needs more backbone. Henry dutifully looks at each item until his eye rests upon the exquisite piece of craftsmanship from Carr's of Sheffield.

'How about that one?'

'A good choice, sir. It's made by Carr's of Sheffield. It's £90, sir.'

Henry recognises the nearby magnifying glass with silver handle, the one he carries around Europe but never needs to buy again. The assistant proffers the gift in his open hand.

'Would sir like to hold it? Be careful. The blade is quite sharp.'

Henry's wondering how he can resist the temptation to knife this guy. But the blade isn't sharp at all. He knows it's as blunt as the one in Diane's bedroom. He can work on that at home in peace.

'That would do nicely.'

The assistant turns over the item to display the hallmark. Henry recognises the RC abbreviation of Carr's, the number 925 confirming the standard of silver as being 92.5 per cent, the mark of the Office of Assay in Sheffield, the rampant lion and the date letter.

'If sir would like me to explain the hallmark ...'

'I'll take it.'

'If I may—'

'I said, I'll take it.'

They walk to the tills together. It's still gloriously quiet in the silver department.

'How is sir paying today?'

Henry takes out five twenties, still warm from the HSBC hole in the wall on Bedford Street. There's no need to hand over unnecessary personal details of Switch or Amex cards.

'Cash, please.'

The assistant rings up the sale and produces the burgundy gift box with the velvet interior.

'The gift comes with a presentation box, sir.'

The memories of Diane thrashing around under him are still too fresh. That kick still hurts.

'I don't need the box.'

'You did say that it was a gift, sir. I'm sure it will look much better in the box. Let me show you.' He slides the blade under the two clasps and holds it up. 'Now, you see. Much better, sir.'

Henry's getting to the end of his patience. He shrugs. 'Maybe. Is that it?'

The assistant shakes his head. 'I assume sir wants this to be gift-wrapped?'

Henry doesn't need a scene. He acquiesces.

'Sure.'

Henry watches him wrap the box in gold paper and knot a black cord around the package. With a broad smile, he hands over the gift in a trade-mark yellow bag. 'Someone's in for a pleasant surprise soon.'

CHAPTER THIRTY-TWO

CANARY WHARF, LONDON, E14: 12.05 P.M.

Adam lives with the mounting tension. There's still no word from the Dublin Garda. Each day at Mitchell's drags. Fear of meeting Henry pervades his working life. There's more edge to the trading floor today. It's only twenty-four hours to bonus day. Somehow the desk made millions in the past twelve months and only Adam seems to wonder how they did it. He watches Diane and Bruce deep in conversation inside her office. The FX desk staff will share the riches. Adam smells the greed. He hopes to be in the bonus pool in some small way but management have not yet approved his three-month probationary period.

Diane calls him on his direct telephone line late in the morning. 'You got a minute?' It's an order.

She doesn't bother to come outside to him. The signs are there already. This is ominous. 'Sure.'

They sit together behind closed doors. Diane has a single Excel printout on her desk. Adam can't read the content but it looks vaguely like a list of staff names and USD numbers, the sort of page used for bonuses. There are some changes circled in red pen. Adam grows anxious. Diane looks for the right words.

She pauses. 'Adam, there's no easy way to say this ...'

It's as he thinks. He has no desire to prolong the agony. 'I know what you're going to say.'

She looks up. 'Do you?'

'Yeah.' He nods. 'And it's okay with me. I understand. Such is life.'

Diane sighs. 'That's great. I could see us having a big argument.'

'I've only been here a few months. Next year I know I'll be in the bonus pool.'

She stares back in slow realisation. 'I think we're at cross purposes.'

His eyes light up. 'Really? Excellent. Then I *am* in the pool this year?'

Her expression hardens. It's the same old Diane he knows. 'Let's go back to before you interrupted me. There's no easy way to say this: you're being terminated. That's what I'm trying to tell you.'

'Serious?'

She rolls a pen in her fingers, her patience rapidly diminishing. 'Very.'

Adam points to her desk. 'What about that page with the bonuses?'

She turns over the page in annoyance at his observational skills. 'Forget about it. You're not on the list.'

'How come?' Adam almost loses the use of his vocal cords. 'What did I do?'

'It's not what you did, it's what you didn't do. You didn't perform. And you won't. Period.'

'That's too vague.'

Diane shifts uncomfortably. 'Let me spell it out for you bluntly. You have the ability and intelligence to be a *good* FX trader but you will never be a *great* FX trader. We need great traders. I've no doubt you will get another job in the City but not at Mitchell's. You haven't got what we need.'

Adam restrains his emotions. 'It can't be that final.'

'This is life at a US investment bank. Risk and rewards. The rewards are for those who excel, and they come tomorrow in hard dollars. The risk is that some don't stay the distance.'

'Don't I have some rights?'

'You're still on probation. Read the small print in Lloyd's offer letter that you signed last year.' Diane produces an envelope. 'Here's your termination letter. It's been checked by HR and by Legal. It's watertight.'

He opens the envelope. His hands shake as he reads. 'Don't I get some help here? Like from HR?'

'They can't help you. No one can. That's all.'

Adam looks around outside in vain. He sees the faces looking in at him. Bruce stares back at him. Muppet, Bookie and the others are chatting, even managing an occasional grin. They all know.

'What do I do for a job?' he asks.

'Go job-hunting. Maybe Kapital will have you back, but I doubt it. Call Henry Simpson again.'

He is tempted to make some jibe but holds back. 'So when do I leave?' he asks. 'End of this week?'

'Today. That's the firm's policy for traders. We'll pay you up until the end of the month. And when I say today, I don't mean five p.m. I mean now.' Diane points outside. One of the security guys from downstairs stands there. It's all been arranged. 'I mean immediately.' Diane is on her feet, motioning Adam to the door. 'Give me the keys to your bank car. I'll have it picked up later today from your home.'

'I never got a bank car.'

'Didn't you ask HR for one?'

'I thought I needed to pass probation.'

'Not so. HR erred. The others should have told you,' Diane shrugs. 'Just as well. No point getting used to one.'

Adam gets up reluctantly, still stunned. 'Is all this because I told you about the scam at the desk?'

'There's isn't a scam, as you call it. I've checked. Your suspicions are unconfirmed. So drop it.'

Adam sees a glimmer of hope. Diane's reaction is too dismissive.

'Maybe I will, and maybe I won't,' he counters.

'You don't really think that one individual like you can take on a giant US investment bank and win?'

'It's not just me. I can get help.'

'From who?'

'The FSA might be interested.'

She's very close to him now. 'No one likes a rat in the City. If you go and make some stupid allegation to the FSA, then your chances of ever working again at an FX desk will be nil. Think it over. Be smart.' Diane opens the door. 'You've got five minutes to gather your personal belongings. Goodbye.'

Adam walks back to his desk in a daze to collect his meagre possessions. The aged security guard follows behind. Bruce passes Adam, going in the opposite direction. No words are exchanged. Even though it's lunchtime there are enough colleagues on the sales floor to rubberneck at the unfolding drama. Those lucky guys and girls still with jobs in bonds, equities, derivatives and syndicate stare over in silence. He wishes that he had someone to share the burden. He misses Samantha. Adam feels like a criminal.

He runs over the wider ramifications in his mind. It's not just the end of a job. It's a potentially fatal blow to his career. He'll have to explain to any future employer how and why he left Mitchell's after only three months' probationary service. They'll think the worst, that he screwed up some trade or lost big money. He wonders what sort of legalistic job reference Mitchell's will give him. He doesn't think the clingy woman in HR will do him any favours this time. He'll have to go job-hunting. Maybe even call someone like Henry. But not Henry.

He opens his desk drawer and removes the contents. There's some loose change and spare apartment keys, a couple of half-read paperback thrillers, recent *Viz* and *Loaded* magazines, his spare toothbrush and toothpaste, some Links cufflinks, a tie to be used in emergencies but sadly of no use today. He finds his old backpack under the desk, stuffs the items inside and is about to stand up.

The FX desk is deserted. Muppet and the others have drifted off to lunch, hopefully more out of embarrassment than hunger. Bruce is in Diane's office and is engrossed in conversation with his boss, his back to Adam and obscuring Diane's view. There has to be some parting shot, some final insult, he can make. The security guard is a joke. He's a pensioner, sixty-plus, of such a slight build that a decent gust of wind would topple him. He's totally lacking in confidence, standing at the far end of the desk, afraid to approach.

Adam has an idea. 'I'll just log off from my PC,' he advises.

The pensioner is about to mumble something conciliatory through a bad set of dentures but nods instead. Adam wavers. It's hardly a wise career move but it is tempting. He doesn't know how organised Diane is but it's worth a try. He doesn't log off. Instead he opens up the Reuters 3000 trading screen. He wonders if his user ID is still active. He taps a few keys on the keyboard. The words appear on screen. His ID is valid. It might work. He types.

ADAM> HIHI KAP

He waits. Someone must be manning the FX desk in Kapital.

ED> HIHI ADAM

He knows with whom he prefers to trade today.

ADAM > BEAMER PLS

There's an immediate response.

BMW> HIHI ADAM

Adam has a moment's hesitation. This is potentially serious shit, bordering on the illegal, even the insane. He thinks about the way Diane and Mitchell's have treated him over the past three months, then decides to continue.

ADAM > EUR 100

BMW > 50 60

Adam eyeballs the buy and sell prices from Kapital. The bid / offer prices are indeed the market rates. It's a valid quote. Now he must see if Beamer will play softball with him. Adam types his trade.

ADAM > I SELL EUR 100 MIO .8960

There's a delay in the reply. He guessed as much. Beamer is puzzled. The rate should be .9960.

BMW > EE?

EE means error. Beamer saw his deliberate rate-error. But today Adam wants to trade at an off-market rate.

ADAM > OK – RPT – I SELL EUR 100 MIO .8960

BMW > R U SURE?

ADAM > YES

BMW > RISK BIBI

The dealt rate is ten per cent off the current market dollar-versus-euro cross-rates on the price feeds. Ten per cent of a hundred million euro trade represents ten million euros profit for someone. Adam thinks, hopes, that this is a legally binding FX trade for both parties. He's a valid user of Reuters. The termination letter shows him as an employee of Mitchell's until close of business today. It must be a valid trade on behalf of Mitchell Leonberg.

'Are you ready yet?' mumbles the watching pensioner, shifting on his flat feet with growing anxiety.

'Nearly there. I gotta power down the PC.'

Adam is still completely unsupervised. It's payback time. Big-time. He knows the clock is against him. Bruce could walk outside to the floor any time. Colleagues have turned away. He's still connected to Kapital.

ADAM > HIHI BEAMER

BMW > HIHI ADAM

ADAM > I SELL EUR 100 MIO .8960
BMW > R U SURE x 2?
ADAM > YES
BMW > RISK – BIBI

Adam switches off the PC and follows the pensioner towards the elevators. They are near Diane's office. Adam works out the numbers on the walk of shame along the trading floor. He passed twenty million euros of trading profit from Mitchell's to Kapital. Right now Beamer in Kapital is long two hundred million euro and is closing out his position in the market and crystallising his profits, counting his blessings, wondering if these magic trades are a dream or reality. Adam sees Bruce turn and open the door.

'See you,' says Adam.

Bruce doesn't know it but right now he and Mitchell's are short two hundred million euro. He probably won't learn the news until later today, maybe not even at five p.m. when he squares the trading book and passes any positions to his colleagues in New York in a more advantageous time zone for late trading.

'Are you still here?' Bruce snarls.

An expert position keeper like Samantha would have spotted the huge trading error immediately, if they still had her services at the bank, if she had stayed, if they'd treated her right at the desk and given her the career that she deserved. Some desk clerk in the back office will eventually spot the off-market rate in the trade verification or confirmation process but by then it will be too late. Bruce will have to buy back euros to square his position. He will be paying closer to .99 rather than .89. He'll be booking a twenty million euro loss to the bottom line. Adam can't see any way out of this for his former colleagues.

'Evidently so,' he replies with an unnerving smile.

Henry walks into a downmarket travel agency at the commercial end of Edgware Road nearest to Marble Arch. It's one of those agents with an unpronounceable Arabic name on the door and a window full of handwritten never-to-be-repeated once-in-a-lifetime around-the-world bargain fares on dodgy Far Eastern and Chinese airlines with a tendency to plummet into mountains. Henry feels like he's the only English speaker amidst the sea of foreign faces and Middle Eastern garb. He approaches the guy at the counter.

'I need to get away somewhere.'

Twenty minutes later he hands over four grand in cash and pockets a Singapore Airlines Royal Orchid Class one-way ticket in the name of Graham Berisford. He spends an hour doing manic shopping on Oxford and Regent Streets including a stop in Tesco Metro near Oxford Circus to sustain him for the next day or so. He hails a cab in the rain to take him and his carrier bags back to Islington.

He is alone at home. Amanda is at another oh-so-essential PR event. He microwaves a low-cal Spag Bol, wolfs down most of the tepid contents and chucks the remaining strands of congealed pasta into the bin. His appetite has faded. He has work to do. He carries the bags down to the basement room. Amanda never dares to enter this room, whether to power up the Dixon's PC, to inspect the crates of fine red and white laid down mostly for effect, or to try the modest assortment of virtually unused Black & Decker power tools.

First he opens the M&S bags. He's bought so much that he might single-handedly assist in the recovery of this former high-street retail star. He packs socks, boxers, T-shirts and shoes into his Samsonite. The Gap bags contain shirts and chinos. There's an Austin Reed suit and a few ties from Tie Rack in case he needs to look smart. Next to go inside is a bag from Boots with blades, foam, shampoo, gel, a comb and dental floss. He throws in a few paperbacks from Books Etc, smiling wryly. One of them is a serial-killer book. Then some pens and paper. He is pleased that the entire contents of a new life fit inside a flight bag.

The last bag he opens is from Selfridges. He listens. Everything is still quiet upstairs. It's safe. He takes the letter opener out of its box. There is a rarely used vice at the end of the pristine DIY bench. Henry wraps the handle of the letter opener in paper to prevent undue damage, slides it between the welcoming jaws, handle side first, and pivots the vice tight. He runs a finger along the edge. The blade is too blunt to use.

He opens the old Victorian canteen of cutlery that lies upon one of the shelves. It's some old handed-down heirloom from Amanda's side of the family. He takes out the bone-handled knife sharpener and begins to draw the ridged metal along the blunt edge of the letter opener. The noise and heat rise as metal grates upon metal. He sees the edges slowly narrow and the point crystallise. Ten minutes of patient and consistent work is enough. Any more and the blade will be too brittle to use.

He holds a sheet of A4 paper from the dusty PC laser printer in his left hand, takes the blade in his right and runs it through the paper. One half of the page remains in his hand, the other flutters slowly down to the bare concrete floor. Examining the edge of the page, he's not quite satisfied with the cut. Not clean enough.

'What's all the noise?'

He stops as if frozen. It's Amanda's voice. He turns. She stands in the doorway.

'Why are you here?' he stammers.

'I live here. Don't ever forget that,' she retorts.

'I mean ... what happened to tonight?'

'The B-list so-called celebs failed to show. So we called it a night, earlier than we'd planned.' Amanda surveys the basement afresh. Her eyes rest upon the open canteen of cutlery and Henry's right hand. 'What are you doing? Is that from my grandmother's inheritance? It is. Jesus, Henry, it's a damn' antique. It's not to be used.'

He feels the urge rising within. This is not going to plan. 'There's no harm done. Leave it out.'

Amanda is closer now. She sees the empty shopping bags and bulging flight bag. 'Where are you going?'

Most fatal stab wounds are homicidal. Often there is only one wound that pierces a vital organ or nerve centre, causing death from shock, haemorrhage, or the ceasing of a vital function. Homicidal stab wounds often appear on the back, neck, and upper chest. Wounds of the same depth, wounds of non-vital areas, scrimmage wounds, and multiple wounds of a vital area strongly indicate a homicide. Several stab wounds to the breasts and genitals are suggestive of a sex-related homicide. And defence-type wounds on hands and arms and wounds to the back or other areas not easily reached by the victim hint at homicide.

He's tired of her questioning. She's invading his personal domain. Henry is seething. Amanda knows too much about him, about his lifestyle, his habits, his likes and his dislikes. She's become a liability. She has signed the sale agreement with Lionel Roberts. The cash is on the way. 'I'm going nowhere.'

'It doesn't look that way to me. Are you running away with that bloody woman from the wedding? Or worse?'

The depth and shape of a fatal stab wound may give a clue to the type of weapon used. The track of a weapon may be clear in fleshy areas. However, when a weapon penetrates inner organs, such as the heart, its track may not be accurate. Inner organs change in shape and position after death and when a body is moved. Also, a strong stabbing force against a soft area like the stomach can depress the area, making the wound deeper than the true length of the weapon.

Henry wonders if he left the airline ticket on the table in the kitchen. He will telephone her PR agency tomorrow and say she is off ill for the day, to buy some time. She has come to the end of her usefulness. He steps forward with an adequately but not optimally sharpened blade in his right hand, his good hand. 'You're right, dear.' She looks blankly.

He moves closer. 'It is worse. Far worse than you can imagine.'

The 37-year-old woman is found dead in a basement room in Islington. She is found fully clothed in trousers, jumper, underwear and shoes and lying on her back on the floor. The room appears undisturbed. The door to the room is ajar. Adjacent to the various stab wounds is a bruise produced as a result of blunt force and possibly as the result of a separate blow to the chest inflicted during the course of the struggle. More likely, the bruise represents impact with the hand holding the blade at the time of the stabbing. This would imply that the entire length of the blade entered the heart and that the blade length is therefore 10cm.

CHAPTER THIRTY-THREE

BARRIER POINT, LONDON, E16: 3.25 P.M.

Adam sits alone at home, unemployed, numbed by recent events. And what's on TV? First there's the Kilroy show with 'I was born the wrong sex', then the Sally Raphael show with 'Grandmothers Who Work as Exotic Dancers', followed by the Jenny Jones show with 'The Polygraph Says I'm Not the Father' and at lunch the Ricki Lake show with 'High School Geeks Who Now Flaunt It'. Daytime reality TV sucks. The phone rings in the hallway. He rushes to answer, the relief evident in his voice. 'Hello.'

'Hi, Adam. Henry here.'

His enthusiasm vanishes immediately. He wonders what the angle can be. 'What do you want?'

'Relax. That's no way to talk to a friend. I heard the news from Mitchell's.'

'News travels fast when you're bedding the FVP of FX,' acknowledges Adam.

'Sorry it didn't work out.'

'It's not your fault. It's mine, according to Diane.'

'We should talk about your future,' asks Henry. 'How about meeting up today? My office. Five p.m.'

'This time I'll go somewhere else.'

'You don't wanna do that. I can drop around, if you like? I got some great FX vacancies.'

'Like last time? Forget it. Bye.'

Adam hangs up and paces the wooden floor of his apartment. A visit from Henry is potentially fatal. Adam's told no one but Samantha, Trish and that cop Doyle of his suspicions. He can't stomach the wait, the sitting around at home, wasting away. He wishes he could be back on the trading floor at Mitchell's, not for the company of Bruce and the others, but for the security. Henry would never try anything at work. Home is a different matter.

He dials Dublin again from the hallway. 'I need to speak to Doyle urgently.'

A switchboard voice replies. 'He's not in the office today.'

Adam has forgotten his movements. 'He's in London, isn't he? Where is he? Tell me.'

The voice sounds vaguely impressed. 'He is indeed in London. But I can't tell you where he is.'

'Jesus! Tell me. This could be a matter of life and death. Mine. C'mon.'

The voice is frustrated. 'I can't tell you because I don't know where he is.'

Adam looks at the card from Dublin. There is no mobile number. 'Gimme his mobile, then.'

'We don't divulge mobile telephone numbers of detectives. Please try later.'

The voice hangs up. Adam paces the apartment. Doyle is in London. But where? He must be with the Met. Adam doesn't know anyone there. Does he call 999 and say that a serial killer is about to make a house call and it's not for a social chat? They'll think he's a loony. He stands by the window and looks down. He is trapped inside the block. He needs to get out. The nearest police station is Barking. He takes the elevator down and revs the Astra out of the gates.

Barking police station is quiet, untouched since the 1980s. Behind the counter a teenage officer with gelled hair, blotchy skin and raw razor rash slowly grows into an oversized uniform. Adam approaches.

'I need to speak to someone in charge.'

The officer looks up and then vaguely around the room. 'That'll be me, then. I'm in charge today.'

'I mean someone senior. No offence meant, mate.'

The officer stares back at him. 'Senior? So this is something important, is it?' Adam nods. 'I think the Commissioner and Deputy Commissioner are both busy. Would the duty sergeant do?'

Adam shakes his head. 'How about someone from CID?'

'Do you watch *The Bill* much on TV?' says the officer.

'I'm serious.'

'Me too. CID will want to know what this is about before they cut short their tea break.'

'It's a bit complicated.'

'I got the time.'

There are no other words. 'I think I'm next on a serial killer's list.'

The officer smiles. 'You taking the Michael? We don't have many serial killers in the UK. You want the USA for that.' Adam remains impassive. 'You are serious, aren't you? Jesus Christ, CID will love you.'

Ten minutes later Adam is in a room with a plain-clothes DC. He summarises the past few months. The DC takes notes as his initial vacant incredulity slowly recedes. He looks up from his scribblings.

'This is either a massive wind-up to waste police time, or else you're about to give me a major push up the Met career ladder. And for your sake, it had better damn' well be the latter.'

'Your career is in good hands. So what can you do for me? Round-the-clock protection? A safe house?'

The DC throws down his pen and watches it roll across the desk.

'We haven't got unlimited resources for that sort of lark. Until I can check these facts out, I'll get the area car to spin by your place at Barrier Point to keep an eye on things there. I'll call you tomorrow.'

'Spin by?' Adam thumps his fist down on the table. 'It's not enough.'

'You don't even fit the profile of the type of people you say died.'

'I know I don't. I'll be the first in the UK. Simpson knows I'm on to him. He just called me!'

'Do what anyone else would do in your circumstances. Disappear. Go to a friend's house. Or to relatives. Anywhere. Leave me your mobile phone number. I'll be in touch as soon as I can. Trust me.'

Adam signs a statement and sits in his car. It's dark. He wonders where to run. He glances in the rear-view mirror at a solo male walking along the pavement. He's becoming paranoid. He needs to be somewhere far away. Now. He dials the pre-programmed number in his mobile. She answers the call immediately.

'Samantha, it's Adam. How are you?'

'I've been better. How's life at Mitchell's? It seems quiet there.'

She doesn't know about his termination. 'I'm not at work. They fired me.'

'I'm so sorry. What are you doing? What about Henry?'

'That's why I am calling. He called me at home and I can't contact the cops in Dublin. I'm scared.'

'Does Henry know where you are?

'He has my telephone number so he must know my new address. Diane must have given it to him from work. And he has my parents' address on his files from when I first moved to the City from home. He knows where I go. I need to be a step ahead. I need a safe house. Tonight.'

She catches his drift. 'Mum would love to see you back. You'll be safe here.'

'Safer, maybe. Does Henry know your mother's home address?'

'I don't know. Mitchell's HR department have it on their files. Diane would know, Henry might know.'

'It's a chance I'll have to take. Right now, Cornwall seems a much safer proposition.' Adam looks at his watch. 'I can be with you by midnight tonight.'

'Why not earlier?' she asks, concerned.

'I've got one more visit to make today and then I'll pack a bag at home in ten minutes. See you later.'

'Supper will be waiting. Take care.' He's sure that she's not referring to the M4 traffic.

Adam hangs up and drives along the A13, away from Barrier Point and towards Docklands. He parks nearby and walks into an office building in a narrow side street. The sign over the reception desk says Financial Services Authority. He asks the girl for an immediate appointment. Damn Diane. Damn Bruce. Damn Mitchell Leonberg & Co Inc. Damn all their kind in their ivory tower in Canary Wharf.

'I'd like to report a scandal in a US investment bank.'

Today is the day. Diane gets in late and immediately closes her office door for some privacy. She powers up Outlook, looking for the vital message plus the attachment. The e-mail is in her in-box, entitled AICPFX and sent by Jerry Horowitz in HO. Mitchell's has an in-house name for everything. Why call it a bonus when some genius in HR dreamt up a Annual Incentive Compensation Plan? Today is Bonus Day.

She opens the Excel file and eyeballs the final set of numbers received overnight. This year she is pleased. Sometimes Horowitz makes last-minute adjustments for some personal gratification but this year he's left Diane's proposed allocation of the bonus pool to her team unaltered. Her fears subside. Someone on the trading floor said that this year the bonus pool would be a puddle. It hasn't been a great year in the markets for most but her inspired team has racked up great profits with that wonderful ECB scam.

She looks forward to breaking the good news. Megabucks always bring smiles. Bonus announcements are embargoed until later so that her New York peers can talk to their own staff. She extrapolates the numbers on the Excel file. Most individuals are up. She should be too. Only Horowitz knows her final number. *Six figures, here we come.* This should be a very rewarding day. There's a knock on the door.

'Yep,' she invites.

Bruce stands in the doorway, appearing reluctant to venture any further. 'Can we talk?'

She nods and closes the file on screen, aware of its confidentiality. 'You're a bit early today,' she jokes.

'It's not that.' Bruce closes the door, something he rarely does voluntarily. She sees his face, oily with sweat, much paler than usual. His eyes are red, the edges of his retinas bloodshot. Maybe he didn't get much sleep last night. She wonders if he's unwell, or perhaps he's going to do something stupid like resign. But no one resigns on bonus day. They always wait until payday at the end of January. Maybe the ECB scam has taken a turn for the worse. She watches him choose his words. 'I've got some bad news.'

She shakes her head. 'I don't want to hear bad news. This is a good-news day.' She's already said too much and given Bruce an explicit indication that the numbers are up. He doesn't lighten up. 'Can't it wait?'

'I should have called you at home last night, only I wasn't sure till very late.'

Diane turns away from her PC and leans closer, concern growing.

'Sure about what?'

He looks directly at her, as if it makes a difference or lessens the pain of being the messenger.

'We lost twenty million euro.'

Diane laughs. 'What the hell are you talking about? You're not making any sense. We made twenty million bucks last year. That's what the year-end numbers from Finance confirm. That's what we told Horowitz. That's what today's bonuses are based upon. You don't dispute that fact, do you?'

'Yes, and no. We *did* make twenty million last year. But we lost twenty million yesterday.'

'That's impossible. We can't lose twenty million anything in a single day. Are you out of your mind?'

'I had to close out a naked euro position last night at midnight with Westpac in Sydney and ANZ in Wellington. Muppet and I spent bloody hours looking at the trading yesterday, trying to find where the black hole had come from. We crystallised a loss of twenty million or thereabouts. What a fucking day!'

Diane is genuinely worried. The mention of any black hole to a head of trading desk is a red rag to a bull. Bruce has his head in his hands and looks close to tears, his career rapidly going down the pan.

'Jesus. I still don't understand. What exactly happened?'

'Someone at the desk did two euro/dollar trades late yesterday morning. We traded twice with Kapital at rates that were miles away from the market. That's where the bloody loss originated. At the close of business we found this short euro position that came from nowhere. Later we found the trader's name.'

'Who the hell was it?' Diane clenches her fist. 'I'll have his balls in a vice. I'll fire him now.'

'Too late. It was Adam.'

'Impossible. He left yesterday. I saw him walk out of here after we fired him.'

'We checked the times of the trades. You know he stopped by the desk on the way out?'

'Yeah, to get his personal stuff. So what?'

'He told the security guard he was logging off from Reuters. Only he wasn't. He was logging on to trade.'

'Didn't you get his user access cancelled by ITS?'

'Only after you and I were in here together. He had five minutes to trade. And he did. With his old mates.'

'Goddamn it!' Diane jumps up and paces the room, looking for a solution. 'Hang on, this won't wash. You say the trades are off-market. We can get them cancelled. We can call Kapital.'

'I already did that at seven a.m. this morning. I spoke to a guy called Beamer who runs the Kapital FX desk. He says that Kapital did the trades on Reuters in good faith. At the time Adam Lewis was a legitimate user of Reuters on behalf of Mitchell's. So Beamer says the trades are good. No joy.'

'Does that mean Kapital made twenty million yesterday?' asks Diane.

'Unfortunately.'

'Then we'll sue the ass off them.'

Bruce shakes his head, the despair evident. 'Do you really want a court case where we fight over a rogue trader who ripped us off? We'd be a public laughing stock. A case where our FX trading profits might be analysed in the full light of day, let me remind you. There's a real risk that the ECB stuff might come to light. I think not, Diane. It's not worth it. Anyway, if I was in Kapital's shoes, I'd tell us to piss off too.'

'Whose side are you on?'

'Ours. But this time we're beat. We spend twelve successful months screwing the ECB and the market every month and then some probationary grunt screws us in turn. Poetic justice or what?'

Diane is now pacing the room, slowly aware of the growing ramifications of the huge loss.

'I'm gonna have to tell Horowitz about this, first thing New

York time. I'd better call him at home uptown. On bonus day too. I'm finished here. We all are. If Adam Lewis was here now, I'd kill him.'

'Get to the back of the queue.'

Henry is at home in the early evening. It's his last night ever in Islington. A final eyeball of his home is required. He grabs his favourite coat from the hook in the hall, ignoring his now redundant briefcase on the floor, and walks down one flight of stairs to the den. He steps over the body, takes the letter opener from the DIY bench and wonders if the Selfridges silverware department will miss his custom. He carefully places the blade inside the pocket of his coat, handle uppermost.

He runs up the two flights of stairs to their bedroom. His assorted effects are on the mantelpiece over the wrought-iron fireplace. He slowly examines his tattered old passport page by page, sees the immigration stamps and recalls a lifetime of exhilarating travel, ignoring the long-ago honeymoon in Bali. He admires his new passport. It's virginal. He folds it back and forth several times to give it that well-used look. He admires his photograph. This passport is a work of art. It's not a fake, it's the genuine article.

He takes his new CK wallet from his back pocket and checks it. Inside there's a few thousand quid in cash extracted over the past few days from faceless cash machines within the environs of Covent Garden. It's enough change to get him to the other side of the world in a few days. He has no credit cards. He will reapply for another card soon with his new identity. In the meantime he feels naked without their plastic security.

He picks up the Bank Julius Baer headed notepaper. Henry watched the account manager personally sign the receipt on a day trip to Zurich. The receipt is in the name of Graham Berisford and is addressed care of the exclusive private bank. Henry runs his finger slowly over the row of zeros shown at the foot of the document. One and a half million pounds is in a high-interest fixed-term sterling deposit. The funds are safe until a wire transfer instruction from the other side of the world will summon them to a new home.

Last into his pocket is a ticket for this evening's 9.45 p.m. Eurostar departure from Waterloo to Gare du Nord. The reservation is in his new surname. In any event the passport check from the UK to France is a hit-and-miss eyeball affair as hassled authorities focus on waves of Albanian and Croatian refugees coming in the other direction. It's a first-class reservation and includes a three-course meal. Henry is already hungry. His convenience food is all gone.

He pulls the hall door closed and walks along Gibson Square for the last time, savouring the tranquillity of the chill evening. He dumps the Samsonite into the boot and slips into the driver's seat of the Saab. In a few hours' time he will abandon it as a suitable decoy in the anonymous car park at City Airport, take the shuttle-bus service back to Liverpool Street station and select a cheap and nasty minicab to Waterloo.

Henry anticipates as he drives. He knows how the UK press will report these events. In a few days, time they will run a lead story about the mysterious disappearance of a City recruitment player, and the terrible fate that befell his wife. But before then, Henry is certain that the same newspapers will run a story about the murder of an unemployed former FX trader in his rented Docklands apartment.

CHAPTER THIRTY-FOUR

BARRIER POINT, LONDON, E16: 7.35 P.M.

Adam is followed into the underground car park. It's the yellow Beetle. He and Lisa get out of their cars at the same time. His mind is miles away, focused on late-night drives to safety in deepest Cornwall. This time he doesn't offer to carry her shopping.

'How are you?' asks Lisa, sounding as if she listens to too many Vodafone adverts.

'Fine.' If only it were true. They take the elevator together. He takes a deep breath. 'Eh – call down anytime,' he says finally.

She smiles. 'I will. Soon. How about tomorrow evening?'

He shakes his head. 'Sorry, I have to go away for a few days. I'll be back as soon as I can. Maybe then.'

'I promise. I will call down.'

Adam sits in his living room, summoning the energy to pack a bag. The noxious air of the storage heating circulates in the narrow confines. He recalls how easily he was fired, imagines what this week's bonus pool is like, wonders how to get another job in the City with such an immovable stain on his CV and how he'll pay next month's extortionate rent. There's a firm knock on the hall door. He smiles. The videophone never rang. It's a local who doesn't need to get past the door on the ground floor. Lisa is indeed keen.

He strides, almost runs, to the hallway, glad of the impetus. He looks out through the magnified peephole but can't see anyone there. He assumes she's standing to one side. 'Welcome!' He unlocks the mortice lever and swings open his hall door to his guest. He's momentarily stunned as recognition dawns. 'You?'

'Adam, great to find you at home tonight.' Henry leans against the door jamb, his shoulders sideways on, waiting to be let inside the apartment like it's a mere formality. Adam says nothing, words seemingly failing his vocal cords. 'I was passing by.'

'You were passing by?' Adam knows that he sounds incredulous. He thinks about slamming the door.

'Sure. In the car. I've got many clients down in Docklands.'

'How do you know where I live?' asks Adam. He could still slam the door. It might work. He should.

Henry searches for the right words. 'I have my sources.' He laughs. 'Mostly in investment banks.'

'How did you get in the main gate?'

'It was open. There was a car arriving. Don't blame me, blame that dumb security guard in the box.'

'And what about the door downstairs?' There is still time to slam this door. But Adam's frozen.

'There was someone leaving on foot. They were polite and held the door open.' Henry moves closer. 'Hey, relax. I know you're stressed out, that's why I'm here. To help. I heard about the bad news at Mitchell's. Thought I could sort you out. So I'll come in, shall I?' It's more of an instruction.

There's an urgency now in Henry's voice. Adam needs time to think. This is happening too fast. He knows too much and too little about his guest. Henry is not getting inside tonight. Adam stands rooted to the spot and refuses to open the hall door any further. He does his best to hide his fear. Maybe Henry will go away if he stands his ground.

Adam is only seconds away from being trapped within his own home.

'You on your own in here?' Henry asks, looking past him and down the hallway.

'So?'

'So you need to talk to someone.'

'I'm fine about it,' he lies.

Henry steps forward. 'C'mon. I feel bad about what happened. I got you the job.'

Henry sees the doubt, sees him relax momentarily. Henry is all smiles as he steps past Adam.

'Thought I'd never bloody well get inside.'

They shake hands belatedly, one party shaking more enthusiastically than the other. Henry's grip is firm. His right palm is sweaty. He immediately puts his hand back into the deep pocket of his coat.

Adam follows him into the living room. Henry seems unimpressed with the view of the Thames and takes Adam's favourite seat nearest the door. Adam is forced to take a seat by the balcony door.

'So, how are you doing, Adam?'

'I've had better days.'

'How's your friend Samantha?' asks Henry. 'I heard she left Mitchell's too. Voluntarily.'

Adam decides the less said the better. 'She's okay.'

'So you know where she is.' Henry leans forward. 'Where is Samantha? I'd like to contact her.'

Adam feels his confidence rising. 'That information is only available on a need-to-know basis.'

'Look, I'm not staying long.' Henry shifts in his seat. 'But I need to know where she is. Is she in London?'

Lisa paces up and down the hallway of her apartment. She's made it back from the shops in the rain, had a vaguely promising conversation with Adam until he blew her out, and now everything is in the fridge or packed away. On the hall table is a white envelope, propped up against a gilt table lamp. It's been a daily reminder, staring back at her for more than a week. Inside is a New Year's Day card that she must deliver in person. She picks up the envelope. There's no name written on the front. Just '1205!'

She kept aside a Christmas card a few weeks ago but it too lay on the table undelivered until it was past its best-by date. She threw it out with much regret. She either delivers this one, or waits days until he comes back from wherever he goes to that's so bloody important and top secret. She knows Adam is still at home tonight. She's heard the apartment door open and close and then some internal doors too. Someone is still at home.

She stands by the door, card in hand. Maybe he's not interested. He didn't volunteer much tonight. He seemed to be miles away, lost in inner thought. Or maybe he is interested. He made the effort to come up to her apartment with her post when he could have binned it or put it anonymously into her letter box. He speaks to her in the car park.

It was a serious error on her part when Adam met Mike. She knows how it looked. Mike and she heading out for a romantic meal for two in some smoochy Italian place and then back home for afters. There was no opportunity to explain. The fact was that they watched a movie in the Surrey Docks Cineplex and got a Chinese takeaway before his flight next morning from City Airport on the ticket that she bought for him. Staff discount, of course, ten per cent of what everyone else pays. Mike plus his rugby mates went skiing in the Alps. Lisa never told Adam that Mike is her younger brother.

She has second thoughts tonight, but Adam's worth it, she just knows it. He smiled at least once and it's a smile worth seeing again, if she can give some encouragement. He looks smart and is out 9 to 5 so he has a job of sorts. Dream on. Maybe he works locally in Canary Wharf, sells bonds or equities to corporates, sells Docklands flats to investors, sells pensions or life assurance to suckers, sells shoes in Barratt's to old dears. Hard to tell.

One last glance is needed. She opens the envelope and carefully reads the short verse. The words she chose are perfect, non-committal yet appropriate. She has signed the card merely '1305'. She wonders with hindsight why she only wrote her apartment number, then closes her hall door and walks down one flight.

Henry waits for the optimal moment, his right hand staying in the pocket of his coat, the blade growing heavier by the minute. There is time to savour the anticipation. He estimates his pulse rate to be close to ninety b.p.m. Almost too fast. His mind races ahead over the next few glorious minutes of closure.

Adam sits by the window. Henry could finish it now but the curtains are open to the world below. It's an unnecessary risk. From his reconnaissance of the interior he knows that the kitchen is the most confined room in the apartment and so represents the best place to make an easy killing. He jumps as the doorbell rings.

'Wonder who that is?' says Adam.

'Are you expecting someone?' Henry replies with unassumed interest.

Adam laughs. 'No one calls around usually. This is more visitors than I've ever had before.'

Adam leaves the living room. Henry is alone with his thoughts. He's breaking many of his Ten Commandments tonight. He will kill on the UK mainland. There are many unprecedented complications. The long-haul exit route is untried and untested. He knows the target personally. He has a definite motive. It's all wrong but feels so right. This time it's personal. He can hear the conversation in the hall.

'Hi.' It's a girl's voice.

'Hello,' replies the target.

Who the hell is out there? Henry wonders.

'I brought you a New Year's card. Before you head off.'

Where the hell is Adam heading off to? Maybe to find Samantha? He knows where she is.

'Thanks.'

Is that it? Why doesn't she piss off and let him sort out things here?

'Won't you come in?' Adam asks.

Why the hell did he have to say that?

'Love to.'

What the fuck is she coming inside for? Doesn't she know what's good for her health?

Henry stands up to greet the girl, releases his firm grip on the blade and offers a handshake. He watches her subtly wipe her hand afterwards on her faded denims. They both know he's too sweaty.

Adam effects the introductions. 'Lisa lives upstairs. This is Henry. He's going soon.' So she'll be able to give the filth an ID but by then he'll be long gone under a new identity. Maybe she's not staying, maybe she'll go back upstairs and get to live a little while longer. 'Lisa, you want a drink, a beer?' Or maybe not.

She nods. 'How about a coffee?'

'No problem.'

'What about Henry?' she asks. They're both staring at him. He feels unloved, unwanted. Does she know something already? Is her feminine intuition working overtime?

'What about me?' he replies.

'You want a coffee?' She's the proper little homemaker.

'I told Adam, I'm not staying long.' Just long enough for you to disappear.

Adam goes to the kitchen. They're alone. He could take the target right now in the kitchen but that's not the plan. She's not supposed to be here too. Why is this all going wrong?

The girl reclines on the sofa and looks at him. 'I think I've seen you before somewhere.'

Henry smiles back. 'I don't think so.'

'I've got a good memory. You fly much?' she asks. This is beginning to feel like the third degree.

'Now and again,' he replies, already wishing she were dead too.

'What do you do?' she asks again. This *is* the fucking third degree.

'I work in the City.'

'Me too. Sort of.'

Maybe he does know her. 'Where do you work?'

'Not that City, a different one. I'm based out of City Airport. Maybe I saw you there?'

'I don't use City. There are too few routes. As an airport, it's a joke.'

'Where do you use?' she asks.

Henry wonders if he should kill them both now. Just for the heck of it. He evaluates the risks and downside. They need to be in the same room. Henry must be nearest to the hall door to block any escape. 'I prefer Gatwick.'

She recoils in horror. 'Gatwick's a nightmare. It's always packed with charters. Big queues.'

'I like it like that. I like the chaos. I like the queues.'

If he kills Adam first, there's a good chance that she'll be a bloody screamer and then the whole block will get to hear her reaction to the blade. If he kills the girl first, the element of surprise is lost and there's a chance the target will tackle him. He's never killed twice at the same place and time before. He wonders if it will feel twice as good.

'What sort of business are you in?' she perseveres.

'The people business. I'm a headhunter.'

'Do you always get your man?' she jokes.

'Sometimes companies hire women.'

There's an uneasy silence. They can hear the rattle of cups and spoons in the kitchen. She stares over at him, looking for some mutual recognition. Henry thinks that she's good to look at. She's got a face that any guy would watch on overtime. Soon she's going to realise that she doesn't know him at all.

She points. 'I've got it,' she announces. 'I *have* seen you before.'

'Where?'

'I saw you here. A few nights ago.'

'I don't think so. I haven't been up here before.'

'I mean downstairs, in the grounds.'

Adam returns. Henry recalls his reconnaissance trip. 'You must have the wrong person.'

She shakes her head. 'I don't. It was a few nights ago in the rain. I was coming back from City in the car and you were walking out. I remember that coat you've got on now. It was you, I'm sure.'

Adam is too interested. 'What have I missed?'

'Nothing.' Henry handles the blade in his pocket. 'I said, I think you're mistaken.'

'Mistaken about what?' Adam holds two steaming mugs of coffee. Henry is getting the distinct impression that he's surplus to requirements.

'I saw Henry here a few nights ago. He was walking around the complex in the rain.'

'You know someone else who lives here?' asks the target.

Henry grits his teeth. 'I said, I wasn't here.'

''Course you were.' She smiles at him. 'Actually, I thought you looked a bit shifty that night. Like you were casing the joint. So anyway, how do you know Adam? What brings you here?'

Henry searches for the right words. 'I'm here to help him get a new job. He was fired this week.'

She's horrified and stands up. 'God, that's terrible. I'm sorry. That's serious. I'll go and let you guys talk.'

Perfect. She's finally got the message that she's not wanted. She'll go. It's killing time.

'Stay,' instructs the target. 'Henry is the one who's going. We can talk shop some other time.'

He fingers the wet blade in his pocket. It's now or never. He must decide. 'But it's your career, Adam. Your future is in my hands.'

Adam points to the door. 'No, thanks. That's enough for tonight. I'll call you. Don't call me.'

Henry stands by the hall door, blade hidden in hand, wondering if he can still strike, weighing up his chances. 'You're a lucky guy,' he says eventually.

'Because someone like Lisa wants to call around to my apartment, you mean?'

Henry steps across the threshold. 'No. Just lucky.'

FEBRUARY

CHAPTER THIRTY-FIVE

NEW SCOTLAND YARD, LONDON SW1:
10.25 A.M.

Adam is in an anonymous office off Whitehall. Across the desk a middle-aged officer with nicotine stained hands is doing his utmost to defend the work of the Metropolitan Police Service Missing Persons Bureau.

'If it weren't for the request from my colleagues then I wouldn't . . .'

'Look, I appreciate your taking the time to meet me,' interjects Adam. 'So can you help with Simpson?'

'Henry Simpson is different.'

'He sure is. He killed people. He tried to kill me. I need to know where he is. I need to sleep at night.'

'Finding someone like Simpson is not what we do.'

'Do you know where Simpson is?' Adam watches the officer shake his head. 'Then he's a missing person.'

The officer produces a twenty-pack of Rothman's cancer sticks, taps one on the desk as if that will make it taste different to the thousands inhaled before, and slowly shares his expertise.

'You don't understand why this Bureau exists.'

'You find missing persons.' Adam points outside. 'It says so on the door to your office.'

'It *doesn't* say that. It says we are a Bureau. The responsibility for finding missing persons in London rests with police stations. We get copies of their missing persons reports and we keep a central index. We get info on people taken to hospital or found dead without any next of kin, people who attempt suicide and vulnerable people found wandering the streets. We try to match up all the names. That's what we do. If we had Henry Simpson's name here, take it from me, we would have told the guv'nor by now.'

'But where do missing people like Simpson go? Are there others like him out there? You must know.'

The officer leans forward, stubbing the butt out.

'There are men who vanish without trace. They're the sort who are overwhelmed by mortgages, loans, marriage or family life. They're being pursued by the Child Support Agency to pay up cash to ex-spouses. They're having a breakdown that even the RAC can't solve. They work long hours, are under pressure, are fatigued or depressed. They think that the world will be a better place without them and they know suicide invalidates all their life insurance policies. So they simply disappear. The Americans have a special term for it, as they would. Pseudocide.'

Adam is only slightly impressed. 'Simpson has no kids, was self-employed and has no money worries right now. He's very flush with cash from his business.' Adam sighs and thinks about leaving. 'Is that it?'

The mention of money seems to jog the memory of the officer.

'There are also white-collar criminals, the bank embezzlers and the husbands escaping divorce settlements. They panic because they see either a jail term or poverty or both. These people have money so they do it right. They change their clothes, grow beards, gain or lose weight, learn a new language, acquire a new accent, go under the surgeon's scalpel. They get themselves complete new identities. Most people want to change something about themselves. These people do it all in one moment of desperation or hope.'

Adam thinks aloud, thinks about Henry.

'Is it easy to change identity?'

'You find a guy through underworld contacts or small ads, meet him in a pub. He gives you a new passport, bank ATM cards, Amex card, flight ticket, even an Air Miles card, whatever you want. The average turnaround time for the finished product is about one week. You get a new life, new town, maybe even a new lover if you're lucky. You give the guy cash in return. Going rate is about twenty thousand. Has Henry got that sort of cash?'

Adam nods. 'About a hundred times over. How do we find someone who changes their identity?'

'We don't. They're long gone. If Simpson has done that, he won't be staying in a B&B in Clacton, in a cottage in Wales or a seedy squat in East London. He'll be out of sight. Maybe he's on an island in Greece, a beach in Thailand or a mountain peak in the Andes. He'll have planned this meticulously.'

'So you think Simpson is safe and well?'

'Safe maybe, not necessarily well. There are serious psychological aspects to identity switches. You lose touch with people, you speak to no one, you fear social closeness, you reject the norms of human behaviour.' The officer toys with the butt in the already overflowing ashtray, then stands up. 'I think you can be sure that your serial killer won't be coming back to the UK. You can sleep easy at night.'

Adam follows him to the open door, inhaling the fresher air of the outside corridors.

'It seems so bloody easy.'

'Give me your wallet.' Adam obliges. The officer takes out the contents and examines them one by one. There's a credit card, an ATM Switch card, a redundant work ID from Mitchell Leonberg, a John Lewis store card. 'We are all essentially what is in our wallet. I know from these that your name is Adam Lewis.

You change the name on all these items and suddenly you're someone else entirely. Easy.'

Samantha rests on an uncomfortable wooden bench in a long corridor. To her left sits her mother who has travelled up from Cornwall to offer her support during the arduous recent days. They hold hands. Next to her mother is Kerys, straight from work at Guy's and still in her uniform. To her right sits Samantha's legal adviser who has brought her to the brink of possible retribution. He hands her today's newspaper.

'I see you made the *Standard* again.' He opens the relevant page. 'You're on page seven this time. Getting better. You'll be front-page news tomorrow. Whatever happens with this case.'

Samantha reads the headline. *Girl Testifies on Sexual Slurs at City Bank*. The content of the article is pitifully limited. Instead there's another photograph of Samantha striding up the steps to the Employment Appeals Tribunal, taken with the maximum amount of exposed calf. Kerys hates the photographs too. Sometimes Samantha wonders if the UK press are any different from an investment bank in the City.

'We'll be back inside soon,' he advises her.

She looks down the sterile corridor. The Mitchell's defensive huddle remains intact, holding a mumbled conference. They avoid eye contact. Obviously planning something. Samantha worries they will dig up some dirt on her, play hardball somehow. Diane sits with a bunch of earnest Law and Compliance types who flew over from New York HO to offer their expert advice, rack up expenses, live in the Savoy and save the firm from public disgrace. Bruce sits alongside. The plummy Sloane from HR sits a few seats away, her velvet hair-band not so pristine, hopefully ruing the day they ever hired Samantha. Muppet is the only one to offer a hostile stare in her direction. She recoils at the bad memories.

The recorder appears from inside and speaks to no one in particular. 'Five minutes, please.'

Samantha gets to her feet prematurely. She'll soon know whether it's all been worthwhile. She looks further down the corridor and through the set of glass swing doors. The press pack is outside, even bigger today. There's a Sky camera crew with spotlights and umbrellas, planning to go live when the decision is known. She sees the array of logo microphones on the steps. She wonders how she'll feel in the spotlight, wonders about their questions, worries about justice.

The Mitchell's guys get to their feet too. One of the American lawyers approaches.

'Can we talk before we go back inside?' There's a distinct New Jersey twang to his voice.

Samantha is about to answer when she realises he's looking past her at her legal adviser.

'What's there to talk about?' replies her brief.

'We're about to get a verdict. It could go either way, ya know,' he drawls offensively.

'But we know it's going to go our way. Samantha's testimony yesterday under your aggressive cross-examination was the turning point. Those tears were real. If I were you, I'd be booking a cab to Heathrow in an hour's time because you won't be doing any celebrating here, chum.'

They both expect some barbed riposte from the heavyweight American. None comes. Instead he looks up and down the corridor as if the next words are difficult to get past his chubby jowls.

'We think we might want to settle before the verdict is announced.'

'You think, or you do? Go on, say the words.' Her brief revels in the moment. 'It won't hurt.'

'We do.'

'You're stalling for time,' replies her brief. He's good. Has been all week. It's paying off.

'I got the okay from New York on my cellphone over lunch. We can offer a cash settlement. Here and now. Think about it. You go inside and lose, you get nothing. You can win now.'

'You're worried the Tribunal is going to hang Mitchell's out to dry in public. All that press coverage . . .'

'I can live with that. It's a hazard of the job.'

'So what's the catch?' asks her brief.

'Same as usual. The girl here drops her case. She says nothing. We don't admit any liability or wrongdoing.'

Her brief points to Samantha. 'The girl here has a name. Use it.'

'Okay, Miss Perry here. Jeez! You're bleedin' me dry. Have we got a deal?'

'What's the colour of your money?'

The American opens a folder and shows a page to her brief. There's a number. 'Here it is.'

Samantha sees the six-figure sum. She hears Kerys beside her gasp. It's more than she ever thought. Her brief hardly raises an eyebrow but answers before she can interrupt with wild enthusiasm.

'Are we talking dollars or sterling?'

'Dollars, of course. We're a US bank.'

'Miss Perry, though, is UK staff. If it's sterling, then you've got a deal.'

He thinks quickly and does some basic FX conversion maths. 'That's a lot of dollars. Gimme a minute. I gotta call New York.'

The American lumbers off, the uneven wooden parquet floor creaking under his weight. Kerys grips Samantha's hand and squeezes it tightly. Her brief turns to Samantha.

'It's like we discussed last night. I hoped they'd settle before rather than lose and risk some damning public pronouncement from the bench inside. They took us to the wire, though. Are you happy with that sort of settlement?' Samantha nods. It's the price of a new house in Cornwall. Several new houses in Cornwall, in fact. It's their financial freedom. She and Kerys could retire. Almost! 'Good. Anything else?'

Samantha whispers something to him just as the American returns, all teeth and smiles.

'We got a deal.' He offers a handshake. The offer is not reciprocated. 'What's up now?'

'One other matter. My client would like an apology.'

'Yeah. Sure, no problemo. We can draft one up and send it over.'

'My client wants a verbal apology from that gentleman over there.' Her brief points.

Muppet sees the summons from the American who pulls rank. He approaches slowly.

'What do you need me for?'

'Give Miss Perry an apology,' the lawyer instructs.

'You gotta be joking,' objects Muppet. 'I've done nothing wrong. The case isn't over yet.'

'It is. Just do it. Words cost us nothing. And we want to be able to hear the apology.'

Muppet stands in front of the assembled party. Finally the words come trickling out. 'Sorry for what happened. Sorry we didn't all get on.' He debates the next line. 'Sorry you and I didn't get on.'

Samantha stands her ground. 'I never would have got on with you.' She kisses Kerys. 'See, Muppet?'

Henry wakes suddenly. The room is pitch dark. For a moment he doesn't know where he is. Then he recalls the past few days. He glances at the alarm clock. It's past ten in the morning. He feels like death warmed up. It's the jet lag after the dash across Europe and the long-haul flight. He wonders what roused him. He leans over and throws the lamp switch. The room could be in any hotel anywhere in the world. There's a hesitant knock at the door. He sits upright in bed, wondering if he's becoming paranoid just because everyone's out to get him.

There's a second knock. He rolls over in the bed, grabs a bathrobe thrown on the floor and vaguely recalls the sordid events of the previous evening. Her side of the bed is creased, the sheets bunched together with an impression left in the plump pillow. He sees white stains in the sheets lower down the bed, most likely his semen. There are some spots of blood too. Menstrual, he guesses. He never touched her. Honest. He can't see her skimpy clothes that hung upon the nearby chair last night, nor can he recall her name. She's done a runner. Never said goodbye. He panics and reaches out. His wallet is still there, and his watch. There's another knock.

The voice is distant. 'Morny, room serbis.'

Henry is not yet convinced. He hasn't ordered any room service today. It could be someone already on his trail, someone with a crested badge, a warrant and a loaded piece. He stumbles along the hallway, wondering who is behind the heavy double doors that guard the only entrance to his luxurious three-room suite on the thirtieth floor of this Leading Hotel of the World.

'I didn't order any room service,' he shouts back.

There's a pause and some shuffling of papers and receipts. 'We took call ten minutes ago.'

'Not from me you didn't.'

'A lady order breakfast for two. From your room extension. 3012.'

The lady is gone. It's some joke she's playing on him. Henry shifts uneasily. He peers through the magnifying spyglass. He can see a waiter in a white uniform. No one else. No breakfast, either.

'I can't see any food.' The waiter wheels out a trolley piled high with edibles, fruits and a single long-stemmed red rose. 'Are you alone?'

'Yeh, Mr Berisford.'

Henry opens the door, accepts the trolley and signs the tab without adding a tip. The waiter insists on individually detailing the items arrayed before them.

'Bayhcem for two, one pry, boy, pooch and strangle ache, san toes and singlish mophins, we bother, copy, tea, mill ... tanjewberrymud.'

Henry is alone. He opens the curtains and allows the morning sun to bathe the softwood furnishings and muted pastel tones. He can see much of the city from his vantage point. Across the river are the towering offices of the UOB and OCBC banks at Raffles Place, below them the dwarfed row of the late-night ex-pat bars of New Boat Quay. Nearer to the hotel are the City Hall to his right, the St Andrew's Cathedral and the extensive manicured lawns and verandas of the Padang, home to the Singapore Cricket Club.

Memories return of too many Tiger beers in Harry's Bar. Then that mixed satay with peanut chilli sauce, cucumber and spring onions in one of the open-air food courts of Clarke Street, where she picked him up. Or he picked her up. He's free to do so. Graham Berisford is a single man.

He stares up at the sun, allowing the heat to energise his senses. No more fucking long dark cold winters in England. The bathroom door suddenly opens.

'Morning.'

It's all coming back to Henry. She's standing with a towel wrapped around her dark hair, wearing the same short skirt and tight pink T-shirt with '69' emblazoned across her pitifully flat chest. Without her make-up and heels she looks like a juvenile who's bunking off school. He wonders what attracted him to her? Was it loneliness or a drunken haze? She was useless in bed, too submissive and eager to please. She never took the lead in the foreplay. He misses Diane.

'I thought you were gone.'

'You get a full night with me.'

Henry points to the food. 'Did you order all this food? You like eggs?' She nods eagerly. 'Why didn't you answer the bloody door? I was asleep.'

'I was in the bathroom. Women's trouble. You know?'

He lets it lie. She eats voraciously, moving on from course to course with a practised ease. She finishes with consecutive black coffees downed almost in one, then finds her bag on the floor.

'I enjoyed last night. You want to meet tonight?'

Henry decides in an instant. Singapore is a city of wealth, a city of technology and techies, a city of mobiles and mobility. It's a fine city; a five-hundred-Sing-dollar fine for not flushing a public convenience, for opening a rear window in a car or bus, for smoking inside a building or in a taxi line, for chewing gum on the street. It's a wired city but only because of the omniscient CCTV. Its four million automatons signed an unwritten contract to exchange token freedom for the dollar bill. It's the world's champion killer with a prison execution every ten days. It's Asia for beginners. Henry is no beginner. He's had his fill of the place. He feels the need for speed.

'I got plans. I've got a flight. I won't be around,' he advises.

'Oh . . .' She looks around the room, trying to find the right words. 'Can you help me out?'

'With what?'

'My expenses for last night.'

'Expenses?' Harry gets the message. 'You a pro?'

'We all are.'

'So what are your expenses?'

'Six hundred dollars.'

'Singapore?' he wonders. She nods. Henry thumbs through his wallet. He doesn't have enough in Sing notes. 'Any discount for the best damn' hotel room and breakfast in Singapore?'

'Afraid not.'

'You take US dollars?'

'I take anything as long as it's legal.'

'Unlike yourself, then.'

He kneels down in front of the room safe inside the wardrobe and keys in his access number. Inside are his new passport and his petty cash. The US dollar remains king. He takes three hundred-buck notes, assured that the other pristine notes remain untouched at the rear of the safe. He stands up but suddenly worries. He's not sure but he thinks she saw the rest of the money. She goes.

Henry ignores the breakfast, takes down his Samsonite suitcase and dumps the safe contents onto the bed. Next stop Changhi Airport, Quantas for seven hours and then touchdown in Oz.

She uses her mobile in the hotel lobby to call two local guys. They're muscle-men who do anything for money. The more, the better. She tells them about the wealthy solo punter from England and gives them the 3012 room number for an agreed ten per cent of the take. She tells them that the punter will be expecting room service to call in about an hour's time to look for the return of a trolley.

CHAPTER THIRTY-SIX

LONDON WALL, LONDON EC2: 9.05 A.M.

Adam has a flashback. He walks along the crowded trading floor between the rows of traders and salesmen but this time it's different. There's some reaction from the others. A few of the familiar faces, guys and girls whose names he never knew last year, now smile back. One bloke gives him a blatant thumbs-up sign. Others whisper to colleagues and swivel their chairs as Adam strides by. One equity group break into modest applause. His pace slows. It's enjoyable.

Other faces appear over the Reuters terminals. The token applause ripples progressively around the huge room and grows louder as he nears the FX desk. Adam walks slower. He is no longer a junior FX trader at Kapital Bank. He seems to be a minor celebrity of sorts. His former colleagues stand up. A few perform a mock bow and wave their hands. 'We're not worthy,' they call.

Beamer offers Adam a firm handshake and slaps him on the back. 'Welcome home.'

Adam is bemused. 'Someone once told me that you should never go back.'

'You never left us. Except for a short unpaid holiday at the black hole that is Mitchell's.' Beamer points beside him to an empty chair. 'Take a seat.'

Adam looks around to the far side of the desk. 'I thought I'd be sitting in my old seat.'

'You're sitting next to me. This is where the action is. You'll enjoy it more.' Adam takes a seat and tries to relax. 'So how do you feel?' asks Beamer.

He looks at the screens. 'Strange.'

Beamer sits alongside. 'Enjoy the moment. You've sure been blooded.' Adam winces. 'Since we last met you've dodged death, uncovered a serial killer and made twenty million bucks of FX trading profit for Kapital. Now that's what I call a productive three months. So you feel . . . ?'

'. . . Lucky.'

'You feel elated, optimistic, bullish. You can take on the world. You've proven yourself in the most hostile of environments. You're gonna make us a shedful of loot this year.'

'I hope so.'

Beamer opens a desk drawer and produces a small box. 'These are yours. The ink's still wet.'

Adam opens the box. Inside is a set of personalised business cards with the Kapital logo. He reads the words slowly, digesting the implications. Adam Lewis. Vice-President. Global FX Trading. 'Since when did I become a VP?'

'Since you made a killing on the FX market. There's more.' Beamer throws a keyring across the desk. 'How about that?'

Adam sees the unmistakable logo. 'Looks like a BMW keyring. *Your* keyring, if I recall.'

'It used to be mine. I got a new motor last month courtesy of Wolfie. This is your bank car. It's a 320i with all the extra kit. It's a beaut. I should know. I did ten thousand careful miles in it. There's a dent in the wing but that's a good thing in a new car. You don't have to worry after the first dent. It's parked below. You can drive it home. You got a space, too.'

'I'm amazed,' admits Adam.

Beamer looks around the floor. Others take the hint and drift back to their own desks.

'I want to know it all. Where is that guy Henry Simpson?'

'I dunno exactly. But I think he's gone for good.'

'What makes you so sure?'

'A guy in the Metropolitan police'.

'You are so well connected, man.'

Wolfie hears the welcome and emerges in a rush, offering Adam a handshake. He seems to have gained a few pounds, lost a few grey hairs since last year but still won't retire from Kapital. 'Come on in.'

Adam sits in the MD's office. Last time was the day he resigned. Wolfie is effusive. 'Delighted to have you back. We missed your experience at the desk. I hope you settle back in straight away.' He sighs. 'I'm sorry to say our bonuses were agreed last week.' Wolfie is actually apologising. 'You won't be in last year's numbers. There's nothing I can do. My hands are tied.'

Adam wonders how he was ever afraid of Wolfie. 'I didn't expect to get a bonus. I just wanted a job.'

'This year will be a very good trading year,' promises his boss.

'You seem sure. There's a long way to go until year-end.'

'Thanks to you we have twenty million in the bag and we're still in quarter one. I'll make sure I see you right at the end of this year. You can look forward to a six-figure bonus from me.'

Adam is puzzled. 'Didn't Mitchell's look for their money back on that trade?'

Wolfie rolls back in his chair and grins. 'I had begging calls from some bitchy American woman called Diane Somebody. Then I had some global FX head called Horowitz on from New York giving me chapter and verse. I had Mitchell's legal department threatening legal action so I took advice. Our legal guys said to play hard and let it run as long as we could stall them, but not to risk a court case in the glare of media publicity. Then Mitchell's suddenly went all quiet on us. I haven't heard from anyone there in weeks. Maybe they've got something else on their mind.'

Adam recalls his own visit to the FSA. 'Yeah, they might have.'

'You know more?'

'There's some dealing scam. Sorry, I can't say more. I was sworn to secrecy.'

'By who?'

'Let's just say by the authorities and leave it at that.'

'*Ja*. You are the main man. You're in the loop. You've come a long way since last year.'

Beamer knocks on the door and barges in without asking. 'Something's up at Mitchell's.' Adam and Wolfie look at him for more information. 'Our bond guys down the floor say they spoke with the bond guys at Mitchell's in Canary Wharf. There's a bunch of heavy-handed suits all over their FX desk now like a rash. They say it looks like a movie and soon it'll be handcuffs for all. There's some insider trading in the euro, they say. Or that's the word on the street, guys.'

Wolfie nods and points.

'Adam already told me about this. He's a player. Now he's first with the news, not last.'

Diane is reclining in her office when there's a sudden commotion outside. She looks up and glances through the smoked-glass partition. Some of the traders and salesmen are on their feet. A small group of purposeful suits stride along the corridor, making directly for her office. Her door is closed. They don't knock but open it and enter in single file to stand in front of her desk.

'Ms Rubin?' asks one suit at the head of the group of four. She nods but remains seated. The suit wears a nasty shirt and dull tie that are a give-away. He is not of the City. Diane is puzzled.

'Who are you? How did you get past our security downstairs?'

'We *are* your security. Of sorts.' The suit opens a warrant card with a well-polished embossed silver and red crest. 'DI Hargreaves of the City of London police. We're here for you.'

She panics as a shocking thought runs through her mind. Then an easier possibility dawns.

'Gentlemen, of course. I know why you're here.'

The DI looks at her long and hard and nods. 'That's good. That'll make it easier for all concerned.'

'I've already spoken to police officers last week about this matter,' she explains.

The suit is momentarily fazed. He stares at his colleagues and then back to Diane. 'You have?'

'I told them all I knew about Henry. They seemed satisfied.'

'Henry?' the DI asks.

'Henry Simpson. You *have* heard of him?

'Of course I've heard of him. Who hasn't? He's all over the papers and TV. But that's not my beat, lady. I don't work CID. I work in white-collar crime. I'm here on a different matter. That's why we all came along.' He points to his right. 'Two of my colleagues here are from the FSA.'

Diane slowly repeats the words. 'The FSA?'

'The Financial Services Authority. The regulator that polices the City. You've heard of them?'

Diane is still lost. 'I know what the FSA do, but what does the FSA have to do with Henry Simpson?'

'You're not getting the picture. We know there's insider trading going on in this office. We're taking you back with us to Barking police station for questioning.'

Diane feigns surprise and shakes her head. 'I don't know what you're talking about.'

'ECB. Euro interest rates,' advises the DI. 'You'll talk later. We have all the evidence on you.'

'What evidence could you possibly have on me?'

'We got a court warrant last Friday. Spent the weekend down with your ITS guys who man the telephone recording system.

A guy called Krish was very helpful. We've been through the tapes of the FX desk on the day of one rates announcement. We know that a Karl called in regularly with information. It's in the transcript.'

'That's the FX desk telephones. I don't work at that desk. It had nothing to do with me ...'

Diane immediately regrets the comment, which was no denial.

'We did the same check on your personal telephone extension. There were some juicy conversations. We've got a transcript of you talking to Horowitz in New York.'

'What did he say?' she asks.

'It's not what *he* said, it's what *you* said. You can read it in the interview room. Let's go.'

Diane shakes her head, still not believing that this is happening. The suits move forward.

'You know nothing about FX or the ECB. You're not smart enough,' she snarls. 'Someone told you all this.'

'Nothing wrong with that. It makes our job much easier to have someone on the inside.'

'Who the hell was it?' she demands.

'Can't say. You'll know later, definitely by the time we get to court.'

The DI has taken her right arm and tries to lead her.

'You can't arrest me today. I have a flight to New York at the weekend. I'm on vacation.'

'You might get bail but we'll keep your passport. You're going nowhere.'

'But Horowitz promised me I could go home often.'

Diane is now conscious that all the staff outside are staring in at the unfolding nightmare. She sees Muppet, Cable Guy, Spoon and Bookie sitting in a huddle, fear etched on their faces.

'What about the guys who work on the FX desk?' she asks the DI.

'We're not here for the monkeys, we're here for the organ grinder. Get your coat.'

Two of the suits move closer to escort her from the premises. She's still in denial.

'I only joined a few months ago. This was all happening long before I came ...'

'Thanks for the admission, lady.'

'Oh, fuck it, you've got the wrong person. You want Horowitz in New York.'

'Don't you worry about him.' The DI looks at his watch. 'He'll have a visit from the SEC in a few hours' time at his Westchester home. I don't think Horowitz is gonna enjoy his breakfast today.'

Diane stands by the door, and turns to them with one last desperate plea.

'You don't want me, you want Bruce. He set it up. But he's not here today. He's away.'

'In Frankfurt,' replies the DI.

Diane wonders how this ape knows so much. 'But he's back in London later today.'

The DI looks at his watch again and smiles at the suits from the FSA. 'Unlikely.'

Bruce takes his usual BA flight and catches a taxi on arrival into Frankfurt city centre. He is deliberately early because it's the first time with a new contact and it needs to be done right. He is uneasy. The arrangements have changed. The contact wants to meet away from the environs of the ECB. Bruce alights at the Oper Platz, an expansive paved pedestrian square in front of the old Opera. A helicopter briefly flies overhead. He smiles. Now he's becoming paranoid.

He sits on a marble bench in an adjacent seating area, hiding behind a screen of dead trees and their outstretched entwined limbs. His eyes roam the agreed rendezvous from a hundred yards. Tourists stop at the impressive Opera building, perhaps wondering what the carved words *Dem Wahren Schoenen Guten* mean. He does too. Bloody foreign languages. Locals emerge from the U-Bahn station. A Movenpick Eis concession does modest business. It's all unfamiliar territory. Bruce worries.

He watches the agreed Operncafe with its red awning. At five minutes to the hour a young guy with an FT takes an outside wicker chair at a chrome table. Bruce is pleased. The new contact won't retire from the ECB for many years. Already this year's trading P&L at Mitchell's looks a little healthier. A waiter takes an order, wearing a gleaming white apron so he can charge more.

The contact seems nervous. He grazes the newspaper but reads nothing. He looks around the plaza, then at his watch. But he should be anxious. He's on the slippery slope to crime and crime pays, in euros now. There's no one else of interest or importance sitting outside in the chill mid-morning air. Bruce is satisfied. He walks over to the contact and sits down silently.

The contact takes off both his gloves and offers an enthusiastic handshake. 'Hello, I am Klaus.'

Bruce nods. 'No formalities today. We don't need to know too much about each other.' He doesn't like the view from the café. He sits up against a brick wall. The Citibank and Deutsche towers are off to his left, the BHF and Helaba buildings to his right. But there's so much empty space out here. There's nowhere to hide. Nowhere to run. If he ever needs an exit route.

The contact nods. He's almost stuttering to get the next words out. 'I understand.'

Up close he's maybe thirty years old, with glasses and a recent tan. He has those eerie whitened polar-bear eyes, the sort you get from a winter skiing holiday wearing shades. He sweats, despite the cold. Bruce likes to see the fear. The contact needs to be afraid. Here is a boring pen-pushing German civil servant up against the ultimate predator, a global foreign exchange player with a US name.

'Relax. This'll be easy,' Bruce assures him. 'It all worked fine with Karl.' He looks around the deserted square, leans over to extract the envelope from his briefcase and places it out of sight between the folded pages of the contact's *FT* as agreed. 'Here's ten K up front, like I said.'

'*Danke.*' The contact nods but doesn't open the envelope. 'So what do I have to do?'

Bruce sighs. 'Didn't Karl tell you?' The contact shakes his head. 'Jesus, don't you ECB guys ever talk to each other at work?'

'Not about matters like this. This is illegal, you know. Inside knowledge.'

'Of course I know that. So you want me to spell it out for you?'

'*Ja.*'

'On the day of the monthly ECB interest rates announcement, you will call me in London.' Bruce produces a business card and points. 'Call this mobile number. Don't call me on the work number. All the lines are taped. Karl did that once, it's a risk we don't need to run. You call me by ten to ten, London time, otherwise I can't build a euro position. Have you got that?'

'So this is the way it worked with Karl?'

'Sure did.'

'For the past three years.'

'Do you like stating the bleeding obvious?'

'I want to be sure.' The contact leans forward, places his hands on the newspaper, feels the bulky envelope of euros, smiles and leans back in his seat. Bruce watches him closely. There is a grey wire like from a set of earphones, curling around his tie and disappearing down into the contact's suit. He is suddenly curious. Who the hell is this guy? 'Do you have any work ID?'

'You said no formalities today.'

'I need to see some ID.' The contact produces an ECB employee identity card with a decent photo. It's the right guy. 'I needed to be sure. What are you going to do with all the money?'

The contact stalls, like he doesn't expect this line of questioning. 'My wife has expensive tastes.'

Bruce looks at his left hand. He's not wearing any wedding ring. It's time to go.

'Don't ever take any vacation on an announcement day. Be in touch at the required time.'

Bruce rises from his seat. His line of vision suddenly improves. He sees the plaza is not as deserted as it was previously. Two middle-aged men in tan trench coats are walking towards them. The trenchcoats are almost identical, like they're wearing some sort of unofficial uniform. One of the men breaks into a jog. There's a moment when Bruce thinks he should run too, but he doesn't. They stop beside the table. One speaks in almost perfect English with a touch of a German accent.

'Bruce Villiers?' Bruce nods. How can this guy know his name? 'We are from the fiscal police. You are under arrest on charges of corruption and bribery of a government official.'

'You got it wrong. Nothing's happened. I don't know this guy. We just met.'

'We're talking about Karl in the ECB. You know *him* rather well. Three years is a long time. Ten spent behind bars is even longer.'

The other opens the envelope and smiles when he sees the cash. 'It's all in here.' He nods to the contact who seems relieved. 'We got all the conversation. You asked the right questions. Well done.'

A mob of uniformed police and a couple of green Polizei cars pull into the plaza. Bruce is ushered into the nearest Opel saloon. He's not sure what's happening here. He stays silent.

The car moves off at excessive speed as they exit the plaza, bouncing over cobbled one-way streets and across sets of gleaming tramlines. Bruce would be thrown left and right on each corner if it weren't for the uniformed officers sitting to either side of him in the cramped back seat. The siren above wails unnecessarily in sheer pain. Pedestrians on nearby pavements peer into the misted rear windows at red traffic lights.

'How the hell did you get to know about this?'

'We have our sources. We were given a telephone number in Germany to trace. The rest was easy.'

He can't see what the hurry might be. There are some road signs and then one showing a plane. He knows where they're going. He'll soon be on a BA flight back home to London. Extradition is fast. They leave the motorway and head towards an ominous grey-brick building off in the distance.

'Aren't we going to the airport?' he asks hopefully.

The uniform on the left shrugs, then smiles. 'We're going to the remand prison. You're now in the care of the German judicial system, and will be for some time, I fear.' He watches Bruce's face turn paler and smiles again. 'For you, I think – how do you say – the war is over.'

JUNE

CHAPTER THIRTY-SEVEN

BARRIER POINT, LONDON, E16: 4.15 P.M.

Adam and Lisa lie out on the balcony of 1205. He wears a pair of shorts and nothing else. She wears a loose freebie airline T-shirt that leaves nothing to the imagination. Inside the Lighthouse Family play softly on her Sony. Track 2. 'Who says you can't be happy all the time?' And all that.

He looks around. 'What do you think of this balcony?'

'Awful. Ten feet makes all the difference,' Lisa advises.

'You should be so lucky.'

Below them, East London has undergone a miraculous transformation. Small pleasure craft zigzag up and down the Thames, naval pennants fluttering from sterns. The sun glistens off the row of silver domes of the Thames Barrier off to their left. A cool breeze belies the burning rays. A few terracotta tubs of parched geraniums gasp for rainwater. The Sunday newspapers lie half-read on the wooden sleepers, their loose pages slowing curling with the overhead rays.

'Don't tell me that you're in there again?' she asks as she points down.

Adam picks up the business section and reads aloud. 'The *Sunday Times* crack insight investigative team retrace the footsteps of a serial killer across Europe and uncover more shocking murders. How two City traders came close to death. Sightings reported in Rio, KL, Alaska, Montana and Moscow, but as yet no definite identification of Henry Simpson'. He holds up the article and points to his dated photograph. 'I get a small paragraph at the end.'

'Any word on the others?'

'Bruce is still on remand in Frankfurt. German federal prosecutions against ECB employees. Diane fired from Mitchell's. The rest of the desk fired too. Horowitz dropped from a great height in New York by his management and by the SEC. Did I really cause all that? Sometimes I wonder.'

She shifts to ensure an all-over tan. 'You're hot,' she tells him fondly.

'I think that's only because it's eighty degrees up here.'

'You know what I mean.' She can see an approaching airplane. 'Did you book those Ryanair flights?'

'Sure did. Trish would never forgive us if we missed her wedding to Patrick. Roll on next month.'

Lisa looks around. 'Hard to believe that it's your last weekend in this place.'

'I'm going to miss it here,' he admits with a wry smile.

'The move's going to be a real wrench. How far away is the new place?'

He points upwards. 'At least ten feet. I heard the girl in the flat above is nice, though.'

'I heard she's noisy. Plays music. Uses the shower. Walks on the floors. Has a wild crazy brother called Mike who keeps turning up at the wrong moment. That sort of stuff.'

'I heard that too. But it'll be quieter in 1305 than in 1205.' He hopes.

'What about the part-time heavy-metal drummer and the insomniac techno DJ in 1405?'

For a moment he's fooled. 'Hah-ruddy-hah! What about my parking space?'

'That flashy BMW! You can squeeze in beside me. It'll be the same as the arrangement we have at night.'

Adam stretches out in the seat and crosses his legs, resting his feet upon the newspapers.

Lisa picks up the bottle of factor fifteen. 'You're burning up. Turn around. I'll do your neck.'

He swivels on his seat, leans back and enjoys the sensation of lotion being kneaded in. She runs her hands across his shoulder blades and up and down his spine, then instinctively delves below the waistband of his shorts. 'What time are Cheryl and Brian arriving?'

'I told them to be here at six. We can dine outside, if you like.'

Lisa leans against the low railing, rolls her head around, loosens her limbs and turns sideways on. 'Do you think we have time before they arrive?'

He stands up, turns his back on the sunlight and takes her hand in his. 'Your place or mine?'

EPILOGUE

Singapore, 16 July – Police chiefs yesterday revealed a sensational development in their investigation into a murder earlier this year in a city hotel. Graham Berisford, a 37-year-old tourist from London, was stabbed to death with a knife in his luxury room on the thirtieth floor of the Westin Stamford Hotel in early February. At the time police officers thought that he was the victim of an opportunist thief.

DSP Koh Teck Hin of the Major Crime Division outlined amazing details at a packed press conference at the CID Tower at the Police Cantonment Complex on New Bridge Road. Lack of information on the deceased and the absence of any next-of-kin initially hampered the murder investigation. Several months of routine follow-up work with relevant UK authorities revealed that Berisford's identity was fictitious. Subsequent inquiries with the UK passport office and the Department of Vehicle Licensing in Wales confirmed the man's real name as Henry Albert Simpson, a former City of London financial recruitment executive.

Simpson immediately showed up on the CID's Interpol liaison wanted-persons list. He was wanted for questioning by the Metropolitan Police in London and by police in

Ireland in connection with the murders of his wife and of an American businessman in Dublin. Police in Madrid and Dusseldorf were also seeking his arrest. Simpson was last seen in January. His car was found abandoned in a London City Airport car park. Two days later his wife's mutilated body was found by her colleagues in the basement of their home, and an international manhunt began. It eventually ended in Room 3012 of the Westin Stamford in the mammoth Raffles City complex. Following the sale of his London recruitment business, Simpson was believed to have been carrying over one million pounds sterling in cash on his person, which as yet remains unaccounted for.

The Singapore Straits Times